ACKNOWLEDGEMENTS

In writing *Crossing the Goal Line*

I must initially acknowledge some of the great mentors I have had the fortune of working for, and with, as I formulated the story of CROSSING the GOAL LINE; Homer Smith, Larry Smith and Mouse Davis. I, also, thank the following coaches who have been there when I got stuck and needed their assistance; Brad Minor, Brent Meyers, Chance Clatterbuck, Gary Bernardi, Preston Jones and Ted Williams.

Special thanks to my three computer whizzes, my son-in-laws; Chris Schuld and Ross Grainger and my teenaged grandson Tyler Grainger, all who have pulled me out of a hole more than once or twice when my sketchy computer skills became dangerously close to blowing up the manuscript a number of times. I'll never forget when my eight-year-old granddaughter, Addie Grainger, helped me with my lack of computer skills by stating "...hit the key twice, Poppa."

Thanks to Dana Nelson, my Author Representative and the folks at Outskirts Press. And last, but certainly not least, special thanks to my wife, Dr. Marie Axman, who I called upon so often to help make *Crossing the Goal Line* feasible.

DEDICATION

To my wonderful wife
and best buddy!
Dr. Marie L. Axman

A ballcarrier scores a touchdown once any part of the football in his possession crosses over the very front of the goal line.

CHAPTER 1

MID-NOVEMBER 2007 (CHICAGO, IL)

"How's your mom doing, Johnny,?" asked the St. Ignatius linebacker coach, Sean Dempsey, with a sincere smile stretched across his face. The two walked side-by-side towards the football practice field. Johnny Larkin's mother was halfway through radiation treatments for a brain tumor. The trauma had been extremely difficult for the young linebacker being so close to his mother. Unfortunately, the doctors were not giving the woman much of a chance to make it. *Too bad,* thought Dempsey. *Johnny's mother is all he really has.*

"She's hanging in there, Coach," replied the youngster sullenly as he took a deep, slow breathe. "It's been so hard. I'm just lucky she's such a tough person and that she has such strong religious beliefs." The two became very quiet finding it hard to formulate words that could have significance. "And, Coach, ...I really appreciate your concern. You've really been a great help to me," as tears started to well up in his eyes.

"Remember, Kid, if you need a ride home, let me know," added Dempsey. "And I can pick you up in the mornings if you're stuck, John. I also want you to know that my wife and I are praying for her. Keep in mind what you just said, Kid. She's one tough lady which is a big part of all this."

"Got'cha, Coach," said the youngster. "I'll definitely take you up on that ride if I'm stuck. Thanks, Coach. Thanks a lot."

"Bend your knees, Sully," encouraged Sean Dempsey, the first year, hard-nosed, varsity linebacker coach at St. Ignatius College Prep as he intensely corrected the linebacker's performance. "Ram your inside flipper right under his grill! Dominate his ass! Get yourself ready to kick some butt, Sully! Make that fullback quit on Friday!" *We can't get complacent just because we made it to the play-offs,* thought the assistant coach. *These kids have to understand it's show time. We can win the whole damn thing and go home state champions again if we can get our act straight.*

"Atta boy, Sully! That's the way to keep your outside arm free. Just keep your pads down, Kid. Be ready to stuff that fullback's ass once you read his run course. You can do it, Sully. I know you can," supported Dempsey, with a warm smile across his face and an arm over the player's shoulders as the two walked back to the huddle. Dempsey was a tough coach, ...often extremely tough. However, he was equally caring and positive when dealing with his boys. "We can definitely get this one done, Sully. I know we can. Blow'em up, Son. Blow'em up. I know you can get after that fullback's ass."

Dempsey reached for a water bottle from one of the student trainers. "Thanks," said the smiling assistant coach as he squirted the power drink liquid into his dry mouth. He then extended the bottle to Johnny Larkin. "Keep your pads down and I know you'll stuff those blockers cold, right in their tracks Johnny. Just keep focusing on maintaining your outside leverage. You'll get it. I promise you. You'll get it, Kid. There's no doubt in my mind, Big Man. You're going to be my hit man in this game. I want you to knock the snot out of any gold colored jersey that crosses your face. And, be sure to get after those running backs every chance you get. Got that, Johnny?"

"Yeah, I got'cha, Coach," said Johnny. "You just wait and see. I'll be taking care of business, ...just like I always do."

"You got that right, Kid," reinforced Dempsey with a haughty retort. *I've got to get the backers to play as physically as they can. They simply have to out-hit Chaminade if we're going to get done what we're capable of doing. It's now or never.*

The burley, well-built Dempsey prowled the practice field with the same intense focus and demeanor that he did as a standout high school and college football player but a scant few years ago. Well known for his ferocious tackling, the rugged, six foot two, 232 pound coach had swiftly transformed his highly aggressive style of play as a first team, all-conference linebacker to his new found profession of football coaching where he was now working at his alma mater. The young coach, whose fire seemed to burn so brightly, was the real deal agreed the staff's veteran coaches. He was a student of the game and applied his trade with a solid balance of toughness, preciseness and a sincere concern and respect for the players he worked with. As intense as Dempsey could be, he was often found smiling and shouting with excitement when one of his players met with even small measures of success or improvement. He loved the game of football with a passion that was easy to see as he roamed the practice field. The players under his wing practiced intensely with great execution and discipline. He pushed young players of average talent into aggressive, hard-hitting, fierce-tackling linebackers of all-conference caliber.

"That was some good stuff out there, Guys," said the linebacker coach assuredly. "You play like that come Friday night and it will be lights out for these dudes."

St. Ignatius was a long time Illinois high school football juggernaut. Large banners of red with silver markings displayed bold inscriptions that declared an overwhelming number of conference and state championships from the past that ringed the St. Ignatius Crusaders stadium. The strength of the team's daily practices matched fierce, game day performance efforts by the players. On a daily basis, significant groups of parents and students filled the practice field bleacher seats, fervently following every practice drill repetition. Loud, excited cheers or adverse utterances of disappointment followed each practice repetition with success or failure.

An even more frantic passion was clearly exhibited by the young, Sean Dempsey whose instructions could clearly be heard all across the practice field.

"You have the front side gap when the ball carrier action is away, Connor!," Dempsey yelled out to his weak side linebacker as the defense practiced their red zone defense versus the scout squad. "You can't forget that!" He expected his linebackers to execute precisely. He could not accept anything but efforts for perfection. "We can't overrun that gap. You've got to pace the ball carrier. Stay home for any cut backs. If you're not patient, that Moore kid will smoke us! We can't let him cut back on us! We can't let that happen! Do you understand that, Gentlemen? No way, no how," as the tough, demanding coach constantly pushed and prodded his linebackers to excel. "Do it right..."

"Or do it again," chimed in the linebackers in a familiar reply to a Dempsey coaching decree. The linebackers had quickly learned that Dempsey would drive them unmercifully. They also knew he would help them to play at their best come game time and that he had great concern for them as people. He was the tough army sergeant type coach who pushed his troops to the limit to help ensure success but then put his arm over their shoulder when they needed words of encouragement or support. And yet, the players greatly enjoyed Dempsey's sense of humor. At times, he seemed ferociously intent. At other times, he would slyly, but wittily, make a coaching point that would send a message to his players putting knowing smiles on their faces.

"You stay that high when taking on that isolation block and you'll find yourself flat on your ass. You can do it, John," stated Dempsey. "Keep your pad level down and get under that fullback's block. You know how to do it so go out and get it done."

This coaching method was true for all of the St. Ignatius linebackers but one, ...Juron Potts. The six-foot, one inch, 205 pound Potts was known as the "...baller..." of the Crusader's football team and everyone knew it. And, if another teammate didn't know it, the star athlete made sure that he quickly did. The brash, cocky Potts was unanimously named the first-team, all-state middle linebacker after his junior season, filling his mind with self-proclaimed greatness. Even more impressive was the fact that he was also named the Defensive Player of the Year at the 6-A division, the highest level of play in the state. Unfortunately, Potts cared about one person and one person only, ...Juron Potts. No one would ever categorize Juron as a team player.

"Man," whined Potts. "I can't believe this turkey they call a coach isn't still working with the freshmen. The guy's a clown, man. Nothing but a clown. And, he's supposed to be coaching me! You got'ta be kid'n. He don't know jack shit, f'sure."

"Oh, shut up, Potts," retorted one of the linebackers. "You might think you're Superman. But, the rest of us have to work our asses off to be good. So why don't you just shut that stupid yap of yours and practice like you're supposed to?"

"Kiss my ass," growled Potts. "All you're good for is kissing Dempsey's ass anyway. And, what the hell do you know about be'n a backer? Man, you're a clown just like that fool."

Potts couldn't stand Dempsey. He couldn't stand the feeling that the upstart coach had crowded in on his own limelight. Juron was the star of the team and felt he didn't need a new, hotshot coach infringing on his notoriety. *They bring in Bozo the Clown to work with me and I'm supposed to feel lucky? All he ever did was get a cup of coffee for a few days as a free agent and everyone treats him like he was an All-Pro.*

In turn, Sean Dempsey had no love for Juron Potts. Dempsey had to work his tail off to be the tremendously productive linebacker that he was. Nothing had come easy for him. He had to toil unbelievably hard to achieve what he had accomplished in his high school and college playing days. In actuality, Dempsey was jealous of the talented Potts. He couldn't accept that Potts was so arrogant, obnoxious and lazy. Secretly, Dempsey felt like smashing Potts in the mouth every time he saw him walking around the practice field or sauntering into the defensive huddle with a routinely smug smile spread across his face. *How could a player be so talented and, yet, be so selfish,?* thought Dempsey. *If I had half of that idiot's ability, I'd still be playing. What a total waste of God-given ability!*

Dempsey finally complained about Potts's lack of effort and poor work habits to the St. Ignatius head coach. The young coach simply had enough of Potts and his obnoxious, spoiled-brat attitude. "You've got to help me out, Coach. Potts is a pompous ass and I'm getting sick of his crap. He doesn't give a damn about anyone but himself. As talented as he is, he's a detriment to our team."

"Sean, I hired you to handle the linebackers for me," replied the wizened, sagacious head coach. "Son, you have to realize that good coaches are a dime a dozen, ...easy to find. Players with Juron's abilities only come along but once in a great while. Do you like being here at St. Ignatius, Sean?"

"I love it here, Coach," said the down-hearted young man. "This is my school. St. Ignatius is my alma mater. I'm extremely proud to be a Crusader and I always will be."

"Well, Sean," said the head coach seriously, "then I suggest you find a way to get this situation straightened out because I sure wouldn't like having to go out and find a new linebacker coach this late in the season."

As impressive a young coach that Sean Dempsey was, he had one major flaw in his personality. He could easily lose his temper. Actually, he could become quite violent. This trait had reached all the way back to his elementary school days. "Nice young man," wrote one elementary teacher on Sean Dempsey's report card "... but Sean fights too much."

"Juron, you've got to open up and burst to the end of the line," shouted Dempsey during a run game drill as he slowly shook his head from side-to-side. Focus, intensity and effort were three of the most important characteristics that Dempsey felt his linebackers needed to be successful at St. Ignatius. *What a shame,!* thought

Dempsey disgustedly. "You've got to move your ass, Juron! You're loafing, Man! You're killing us! There's so much at stake and you don't give a damn, do you? All you care about is your punk-ass, Juron," as the angered coach closely trailed Potts back to the offensive huddle.

"Hey, don't worry about me, Home Boy," barked out Potts. "When Friday night comes, you'll get all the action from me you want. Right now, I'm pace'n myself, Dude, so I can get game-time ready. You dig, Coach? I need fresh legs, Bro. You know what I mean, COACH Dempsey?"

"Get off the field, Potts! I don't need your crap anymore," stated a riled-up Dempsey as a hot-tempered rage began to roil within him. He needed to back off and let the situation calm down. Unfortunately, he did just the opposite.

"You're a joke, Man. You don't know noth'n! I don't need your bull shit, that's f'sure!," yelled Potts as he continued strutting back to the defensive huddle.

A crazed look of rage suddenly lit up across Dempsey's face. *Enough is enough,* thought the young coach. His fists were clenched tight and he reached his limit with the loathsome player. At this point, Dempsey didn't bother to think about the possible consequences of what he was about to do. He simply didn't give a damn.

Dempsey fought through the myriad of players hustling back to their respected huddle spots. He sprinted directly to Potts. Dempsey dipped down low to get under Potts' shoulder pads just as he did so many times in his linebacker playing days. However, instead of tackling Potts to the ground, he reached underneath and through Potts's legs with one arm and over-the-top of his shoulder with the other to put the repulsive player in a wrestling carriage hold. Dempsey then lifted Potts up into the air and violently slammed him to the ground.

"My shoulder! Oh my god! My damned shoulder!" Potts laid on his back, screaming out in pain, rolling around on the ground from side-to-side. "Why did you do that, Coach! You broke my shoulder! You broke my damn shoulder!," as the players and coaches alike hustled over to Potts and Dempsey, shockingly mesmerized by the chaotic scene in front of them.

Dempsey's head started to spin. He had just committed an extremely egregious act and he knew it. His entire body seemed to freeze into a locked position. Unfortunately, Potts did have a broken shoulder.

"What did I do!," whispered the shocked coach to himself. "Oh my God. What did I do?," as he hung his head down to the ground.

CHAPTER 2

EARLY SEPTEMBER 2012 (AFGHANISTAN)

Sean Dempsey had risen quickly to the level of being a United States Army Ranger Sergeant and squad leader. As in his high school coaching days, Dempsey was highly respected and greatly appreciated by his squad members. "At least he isn't one of those sergeant assholes who have rifles stuck up their asses thinking they're God knowing everything," said one of Dempsey's squad members. The sergeant's squad truly felt they were a team, ...a bonded family with locked arms when in battle, side-by-side. The squad members, to a man, believed that if someone would take a bullet for them, it would be Sergeant Sean Dempsey as they kept their heads moving on a swivel looking for Taliban insurgents. Dempsey carefully followed the rule of taking care of the small things believing that to do so helps take care of the big things.

"O.K., Guys. Let's take five," said Dempsey to his Ranger squad. "We've made some good time coming over those hills so we can now pace ourselves a bit. Make sure you water-up. We're getting pretty near the target. Hopefully, this is a quick in-and-out job like command says it should be."

The squad physically relaxed somewhat. However, almost all still followed the actions of their sergeant leader. "That's probably the reason why we should worry, Sarge," stated Corporal Bo Harris. Bo kept his head moving on a swivel looking for Taliban insurgents. "Whenever it's one of their quick, in-and-out jobs, things seem to end up as out-and-out slug fests. That's why I don't trust a damn thing those idiot colonels have to say."

"I hear you, Bo," stated Dempsey. What worried the sergeant the most was that he had a strange feeling that Corporal Bo Harris might be quite right as he started rotating his head and eyes from side-to-side as well. "At least we have a coordinated envelopment that will box them in. All the other leaders say they're about set and ready to go. We're going to hit the objective just before dawn to give us better cover."

"Yeah, but it's still that 'coordinated' stuff that worries me," replied Bo. "Always has and always will," answered the negative thinking Harris. Dempsey had been with Bo since the day the two had enlisted and they had quickly become best of friends. As a result, they had formed sort of an odd couple, but close, relationship. Dempsey often let Bo's negativity fly over the top of his head, especially when his buddy got cranky. Dempsey knew it was the small price he had to pay to have such a loyal, savvy, veteran soldier and close friend at his side.

Bo Harris was a wiry, raw-boned cowboy from Montana. He drove and branded cattle and made good side money as a rodeo roper. Bo was only five foot seven weighing a mere 160-pounds. However, he was most well-known for his effective fisticuff abilities in, and out, of local bars where far too many cowboys made the mistakes of attempting to pick on the small sized Harris. Bo's fighting skills often helped him stuff bulging wads of victory money into the pockets of his jeans. All of this came to a head one day when Bo found himself standing in front of the county judge for the eighth time.

"Bo, you're the dumbest smart guy I've ever met," stated the judge. "Wipe that smile off your face, Son, because I'm sick of you standing in front of me because you're a dumb ass. You need to grow up boy and I do mean boy. I'm giving you a choice, Son. Six months in the County Jail with no ability to lessen your sentence or you join one of the armed services." The judge banged his gavel and swiftly disappeared into his backroom. Bo Harris enlisted in the Army the next day.

Dempsey crept around to supply pats on the back and words of encouragement to his squad. Sergeant Dempsey was well respected by his squad. His leadership had an undaunted reputation. His squad felt that being under Dempsey's wing was good luck. However, they were well aware that it was Dempsey's forced focus and attention to detail that helped to create such luck. "Stay sharp Guys," ordered Dempsey at just above a whisper. "I'm not too sure about this situation. Bo, keep your eyes behind me till we get a better read on that gate."

"Got'cha, Boss," said a wide-eyed Harris following his leader.

Dempsey was a confident, well prepared leader. He was always sure to check and recheck every move that needed to be made in any plan that he and his squad were assigned to execute. And then, ...he would check again. This was his squad, ...his men. He knew mission success was paramount. However, deep down in his heart, his major goal was to get every member of his squad back to base alive and in one piece.

A pile of rock suddenly slid down the side of the mountain they were traversing. The squad all quickly tensed and hunkered down, trying to make themselves as invisible as possible. Their eyes were opened wide as they scanned everything they could see in the pre-morning dark. An unexpected bbbaaahhh suddenly filled the pitch-black air as the soldiers worried that an unfriendly sheep herder might be close at hand. Fortunately, the goat seemed to be a harmless stray.

Dempsey then continued to finish his comforting, assuring efforts for his squad. He thought back to Bo's whining. Bo was a constant complainer, Dempsey well knew. However, for some perplexing reason, Dempsey felt a strange wave of worry pass through his body again as he recounted what Bo had said, "...it's still that 'coordinated' stuff that worries me."

Dempsey reached inside his combat shirt and pulled out the

picture of his pretty wife, Mary Elizabeth that shared the chain with his dog tags. He gave the picture a short, but slightly lingering, kiss. "Love you, Sweetheart," he murmured to no one but himself as he felt a wave of apprehension wash over him. Loving his wife, Mary Elizabeth, was the one, true rock that helped to make him a tough, combat, U. S. Army Ranger sergeant.

"O.K., water-up again and let's get ready to move," ordered Dempsey at just above a whisper as he, himself, took one last swig. He got up off the ground and raised up into a low crouch. From his hunched body position, he moved again from squad member to squad member to give fist bumps or to provide reassuring head nods. "Good luck, Guys. Remember, I got the first round when we get back."

Recently married with a pregnant wife and being out of work after being fired by St. Ignatius, Sean Dempsey was at his wit's end in his effort to support himself and his wife and get the bills paid. Fortunately, his older brother had a basement apartment that he let the young Dempsey family use. Sean demanded that he, at least, pay a small rental fee as best he could. His wife, Mary Elizabeth, was a nurse with medical insurance that helped to take care of many of the heavy expenses, especially the medical bills. However, Sean Dempsey was, by no means, a slacker. He worked long and hard to help keep the boat afloat on the home front taking almost any available job he could to make a few dollars.

"You'll figure it out, Sean," replied his wife. "You've always been able to get yourself out of a hole when things weren't going well. You'll see. Just keep plugging away. Something good will pop up. I know it!," said the loving wife even though she, herself, was starting to have some serious doubts. *Why did he have to lose his temper and hurt that kid? He has such a good heart trying to help people. What a shame. The worst part is that it was his own fault, ...no one else's.*

Unfortunately for Dempsey, the harder he tried to financially support he and his, now, pregnant wife, the further he seemed to fall behind. "We've got to eat," mumbled the ex-coach as he scoured the classified job section of the newspaper. As an extremely proud man, Sean Dempsey refused to take family or government handouts. Depression started to set in and so did heavy drinking. After one night of overindulgence and participation in a nonsensical barroom tussle, he was pulled over by a local policeman as his car weaved back and forth between lanes.

"Sean, what the hell are you doing,?" said the patrolman, as he lit up the cab of Dempsey's truck with his flashlight. Fortunately, the patrolman was Ron Bakersley, one of Dempsey's old, former high school football teammate buddies. Bakersley pulled Dempsey out of his truck and pushed him into his patrol car. He then parked Dempsey's truck to the side of the road.

"I can't believe I'm doing this," stated a worried Bakersley as he drove Dempsey home. "I better not get in trouble for this because of you, ...you stupid ass," stated Dempsey's angered, close friend. "You're a real idiot, Sean. You know that, don't you? Driving around all drunked up like this," as Dempsey mumbled out something incoherent. Once Bakersley arrived at the Dempsey home, he pulled up into the long driveway next to the side door entrance of the Dempsey basement apartment with the lights of his patrol car doused. The patrolman was hopeful to avoid the neighbors from seeing the ruse. He had to carry the, now, passed out Dempsey over his shoulder. "Damn, Sean. You're an absolute load."

"Who is it,?" asked a frightened, worried, Mary Elizabeth Dempsey as she answered the doorbell.

"It's Ron, Mary Elizabeth. Open the door fast!"

"Oh no, Sean!," stated Dempsey's wife as she saw the inebriated condition of her husband. She quickly flicked out the lights. "Thank you, Ron. Thank you, thank you," whispered Mary Elizabeth. *Why, Sean? Why,?* thought the distraught wife. *We'll get through this, Sweetheart.* "He'll bounce back, Ron. I know he will. You'll see."

Two days later, Dempsey took the only option that he felt was proudly left open to him. He joined the U.S. Army.

"Red Leader, this is Blue leader," said Dempsey quietly into his attached microphone. "We're in position and ready to go. We'll wait for your signal," as the squad leader studied the dusty, dirty, ancient looking compound.

"Copy that, Blue Leader. When we're a go, we'll be looking for you to take the north, back gate."

"Copy that, Red Leader," as Dempsey took a deep breath and exhaled slowly. When entering combat, the sergeant always seemed to exude a tremendous amount of confidence. In reality, he worried enormously for his squad members and for the fact that he might never again see his wife nor his new born son.

Once the "go" signal was given, Dempsey, and his squad carefully approached the back gate of the Afghanistan compound. "Go, go, go," ordered Dempsey. "Keep your head down and your eyes on a swivel. We can't miss anything. Be sharp, Guys. Be sharp."

Dempsey's squad attached explosives to the large, north door hinges and backed off for cover. At the designated time, effectively synchronized explosions rocked the compound blowing open the North and South gates. Dempsey's Blue Team quickly, but cautiously, entered the compound. Sergeant Dempsey was the first to enter with Bo Harris right behind him.

"GO! GO! GO!," yelled Dempsey. "Keep your heads down. Take cover fast."

At that moment a fellow Ranger spotted a Taliban insurgent on the rooftop of the building to the right of the squad. "Bogie on the roof. Three o'clock!" He immediately unloaded a volley of gunfire at the enemy soldier. However, the Ranger wasn't able to negate the insurgent before the Taliban fighter had tossed a grenade directly in front of the squad. "Grenade,!" shouted the Ranger.

"Stay down! Stay down,!" shouted out Dempsey as a bright, white light and a tremendous, deafening sound filled the open, courtyard area. Dempsey felt himself flying backwards into the air with all sorts of pieces of debris spraying his body. For a quick second, the delirious Dempsey wondered what kind of football player could possibly deliver such a vicious blow to his chest. He desperately worked to suck some air back into his lungs. He could hear voices at that point although he couldn't understand any of the words. To him, it was just a bunch of jumbled noise, ...extremely loud jumbled noise. People seemed to be running all around him but he couldn't make out who they were. He shook his head in an effort to clear it. It was then that he realized he was lying on top of a body. Looking into the person's face, he gasped. It was Bo's.

"Let's get out of here, Bo," shouted the barely coherent Dempsey. "Come on, Bo. Wake up, Buddy. We got to find some cover," as Sergeant Dempsey began to unsuccessfully pull Bo back outside the compound while still lying flat on his own back. "Don't worry, Bo. I got your back, Bo. You're gon'na be just fine. I promise you, Bo," as he continued to attempt to drag his good friend back away from the gunfire and explosion.

"I got'cha, Sarge," stated another member of Dempsey's squad as the Ranger dragged Dempsey backwards. "Stay in this doorway until I get some help."

"Get the medic quick,!" ordered Dempsey. "Please hurry. Bo needs help right away!"

"Sarge, ...Bo didn't make it."

CHAPTER 3

MID-NOVEMBER 2015 (TUCSON, AZ)

Three years later in Tucson, Arizona, Tyler Douglas was told to start warming up. "You might have to go in, Ty," said one of the assistant coaches. "Get yourself ready and you better do it fast."

"You sure, Coach,?" replied the surprised sophomore quarterback as he quickly started to toss the football back and forth to one of the back-up wide receivers.

Ty had just finished leading the North Tucson Tigers junior varsity team to a perfect 8 and 0 record as the team's quarterback. North Tucson High had an extremely strong football program and was rated highly in USA Today's national high school rankings each of the past four seasons. They were presently on a 39-game win streak and were now playing for their fifth straight Arizona State Championship. However, the Tiger's had just lost their starting quarterback in the previous semi-final play-off game and were now staring at their back-up quarterback as he laid on the ground in the final game. The Tigers were trailing by four points with a little over two minutes remaining in the game.

"Doesn't look good, does it, Smitty,?" the Tigers' head coach Ben Marion asked of his trainer as he started to feel the making of an immense headache.

"No it doesn't, Ben," replied the trainer as he attended to their newest injured quarterback. "Unfortunately, I'm pretty sure it's a lateral ligament. One way or another, this will be all for this young man tonight."

"Let's get some players over to help him off the field," ordered Smitty.

The head coach sighed. *What a way to lose a championship. And, to think we were so close.* During the regular season, his team had crushed the two opponents they were now facing in the semi-finals and finals of the state play-offs. However, in the semi-finals, his starting quarterback was blown up by a blind side tackle knocking the quarterback senseless.

"Concussion," stated the team doctor. "He's still trying to figure out if he's watching a hockey game or dancing at the prom."

Marion's second team quarterback was also an excellent player. The head coach's smug confidence was, however, quickly shattered as the substitute quarterback's knee was torn-up. He was now watching his second quarterback being helped from the field by two of the team's substitute players.

"You better step up the warm-up, Douglas," stated the sideline signal calling coach. "Coach Hawke thinks they might be needing you." Ty's mother, Addison Douglas, was startled to see Ty loosening up. "Oh, my," stated the mother. "I think Ty might be going in."

Ty Douglas did step up his warm-up as he threw behind the team's benches. The fans in the stands were all groping for their game programs trying to figure out who the new quarterback was. *This is some heavy shit,* thought Ty. *On Monday, I'm moved up to the varsity as a back-up. Now, I might be going in for a last-minute touchdown drive to win a state championship. This is a definite trip! I guess it's time to let it rip.*

Putting his head phones back on his head, Marion walked back to the sidelines in shock. The head coach asked his offensive coordinator, "What do you think, Ed?"

"I guess we have to go with Gus," replied Ed. "What choice do we have? He's all that's left. Just keep running the ball on the ground and see what we can do. Hopefully, we won't have to throw a pass."

"Behind by four points in a two-minute offense situation and we're hoping we don't have to throw the ball," stated Marion. "That doesn't give us much of a chance to win, does it, Ed?" *Gus can't play dead,* thought Marion. Gus Tremont had no ability to lead an offense in a real game and everyone on the staff and team knew it.

"Ed, we're 83-yards and a touchdown away from a state championship with a little over two minutes to go," continued Marion. "We have to do something! We just can't fold our tent and give up."

"You could put in Ty Douglas," said the junior varsity head coach, Jarred Hawke, the varsity, game day, offensive press box spotter.

"Douglas? What the hell are you talking about, Hawke? You mean your sophomore Q.B.? The one we just brought up Monday in case of an emergency?"

"That's right," answered Hawke. "He's a heck of a player. He's the main reason the J.V. went undefeated. We use the exact same offense as you do. He knows what to do and he's real smart. And, he has the balls to do it! You just said we brought him up in case of an emergency. Well, that's what we've got right now, Coach, ...a big-time emergency!"

"You about ready to go," asked the referee as the injured quarterback was just about helped off the field.

The head coach hesitated for a few seconds of thought. "Yeah, just give me a few extra seconds, will you, Ref?" Marion looked into the face of Gus Tremont who was standing next to him. He saw a look of terror spread across the back-up quarterback's face. Behind the bench, he saw the young, sophomore quarterback, Ty Douglas, hard at work warming up.

"Douglas," yelled out Marion. He turned to Gus. "I'm going with the Douglas kid, Gus. Let's see if he can give us a spark."

"I understand," said Gus, the third string back-up. A tremendous look of relief suddenly appeared on the senior, substitute quarterback's face.

Marion waved his sophomore, J.V. quarterback over to him. "Tom, if I put you out there, you won't soil your pants, will you,?" asked the forward head coach in an effort to see what type of reaction he would get from the young, 16-year old athlete.

"My name's Ty, Coach, and soiling my pants is not going to happen," said the brazen, intent looking young man. "We only have two minutes and three seconds left to go home as Arizona State Champions. Turn up the heat with the play calls mixing in some base passes and I promise I'll get you the touchdown you need," stated the audacious quarterback.

Marion was quite surprised by the bold, sophomore quarterback's words. He also noticed the youngster's steely blue eyes peering directly into his own. Well, h*e's all we have left,* thought the head coach. *What a way to make a living.* "Let it rip, Son. Let's see what you can do."

Ty Douglas ran out towards the huddle assuredly to find ten sets of eyes locked onto him in disbelief. The North Tucson fans were in shock without a word being uttered from the stands. Even the band and cheerleaders were silent.

"Who the hell are you,?" asked the center.

"He's the hotshot quarterback from the J.V., Ty Douglas," answered one of the receivers.

"You got to be kid'n me," stated the offense's tailback. "From the J.V.!"

"Hey, it's him or Gus," added the center.

"Enough said," replied the left guard with a smirk. "Let's cut the crap, kick some ass and go win us another state championship."

"Thanks for the confidence, Guys," said the peeved new quarterback, Ty Douglas, as he saw the "all-set" signal being given by the referee. "Don't worry, Guys. I'll do my job. Just make sure you kick some butt and do yours. Be ready to handle their pressure. I'm sure they'll bring some heat. Slot left, 33," stated Ty calling an inside run play as ordered on the sideline by the coaching staff. "Be ready for possible checks."

When Ty got to the line of scrimmage, he saw the defense's linebackers up tight, ready to blitz. The secondary was aligning in tight, man-to-man coverage. "Green, 232. Green 232," checked Douglas as he changed the called run play to a double slant pass pattern.

"What the hell's he doing? Just run the damn play, Son," yelled out Marion even though he knew his new quarterback wouldn't be able to hear him. With the defense showing blitz, Douglas took a quick one step drop from his shotgun alignment and fired a strike to the open slot back's inside slant route. The slot back caught the ball for a six yards gain and broke up field for an additional five for an eleven total yard gain.

"Great pass, Ty," yelled-out the excited mother. "Just show them what you got, Son."

That should calm down that blitz crap, thought the new quarterback.

"First down," yelled out the stern looking official, well aware of the gravity at hand.

"Nice job, Ted. I mean, Ty," yelled out Marion. *No, it doesn't look like you're going to soil your pants, does it, Kid? Actually, it looks like you have some balls.*

"Nice job, Rookie," said the split end. "See if you can do it again," as the huddled players started to feel a sense of renewed confidence.

"On-the-line, on-the-line," yelled out Ty as he took the signal from the sideline. The play was a slot cross pass, another good blitz beater. *So you assholes want to pressure me again,* thought Ty. The new quarterback immediately felt pressure from up-the-gut by a nose tackle, linebacker cross blitz. As he was quickly hit by the line-backer, Ty rifled a side arm throw to the slot back. The receiver crossed the formation five yards deep negating a second blitz effort in a row by the defense. The total gain was for twelve yards and another first down as Ty Johnson struggled to get two of the defenders off of him from his flattened position. He smiled as he saw the wide receiver bursting upfield.

Ty was quickly picked up off the turf by two of his offensive linemen as he shook off the linebacker's crushing hit. He immediately put the on-the-line offense in motion with no panic or worry in his voice. However, there was hesitation and confusion with the play call signal being sent in from the sideline. Amidst the mix-up, Ty took it upon himself to call a basic run play to help untangle the confused situation in the huddle. It was a draw play to the running back. Unfortunately, the back slipped and fell to the ground. With the football still in is hands, Ty deftly spun out of the grasp of another blitzing linebacker, evaded the rush of a defensive tackle and raced up field for a nine-yard pickup.

"Sorry. I missed the defensive tackle," grumbled the right guard as the two-minute offense worked quickly to get back to the line of scrimmage.

"No problem, Big Man," replied the supportive, substitute quarterback. Just get it done on the next play!"

On the draw play, Ty had noticed that the flanker's deep post route was wide open. As a result, Ty ran over towards the sideline to inform the offensive staff what he had seen. He was quickly given a green light, go-ahead signal to take the deep shot.

"What do you have, Ed," asked Marion.

"Might be going for it all, Ben," said the offensive coordinator. "It could be six points to the post route."

I hope we know what the hell we're doing, thought the head coach as his heart raced and his head pounded. The head coach then saw what his new quarterback had read from the alignment of the free safety.

"Give me some time, Guys. I think we have a clean shot to the post." Douglas read the play perfectly but was, once again, blitzed up the middle by a different blitz stunt. Ty scrambled out to the left, saw pressure coming hard from the outside and peeled back deeply to the right side of the formation. There was green grass in front of him as he sprinted to the outside. He looked up to see his flanker racing down the middle of the field. The young quarterback let go a deep, arcing post pass. The stadium suddenly went into a hush as the tightly thrown spiral cut through the air. The football fell flawlessly into the flanker's hands as he ran full stride towards the end zone. 18-yards later, the receiver crossed the goal line for the go-ahead touchdown.

"YES,!" screamed-out Ty Douglas as he sprinted to the end zone to congratulate the touchdown scoring wide receiver. The Tiger fans screamed wildly. He then bumped hips and slapped hands with the rest of the offfense as they pounded Ty's back and smothered him with giant bear hugs. When he broke free, he spun his head to the location in the stands where his mother was jumping up and down, screaming and hollering. A giant smile spread across his face.

I listen to my staff, stick in a sophomore quarterback whose name I don't even know and he takes us down the field for a two-minute drive for 83-yards and a game winning touchdown. And, I thought I had seen it all. "I owe you a cold one, Hawke," said the smiling Marion as he watched the extra point kick go through the uprights. "You're right. Terry certainly has some gumption."

"It's Ty," stated Coach Hawke.

"Ty, Terry, Tom," said Marion. "It's going to be fun watching this kid the next two years," said the head coach. Little did he know, he couldn't have been more wrong.

CHAPTER 4

The young Sean Dempsey had seemingly ended a promising career of being a teacher and a football coach as a result of that one, uncontrolled, crazed moment when he lifted Juron Potts up into the air and slammed him to the ground. As hard as he tried to get another opportunity, no school district would touch him. To the educational world he was a pariah, ...an untouchable. Eight years after his disaster, he got a call from his old college teammate and friend, Daryl Hoskins.

"Sean, this is Daryl. As you know, I'm now the principal here at Roosevelt High School and I have a teaching and head coaching gig open for one of the best linebackers I've ever seen play. I'd like for you to come in and visit to talk about the possibility."

"Wow! That's really something, Daryl," said the taken back, surprised Dempsey. *This has to be a crank call.* He drew in a deep breath hoping the proposal truly was a reality. "It's really nice of you to think about me after all these years, Daryl. But, honestly, I just don't know about trying to start all over again. I've been away from the classroom and football for eight years now." *This isn't a joke, is it? If it is, it's really a bad one, Daryl.*

Dempsey suddenly got light-headed. "Daryl, are you really talking about a teaching and a coaching job? Don't you know what happened eight years ago. This all sounds wonderful but I think you'll have to check in with your school board. I really doubt that they'd be interested." The ex-teacher and coach could, simply, not believe what he was hearing. *Coach and teach again,?* questioned a pensive Dempsey. *What the hell is Daryl thinking about?*

"The classroom would be your biggest adjustment, Sean. But I have a great buddy teacher I would team you up with. She'll get you on track in no time, I'm sure."

"What if I screw up again, Daryl? What do I do then,?" asked the puzzled Dempsey.

"Then you go back to your old life. Sean, you have a wife and three kids now. Wouldn't it be nice to have steady employment, health insurance for your family and some vacation time to spend with Mary Elizabeth and the kids?"

"Why me, Daryl? There's got to be hundreds of excellent candidates out there who would jump at such an opportunity." *Something's got to be wrong with all this. It sounds too good to be true.*

"Because, you'll be teaching at Roosevelt High School in the Latimore Heights section of the city, Sean. We're smack, dab in the middle of 'The Hood.' Heck, Sean, we've had race riots here the last two years. I have to hire good teachers. But, I also have to hire teachers who can teach and physically and mentally handle themselves and I'm definitely serious when I say that."

"But what about my track record, Daryl? The school district has to be concerned about my past incident."

"Not at Roosevelt they won't, ...especially if I'm the one pushing for you. I've done a good job of controlling many of the problems here. Not all, ...but many. As a result, they wouldn't dare mess with me. The only thing people now worry about when it comes to Roosevelt High is that we don't hit the media with too much negativity. Besides, I've been doing some checking up on you. Everyone's been telling me you're all grown up now. And, to boot, you're a highly decorated ex-Army Ranger sergeant. Heck, Sean. You're a war hero."

"No, Daryl. I'm not a war hero," said the veteran humbly with a sudden empty feeling in his chest. "I tried to do my job like I was supposed to, to the best of my ability. Unfortunately, that always didn't happen. Combat has a funny way of dictating what's going to happen to your life, Daryl."

The principal was quickly able to pick up on his old friend's dismay. "You served with distinction, Sean. That's one of the reasons I'm still proud to say that you're one of my good friends after all these years. And besides, the only negative I hear about you now is how much you complain about worn out knees and how you gulp down ibuprofen and coffee all day long. Sean, when you think about it, ...what do you have to lose?"

CHAPTER 5

"Bo! Bo! Get out of the way, Bo! Get out of the way," screamed a still asleep Sean Dempsey. In a dream, he pictured Bo Harris, his Army buddy being blown backwards into the air. "Medic! Medic! We need a medic," he continued to shout as he squirmed from side-to-side in the married couple's queen-sized bed four years after the Afghanistan compound skirmish. The bedding and his pajamas were soaking wet from Dempsey's nervous sweating.

Ease up, Chief. I'm right here, stated the apparition of Bo Harris as the corporal sat, leaned up against the wall, lighting up a cigarette. *Don't stress yourself, Sean. Everything's all right, Sergeant. Just remember, I got your back, Pal. I got your back.*

"Wake up, Sean. Wake-up,!" cried out Mary Elizabeth as she tried to grab her husband's flailing arms. It's all-right, Sean! You're in your bed. You're with me. It's all right!"

"Oh no," cried out Dempsey as he shot up, trying to shake off his sleep delirium. "It was Bo talking to me, Mary. He told me he's got my back again."

"It's O.K., Sweetheart," stated the apprehensive wife. "Everything's O.K. You were having another nightmare. But, you're all right now, Sean. You're with me. It's O.K. You're in your own home, ...your own bedroom."*Dear God, please help this poor man. Deep down he's such a good person, ... a good husband, ...a good father.*

"It's so dark in here," stated the new Head Football Coach at Roosevelt High School. "I'm so sorry, Mary," replied the distraught Dempsey as he continued to try to shake off the cobwebs in his head. "I didn't mean to scare you," as he started to slow down his heavy breathing. "I saw Bo again. He was sitting on the ground right next to me. He was telling me he has my back again. When are these dreams going to go away, Mary? I just wish they would stop. I keep seeing Bo and the others in the squad who didn't make it. I just want those dreams to stop!"

"Let's get up now," said his wife. "It's almost 5:30, anyway. You go take a shower and I'll put on some coffee. How about some pancakes and sausage,?" well knowing it was his favorite breakfast. "We still have some of that pure maple syrup your mom brought over." Mary Elizabeth Dempsey sighed as she threw on her bedroom robe and turned away from the husband she so devotedly, and truly, loved to make it to the kitchen. *All this medicine and therapy and doctors. When's the sleepless nights, the anger, the depression, the headaches all going to end. It seems to be so endless.* It was called Post-Traumatic Stress Disorder, PTSD, and the stress had become something that the medically discharged, Purple Heart, Army Ranger , Sean Dempsey now had such tremendous difficulty dealing with.

We'll find a way, Dear, thought the troubled wife. *Sooner or later, we'll find a way!*

After showering and dressing for the first day of his new job, Dempsey walked into the kitchen where his wife was flipping over the pancakes. "Wow, don't you look spiffy in that new shirt and tie," said Mary Elizabeth as she made a concerted effort to smile and help her husband smoothly shift over to a more pleasant mental state. *Now I just hope this diversion of a new teaching and coaching job will put an end to this anguish.*

"Thanks, Mary, but don't get any ideas about this shirt and tie stuff being a normal occurrence," said Dempsey with an ironic smile. "One day of this will definitely be enough, so let's not get carried away." Dempsey's wife covered his hand with her own hoping her new teacher and coach husband was ready for this new challenge.

It's going to really feel strange walking into that school today. I can't screw this up. I can't, thought Dempsey as he pushed his pancakes around his plate. He knew that the stress of the new teaching and coaching job is what triggered the early morning dream episode. And yet, he was also not sure that this was totally correct. He had long thought his football life was over concerning the Juron Potts incident and his resultant firing from his assistant coaching and teaching position at St. Ignatius, a fact that he was never fully able to accept. Then, like a bolt of lightning out of the sky, Sean Dempsey was offered an opportunity to drape a whistle around his neck once again. Although it might not have been the greatest of job opportunities, he was still getting a chance to be a part of his passion, ...football coaching, after his lengthy, forced hiatus. Maybe his long-desired goals had disappeared on him that horrific day when he slammed Potts to the ground. But, this time, he was determined to not let such an opportunity slip through his hands again.

After his medical discharge, Dempsey had returned to his home town and quickly found work as a housing framer. The housing market had improved greatly during his Army days in Afghanistan creating a need for house building workers once again. His injured body did not allow him the flexibility and nimbleness that he had before his combat injury. However, the tough, ex-Army Ranger pushed through the aches and pains in an effort to not let others realize his true condition. Seeing the ex-Sergeant pop down ibuprofen on a regular basis was about as far as others got to know about his discomfort. Most people didn't even know about him being an ex-Army Ranger and that's the way Dempsey wanted it. He had enough nightmares to remind him of what he had gone through but a short time ago. *If only I could get some decent sleep,* thought Dempsey. *If only the headaches would go away.*

Mary Elizabeth, the pretty, long, dark-haired wife of Sean Dempsey felt a quick wave of happiness run through her body as Dempsey suddenly bounded off the breakfast room stool to get to the school that had offered him this new, exciting opportunity. A big smile suddenly appeared across her face. She loved her husband dearly and was now full of hope that things were starting to go his way. For the first time in a long time, the flame in his heart that had once blazed so fiercely seemed to be reigniting. She prayed that the road to recovery was truly starting to happen for her husband. However, she also wished she could get rid of the feeling that it might not.

CHAPTER 6

LATE AUGUST 2016 (CHICAGO, IL)

Nearly nine months after leading North Tucson High School to its fifth straight Arizona State Championship, Ty Douglas stepped out from his mother's car. He leaned back into the vehicle with a smile to give his mother a hug and a kiss. It was then that he realized that it was almost two years to the day that his father had been killed when a drunk driver crossed an intersection causing the deadly collision. People told him that his father was fortunate to have died immediately, without pain. That did little to fill the tremendous hole left in Ty Douglas's heart.

Here we go again. This stuff's really getting old, thought Ty to no one specifically. *Another school and a total dump at that.* The school was Roosevelt High School, an old, downtrodden, beaten-up institution in the middle of a tough, dangerous, inner-city ghetto. *What the hell did you do to me this time, Mom? This sure isn't North Tucson High!*

"I love you, Mom and you hang in there."

"You hang in there too, Boy," urged the mother with tears streaming down her face. "I love you so much, Ty!"

And remember, Ty heard in his head from his deceased father, *...don't take shit from anybody,* as a knowing smile spread across the youngster's face. Accepting guff from somebody was not an option for Tyler Douglas. Not taking crap from anybody was, in reality, the family motto. That slogan had been drilled into his mind by his father for as long as he could remember. And, if it resorted to fisticuffs, Ty was well equipped to handle himself. He loved to box and was good at it with quick hands and a powerful left uppercut. Switching states as a result of his father's job changes lead to the loss of numerous boxing opportunities. However, a quick change to Karate led to rapid success and a black belt. Not knowing anything about the new kid at school was often a mistake for many a school's bullies who made the error of trying to pick on Ty Douglas.

Most people would describe Ty as nice looking, in a strong-featured, good-looks sort of way. He had long blond hair that covered the back of his neck and piercing blue-green eyes that quickly caught many a stranger's attention. He was well over six feet tall and tightly packed with muscle from rigorous weight lifting workouts. With the teachers and students, Ty was well received, quickly liked and had almost no trouble with his studies. However, his normally easy going, smiling demeanor and quietness didn't prevent him from being well known for his many "frequent flyer" trips to the principal's office for fighting. School counselors pointed out his occasional violent, hot temper to anger management needs. Ty looked at it as living up to the family motto. Unfortunately for Ty, he had already lived up to the family motto far too often in his limited years as a student. As Ty turned and looked up at the failing brick façade and the cracked, uneven, concrete stairway of Roosevelt High, he immediately thought of how the school must have really been awesome looking at one time. *Reminds me of all those big historical homes in D.C.* The high school, like so many of the buildings in the Latimore Heights area, had long been let go. The streets bordering the high school were lined with dilapidated buildings between old, worn-down store fronts and ancient, beat up looking apartments. Door-less apartment entry ways showed single light bulbs hanging from ceiling wires if there were lightbulbs and wires at all. Tireless, stripped down cars sat in weed filled, empty lots smothered with trash.

A little bit of community service cleaning and some paint would go a long way to, at least, making this place look decent, thought the new student. Realistically, Ty knew it would take a lot more than cans of paint and clean up efforts to revitalize Roosevelt High School and its surrounding neighborhood. "Taking down the eighteen-foot cyclone fencing with coils of barbed wire at the top would certainly help," said Ty quietly to himself.

"You've got to be kidding me," shouted out Addison Douglas to her real estate agent. "I spend all this money to have my son and I live in a decent community and have my kid go to a decent school and now you tell me he has to go to that abomination of a high school. This is a lot of crap!" Ty's mother, in her rush to get settled, had not checked the school boundaries. She assumed her son would go to Eisenhower High School as everyone else in the Stratford Hills community seemed to. Unfortunately, his mother's assumption was incorrect and all of the efforts in the world could not get the district administration to budge on the matter. The fear was of one student setting a precedent for others to be able to utilize. Being so close to the starting of the school year made it impossible for Ty to register at any of the crowded, private or parochial high schools in the area. They were, quite simply, all filled up with the children of parents who desperately did not want their children to have to attend Roosevelt High School.

CHAPTER 7

As Ty began to walk up the long flight of stone entry way stairs towards Roosevelt High School's doorway and metal detectors, he heard a nasty sounding voice with a heavy street accent taunting in his direction. "Hey, White Boy!" Ty looked up to see a somewhat tall, skinny Afro-American male, about the same age as himself, staring in his direction. Ontario Mosely was decked out in brightly colored clothing underneath a full length, black leather trench coat even though the temperature was well into the nineties. With the clothing all looking too big on his exceptionally thin frame, Ontario was holding on to a short, extremely heavyset, Afro-American girl. The girl's face was overly made-up with heavy layered eye make-up. Surrounding Mosely, the gang leader, was a group of ten or so of his cronies, all dressed in the same gangster style, sneering and snickering at Ty.

Ty's first reaction was to look behind him to see who the gang leader was talking to. Once he did, he realized the gangster was talking to him.

"Hey, Whitie, I'm talk'n to you, Pal. Or, should I call you Sweetness with that long, sissy, yellow hair,?" asked Mosely.

"I'm not looking for any trouble, Buddy," said an annoyed Tyler Douglas as he turned away from the thug disgustedly to walk towards the school's tattered front doors. As he did, he found a small wall of Mosely's accomplices blocking his way. Ty started fuming and was getting close to losing his temper. His smoldering anger started to build amidst his fear of being so thoroughly out-numbered.

"But you were look'n for trouble when I caught you check'n out my lady." Mosely glowered at Ty. "I don't like it when someone checks out my woman, you got that, Whitey!"

"I wasn't checking out anything other than where the front door was for this wonderful bastion of education," replied Ty. "So, why don't we just end this discussion before it becomes a problem for the both of us?"

"And, Sweetness uses fancy lingo too," announced Ontario to all of his gangster buddies who all snickered as if on cue. "Dude, I don't see this as much of a problem except your say'n my lady isn't anything," whined the provoking gang banger. "So she's noth'n, huh Pal?! I don't like it when someone says my woman's noth'n. That's very insult'n to her and to me."

Ty wanted to avoid an altercation. He knew he didn't need to get into a fight his first day of school getting to personally know the principal so rapidly. It was at that moment that Ty felt the movement of Mosely's people as they compacted around him.

Ty turned angrily to the gang bully with rage on his face. He started talking in a low, deliberate, menacing tone. "Listen, shit bird, ...if you want to go around back, you and me, one-on-one, then I'm all for it! But it wouldn't be that way, would it, Man? It would be me against you and all your dirt-bag friends because you're too gutless to go against me by yourself. Isn't that right, Dude?"

Mosely lifted his fist to deliver an overhand blow to Ty's jaw. As the gangster's fist came forward, Ty bowed his head backward forcing Mosely's wild swing to miss drastically. Ty then stepped forward to deliver a vicious left hook to the gangster's belly followed by a right uppercut to his jaw. Ontario Mosely melted to the ground as his eyes rolled up into his head.

Ty instinctively knew that Moseley's gang buddies would continue the attack from behind. He swung around, whipping his elbow into the chin of the closest attacking gangster. He, too, crumpled to the ground as Ty continued his defensive attack. Ty then punched a gangster closing in on him from the opposite side in his throat. Having totally immobilizing that threat, he slammed upward with the heal of his right hand into the next attacker, catching him just under his nose. Blood quickly poured out from the nostrils of that attacker as the gangster brought up both of his hands in an ineffective attempt to make the blood flow stop and to get the pain to dissipate.

Ty loaded up his righthand fist to take on the next assaulter when two of Mosely's attackers emerged from Ty's rear to pin his arms back behind him and drive his face down to the ground. Three new attackers then joined into the melee taking a clear path to Douglas. From the ground, Ty then explosively whipped his right arm and elbow free allowing him to spin his body around to pound his right foot into the crotch of the nearest attacker. However, he was now about to be totally overwhelmed by the remnants of Mosely's gang.

An extremely loud yell and awkward, backward movements by the gangsters seemed to dissolve the attack of the thugs. Ty suddenly saw a giant, mountain of a man in front of him, grabbing and powerfully throwing Mosely's gangsters left and right. Julius Goodman was assisted by four of his fellow football players. With the fear of facing Big Julie Goodman and his players, Mosely's gangsters quickly melted into the crowd.

"Hey, Man. You all right," said the mountain as he reached down to help pull up the battered and bewildered Tyler Douglas.

"This ain't over, Man," spit out Mosely as he got up off the ground holding his left arm and started to push his way through the crowd.

"It's been real, Bro," replied a bloodied Tyler Douglas. "You gutless bastard."

Big Julie chuckled at Ty's response. "Standing up to that jerk showed some balls, Man."

"If I went one-on-one with that fool, I'd crush him," stated Ty.

"Dude, from what I just saw, I don't doubt that. But the reality is, you would've been taking on ten or eleven of those other brothers as well, ...like you just tried to do. Now you might be one tough sucker, but you and I know those ain't very good odds. Stay away from that fool. That gang usually has blades. You might be tough. But I doubt you're that tough."

"Thanks for helping me," said Ty as he began to calm down.

"No problem, my man. Mosley's a turd. He's a bad dude, an evil person. And, you seem like a pretty good dude, ...for a white guy," chuckled Julius Goodman.

"I'm Tyler Douglas," as the still peeved teen stuck out his hand. "Ty for short. Man, that's the biggest hand I've ever seen. Matter of fact, you're the biggest human being I've ever seen. You're gigantic!"

"My momma says I'm thick boned. My name is Julius but everyone calls me Big Julie. And, these guys are my buddies. They're all football dudes. They can get a bit rambunctious. But, for the most part, they're really good people."

Ty noted the "rambunctious" word being used by Big Julie. *This guy's no dummy,* thought Ty, *even though he works* hard *to sound like a street guy.*

"What the hell just happened," asked Rod Franklin, a security guard and the Defensive Coordinator for Roosevelt High's football team. "This looks like a war zone, Julius. Was this a gang war or something? I leave for five minutes and all hell breaks loose!"

"Nah, Coach," replied Big Julie, Roosevelt's mammoth, star offensive tackle. "Mosely just tried to reestablish his dominance of being the leader of that dumb ass gang of his. Looks like he picked on the wrong dude to mess with. Got'ta say, Coach, that white boy over there sure can fight," as he pointed to Ty who was now being treated by the school nurse for cuts and bruises. "He took out half of Mosely's dirtbags for the count. But then he just had to take on a few too many."

"And, that's where you came in," stated Franklin.

"Someone had to help the dude," replied Big Julie. "Besides, I'm pretty sure he's the new quarterback who just transferred in and you know how much we need a quarterback, Coach. He might not be any good but he sure can fight. What he now doesn't realize is that the embarrassment of taking down Mosely in front of all those people won't be good for the dude, especially with him being a white boy."

Big Julie's right, thought Franklin. *The poor kid's going to have to watch his ass from here on out.*

"I have to call who,?" asked the Principal, Daryl Hoskins.

"A Mrs. Douglas, ...Addison Douglas," answered the administrative assistant. "She's the mother of Tyler Douglas, a newly registered student who was, as she said, 'accosted by a gang of thugs on the school's entry way steps before school started today.'"

"And, let me guess," interjected Hoskins. "Another Ontario Mosely incident."

"You got that right, Boss," answered the assistant. "I think you better be careful with this one though. She was a fireball on the phone, ...to say the least."

"Just what I need to start off the school year."

CHAPTER 8

"Come on in, Sean. Come on in," said Daryl Hoskins with a forced smile on his face as he sprung up from his desk chair to greet his new Head Football Coach. "Need some coffee? Renee just made a fresh pot."

"No thanks, Daryl. Another cup and I might go into orbit. So what's up, Daryl,?" asked Dempsey knowing that getting called into the principal's office usually meant trouble. "Did I screw something up already,?" with a questioning smile.

"No, no, Sean, It's nothing like that. It's just one of those nagging principal-type problems that I wanted to warn you about amidst about a thousand other such snags. Actually, this one's more of a nuisance-type problem concerning one of your assistant coaches. Now I know you were aware when I hired you that you couldn't hire any new assistant coaches since last year's staff had the option to stay on at Roosevelt as they all did. Those contracts were signed at the end of the school year this past spring."

"I clearly remember your concern when we discussed the assistant coaches last month. Your, ...or should I say our, problem is Carlo Martelli, ...our Offensive Line Coach. He certainly seems to be a different cat, that's for sure," stated the new Head Coach. "From what little I've been around him, he's certainly not what I would consider a team player."

"You hit the nail right on the head," said the principal.

"Don't forget now, Daryl. I'm a certified carpenter and a pretty good one at that," replied Coach Dempsey with a chuckle.

"Unfortunately, this nail is a pain in the ass, Sean. I get more negative calls from parents about him than the rest of the entire school.

"I get a kick out of his well-groomed, fifties-styled haircut and his steroid, muscle look. I think he would explode out of his coaching gear if he bent over the way their so tight.

"I think he has a definite forty plus year-old complex," added Hoskins. "Just be careful with him, Sean. He's a definite whiner and complainer. He goes out of his way to cause problems. To be honest with you, I wish I could get rid of him right now but that's tough to do with a tenured teacher."

Sean Dempsey sat behind his large, ancient looking teacher's desk awaiting the potential candidates for his varsity football team with an uncertain and, yet, pensive look on his face. His life had been flipped upside down with the sudden offer of a high school social studies teaching position and the head football coaching job. This all seemed so new to him. Being named the new Head Coach was so much more involved than being an assistant coach and he had only slightly less of two seasons of experience doing that.

Dempsey's classroom had become the designated team meeting room. Actually, there really were no specific rooms with enough chairs and desks at Roosevelt to be utilized as a football team room other than a classroom. As a result, Dempsey took it upon himself to spruce up his own classroom in an effort to create a fun environment for the team. The City Football Conference, itself, was predominately made up of inner-city schools with little money for early, preseason football practices. This resulted in the late, seasonal practice starting dates.

As the players walked into the room, they immediately noticed the smell of fresh paint. Dempsey had brought his coaching staff, minus the absent Coach Martelli, into school a few days early for a do-it-yourself makeover to help change the dour looking classroom. They also observed a large variety of eclectic football paraphernalia: prints of paintings, pictures, sayings, newspaper articles, pennants, old helmets and cartoons. The classroom had been changed into a small football museum.

The last of the football prospects were finally making their way into the classroom, working their way to empty seats. *Wow! Did I really look that young when I was in high school? Some of these kids look like youth league players. And yet, some of the others look like they were twenty or twenty-five. Not a lot of studly looking kids, that's for sure. Well, let's see what we can do with these guys. First of all, I've got to get them to believe in themselves.*

"I'm Coach Dempsey," stated the new coach. "I'm your new Head Varsity Football Coach. I'm very happy and excited to be a part of the Roosevelt High School family and to be a member of this team," he said sincerely. "The first thing I want to do is have every one of you stand up and tell us your name and what position you intend trying out for." The concept of a try-out for a position on the team was, actually, a bit of a stretch. The year before, Roosevelt had to forfeit their last four games when the team couldn't meet the district's required number of twenty-two participants suiting up for a contest. This situation occurred once a large number of the team's players were declared academically ineligible at the end of the first eight week's grade check period.

"I'm Dino DeTaglia and I'm THE middle linebacker here at Roosevelt."

"Ooohhh!," chanted the players out of respect for the linebacker. The book on DeTaglia was that he was a fierce hitter and had explosive speed.

I'm glad the middle linebacker is one of the players who looks like he's 25. Dino's certainly physically impressive looking, thought Dempsey.

"My name's Julius Goodman," said the team's behemoth offensive tackle. "But everyone calls me Big Julie. I'm an offensive tackle and I like to eat. Actually, it's kind of my hobby. Those foot-long sandwiches are my favorites, especially..."

"AWWWW! All you got'ta do is throw a sub in front of Big Julie and you'll have a free pass to the quarterback," stated Dino.

"At least I'm not ugly like you, Dino," retorted Big Julie. "That mug of yours frightens people."

"Let's try to be a bit more serious," stated the new head coach with a pleasant smile lighting up across his face. He had, long ago, learned to enjoy the fun and comradery of being a football player and being part of a football team. "I want to be sure that everyone gets a chance to stand up, tell us his name and what position they're going to try to play."

"I'm Jarvis Means," said the big outside linebacker. "I love knocking the snot out of anything that moves!" There were no smart guy retorts to that. Jarvis was another player who the team didn't want to mess with.

"Guys, let's stick to name and position," said Dempsey. "At this rate, we'll be here until ten o'clock."

"I'm Hug Wilson," said the rocky looking, six-foot one athlete. "As many of you know, I missed all of last season when I broke my leg in a practice warm-up, of all things. I'm a quarterback and I'm really glad to be back play'n again."

"Big Hug's back,!" yelled one player.

"Happy for you, Hug," said another as a chant of "Hug!, Hug!, Hug!" began to fill the room. Hug Wilson was one of the best athletes on the team and one of the most popular students at Roosevelt High School, football player or not.

"I'm Ty Douglas," said the recent transfer student athlete brandishing a series of cuts, welts and abrasions from his morning skirmish with Ontario Mosely and his gang. Everyone in the room knew about Tyler Douglas by the time the football meeting had commenced. The players discretely, or indiscreetly, stole looks of the new quarterback wondering what he looked like and to see how badly he had been beaten.

"I'm new here, transferring in from Arizona," said Ty, unashamed of his freshly displayed battle scars. "I'm a quarterback too. I'm really excited to be a part of the Rough Riders' football team." Ty's statement was said sincerely. No matter how tough another move was for him, he was always able to feel instantly comfortable among fellow football players. The big change for him, he noticed, was that for the first time in his life as a white person, he was now definitely a part of the minority. The room was full of a mixture of Afro-Americans, Hispanics, Caucasians and a mishmash of other ethnicities.

"Welcome, Dude," said Dino as he grimaced at Ty's beaten face. "It's nice hav'n you here, Man."

"Glad you're here," stated an earnest Julius Goodman, with a positive nod of his head.

Sean Dempsey felt thoroughly disgusted as he observed the condition of Tyler Douglas, no matter who he was. The new head coach was quickly getting a sense of some of the ills of Roosevelt High School.

Well, I guess I'm the guy who has to find a way to fit in this time, thought the new quarterback, dismissing the disfigured looks of his face.

"I'm Brock Jamal," stated the smallest player in the room. "I'm a cornerback..."

After the introductory exercise and going over of all the procedures needed to get everyone eligible to participate, Dempsey asked the group if they had any questions.

"Where'd you get all this cool football stuff,?" asked Ty.

"Well, I've loved football for as long as I can remember," said Dempsey proudly. "I started collecting any kind of football item I could find when I was a kid. Believe it or not, all this stuff was crammed into one, small bedroom."

"I like that picture of those three funny dudes making like they're place kicking a football," stated Big Julie. The big man had established himself as a local Latimore Heights folk legend. One of the few touchdowns scored by the team the season before happened when the running back broke off of one of Big Julie's famous pancake blocks. He knocked the opposing player flat to his back and then sat on top of the defender for the rest of the play as he watched the ball carrier scamper for 76-yards to the end zone.

"Are those the type of helmets you used when you played, Coach D, the ones with no face masks,?" joked safety Pete Logan.

"No wonder he looks like he does," said Dino DeTaglia good-naturedly and, supposedly, at a low enough volume for only the players to hear.

"No," answered Dempsey with a big smile. "They had face masks when I played."

"I guess they didn't work too well for you," said Dino to an outbreak of loud laughs by the players.

"O.K., O.K.," said the still smiling Dempsey. "The three people in that poster are The Three Stooges, a comedy group back in the days of black and white movies before we even had television. And, by the looks of it, I might have a lot of 'The Stooges' descendants in this room right now!"

The response by Dempsey was met by a number of sarcastic, but jovial, ha-ha's by the team. Dempsey was, inwardly, starting to like the make-up of this gregarious group. *They certainly seem to have some spunk. Now if they can only play a little football*!

"I like all of those sayings you have up there," said Hug. "Which one's your favorite?"

"I'd have to say that my favorite is the one behind me by Vince Lombardi, the famous Green Bay Packer coach. 'It's not whether you get knocked down; it's whether you get up.'"

"That sounds like something a boxing dude would say. What does that have to do with football,?" asked Leotis Brown, Roosevelt's best cornerback.

"I think Lombardi was trying to say that when life, in general, knocks you down, there's two things you can do. You can lay there and give up. Or, you can get back up and get back in the fight. Getting back into the fight doesn't guarantee success. But, staying on the ground certainly guarantees failure."

"Man, that's some heavy stuff, Coach D," said Big Julie. "You're one of those dang philosophical dudes aren't you?"

"I don't know about that," responded the new, smiling head coach. "But, I'm glad to see you guys taking notice of such important thoughts."

"Why's the back wall left blank,?" asked Ty.

"That's going to be the Roosevelt Football Wall of Fame. There's been a number of Rough Riders who have gone on to be great college and pro players. There have also been some former Rough Rider football players who have gone on to great heights in their business and professional careers: doctors, scientists, politicians. We've even had an astronaut flying around in outer space."

"Maybe one of us can get our picture on that wall," stated the team's center, Bernardo Diaz.

With a warm smile, Dempsey replied, "that's the plan. Although I hope it will be a good number of you. Not just one."

"How come you took this job,?" blurted out Leotis. "I thought nobody wanted it."

"That's exactly why I got the job. I'm the only knucklehead who was dumb enough to say yes," to another chorus of laughter and smiles.

"Coach D, what happened to the side of your face and your neck and your ear,?" asked Jarvis Means. "Man, that looks like a real bad burn or something?" The rest of the room of players became wide-eyed and dead quiet, definitely surprised by Jarvis's audacity.

Sean Dempsey suddenly clammed up for the next few seconds. "You were wounded in the war, weren't you,?" asked Leotis Brown.

After a few more seconds of delay, Dempsey replied, "...yes I was Leotis."

"My older brother was over there," continued Leotis. "Thank you for your service, Sir."

CHAPTER 9

Dempsey felt the need to pick-up the pace of the meeting. As excited as everyone was for the start of football, the late-summer, hot classroom started to drain the energy of all involved.

"Gentlemen, the Roosevelt Rough Riders football team has not won a game in over four years. The streak is now 43 losses in a row!"

"Gee, I'm really glad you reminded us about that,!" said Big Julie facetiously.

"Big Julie, I know you're trying to be funny. But to be honest with you, that's what really excites me! We only have one way to go and that's up. And, the best part is there's not a person in the Greater City Conference who thinks we can." *There's a lot of people who probably think success is impossible at Roosevelt. I sure hope to hell they're not right.*

"Bam!" The classroom door burst open and slammed against the wall. In strutted Ontario Mosely. The tall, mouthy gangster was, again, wearing his trademark, full-length leather trench coat even though the temperature in the room was stifling. Mosely, and his boisterous entourage of seven other gang members, disturbed the meeting as they loudly aimed demeaning put-downs towards some of the players.

"Hey-hey-hey," chided Mosely to Big Julie. "If it isn't Fat Albert, himself," referring to the big, overweight 1970's and 80's television cartoon character. "It sure looks like you didn't miss any meals this summer. Nigga, you couldn't be but a biscuit away from four hundred." Dempsey cringed as he heard the "N" word used aloud.

"And look what we have here, ...the new white boy quarterback all set to be my back-up. My-oh-my, if I were you I'd get some work done on that face of yours, Whitey. Looks like you got run over by a truck or someth'n."

"Hey hero. Just keep in mind that I only needed two punches to take you out for the count and that's with all your gangster dudes helping you," stated Ty as the players all pounded on their desks and let go a chorus of oooohs. "I'd love to go mano y mano with you Ontario. Too bad you don't have the balls to do it." The embarrassed Ontario Mosely's eyes opened wide as he suddenly couldn't find words to come out of his mouth.

"I'll tell you what, Ontario," said Big Julie as he stood up in his six foot six plus frame." Why don't you and I go outside where we could discuss my weight problem. You could even bring along Marcel, that mini crime boss runt of yours if you like, so we could get this all straightened out."

"Aw, you guys know I'm just mess'n around," said Ontario as he quickly, and nervously, backed off his verbal attacks on Ty and Big Julie.

"Just what we needed," murmured Coach Franklin. "I thought they locked this idiot fool up for good this past summer." *We've got to find a way to get rid of this degenerate and we better do it fast.*

Sean Dempsey's blood pressure skyrocketed. "Sit down, please, Julie. I'll handle this. Is there something I can do for you, Ontario,?" asked the extremely annoyed head coach. "And, if I have one more smart-mouth comment from you or any of your home boys here, I'll have the security people here in a heartbeat. Matter of fact, Coach Franklin, why don't you help me out and go and see if you could invite a few of those security folks to come and join us, would you?"

"With pleasure," replied Franklin as he sprinted to the classroom door.

"What'cha talk'n about,?" asked Mosely. "Your leader is here, Homie! I'm the man! I'm Ontario Mosely! The quarterback of the Roosevelt Rough Riders! The star of this show, ya dig?"

"First of all, I'm not your homie," said the peeved Dempsey. "And, it's Coach Dempsey to you and your buddies. You're all late to this meeting so turn your disrespectful butts around and wait out in the hall. When this meeting is over, I'll then talk to you and any of your buddies here who might still be interested in trying out. Got that, Homie?"

"Man, this here's a joke, Clyde," stated the now embarrassed gang leader. "Without me, there ain't no team, COACH DEMPSEY!"

"There's the door, Ontario."

"How are you gon'na run this show if you don't have me? What'cha do'n, Man?"

"Dialing security."

"I'm so glad you stood up to Mosley in front of all the players, Sean," said Franklin. "The kid's nothing but a gang-banging hoodlum. You made a big statement by not putting up with his rubbish. Last year's head coach was terrified of Ontario and the players knew it. He let Ontario rule the roost. We had no control over the team what-so-ever. You gave Ontario and the team a big notice of the fact that a change is being made. And, a dramatic change at that."

Dempsey hesitated for a few seconds before he made a reply. *Oh boy! What the hell did I do? No one else wanted this job for a reason. I was the only one stupid enough to jump into this fire.* "This problem is not going to go away easily, is it Rod?"

"No, it's not," answered Franklin. "It's probably going to get a lot worse now that you've dug your heels in. A lot worse."

"Tyler, what are we going to do about this situation,?" asked Addison Douglas, Ty's mother. "I understand that you were the victim but you look awful. You were the one who got jumped for no reason by a pack of those hooligans. Ty, I'm as scared as hell that these punks are going to hurt you, or even worse. I can't live with that. I just won't be able to live with that. I still can't deal with the fact that Daddy's gone. You're all I have left, Son. I'm so, so sorry that I screwed up leasing a place just over the Roosevelt School District border. Unfortunately, there seems to be nothing I can do about that now. You tell me, Honey. What can I do?"

CHAPTER 10

"Hi," called out the energetic voice of Marge Strausser as the 50 something Social Studies teacher flew into Sean Dempsey's classroom. "I know the homeroom bell goes off in a few minutes," said the fireball teacher. "I've been busy putting together a good plan for you. I'm glad you're only teaching one grade subject for your five classes. After a while, that might get a little boring. However, when you get hired right before the school year starts, that's the best way to go."

"O.K., said Dempsey with a broad smile across his face. "I'm sorry. But, I really don't know who you are."

"Oh! Sorry! I'm Marge Strausser," replied the veteran social studies teacher. "I'm your assigned teaching buddy. We'll be working together for a while. I've been told you're pretty sharp so I'll just leave you the first month's lesson plans and let you come see me when something isn't clear. Actually, you can go off on your own when you feel confident enough. In the meantime, here are outlines to follow, ...homework assignments, quizzes, tests and a lot of other good stuff. I've arranged for the tech people to get you up to snuff on working the newer, technological equipment. The world of technology in the teaching field is what has exploded in the last eight years since you've been gone. I imagine you're pretty good with computers, right?"

"Well, thanks, Marge," said Dempsey after listening to the barrage of words. "And, yes. I'm pretty good with computers."

"Now you know this is a two-way street, don't you, Coach Dempsey?"

"I'm not sure what you mean, Marge," said the Head Football

Coach with both a frown and a smile. "And, by the way, I'm Sean."

"Well, Sean. I've agreed to help you with the understanding you have to check in on me if there are any problems. My room is right next door. You don't follow me, do you Sean?"

"Not really, Marge."

"If one of our famous Roosevelt riots breaks out or if you hear screaming or yelling, you get to my room as fast as you can to make sure I'm O.K."

"You're kidding me, right,?" responded Dempsey.

"Do I look like I'm kidding, Coach Dempsey,?" answered Marge.

CHAPTER 11

The first practice was called a try-out day. With the low number of participants out for the Roosevelt football team, very few, if any, would be cut. The air, on the warm, muggy day, was filled with excitement. There was a definite feeling of enthusiasm from the players and the coaches. This was true despite the fact that during early practice sessions, the only uniform equipment that could be used was helmets for the first three days by state law. This was done to help the players properly acclimate themselves to the, often, intense summer heat and humidity of preseason practices.

The football fields, of which there were three, had one game field and two practice fields. They were a shamble. The waning heat of summer had dried up the majority of the grass. Actually, the practice fields had far more hard packed dirt than any form of grass. Dempsey was able to, at least, get the grounds keeper to line both practice fields. The game field had some late summer grass. The plan was to stay off of the game field for as long as possible.

Even though it was a weekday, the sideline was still loaded with overly encouraging parents, all sure that this was a big, although unrealistic, step in their child's road to the NFL. From the start, the young prospects were flying around the field at a speed that would be tough to maintain.

The new Head Coach was in a great mood. It felt so good to be back on a football field, even if it was Roosevelt High. For the last eight years, the football itch would take over his mind and body when a summer's end would start to settle in and he could feel the cool evenings starting to bring in the fall weather, ...football weather. *Time for some ball,* thought the head coach. *Time to get it on!*

"How long do you think this will last at this pace,?" asked Dempsey.

"About another ten minutes or so," answered Rod Franklin, the Defensive Coordinator. "Some won't even last that long."

"A cold one says number 67 will up-chuck in the next three minutes," stated Dempsey.

"I'll take that bet," said defensive coordinator. He grabbed the stop watch at the end of his neck lanyard and punched the start button. Dempsey and Franklin had started to form a strong bond in the short period of days they had been working together. They both loved football and coaching and found they enjoyed working with one another, wise guy antics and all.

Rod Franklin was an ex-NFL cornerback who played for the Giants for eight years. He was All-Pro three of those seasons. Sean Dempsey had been around a number of former NFL players during his football days. Many former pros worked hard to extend their days of glory on the field into their everyday lives. Schmoozing with big money people, picking up high prized television and radio commercials, working the crowds of parents and young players at summer football camps all played to their celebrity status. A smaller group of dedicated former pros worked hard to stay in the world of football by becoming coaches. Fortunately for most, it was not to continue the efforts of making the big bucks of the NFL. Instead, many found solace coaching at colleges and universities, big and small, all across the United States. Some coached at junior colleges and at high schools and junior high schools and even in youth programs. They did it for the love of the game and a sincere desire to work with and help young people. Rod Franklin was one of those ex-pros.

"Uh-oh!," cried out Franklin. "He stopped running," now describing the action of the bet on the player as if he were a radio show sports play-by-play announcer. "His face is now chalk white. He breaks to the clump of bushes by the fencing. Ohhhhh! The wannabe football player suddenly up-chunks all over the practice field and himself. Man, he didn't even make a minute."

"And, of course, you now have him for the rest of practice since his puking makes him a defensive player, ...at least for today," added Dempsey.

As far as cutting prospective players, Dempsey's only concern was being sure to not allow any youngster to be on the practice or game field who physically shouldn't be. As much as anyone, he knew that football was a dangerous game. Football was not a contact sport. It was classified as a collision sport and rightfully so.

"Who do you like so far, Sean,?" asked Franklin.

"I like those two kids who are working out with Ontario Mosely at quarterback," answered Dempsey. "That Douglas kid is an excellent athlete with good speed and he sure can chuck the ball around. It will be fun to see what he can do in the forty," referring to the soon-to-be timed 40-yard dash. "He's the kid who transferred in from Arizona, isn't he?"

"That's him. I don't know if you heard about it, Sean, but Douglas got into a big-time tussle with Ontario Mosely and his gang yesterday. Luckily for him, Big Julie came to his aid. I have to say, Douglas stood his ground. The problem is Mosely's a real thug."

"Let's keep an eye on them both," said Dempsey. "I got the feeling that they both might be needing some help." *We're the ones who are going to be needing some help before this situation shakes out, ...IF it shakes out.*

"Got'cha, Sean."

"I also like Hug Wilson, but not as a quarterback," continued Dempsey. "It also looks like he has some jets. He's a horse and punts as well. Hug mentioned in the meeting how he didn't play last year. What happened?"

"Broke his leg the first day of practice," replied Franklin. "He was a man among boys when he played on the freshman team. He flat out ran over people. I think he'll be a heck of a linebacker, Sean," to which Dempsey didn't reply.

"Those wide receivers, Rayshawn Davis, Wooley Woolridge and Seamus Collins look like a good crew. With their speed and quickness, we could have some legitimate deep threats. I really like having one, tall wide receiver like Collins to play split end. You can get some great mismatches with a big receiver like that versus small cornerbacks. The Big Julie kid looks like he's the real deal. He's a big, big man for a person who moves so well. Just wish we had some more linemen like him. Did he already know the Douglas kid when he came to Ty's aid?"

"No. It's that Big Julie hates Mosely. He almost goes out of his way to hassle Ontario. Mosely's terrified of the Big Julie."

"I'm really concerned about that little number 14, Brock Jamal," said Dempsey after scanning his practice roster sheet. "I fear for his life when I watch him running around out there. He might be too small, Rod. And, he doesn't seem very strong."

"He's a heck of a kid, Sean. And, he loves football. His brother Jordan played for us and was one of the best corners this school has ever produced. He now plays for the Chiefs in The League. He looked just like Brock did when he was the same age. All of a sudden, he shot up almost five inches in a year. I'd really like to keep him. He's a tough little sucker. He doesn't have the nickname Brock the Rock for nothing."

"I'm still not so sure, Rod," replied Dempsey as a frown lined his forehead. "You'll have to promise to keep an eye on him for me. I really don't want him to get hurt."

"I'll stay on top of him, Sean. I promise."

Dempsey turned around to look back on the field and saw two wide receivers, both running square-in routes from the opposite sidelines, going directly at one another. Unfortunately, the wide receiver coach, Sonny Walters, didn't see the receiver to his backside mistakenly running the route. A perfect line drive pass was thrown by Ty to a point that split the two in-coming receivers. "WHACK!"

"What the hell's going on,?" yelled out Dempsey as the two receivers slowly got up from the ground. "We have to be careful! We can't lose two players because we have two receivers running the same routes into one another. Wise up, Coaches!"

CHAPTER 12

"O.K., let's have the offensive and defensive linemen go to the north end of the practice field by the blocking sleds," said Dempsey as the first practice continued. Dempsey didn't realize it but his coaching fell right in line with his eight years away from the game. "All the skills position players go to the south end of the field for a One-On-One pass drill. The quarterbacks are doing the throwing."

Ty Douglas and Hug Wilson stood around absent mindedly as the passing drill was being set up. They fiddled around with footballs in their hands as they waited to be told what routes were going to be thrown to.

"Hey, my name's Hug," said Hug Wilson as he introduced himself with a look of worry stretched across his forehead. *The word is, this dude's good, really good.* His warm smile, however, showed a definite sense of sincerity. "You're the new guy from Arizona, aren't you? I heard you're pretty good."

"Ty," said the new quarterback with a happy smile. "Nice to meet you. I heard you're pretty good yourself." *Man, this guy's a little thick to be a quarterback. He looks more like a linebacker or a fullback. He's all packed up.*

"I'd like to think so," replied Hug. "They say competition brings out the best in everybody. So, I guess we'll see," as they smiled at each other.

Ty was lightly flipping the football up into the air as he talked to Hug. Unexpectedly, Ty didn't feel the football falling into his throwing hand.

"I'll be take'n that, Man," said Ontario Mosely. "Just so ya know,

Dude, I'm the quarterback around here. So, you won't have to worry about that competition garbage." Ontario turned his back on Ty and Hug to walk to the line of scrimmage.

The switch on Ty Douglas's short fuse flipped to fight mode. "Hey Home Boy," called out Ty as the hairs on the back of his neck bristled. "If you ever try to take a ball out of my hands again, I'll shove it right up your ass!"

The strutting Ontario wheeled around aggressively to attack Ty. As he approached Douglas, Ontario took a big windup with his right arm and fist in an effort to deliver a punch to Ty's head. Ty ducked under Ontario's wild swing and delivered a fierce, right hand uppercut into Ontario's stomach. Ty then ripped off a left-handed hook to the side of Ontario's head. Ontario immediately dropped to the ground. He had a tough time regaining his breathe and shaking off the dizziness in his head. He then started retching but nothing came out of his mouth. One of Ontario's cronies then started to attack Ty, going to Ontario's aid. He was suddenly clotheslined by a huge club to his chest in the form of Big Julie Goodman's right arm.

"Not a good idea, Bro, if you know what I mean," said Big Julie to the flattened gangster. "Let's let this work itself out in a one-on-one fashion, man-to-man. I know that concept is a little difficult for you to understand but I'm sure you know where I'm coming from, ...right,?" as the silent gangster melted back into the crowd of players.

"Whoa, whoa," yelled Hug as he stepped in front of Ty to make sure there was no further altercation. There was dead silence by the players as they saw the deflated Mosely hovering over the ground.

"You know, I don't think our boy Ontario really knows how to fight very well," stated cornerback Leotis Brown.

"You might be right," replied Big Julie. "But that white boy sure does!"

"This ain't over, White Bread," uttered Ontario, still unable to get up off the ground.

"Hey, Ontario," replied Ty. "I still only had to throw two punches. Are you really that soft?" *I guess I better not turn my back on this*

Ontario dude. Like Big Julie says, this guy's a bad man.

"What's this all about,?" yelled Dempsey as he ran over to the drill once he saw trouble brewing.

Ty Douglas said nothing. His squinted eyes were angrily locked on his adversary.

"This cracker punched me in the stomach," whined Ontario.

"After you took a swing at him," said Coach Franklin.

"Whose side are you on, Nigga,?" asked Mosely bitterly of the defensive coordinator.

"Don't nigger me, Ontario," answered the Afro-American coach acidly. "And for your information, I'm on the side of the Rough Riders, no matter who the player or what the color."

CHAPTER 13

"What was that all about,?" asked Dempsey.

"Another attempt of intimidation by one of our fine, young gang members at Roosevelt High School," answered Franklin. "Ontario tried to hassle the Douglas kid but it backfired on him again."

"Douglas seems like a good kid. But, from what I understand, that's the second time in two days that he's gotten into scrapes with the wrong guy. He won't last long if he keeps that up. I probably need to talk to him before this gets out of hand." *Great! That means I'll have to talk to the Ontario kid too.*

In a drill later in the practice, Ontario took the football from the snapping machine, dropped back awkwardly and threw a pass downfield. The pass wobbled like a wounded duck and flew over the intended receiver's head by a good three feet. "He's not very good, is he,?" asked Dempsey.

"You're being real polite when you say it that way," answered Franklin. "Actually, he's terrible. Always has been since he played Pop Warner football."

"And, all he talks about is his rocket of an arm," said Dempsey.

"It's more like a misguided Scud missile, if you ask me," replied Franklin. "Ontario Mosely couldn't hit the side of the proverbial barn from ten yards away if his life depended upon it."

"Then how the hell was he your quarterback last year, Rod?

There had to be other players who could have done a good job for you. There's always a good athlete or two who could make it as a decent quarterback, especially on the high school level."

After a slight pause to gather his thoughts, Franklin replied. "Because no one else wanted to play quarterback once Ontario got to him. They were too scared."

"You mean to tell me that our quarterback, who's no good, was the starter because he intimidated anyone else who wanted the position with that gangster shit?"

"That's the way it was last year."

"Well, that sure isn't going to happen this year, Rod, or any other year that I'm here," spit out Dempsey with vehemence. I'm rapidly getting tired of hearing about this tough guy, gangster nonsense at Roosevelt High School, I can tell you that!"

"Unfortunately, Sean, you're going to have to prepare yourself for a lot of the crap that goes on at Roosevelt. You're going to see a lot more of it if you intend to teach and coach here for any length of time. Football's important to people like you and me. The fact is, you're going to see a lot more than you want and that's not just on the football field."

As the simple One-On-One pass drill wound down, Ontario interrupted the flow of the drill. "Red, Slider," Ontario barked out to the wide receiver to his right as he called an audible signal from the previous year's season. He also gave the receiver a hand signal to check, and change, his route. "No, no," rechecked the quarterback. "Geronimo, Geron..."

Dempsey blew his whistle loudly. "Ontario, what the hell are you doing, Son," asked Dempsey.

"I'm check'n off, Man! I'm check'n off!," shouted out the quarterback. "What'cha think I'm do'n? I was tired of just throw'n stupid curl routes and thought I'd fresh'n up this dull, boring practice. Ya know what I mean, COACH?"

With a finger squarely pointed at the pompous player, Dempsey barked out, "...Ontario, let's get something straight. If you want to be the quarterback here, you're going to throw to who I tell you to and with the type of pass I want thrown. Got that?"

"Hey Dude, I'm the field general here. When the whistle's blown, I'm the man,!" spewed out Ontario venomously. "Not some run down, flunky old dude who pounded nails for the last hundred years," as he beat his chest with the fist of his right hand. Dempsey suddenly clenched his own fist as a look of rage exploded onto to his face. He started to rapidly move forward towards Ontario.

"Sean,!" yelled out Franklin as he ran up to the confrontation wide-eyed, shaking his head negatively from side-to-side. "I need you over here for a minute!"

Dempsey stopped in his tracks. He then took a deep breathe to calm himself down. "Ontario, I'm sorry to say that I got a feeling this team may not be big enough for the two of us."

"That's funny. This is one time I'm in total agreement with you, Coach Dempsey, f'sure!" Ontario turned his back to Dempsey and strutted back to the line as the team listened to the verbal interchange intently.

CHAPTER 14

"O.K., Guys," said Dempsey to his staff as they took seats on the locker room benches. "That was a good day's work out there. It looks like we have some talented players and some excellent speed. We just might be able to put something together that's not too bad. I just worry about our depth. And, we're going to have to keep an eye on the situation between Mosely and Douglas."

"I've been here for a long time and never thought I'd see it look this decent," said Franklin. "Now, I'm not saying we're any good right now. But, I like the direction we're going."

"I like how you're keeping a tight leash on things, Sean," said Coach Williams. "We'll lose a few kids who won't be able to handle the discipline. But, most of those kids wouldn't be of help to us in the long run anyway. And, like we talked about out on the field, you're correct to worry about Mosely and Douglas. That could be a tough one if we don't stay on top of it."

"Carlo, you seem to be acting like this is all one big joke," said Dempsey with a wry smile set across his face. "Maybe you can share your thoughts with us."

"Come on! Who's shit'n who,?" said Martelli. "We're the clowns of the conference and everybody knows it and that includes YOU, Coach. Yeah, we'll fire these kids up for the first game, which I'll remind you is Eisenhower, the perennial state champs and then we'll quickly fold our tents. And, wait till mid-semester grades come out and you have to forfeit half of your schedule. That's when you'll figure out what Roosevelt's all about. So do yourself a favor, Coach, and start pounding down the ant-acid tablets now before you get an ulcer.

"You're quite the positive person, aren't you, Carlo,?" stated an annoyed Dempsey facetiously.

"Nah. I'm just a realist, Coach," retorted Martelli. "And it won't take long for you to become one too."

"Rod, can I see you for a moment, please," asked Dempsey as the two coaches walked out of the coaching room to get to their cars. Franklin immediately thought he was about to be dressed down for jumping in between Dempsey and Ontario Mosely towards the end of practice. Dempsey placed his hands on his hips and pressed his lips together as he stared at the ground for a few seconds. A heavy scowl creased his forehead. It was obvious that he was distraught about the on-the-field altercation.

"Thanks, Rod," stated Dempsey. "I was close to screwing things up again big time. I definitely have to get a better handle on myself or this is all going to be for nothing."

Franklin delayed replying, trying to organize what he was going to say. Though the two had been working together for only a matter of days, he felt he needed to cut through the honeymoon period and be frank and honest. "Sean, you're going to have to keep your cool if you're going to make it here at Roosevelt," stated the defensive co-ordinator. "I know about your background. The principal filled me in on everything. He asked me to keep an eye on you and help you get accustomed to the culture here at Roosevelt and in Latimore Heights. I'll tell you right now, Sean, you can't allow a confrontation like that with a player, or a student, get to you. You have no wiggle room. And Sean, there's a lot of Ontario Mosleys here at Roosevelt High School. You're going to have to find a way to handle such people the right way if you're going to last very long. And, believe me, Coach, we've had a lot of teachers and coaches here who couldn't do that."

Dempsey pensively stared at the parking lot floor. "Quite the afternoon, huh Rod?"

"Quite the afternoon, Sean."

As Dempsey walked towards his jeep, he noticed something seemed odd. He immediately thought there was a flat tire on the far side of his jeep, the side that was shielded from the view of the locker room. He was wrong. There were two flat tires. The front and back tires had been slashed. "WUZ UP DEMP," stated the white spray paint on the jeep's side door. Dempsey fumed. "You got'ta be kidding me!"

"Ty, I got a phone call from one of the mothers this afternoon saying you had another altercation with that Mosely gangster," stated Ty's mother.

"Who told you that, Mom?"

"Does it matter, Ty?"

"No, ...I guess not."

"Ty, you promised me you would get this situation under control. You've got me so worried, Son. Maybe I should call your coach. I don't like hearing about all this gang-banger stuff. That's far more than you should have to handle. What happened, Ty?"

"I got in a fight with Mosely today. He tried giving me some crap. I told him if he did it again, I'd shove the ball up his ass and then he came at me. He took a wild swing and I nailed him in his belly and then to his head and dropped him. Mom, let me try handling this by myself for starters. If there's any more problems, I promise I'll talk to Coach myself and you can come with me if you want."

"O.K., Son. Let's start out that way. Ty, I know you can take care of yourself. But, you don't want to mess around with a bunch of thugs. Promise me you won't let that happen."

"I promise you, Mom. I don't want problems any more than you do." *How do I get out of this mess,* thought Tyler Douglas.

CHAPTER 15

The doorbell rang unexpectantly. Ty's mother went to the front door and saw a mass of dark clothing clogging up the peephole. "Who is it,?" answered Addison Douglas.

"I'm Julius Goodman, Mrs. Douglas. Ty and I made an arrangement to pick him up for weight training this morning." Ty's mother opened the door's chain lock just enough for her to see the biggest person she had ever seen.

"Mom, it's O.K.," as Ty rushed to close the chain lock door to get it opened. "Come on in, Julie," said Ty "and meet my mother."

"This is my friend, Julius Goodman but everyone calls him Big Julie." Ty's mother was being besieged by all the information suddenly being thrown her way. "Big Julie volunteered to pick me up in the morning and take me home after practice since he really doesn't live that far from us. And, we're in three of same classes and he's real smart too. I would have told you all of this last night but you fell asleep on the couch early."

"Well, that's all great," said the still overwhelmed mother. "Now you won't have to take the bus, Ty."

"And I have an old 83 Chevy that's in great shape and I'm a very safe driver," said Big Julie with a broad, goofy smile across his face.

"Well," said the mother. "I'm very glad you're able to help us, Big Julie."

"We better get going, Julie," said Ty.

"Uhhh, ...can I ask you what's that great smell, Mrs. Douglas," said Big Julie. "It sure smells good!"

"Oh, that's a batch of apple, cinnamon muffins," answered Ty's mom. "Would you like to take some with you?"

"Oh, no. Thank you, Mrs. Douglas. But, I do appreciate your offer and it sure does smell good."

"Mom, can you just give him three muffins so we can get out the door. He'll have them all eaten by the time we get to first period anyhow."

The two football players started to leave when Big Julie stopped, turned to Ty's mother with a smile on his face and whispered, "... don't worry Mrs. Douglas. We'll be sure to take care of Ty." As a result, Addison Douglas now had a bag of some sort of bakery goods ready for Big Julie every morning.

A peeved Sean Dempsey got to school early, driven by his wife, Mary Elizabeth. He seethed as he had to wait for the local car dealership to locate two of the special-order tires he needed for his Jeep. Dempsey had no tolerance for people he thought of as thugs. His problem now was that he had a number of such people on his team and he now knew it was only a matter of time before it would all come to a head. The leader of that crew, he well knew, was Ontario Mosely. As Dempsey stood next to his vehicle sipping hot coffee from his to-go cup watching the mechanic install the tires, he realized that Mosely and his band of thugs were the enemy. They might not be the type of enemy he faced in Afghanistan as a soldier. Never-the-less, they were now the enemy.

The mechanic finally stood up. He looked at Dempsey, shrugging his shoulders. "Looks like someone doesn't like you very much, Coach."

From the get-go of the first practice, Dempsey saw that the basic fundamentals of the Rough Riders' players were dreadful.

Quarterbacks and running backs couldn't exchange the football on hand-offs. Linebackers and defensive linemen didn't know how to shed blocks. Offensive linemen crossed their feet when stepping to a blocking target. The list went on and on.

"Wow,!" said Dempsey with a sinking feeling in his stomach. *This is atrocious,* thought the Head Coach. *The kids don't have a clue. It's almost like they've never been coached, ...never been taught.* "You almost don't know where to start, Rod," he stated to his Defensive Coordinator. "We're consistent, though. Unfortunately, we're consistently awful."

"What do you mean by almost,?" asked Franklin.

"Blocking and tackling, Rod. No matter how good you are, or think you are, you start and end with blocking and tackling. That's the foundation of the game of football. For us, the good thing is we can only get better." *Or, at least I hope that's true!*

Dempsey walked over to the far end of the football practice field to observe the offensive line run blocking drills. He quickly became dismayed to hear the constant yelling, screaming, shouting and negative vibes he heard in the timeframe of his two minute or so walk to observe Coach Carlo Martelli and the offensive line. What then shocked the head coach was, simply, to see extremely poor coaching for the entire fifteen-minute practice block of time.

When practice was over and the players dismissed, Dempsey walked over to address Martelli. "Carlo, I need to talk to you for a few minutes," as Dempsey waited for the rest of the team to clear the field. Martelli, realizing he had been observed, folded his arms, throwing off a disgusted look towards the new head coach. "To be very honest, Carlo, I'm quite concerned about the quality or, more precisely, the lack of quality football coaching I just observed."

"But, that's how I..."

"Whoa, whoa," said Dempsey. "This is not a discussion, Carlo.

I'm the head coach now and you need to understand where I'm coming from if you're going to remain a coach on MY staff. You need to understand that, Carlo."

"These are still young kids, Coach," continued Dempsey. "For the most part, they're here because they love the game, ...because of the friendships and the joys and fun they have being members of a team. To be honest, Carlo, I wouldn't have been very happy if I had known you were my coach."

Martelli stewed with anger. "Are you finished now, Dempsey,?" asked the belligerent offensive line coach. After a short delay in which the offensive line coach glared at Dempsey with a sense of disgust, Martelli continued. "Don't give me that soft, cuddly, 'foofoo' bullshit. You played the game. When you're an offensive lineman, you've got to start out with a tough, mental attitude. You need to hit, hit, hit and grind defenders into the ground to physically hurt them, ...something that YOU don't seem to understand. Tough people make tough players."

"And tough players rely on proper skills and techniques to be effective. Your drill period practice plan seemed to totally ignore that. If you're going to continue coaching here at Roosevelt, I'm going to want to see sound teaching and coaching instruction of basic offensive line fundamentals. Am I being clear enough for you, Carlo."

"This is bullshit, Dempsey," growled Martelli. "What the hell do you know about offensive line play?"

"It's obvious to me, ...a hell of a lot more than you do, Carlo," shot back the head coach calmly but firmly.

"So what are you going to do, Coach Dempsey, ...fire me,?" queried Martelli. "If that's what you're thinking, forget it, ...I'm tenured!"

"You know, I checked on that, Carlo," shot back Dempsey. "You're right, you do have tenure. However, I think you forgot to check the fact that tenure is for full time teaching contracts only. There's no such thing as tenure for extra-curricular school activities such as football."

As the players were walking out of the locker room, Dempsey suddenly asked, "have any of you guys seen Ontario today?"

"No," answered a bunch of the players.

"Didn't see him in English class," said Big Julie. "But that's not abnormal."

"He wasn't in either of the two classes we have together and I didn't see any of his buddies either," answered Hug.

"What's with Martelli,?" asked the Defensive Coordinator.

"I don't think he was very happy to hear what I had to say," as Franklin smiled.

CHAPTER 16

Ty was walking down one of the Roosevelt hallways in an effort to get to his next class. As of yet, he still couldn't figure out the complicated hall patterns, Over the years, a number of additions had been built onto Roosevelt High School creating a confusing hallway maze.

As large as Roosevelt High School was, it was still extremely overcrowded. As Ty was walking down a hallway, he found himself traveling behind a petite, blond-haired girl. She had two, long, pig-tailed braids. The braids bounced off her back just above short cutoff jean shorts and shapely legs. Ty found himself entranced by the sight. Abruptly, a male student flew by Ty, reached out and punched out the girl's belongings from under her arm. Books and papers scattered all over the congested hallway floor. The individual stopped and turned around to laugh and taunt the disheveled and shocked girl.

Although he had never really thought about it, Ty Douglas abhorred bullying. He simply couldn't understand why people would physically, or mentally, torment others, especially people who didn't have the ability to fight back. Ty put his own books on the ground, burst forward and grabbed the male intruder. With a strong hold of the student's shirt, Ty threw the student into the wall lockers producing a loud, crashing sound. He then grabbed the student's shirt again with both of his hands and pulled in his face to within inches of his own. "You're a real asshole, you know that. Now you go over to that girl, apologize and help her pick up her stuff. Got that, Stud?"

"Yeah, I got that, Whitie! But, Ontario ain't gon'na like that you messed with one of his boys!"

"You can tell Ontario to kiss my ass," responded Ty as he threw the gangster down to the hallway floor to pick up the strewn books and papers. Ty then bent down to additionally assist the frazzled girl. After gathering a few of the papers, he looked up to see an extremely cute, sandy blond-haired girl with the biggest blue eyes he had ever seen. Ty found himself strangely speechless although he suddenly felt the need to say something meaningful. Unfortunately, no sounds came out of his mouth. *Wow! This girl's beautiful! I don't think I've ever seen such a pretty girl.*

"Hey, Hero. Next time, mind your own, business. I didn't need your damn help," said the angry Kayleigh Logan. "I can take care of myself, tough guy!"

A wide-eyed Tyler Douglas continued to find himself strangely clammed up, unable to utter a word. To this stage of his life, Ty had never had a serious girlfriend. Or, for that matter, a girlfriend at all.

"My glasses, my glasses. I can't find my stupid glasses,!" yelled out the girl furiously.

"Here they are, Sweetie," said one of the group of girls helping to pick up her books and papers.

"Thanks," growled the distraught girl. "Oh, no, they're broken. My mother's going to kill me!"

"Here," said Ontario Mosely's gangster buddy as he handed the last of the books and papers to the girl.

"Now the apology," said Ty as he stood up.

"Yeah, right," said the gangster.

"What's going on,?" called out a security guard. "Are you the two who've been fighting? What started all this?"

"That asshole purposely knocked my books and papers from under my arm and they flew all over the damn hallway," yelled the feisty, pigtailed girl. "He's a real turd," as she surged forward in an effort to gouge the punk's face with her long fingernails.

Ty found himself grabbing the female wildcat around her waist in an effort prevent her from making contact with the gangster. "Hold on, Girl. You don't want to get yourself in trouble," said Ty as the gangster backed up to avoid the tigress's onslaught.

"O.K! O.K! Just let me go,!" ordered the girl as she ripped out of Ty's hold.

"Look," said the gangster as he continued to back up in the effort to avoid the girl's ferocious attack. Once at a safe distance from the threatening female, the hoodlum rolled his eyes and stated, "I accidently hit her books when I was running to get to my advanced physics class. I'm sorry, Girlie. Does that make everything all right for your tight, little ass?"

"No, way,!" yelled the girl as she exploded forward and delivered a vicious kick to the gangster's crotch. The bully felt an exploding pain ripping through his groin and igniting into his belly. Grabbing his groin area, he fell to his knees and projectile vomited on the newly arrived security guard.

"What the hell,!" yelled out the security guard. "You got that crap all over me."

"Time to get out of here," said Ty as he broke his silence, grabbed the girl's right arm and pulled her into the overly packed hallway crowd. No sooner had Ty pulled the girl into the mass when he felt a twist of her wrist as she vanished into the depths of the crowd.

Ty was late for his American History class. As he hunted for an open desk, he saw the mystery, blond haired girl who so feistily stood up to the lowlife but minutes ago seated in the middle of the classroom. She looked at him with a with a callous looking scowl. *So much for helping the damsel in distress,* thought Ty. *I'm getting the feeling it's better to mind your own business in this place,* as he put a perplexed, wide-eyed look on his face.

There was a knock at the class room door fifteen minutes into the period. The student helper was waved in by the teacher as she brought in two hall passes. The eyes of all of the other students in the classroom quickly focused on the two students who had arrived late for the class.

"Miss Logan and Mr. Douglas, it seems that you're both wanted in the Principal's Office."

"Mr. Douglas, you have only been here for three days and you have already had three physical altercations," said the principal, Daryl Hoskins. "That is not what I would qualify as a stellar beginning here at Roosevelt High, wouldn't you agree?"

"Yes, Sir," said Ty. A flash of Ontario's beady eyes appeared in Ty's head as he squelched the thought of becoming a nark.

"Tyler, you're a bright young man with an excellent academic record. I wish all my student's grade transcripts looked like yours. But, there is one exception, Son. And, do you know what that exception is, Mr. Douglas?"

Ty hesitated for a few seconds. "Unfortunately, I think I know exactly what you're going say, Dr. Hoskins." It had been Ty's one problem since he had started elementary school. Actually, Ty's mother had to return to Tyler's pre-school on the second day of school to take him home. Ty had punched a fellow student in his mouth when that student tried to push Ty out of the way to get towards the front of the lunch line. At a very early age, Tyler Douglas's fists made a habit of punching anybody who acted like a bully.

"It's the comment that says, '...history of repeated aggressive behavior and physical altercations.' I'll not have that here. You're not a little kid anymore, Tyler. Do you understand what I'm saying?"

"Yes, Sir. I do."

"Be the student you're capable of being," said Hoskins, "...academically, as a quality person and, as I understand, an excellent athlete. Now get your butt back to class."

"Yes, Sir," said the discouraged and frustrated new student.

Once Ty closed the principal's office door, Hoskins let out a big sigh. *Please don't tell me I'm going to have to deal with Mrs. Douglas again.*

Ty and Kayleigh's eyes met uncomfortably as the two passed by one another. Ty was able to hear the principal's words as he swiftly dug into her. "Kayleigh, you cannot physically attack another student even if that student is harassing you. How many times have we talked about this?"

"Kayleigh, you leave me no choice. You're now under suspension and will remain so until I get a chance to talk to one, or both, of your parents. Once I get to meet with them, I will then decide what I'm going to do."

"Kayleigh, what do you really think about all of this,?" asked Principal Hoskins.

"So, this gangster asshole knocks my books all over the hallway and taunts me and I'm the one who gets suspended," responded Kayleigh. "I think that this is a pile of shit and the next time this happens I'll kick him in the nuts a lot harder!"

"Mom, you know how you've always told me you wanted to hear something from me first before you heard it from someone else?"

"That's right, Son."

"You might be getting a call from the Roosevelt principal, Dr. Hoskins."

"For what,?" said the concerned mother.

The words then exploded from Ty's mouth. "Mom, there was this girl in front of me in the hallway. This punk runs by, knocks her books from under her arm and then starts laughing at her and taunts her. I grabbed him and threw him into the lockers and then flung him down to the floor and made him help pick up her stuff."

"Was this that gangster guy again?"

"No, but he was one of his buddies."

"And you never hit him?"

"No, Mam. But the girl ended up taking this guy out by kicking him in the balls. Man, he was hurt'n. The dude puked all over the place."

Ty's mother chuckled although she realized that her son's consistent fighting problems were cropping up once again. "Was she, at least, worth the effort,?" asked Addison Douglas in an effort to soothe the situation.

"Well, it turns out we're in a bunch of the same classes. I'll tell you this, I wouldn't want to mess with that girl. She's one wired-up lady."

"Let me guess," said the mother warmly. "A cute blond, right?"

"Actually, she is very pretty."

CHAPTER 17

Stretch was the assigned period of pre-practice time designed to allow players to loosen up their muscles and get focused on the physical and mental stresses of the practice to come. It was also a time for friendly chatter and banter between players and coaches.

"Oh no, ...not you,!" yelled Dino DeTaglia as Hernando, "Hondo," Rodriguez made his way onto the practice field. Hondo was late and had missed the previous days' meetings and practices. There was a breakdown of his family's mini-van on a return, out-of-state, family trip. "I thought we finally got rid of you," said the middle linebacker with a big smile across his face.

"Nah, I'm still around to drive you all crazy," said the teen. "Let's face it Dino, you guys wouldn't know what to do without me."

"We'd probably win some games and have some sanity," said Leotis Brown.

"I can't believe they let you have a uniform," stated Big Julie. "Actually, I'm surprised they found one small enough to fit you. Somehow it seems like you shrink every year? Do they have extra, extra petite uniforms now for football players?"

"You're really funny, Big Julie," said Hondo. "You, of all people, shouldn't talk about someone's size. Look at you, Man. You're busting at the seams. You look like an overstuffed sausage."

With a smirk on his face, Big Julie retorted, "...you better watch what you're saying or I'm gon'na grab you and sit on you, ...you runt."

"You got'ta be kid'n me, Julie," replied Hondo as the two, long-time friends continued their jest. "How would you catch me? You're slower than molasses on a cold day." The verbal jousting went on until Dempsey blew his whistle to gather up the players. Although extremely well liked and popular, Hondo Rodriguez never seemed to stop talking. As a result, he continually took plenty of guff from his teammates for his continual verbal barrages.

"O.K., Guys, let's knock it off," said Dempsey. "I've got a headache today and I don't need all the extra jabber."

"Coach D, you're gon'na have to buy an extra-large bottle of Tylenol now that you let motor mouth come back out for the team," said Big Julie. "Mark my words, it won't be long before he drives you crazy too."

"Guys, that's enough, although I certainly appreciate your making a teammate feel so welcomed back to the team," said the head coach facetiously.

"My ears won't be so welcoming," stated Hug. "I'm gon'na have to go out and buy a new set of ear buds to drown him out. Half the time I don't even think he knows what he's say'n. One way or the other, he just keeps on talk'n and talk'n and talk'n."

"Man, you dudes are full of it," said Hondo. "There's plenty of guys on the team who talk as much as me."

"Name one," said Big Julie.

Hondo had no reply to the verbal challenge. "Man, you guys are haters," Hondo finally uttered.

"Hey, for starters, do you guys want to warm up doing fifty up-downs,?" asked Dempsey. The question finally got the team to calm down, stop laughing and get ready to practice, ...for the time being.

As Dempsey and Coach Walters jogged together to get to the next practice drill, Dempsey asked, "What's the story on the Rodriguez kid?"

"Ever hear of the old term 'greased lightning?' Well that's the definition of it right there," as he nodded towards Hondo. "The kid is quick and fast. Get him the ball and he makes things happen. He's an absolute speed demon!"

"So he's played before?"

"He was the M.V.P. of his seventh and eighth, freshman and junior varsity teams.

Why didn't he play varsity last year?"

"You see how little he is now? He was six inches shorter last season. He was so tiny that everyone was afraid for his life. Some of the coaches didn't even want to allow him to play. Even the administration was concerned."

"Six inches shorter last year,?" exclaimed the disbelieving Dempsey. "Do they make equipment that small?"

"They had to go out and buy junior football equipment for him."

"Is he a tough kid?"

"As tough as they come, Sean."

"Thank goodness for that. And to think I was concerned about the size of Brock Jamal. Brock's a giant compared to Hondo."

It didn't take long for Sean Dempsey to see how special the diminutive Hondo Rodriguez could be. From the slot position, the elusive ball carrier caught a few, quick, short passes to show what Coach Walters was so excited about. During the one-on-one pass drill against the defense, Hondo caught the first three short passes thrown to him and used some head fakes, twists and turns to embarrass all three of the defenders who tried to cover him.

"Hey, Pete," yelled out the playful slot back. "I'll give you ten to one you won't be able to cover me."

"Just shut up, you idiot, and play," said an annoyed Pete Logan, one of the Rough Rider safeties as he nervously lined up to cover Hondo. Pete knew this was a speed match-up that was definitely not in his favor. He also saw that everyone else who was a part of the drill was now watching the one-on-one challenge.

Ty, at quarterback, was surprised by the receiver's quickness. He threw what seemed to be a precise slant pass to Hondo. However, Ty hadn't had the chance to judge Hondo's blazing speed forcing the pass to be thrown behind the elusive receiver. The pass seemed clearly doomed for failure. At the last split second, Hondo reached back to grab and catch the errant pass one handedly. He then accelerated into the slant route course, stopped and spun back tightly the opposite way. Logan totally whiffed on his effort to tackle Hondo. The receiver burst upfield off of a hard break and raced to the end zone untouched.

"Hey, Pete, don't feel bad," said the smiling Hondo. "At least you came close to make'n a play on me. That's got'ta be worth someth'n."

"Shove it, Hondo," replied Logan. "I'm not in the mood to hear any of your crap today."

As much of a motor mouth and wise guy that Hondo was, his teammates knew his antics were all done in fun. He was everyone's buddy once people actually got to know him. When they did, they soon found themselves befriended to the hyper, non-stop talking player.

"He definitely has some shakes, doesn't he,?" asked Sonny Walters. "You're thinking of making him a slot back, aren't you, Sean?"

"Maybe," answered Dempsey with a mischievous grin.

"Good practice, Riders," said Dempsey as the team huddled up around him and took a knee. "We've only had a handful of practices so far but some people are really starting to show up. Remember, players make plays and great players make great plays."

"Hondo really tore it up today," said Ty as the team jogged off the practice field.

"Ty! Please don't say anything like that in front of Hondo," stated Big Julie. "If you do, you'll never hear the end of it. My head's hurt'n enough now. I don't need it to get any worse."

"Come on, Guys, Hondo can't be that bad," stated a smirking Tyler Douglas.

"Just wait," said Hug with a serious demeanor. "You'll see!"

As Ty and his new friends continued to jog off the practice field, he saw Kayleigh Logan, the pert blond he had recently had the hallway altercation with walking towards the student parking lot. Once she saw that Ty was looking at her, she turned abruptly and walked away briskly picking up her pace to get to her car. *I wonder what that was all about,* thought Ty. *That's one strange girl, for sure.*

After showering and dressing, Ty left the locker room to get to Big Julie's car in the student parking lot. "Hey Douglas," called out a serious sounding voice. "I want to talk to you for a second if I can," said the team's strong safety. "I'm Pete Logan," as he held out his hand to shake. "I want to thank you for helping my sister Kayleigh yesterday. Most of the people around here would be terrified to help someone out like that especially when dealing with one of those gangster punks."

"You mean, that girl's your sister,?" responded a surprised Tyler

Douglas. "Wow,! did she ever get after that guy. People shouldn't treat others that way, especially like that idiot picking on a girl the size of your sister."

Pete laughed at Ty's comment. "Actually, if I had to bet on that situation, I would have put my money on Kayleigh. That's one girl I wouldn't want to mess with. She's a definite tiger cat. When she knows she's going to be outsized, she just fights dirty. Most guys just say hi to her and then run! They're definitely afraid of her. Let's just say she doesn't get asked to go out on a lot of dates."

"You all right, Sean,?" asked a concerned looking Rod Franklin. The defensive coordinator noticed the head coach sitting in front of his locker rocking back and forth, rubbing the temples of his head. He then saw Dempsey's right hand shaking heavily as the head coach dropped it to his lap. "You really don't look too good, Coach."

"I just got a headache, Rod," answered Dempsey, forcing a smile to his face. "I forgot to take my medicine this morning and I'm paying for it now."

"You need a ride home, Sean,?" questioned the concerned assistant.

"No, I'll be fine, Rod. I'll take my medicine as soon as I get home. I'll be all right then. But, thanks for your concern," answered the head coach as he put a weak smile on his face and tried to conceal his shaking right hand.

"I heard Coach Dempsey got his jeep decorated," said Ty's mother as Ty put a frown on his forehead wondering how she got that information.

"It was easy to see Coach D wasn't too happy about that.

Supposedly, some of the players saw Ontario and his boys doing the damage but they're afraid to say anything."

"Well, that's probably the best for those guys. No sense looking for extra trouble. What players do you like?"

"Hug Wilson is a load. He's a Q.B. right now but I'll bet Coach D moves him. This guy Hondo Rodriguez showed up today. He's a good guy but he's absolutely crazy. He's the smallest player I've ever seen. But, man, can he fly. And, you've already met Big Julie. He's really a good person."

"I'm glad you sound happy today, Son." *No bad news today,* thought Ty's mother. *Thank goodness.*

"Hello," said Kayleigh with a quizzical look on her face. She didn't recognize the incoming call number on her cell phone.

"Kayleigh, this is Ty Douglas," said the shy, nervous sounding teen.

"Who,?" asked a coy Kayleigh Logan. Since the hallway melee versus one of Ontartio Mosely's gang members, the thought of the shy Tyler Douglas had kind of grown on the sassy Kayleigh Logan a bit. *After all, he's the only guy that has ever stood up for me besides my brothers. And,...he is sort of cute.*

"I'm the guy who helped you when that gangster dude tried to mess with you the other day."

"Oh," said Kayleigh. "I never did thank you, did I,?" responded the suddenly regretful girl. "I guess I was too pissed to be thinking straight," as anger started to roil in her mind thinking of the hallway incident. "I'm not very good at apologizing, never was and probably never will be. But, anyhow, thanks for sticking up for me. That was very good of you. Thank you."

"Other than that, what's up? And, by the way, how did you get my cell number,?" asked the pretty girl as the softened look on her face turned into a questioning frown.

"Your brother Pete gave it to me," answered Ty "I hope that was alright," said the nervous teen.

"Ehhh..., that was O.K., I guess. Actually, that's a good sign that you're a decent guy. Pete never gives out my number to a guy unless he thinks he's a nice person. So, that's a plus in your corner."

"I was calling to see if you had that American History assignment we got today when you were sitting in the desk next to me? I kind of lost it," fibbed Ty.

Kayleigh smiled at the request. "Do you have that red spiral notebook you were using to take notes in today?"

"Yeah, I got it right here," said a more confident Tyler Douglas as the conversation seemed to be loosening up.

"Well, if you turn to the second page, you'll see the assignment inside a big circle that you drew around it. I know because I glanced over to see if I had the page numbers right."

"Oh," was all that was said by the uneasy Tyler Douglas.

"Tyler Douglas, you don't have to call me to get an assignment you already have just to say hello," said Kayleigh with a smile on her face. Caught in his deceptive effort, the embarrassed teen simply didn't know how to respond with the exception of his silence.

CHAPTER 18

Dempsey sat alone at his desk in his classroom. He was enjoying a few minutes of solitude in his new combination classroom, football meeting room. He had an appointment with three of his key players; Hug Wilson, Hondo Rodriguez and Ty Douglas. He knew he had an extremely tough challenge in front of him as Head Coach of the Roosevelt Rough Riders. And yet, it just felt so good to be back in the saddle, coaching football again.

Until Hondo Rodriguez showed up, Dempsey was afraid that he didn't have the run game spark plug he needed at quarterback to run his version of the spread offense. Hondo had never played quarterback before and Dempsey needed a true option quarterback, first and foremost. Hondo's physical skills seemed to be just what he was looking for. Actually, he felt good about using Ty Douglas. However, he thought that Ty was definitely a passer first and a runner second. In Hondo, he saw something quite special in relation to leading a run option style of offense. *He has some magic, that's for sure.*

"I've called all three of you in to have an important talk. I want you to know exactly what I'm thinking because I need to solicit your help to make this all work." Ty, Hug and Hondo sat nervously in front of their head coach. "As I said to the team, we're going to have to think outside the box a bit in our efforts to have an effective offense. We need an offense that can score a lot of points and give ourselves a chance to win some games. Guys, you're three of the best athletes that we have on this team. What's important for me is to have all three of you featured in our offense as a triple threat. When I look at the offensive talent, I seriously doubt we would have much success with a Pro-style throwing attack. We, simply, don't have the quantity of quality linemen you need to throw the ball. I don't think we could be very effective pass blocking on a consistent basis."

"And, that's why you want to run the spread offense," stated Ty.

"That's exactly right. Spread the defense out. If the defense tries to pack the offense in, the outside, quick pass game and wide receiver screens can eat it up. If the defense spreads out to stop the outside passes, the option run game is able to explode."

"So what can we do to help all this, Coach,?" asked Hug.

Dempsey hesitated for a few seconds. It was easy for the three players to see a disturbed look on their head coach's face. "You can let me put all three of you on the field at the same time in the back-field. Ty, Hug, I want you two to be our running backs who can also be flexed out as slot backs to catch passes out in the open."

Ty froze in his chair. *Running back*, thought the determined quarterback! *He wants me to be a running back?! I'm a quarterback and I'm a damn good one. Hugs a good athlete but doesn't throw very well. Ontario's awful. What the hell is coach thinking? I'm the only one who can throw the ball downfield and he wants me to be a running back*? *And, I'm still an effective option quarterback. I'm not even being given a chance to show what I can do.*

"Why such a move, Coach D,?" asked Hug. "That's a big change for me and Ty."

"Because, whenever we can get the ball in the hands of either of you or Ty, you're going to find a lot of green grass for your speed and running abilities."

I can't believe this,! thought Ty. *Here I am stuck in this dump of a school and I can't even play the position I'm best at. How the hell am I going to get a scholarship as a running back? This is unreal! I can't do this. I just can't*!

Dempsey quickly felt he was losing the three standout players. Or, in the least, he felt he was losing Ty Douglas whom he felt was the key figure in the proposal. The real problem was that he, himself, was not sure if he was doing the right thing. "What really excites me, with you being experienced quarterbacks, is that we'll have a fourth option in the form of halfback passes. Give, keep, pitch and halfback pass. That package can be unbelievably dynamic for us. It could give us an offense that has explosive capabilities from anywhere on the field."

Maybe I should just ask to go over to the defense and play safety, thought Ty. *At least college scouts will be able to see me in action at a position I've played before. Oh, man. This is turning into a horror movie*!

Dempsey had anticipated the look of astonishment he saw on Ty's face. *I'd be shaken up too. The kid really looks like an excellent quarterback. It's just that the spread offense really can be the difference for us.*

"So that means Ontario will still be the starting quarterback,?" asked a puzzled Hondo.

"No, Hondo, it means that YOU will be the quarterback," answered Dempsey. "We're going to use your smarts, quickness and speed to be the sparkplug of the spread offense, the man who starts all the read option action."

"But Coach, I've never played quarterback," said the now nervous speedster. *Me, a quarterback? I can't play quarterback. I have no idea what to do!*

"Hey, Hondo," said Hug. "I've never been a running back before but it sure sounds like fun. When you watch some of those college teams who run the spread offense, the backs and quarterback always seem to be running forever. I think you'd be a great spread offense quarterback."

Man, I don't even get a chance to win the job, thought Ty. *Coach has his mind all made up and Hondo's never even taken a snap in his life. It's taken me years to learn how to be a good quarterback. Now, Coach is going to hand the job over to a brand-new quarterback because he's an excellent athlete? I can't believe this is happening. Maybe I should try to transfer. Maybe, ...oh, this really sucks*!

"Hondo, the quarterback in the spread offense is a hybrid Q.B.," said Dempsey. "He's partly a running back, partly an option quarterback and partly a passer. You never know who's going to end up with the football. But, when properly executed, the option action can make a defense look silly."

"Hondo, I've been listening to all of your baloney about how you're 'The Man' for eight years now," said Hug. "You know Ty, it's starting to seem like it's all been a lot of bologna."

"I'm sorry. What? What did you just say,?" asked Ty as he somewhat broke from the shock he had just received. There was no doubt that Ty was the best passer on the team, a possible college scholarship type thrower. He now felt that his scholarship possibilities were circling the drain.

"I said, it seems that Hondo is just all talk after all these years," answered a now puzzled Hug. "Either that or he's afraid to compete with Ontario," continued Hug as he came to the realization that something was wrong with Ty.

"Compete with Ontario,?" replied Hondo answering with a question. "You got to be kid'n, Man! I could beat out Ontario with my eyes closed. He seriously stinks. I'm in, Man! Let's rock and roll with this spread stuff. Wow! I actually get to be 'The Man!"'

"Let's sleep on this tonight," said Dempsey now extremely worried about Ty being so upset. "This is going to be a big change for all of us. We have to be one hundred percent committed to this together if it's going to work." *I can't lose this kid. He's got a lot of ability,* thought the head coach as he watched Ty storm from the room.

"Hey, that reminds me," said Dempsey. "Has anyone seen Ontario or his buddies?"

“Mom, didn’t you hear what I just said,?” asked the exasperated son. “Dempsey wants me to play halfback!”

“I heard you, Ty,” answered the distressed mother. “Take a deep breath, Son. We’ll get this straightened out, I promise you. I’ll call Coach tomorrow. I’m sure we can get this worked out for everyone.”

“Mom, I’m sorry. I’m just so pissed! Being a quarterback is what I’m all about. And, no Mom, I’m not a little kid anymore. I’ll have to find a way to straighten this out myself.”

“That’s fine, Son. I can certainly go along with that and support you one hundred percent. But, the one thing you need to understand, Son, is that Tyler Douglas is about a lot more than just being a quarterback.”

CHAPTER 19

Daryl Hoskins, Roosevelt High's principal, poked his head inside the door of Dempsey's class. "Mr. Dempsey, could I see you for a moment please?"

"Everyone get a start on your homework while I talk to Dr. Hoskins. Your assignment is written on the board."

"What's up, Daryl,?" asked Dempsey.

"Sean, Ontario Mosely and five of his gang members got arrested last night."

"What did they do, Daryl?"

"Armed robbery, Sean. They broke into the back of a convenience store. A patrol car saw something suspicious and spotted the robbery in progress. They got immediate back-up and cut off all the exits to the store enabling arrests without force. Fortunately, Ontario and his gang members dropped the three guns they had along with an assortment of knives."

"Ontario's a tough one, Sean," continued the principal. "He was running dope for his two older brothers when he was eight years old. The older brothers are in the state penitentiary and won't be getting out soon. Ontario has a long, long juvenile record and efforts to get him straightened out have, simply, not worked. Unfortunately, it seems like he was lost a long time ago. And I still think that you need to be real careful concerning the new Douglas kid. Ontario has made it real obvious that he intends to harm Tyler Douglas and I don't want to see that happen. I have a bad, gut feeling about that one."

"Well, it finally looks like we got rid of that Nigger," stated Coach Martelli seeing that the only other person in the coaches' locker room was Coach Dempsey. "Now we need to get rid of the rest of Mosely's Spook buddies."

Dempsey was stunned. For a few seconds he was speechless. "You're gone, Carlo! I don't ever want to see you around our team again. And, be sure to clear out your locker. I won't tolerate such a racist attitude."

"Who you shit'n Dempsey,?" with his patented smart-ass smirk on his face. "Don't tell me you're one of those Nigger lovers yourself. And, if you try to report this it will just be your word versus mine."

"That's not quite correct, Carlo," stated Rod Franklin. The Defensive Coordinator had been quietly sitting on one of the locker room benches in between the next bank of lockers. He was looking over and studying the afternoon's practice plan. "And by the way, Carlo," as he walked into Martelli's view, ...am I Coach Nigger or Coach Spook."

That evening, Coach Sean Dempsey made an early morning appointment with the principal concerning the Carlo Martelli situation.

CHAPTER 20

"So what are we going to do for a new offensive line coach,?" asked the principal now that Coach Martelli had been officially dismissed from his football coaching position.

"It's slim pickings right now," replied Dempsey, "being that almost all coaching vacancies are all filled up at this time of the year."

"Any thoughts, Sean?"

"A veteran fireman I know pretty well is known to be an excellent Pop Warner type coach, especially in developing offensive lineman. He's a bit older but that gives him the security to arrange for any type of work schedule he wants. He's a fine man and I'm sure he'd do a great job for us."

"What's his name,?" asked Hoskins.

"Alejandro Lopez," answered Dempsey. "Al, for short."

"You want to hire another minority," answered the surprised Afro-American principal with a quick laugh.

"Hey, you're the one who said you want diversity," answered Dempsey with a smile.

"Hoskins let go a chuckle. "A white head coach and five minority assistants. What has the world come to,?" as the Afro-American principal shook his head from side-to-side pleasantly. "How long will it take to get him here?"

Dempsey hesitated and dropped his head down a notch. "He's in the equipment room now picking up some gear."

"That was a good practice," said Dempsey diplomatically with the team surrounding him and everyone taking a knee. Actually, the players' skill sets were way off satisfactory and the head coach knew it well. "I like the way the defense is progressing and I see good things happening on special teams already. The offense is going to take a little longer to come around. The timing of all that spread offense stuff is pretty tricky." *We outright stink offensively right now. I might be making a big mistake trying to cram this spread offense stuff in such a short period of time. Maybe I should just go back to a traditional, pro offense.*

"The key is to get better and better every day. Check yourself after every practice. Ask yourself, did you get better or did you get worse? If you stayed the same, then you get worse because you're letting others get past you."

Dempsey paused meditatively for a few seconds trying to get his thoughts together for his next topic. "Guys, as I'm sure many of you have already heard, Ontario Mosely and five of his gang members were arrested for armed robbery." There were, now, no jesting comments. Blank, flat looks appeared across the faces of the players. All ears were fixed to the coach's words.

"Ontario and his gang members are down at the juvenile detention center right now. I'm not sure what the procedure is going to be. But, I do know they won't be going to school here for a while, if at all, and that they will no longer be a part of this football team. Such actions will, simply, not be tolerated by me or this program in any way. Do what's right, Guys. Do what's right."

"It was only a matter of time," stated Big Julie. "Got'ta stay away from those brothers or you'll get sucked in."

"Still too bad," said Rayshawn Davis.

"Gentlemen, we're not going to have a lot of rules around here," stated Dempsey. "Actually, we'll only have two basic rules. The first basic rule states '...don't do anything that hurts the well-being of the team.' That means no guns, knives, alcohol, drugs, stealing, lying or cheating. Go by the thinking that everything is either right or wrong. If you're not sure about something then don't do it and you'll almost always be right. Do the right thing and you won't have problems."

"The second basic rule deals with your academic efforts," continued Dempsey. "You are required, by me," continued the head coach, "to go to school every day, attend all your classes and be on time." There was, immediately, a low grumble of the players as most all displayed definite feelings of disbelief. "Last year, you had to forfeit four games because you didn't have enough academically qualified players after the mid-semester grade check period. We may get beat on the field, Gentlemen. But I refuse to get beat in the classroom."

"Do you think that talk pushed the players over the edge,?" asked Dempsey as he entered the coaches' locker room with the rest of his staff. "I sure got a lot of surprised looks on their faces."

"Coach, I hope not," said Franklin. "The problem is that they're not used to hearing about structure and work ethics. But, it's exactly what most of these kids need. I think most will hang on. Or, at least I think they will. Some will go by the wayside. We'll just have to hope it's no too many."

"Stick with what you're doing, Sean," said Coach Williams. "You're doing it the right way and, deep down, the players are seeing that. Whatever you do, don't let up. Keep believing as you do and each day a few more of these kids will buy in."

"I sure hope you're right, Coach," said Dempsey. *And, I sure hope this all isn't going to blow up in my face.*

"I don't know, Kayleigh," said Ty as the two students were finishing their lunches. The two rapidly found out they were in most of each other's honor classes. They also found out they liked each other as friends. Or, maybe, even a little more than friends. Ty Douglas had never been known as a person who easily opened up to others. More often than not, he kept his feelings to himself. Kayleigh Logan, however, was the first person in his life that Ty truly felt he could talk to freely other than his mother.

"I'm really a pretty, damn good quarterback," said the disturbed Tyler Douglas. "I was the starter on the J.V. at the high school I just left and we went undefeated. I even got brought up for the final state playoff game and ended up leading a two-minute drive for the varsity to help win the state championship. I've got a live throwing arm and I'm accurate. Now, coach wants me to change positions to, hopefully, help the team's chances of winning. I guess that's possible. But, this will definitely screw up my hope of getting a scholarship."

The rambling teen suddenly stopped talking and stared at the ground. "I know I'm sounding awfully selfish but being a college quarterback has always been my dream. I really believe I'm good enough to play at the next level if given the chance."

As the youngest sibling of three older, football playing brothers, Kayleigh was able to assimilate almost all of Ty's words. For Ty, it was not that she understood everything he was saying. It was that she truly seemed to care. "It sounds like Coach Dempsey is trying to make changes for the good of the team, Ty," stated Kayleigh. "And, he's hoping that everyone will hang in there no matter who they are."

"You know, that's what's bothering me the most. I know I didn't come here with the greatest of attitudes. This is a broken-down school with a broken down football program. Coach D is so excited for us. He actually believes we can turn this mess around."

"You never know," said Kayleigh. "You seem to think that he's pretty cool. He just might have a magic wand up his sleeve."

"He might need some magic dealing with the likes of us. Man, that sure would be nice though. There are some really good dudes on this team. They're ballers who would really appreciate winning.

A lot of them come from almost nothing. Some of them are way out there, but in a fun way. But, for the most part, they're really good people. I'm enjoying being around them more and more every day."

"You know, my oldest brother is on a football scholarship at The U. I've heard him tell my other two brothers many times that the scouts never miss much. He says if you're good enough to play on a big-time level, they'll find you. Ty, if I were you, I wouldn't stress about this as much as you are."

"Why do you say that, Kayleigh?"

"Because, deep down, I think you already know exactly what you're going to do. And, I'll bet anything it works out just fine."

"Gentlemen, I want to take this opportunity to introduce to you our new offensive line coach, Coach Al Lopez," stated Coach Dempsey. "He's an exceptional coach and, as you will quickly see, a fine man. Please be sure to welcome him to the Roosevelt football family as soon as you can. Anyone have any questions for Coach Al?"

Big Julie threw a hand up. "Coach, do you yell and scream a lot?"

CHAPTER 21

Eduardo Ibanez, the big defensive end who had impressed the Rough Riders' coaching staff during early workouts, nervously awaited his head coach. He sat in one of the student desks directly in front of Dempsey's large, oak, teacher's desk. As Dempsey pushed open the old heavy door with his body, he tried to not drop any of the items he was carrying. Eduardo sprung out of his seat and ran to the door. He was just in time to catch a batch of the student notebooks before they crashed to the ground.

"Eduardo,!" said Dempsey as he huffed and puffed from the load of materials he had been carrying.

"I got it for you," said the young man with a measure of broken English.

"Thank you, Eduardo. You saved my butt. How come you're in here so early, big man?" Usually, such action by a player early in the season meant he was going to quit the team. *I can't let this guy get away. He could be a good one and he really seems to be a nice person.*

"Coach, I think it is very important that I talk to you. Me madre said I should talk to you too, hombre y hombre."

"That's very good advice," said the concerned coach. *Dang it, he's going to quit.* "If you have a problem, I'll always try my best to help. So, what's up, Eduardo?"

"Coach Dempsey, you said yesterday that if we don't do good in school we will not be able to play football. I am very worried that I will not do good and not be able to play. I love very much playing football and like being on the team with my friends."

"Eduardo, what did I say you had to do to play football?"

"You said I had to go to school every day and go to all of my classes."

"Can you do that?"

"Oh yes, Coach. I do that now."

"Do you try to do well when you are in class, Eduardo?"

"Coach, I try to do my best all the time." Eduardo then dropped his eyes to the ground and lowered his voice. "But, I am not very good at the reading."

"So, you have a tough time reading English?"

Eduardo hesitated with his answer. "Coach, I have trouble reading English y Espanol."

"Eduardo, let me think on this. Right now, I want you to keep going to class and continue trying to do your best. I know you're a good person and wouldn't create problems for your teacher, which is good. I need a little time to sort this all out and see what's the best way to get you some help. Does that sound O.K., Eduardo?"

"Si, Coach. Muy gracias! Muy gracias!"

Dempsey walked down the steps to the basement level of the school to find the office of Melissa MacDougall, the reading teacher specialist who is the wife of an ex-college football coach. There were stacks of reports filling every shelf in the room. The pleasant, but tired looking woman took off her reading glasses and looked up to see the head football coach enter her small office.

"Coach Dempsey, what a surprise! I didn't know any of the coaches knew where I worked."

"To be honest, Melissa, I had to find out and it took some time," answered the head coach. "You really have some sweet digs down here," said the head coach playfully. Dempsey was shocked to see a professional educational administrator working in such a dingy, depressing work environment. "I like all the natural lighting. It looks like that tiny window hasn't been opened in a hundred years."

"I doubt that it has," said Melissa with a grin and a quick laugh. "What can I do for you, Sean? I don't mean to cut you off, but I have a meeting with the guidance office in ten minutes."

"What can you tell me about Eduardo Ibanez?"

"Eduardo's a tough one," answered Melissa as she shuffled through a large file of testing scores. "For starters, he's a real sweet-heart, a very nice young man. He's one of those kids who sits in class, smiles a lot and doesn't cause any trouble. His problem is that he can't read or write. Here he is," as she finished leafing through the latest reading and writing test results. "He has a second-grade reading level and his writing is worse. When we tested him in Spanish, his scores weren't much better. What else can I tell you?"

"What can we do to help the kid,?" asked Dempsey as the reading specialist got out of her chair, gathering up some paper work for her upcoming meeting. "He's a great kid and I'd really like to help him if we can."

"Sean, we have three reading aids and me to work with over twelve hundred students who read and write below their grade level. Check with our school's Service Club for possible tutors. See if some of your players who are good students can help. I'll bet a number of them are bilingual."

"Sorry, Sean, but welcome to my world. Down here we beg, borrow and steal to make do as well as we can." Melissa watched as the new head football coach made no effort to move from the only chair in the room besides hers. Dempsey stared trancelike at the ground, deep in thought.

"Sean, the reason our football program has such terrible teams year-in and year-out is not because we didn't have enough good players. When the mid-semester grades came out, the football coaches would lose half their players to academics. No grades, no play. We've had players who made it in the NFL who couldn't play here because their academics were so bad."

Dempsey continued to sit in his chair in a daze. Once again, he wondered if he was over-his-head in regard to being the Head Football Coach at Roosevelt High School. *How do I get this show on the road? Every time I turn my head, there seems to be a new problem, a new roadblock to deal with and they never seem to be small problems. Every problem seems to be catastrophic. And, in some way, they always seem to be connected to another big problem or mess. Why didn't Daryl tell me any of this?*

"Didn't you know about this, Sean? Weren't you told about this before you took the job?" The shocked head coach now stared at the woman with wide open eyes and a mind spinning.

Dempsey stood in front of Daryl Hoskins who was seated behind his messy office desk. Actually, the office was cluttered from wall-to-wall. The overwhelmed principal felt he had far more important things to do than keep an orderly office.

"Why didn't you tell me this, Daryl,?" asked Dempsey. "I'm busting my butt to improve the worst football program in the city and you don't inform me I'll lose half of my team due to mid-semester grades! You could have told me this when you called me and made the offer. I've put my life on the line for this job, and my family's as well. You're one of my closest, oldest friends, Daryl. Why didn't you tell me?"

The school principal sat in his chair and stared at his football coach. With a defeated, bewildered look on his face, he couldn't think of anything to say.

The next morning at seven a.m., Eduardo Ibanez was working on reading an elementary grade school level book about football out loud to Hondo Rodriguez. The next week, twelve of the better students of the Rough Rider football team tutored thirteen team members in reading, writing and math skills.

"So you're a professor, now," said Kayleigh sitting, pressed closely to Ty.

"Naahh, just a tutor," replied Ty. "But, this is some pretty cool stuff. I'm working with Wooley and Bernardo on their geometry. Both are trying pretty hard. I think the player tutors can make a big difference for many of these guys. It seems like the team tutoring stuff might work. And, it's nice to work with someone who appreciates your help."

CHAPTER 22

The quarterbacks and running backs sat together under the shade of a big oak tree during the five-minute water break period. They squeezed out cold water into their mouths and onto their heads from plastic water bottles. The hot humid air was stifling as the players' sweat soaked t-shirts stuck to their bodies.

"Man, we suck at this option stuff," said Hondo. "I'm not get'n anything right." Hondo's move to quarterback was now being met with more of a guarded degree of excitement. His lack of success was starting to frustrate him. He had always been a natural athlete in whatever sport he played. Hondo didn't like looking bad in front of his friends and teammates. The pressures of being the offense's leader were obviously piling up on him. "Maybe Coach Dempsey should switch us back to our original positions," said the quarterback to Hug and Ty.

"Don't get so worked up about it, Hondo," said Ty. "It's like Coach D said. We have to rep this stuff over and over and over for it all to sink in. Putting in a new offense doesn't happen overnight."

Ty still had some questionable feelings about the position changes himself. It was easy to see that Ty was, by far, the team's best passer. Many of the players, assistant coaches and Coach Dempsey, himself, were all starting to wonder whether Ty should be the quarterback, period, ...option game thinking or not. His obvious leadership skills alone were, perhaps, the reason the assistant coaches fell in line with such thinking.

This is a big change for Hondo, thought Ty. *You can't learn to be a quarterback overnight, ...no way. There's so many minute points to quarterback play. I might not have Hondo's quickness and cutting abilities. But you still have to know what it takes to be the offensive leader, the offensive sparkplug.* "Just hang in there, Hondo," said Ty. "It will all fall in place as long as we all hang in there together. We have to believe in what Coach D is telling us."

"I'm starting to feel like it will take five hundred thousand reps to fix this," exaggerated Hug. "We look more like those Three Stooges Coach D was talking about than an offensive backfield. And, I'm screwing it up the most. I feel like an idiot."

"I don't know, Man! Maybe this stuff is just too tough for us," said Hondo.

Dempsey overheard the last part of the conversation as he walked over from another drill. He felt that he had to get three of his best, most explosive, players to jell if he was going to have a chance to develop an effective offense. "Hondo, you're thinking too much. Hug, Ty, you're not focusing on your progressions. Focus on the option and build from there. When this stuff starts clicking, the three of you are going to tear up this conference. Stick with me, Guys. Can you do that?"

"Yes, Coach," said Hondo sincerely. He, still, really wasn't so sure they were doing the right thing with the spread option offense. However, in the short time he had gotten to know Dempsey, he felt a strong sense of loyalty to the intense head coach creating further conflict in his head.

"I'm with you, Coach D," said Ty, surreptitiously, still feeling the disappointment of no longer being a quarterback. *Maybe Coach D will come to his senses soon and switch us all back to a more conventional pro throwing offense.*

"We'll get the job done, Coach," added Hug as all three of the key backfield players fought through a lack of confidence in their belief pronouncements.

"It will all fall into place, I promise you," said Dempsey. *I sure hope it does. I'm putting a lot on this stuff working. I've got to get these guys to come through. There's not a lot of magic on this team to begin with. If these three can't get this done, the show might be over quickly.* The horn blew signaling the start of the next period.

"Breaks over, Guys! Let's try it again," said Dempsey.

Hondo and his two running backs aligned in a shotgun set. "O.K., 3 option," ordered Dempsey.

"Set, go,!" barked Hondo. This time Hondo pulled the football cleanly from Hug's belly. He then attacked Billy Pierce, the back-up quarterback, acting as the outside linebacker. Hondo pitched the ball to Ty. The pitch was high and over Ty's head.

"That's O.K., Guys," said Dempsey. "Now Hondo, make sure you're looking at the pitch key and seeing the pitch back as well. Get that pitch down by rotating your thumb down. Take a camera type picture of a spot one and a half yards ahead of the pitch back with the palm of your pitch hand. Do that and we'll be taking a lot of these plays to the house. Do it right or do it again."

"Set, go,!" said Hondo. This time, Billy sat on the line of scrimmage. Hondo should have given the football to the running back.

"Nope, that's not it," said Dempsey. "Do it right or do it again. Same play, same reads."

"And I'm sure he means again and again and again," muttered Hug to Ty.

"You got that right," said Ty as he wiped sweat from his eyes. "I guess we need to do it right before we all go crazy." *I don't know about the rest of these guys but I know I'm close to going crazy myself.*

The practice was scheduled to end with a team thud drill. In thud, the ball carrier could be wrapped up but not be tackled to the ground to help minimize injuries. The first offense was working on the option versus the defense's multi-front alignments.

"Tough day for the offense," said Coach Walters. "And yet, it's only the first day that we've practiced team play. I definitely think your idea of extra focus on individual blocking and tackling skills will pay off for us in the long run. And, I think we have to continue such a period of blocking and tackling practice every day."

"Yeah, I think that too," said Dempsey. "I just hate looking so bad when these kids don't have much confidence to begin with. We need to help them find some success fast or we're going to lose them." *We can't lose them. We just can't.*

"Gun, slot right, 3 option on two," called out Hondo in the huddle. "Ready, ..."

"Break,!" called out the rest of the offense. "Set, white 8, white 8," called out Hondo to set the snap count cadence in motion. "Hut, hut..." The center, Bernardo Diaz, shotgun snapped the football high, over the head of the short quarterback.

"Hondo, let's try a simple quick set pass on this play," said Dempsey. "Go with gun, slot right, 94 on set. Let's see if we can catch them on the first sound, Kid."

"Got'cha, Coach." A few seconds later, Hondo was smothered by four different defenders for the fourth sack of the drill.

"We can't even get a quick pass off. And, from shotgun, no less," stated a highly frustrated Dempsey. What he was really worried about was the players' concern that the difficulty of the offensive design might be correct. *Worst of all, the defense isn't even blitzing. Definitely not the start I had envisioned. Not at all!*

"Maybe this might slow them down," Dempsey said to Hondo. "Let's try a little misdirection, Kid."

"Gun slot right, 3 naked right," ordered Hondo as he called the designed misdirection play on the first sound. "Set," barked out the quarterback. He faked the 3 zone run play going to the left and then ran a half circular, naked bootleg sprint out action to the right as he hid the football on his belly with his back turned to the line of scrimmage. The defense was fooled chasing the zone play. Hondo saw the slot's flat route was covered so he scanned inside to try to find the split end's over route. The over route was nowhere to be seen as the split end, Wooley Woolridge, got jammed by Dino DeTaglia, the middle linebacker. Hondo took the third option. He ran with the football.

Hondo broke past the line of scrimmage and through the

linebacker level in a flash. Before anyone realized what happened, the offensive leader was ten yards past the defensive backs as he smoked into the end zone untouched.

"Now that's what I'm looking for," stated Dempsey firmly. "That's the magic I'm talking about, ...pure magic!"

"That boy sure has some quicks," said a slightly befuddled Coach Walters with a smile across his face. "No wonder you stole him from my wide receiver group."

"Nice practice, Gentlemen," said Dempsey as the players huddled up around him. They all took a knee. "We got a lot of good work done today. The defense certainly took the upper hand in the team segment." Making such a statement was tough for the, now, offensive minded head coach. "Good job, D!"

Now we're going to start finding out if this group has what it takes to win. "Today is going to be the first day in our efforts to get in great shape. We're going to run a series of sprints, six forties to be exact."

"Oh, Coach," said Big Julie. "I can't tell you how much I've been wait'n for run conditioning," as the rest of the team laughed. "I just love get'n in all the extra running I can."

"Well, Big Julie. I could easily make it eight forties if you'd like."

"Oh, no, no, no, Coach! You don't have to do that for me," said Big Julie. "You know, there's a lot of other guys here who don't like to run like I do. I wouldn't want you to make it tough on them just for me."

"Well that's real nice of you, Big Julie. AS I was saying, we're going to make great conditioning a major edge for us in our efforts to become a dominant football team. Conditioning, discipline, hard work and toughness all feed off of one another in run conditioning drills. I only have six forties lined up for you. But, they must be six perfect forties."

"When I say "set," everyone will be in a three-point stance with their down hand BEHIND THE LINE," continued Dempsey with his Army drill sergeant training clearly showing. "If one person's hand is not behind the line, the entire group will go back and do it again. You will each run at top speed and through the line forty yards away. It's a forty-yard sprint, not a thirty-eight or thirty-nine yard sprint. If one person in your group slows down before he gets to the finish line, everyone will go back and run it again!"

"No!, No! Number 19 and number 24 didn't run through the line," yelled Coach Franklin.

"Skills position players, bring it back," said Dempsey. "Do it again, Guys! Do it again!"

"This is getting old fast," said Hug. "I think running the sprints correctly the first time would be a lot better."

"I think that's exactly what Coach D's trying to tell us," said Ty as he gasped for air. "He's trying to install discipline, I guess."

"Skills positions, ...set, go,!" said Dempsey.

As the skills position players ran their repetition over, the big linemen started lining up for their repetition. "Do it right,!" yelled Big Julie. "Run through the damn line!"

"Number 76 was off sides," stated the Offensive Line Coach.

"I'm gon'na tear apart the next dude who screws up,!" growled Big Julie.

"Back on the line," said Dempsey.

CHAPTER 23

"Uh, excuse me, Coach Dempsey," came a soft voice from behind as the head coach and Coach Franklin walked off the practice field together. An old Afro-American man, looking to be well into his seventies or more, nervously holding up his ball cap just under his chin with his two hands, limped heavily towards the head coach. The elder statesman fought off looking at the ground for this impromptu meeting with the new head coach.

"Hey, if it isn't Old Irv,!" stated Franklin enthusiastically. "Sean, this is one of the all-time greatest human beings you will ever meet. And, he's a Rough Rider through and through. When did you play your last game, Old Irv? It was only about 15-years ago, right?"

"Huh, huh," chuckled Old Irv. "Coach Franklin is just being nice. I refuse to tell anyone how old I really am because I'm afraid they might fire me. But, I'll say this. I was play'n in the tough days when we didn't have faceguards on our helmets."

"Irv's the equipment manager for all the Rough Rider sports, both boys and girls," finished Franklin. "I've got to get going," said Franklin. "My wife's picking me up for a back-to-school night function. You want something done, you go see Old Irv, Sean. He's the man, I can tell you that."

"Thank you, Coach Franklin. That's certainly kind of you," replied Old Irv with a gentle smile.

"I've got to apologize for not being able to get downstairs to see you yet, Irv," stated the head coach earnestly. "I've been running in circles since the moment I got here."

"Oh, that's all right, Coach. That's all right. And, when you do come down, I got the best coffee pot in the building," said Old Irv.

"You're welcomed to it an time, Coach. Any time! And, I think you'll like stopping by every now and then to sit and relax a bit."

"And, you're welcomed out to practice anytime as well," said Dempsey warmly as he stuck out his hand for a shake.

"Uh, Coach. There is one thing I'd like to talk to you about if I could have another minute of your time."

"No problem," replied Dempsey. The head coach had quickly taken a liking to the older, polite gentleman.

"Coach, I think it's wonderful that you're having early morning tutoring for the boys. There's certainly a lot of them who need it. But I'm having a little problem. You see, now that they have to be here so early, they have to rush to your classroom all the way from their homes. And, since your classroom is all the way on the other side of the school from my equipment room, many are not having enough time to pick up their breakfast bags."

"Their breakfast bags,?" questioned Dempsey with a sudden frown appearing across his forehead.

"Yes Sir, Coach, their breakfast bags. You see, Coach, a lot of these kids don't get much to eat when they get up in the morning and have to wait for their free lunches at noon before they get some food. So, a lot of the boys, and some of the girls too, come down to the equipment room to get a breakfast bag. It ain't much. Lots of times it's just peanut butter and jelly sandwiches and a carton of milk. Other times it's bologna and cheese. When we're lucky, maybe ham or turkey. And, I'm usually able to get some type of fruit and maybe a granola bar. Actually, it's whatever I'm able to hunt up in the community for that day."

"And a lot of the boys might miss getting breakfast because they're up so early hustling to not be late for tutoring," added the head coach. Since being at Roosevelt, Sean Dempsey continually felt humbled by the basic needs of the students and student athletes at Roosevelt. "How can I help you, Irv," asked Dempsey sincerely.

"Well, I was kind of think'n that maybe you could have one of your players or assistant coaches bring the breakfasts to your room for the players who are needy. In that way, they could eat quickly to start the day and then get tutored. I'd do it myself, Coach, but my old knees don't work too good no more and I think I'd have a tough time getting up to your room. I'm also worried that the wrong person might find out what I'm doing which would be awful. I've got to get my kids fed."

After a quick, thoughtful moment, Dempsey replied. "First of all, I got just the guy to help you make such a delivery every day," stated Dempsey allowing a big smile to light up his face. "And I'll make sure no one finds out. I promise, Irv. This is a super thing that you're doing for these kids, Irv. But how do you make this all happen?"

"I beg, borrow and steal, Coach," said the chuckling equipment manager with his patented warm, soft smile as his words mimicked the words of Melissa MacDougall, the school's reading teacher specialist but a few days ago. "The bread and bakery store holds their day-old bread for us and sometimes gives us muffins, rolls and donuts. The Food Kitchen helps a lot. So, do some of the restaurants and grocery stores in the area. What the kids get may not be first class and a day old, but it's a lot better than going hungry."

Ty and his mother sat together in the dining room of their small, but comfortable, condominium. They both were enjoying their daily evening meal that was a relaxing, reflective part of their day. Nothing other than some smoothing, low volume music was allowed. Addison Douglas had found herself a lonely, broken-hearted, single mother after the 2-year car collision that had led to her husband's untimely death.

"Good sour cream coffee cake, Mom," as a smile lit her face knowing that the sour cream cake was her son's favorite. "You sure do a great job of making it."

"I'm glad you like it so much, Ty. It's your Grandmother's recipe, you know."

"I know, Mom. I just think it can't get any better than this. You should enter this in some type of cake contest. I'll bet you'd kick ass."

The mother beamed from ear-to-ear as she heard her son's words. Ty shoveled the last few morsels of the cake and washed down the remnants with a glass of milk. The mother froze as she, suddenly, saw a spitting image of her husband as a young man. Tears welled up in her eyes.

"So, how do you like the new Head Coach, Ty,?" asked Ty's mother as she forced a smile back on her face.

"I really like Coach Dempsey, Mom," said Ty. "He's really into everything whether it's the offense, the defense or special teams. He's a real perfectionist. He's one tough sucker. But the nice thing is that he really seems to be a good guy. He really likes the players and stays on top of them. And, he can be as funny as all get out. He loves to laugh."

"Those are all great attributes of a good coach," replied Ty's mother. "How's the halfback stuff coming?"

"It's coming, I guess. It's tough for me because I know I'm a lot better quarterback than Hondo. But, I also see where having me, Hug and Hondo in the backfield at the same time could be big if we can iron out the timing. There seems to be a lot of big play potentials in this package."

"Hang in there, Son. I have a feeling you're going have a big season," said the mother, not fully understanding all that was said when it came to the football jargon.

"You know, Mom. That's exactly what Kayleigh says."

The next morning, Big Julie used a child's red wagon to bring up twenty-eight breakfast bags to Coach Dempsey's social studies room. Twenty-seven were for the players and player tutors. Although the behemoth Big Julie was well fed at home by his mother, a twenty-eighth breakfast bag was awarded to him for the giant tackle's delivery efforts.

"Got some good stuff this morning," announced the huge offensive tackle as Big Julie hauled the old red wagon. "We got a bunch of Hoagie sandwiches from Super Mart that really looks good. Also got some Gator Aide and Power Bars for dessert and fruit if you want some."

"That means you better grab your breakfast bag fast before Big Julie stashes some away," announced Hondo as Big Julie had already devoured his own personal Hoagie.

CHAPTER 24

The mundane practice field had been transformed into a game day football field. The field was freshly lined. The yard markers clearly stated 50, 40, 30 down to the goal lines. Orange pylon markers defined the end zone. The down and distance chains were set and ready to go. The popular Kayleigh Logan held court with her girlfriends on the 40-yard line just behind the offensive players and, not surprisingly, Ty Douglas. Mary Elizabeth, introducing herself and her children, sat on the 50-yard line amongst many of the parents and assistant coaches' wives. Mothers garnered sections of the bleachers for friends and family to congregate. Picnic baskets, beach bags and coolers added to the festivity. Fathers hung out together outside the south end zone fence waiting impatiently for the action to start.

The referees were warming up and chatting with one another going over the new rule changes. The coaches and players all felt the excitement of a game day even though it was only an intra-squad scrimmage. Nervousness produced tight feelings for both the coaches and players.

"Good warm-up, Guys," said Dempsey, excited to see what his new team could do. "Now we get a chance to get it on."

"About time we get to hit someone," said Big Julie, the massive offensive tackle who wolfed down a last-minute power bar to make sure that he wouldn't lose energy.

"Time to get this offense roll'n," said Hondo, sounding more forced than confident.

"Let's shut these suckers down," growled Dino DeTaglia, the Rough Riders' physical middle linebacker. "Dominate, defense! Dominate!"

"Watch for the option," said outside linebacker Jarvis Means. "Know your assignments!"

"We'll start out with the first offense versus the first defense," said Dempsey as the head coach position was starting to feel more and more comfortable to him each day. "The coaches will be looking to find out who the players and the tough guys are. The best way to show up well is to play hard and play smart."

"Let's bring it up. Riders on three. One, two, three..."

"RIDERS,!" shouted the team.

"O.K., Guys. It's show time," stated a tense Hondo. "Coach D wants us to start with wing, doubles left, 2 bubble. On one, on one, ready..."

"Break,!" yelled the rest of the offense as they turned to hustle out to the line of scrimmage. The linemen readied themselves for the zone blocking scheme making any needed line blocking calls prior to the snap.

"Set, black 7, black 7," yelled Hondo. The "hut" call set the play in motion. Hondo read the wide alignment of the outside linebacker and smoothly exchanged the football with Ty. Ty broke back underneath the play side guard's block to cut up field for an effective eight-yard gain.

"Nice hole, Guys," said Ty to the offensive linemen. "Keep it up! Keep it up!"

"Same play, other way," said Hondo. "Wing doubles right, 3 bubble on two." The quarterback made another good read. The outside linebacker was tucked in tightly to stop the run. Hondo cleanly took a one step drop to throw a perfect, arcing, swing-type bubble pass to the slot back, Rayshawn Davis. Rayshawn cleanly made the reception and ran behind the block of the split end for a 16-yard gain.

"Nice route, Rayshawn," said Hondo. "Way to get up field. Almost a house call!"

"We have a hold on the left tackle, number 77," said the referee as he walked off the ten-yard penalty from the spot of the foul.

"Just what we needed," said the irritated Dempsey to his assistant coaches. "We finally get rolling and then put ourselves in a hole with a damn holding penalty. Who was that?"

"Big Julie," answered Coach Walters.

"Come on, Big Man," said the disappointed coach. "You don't have to hold someone to block them. You're better than that, Kid!"

"Ah, man. I'm sorry, Guys," stated the disturbed Big Julie. "That was stupid of me. I got sloppy with my hands. I won't let that happen again. I promise."

"No problem, Big Julie," said Hondo as he wiped the sweat off of his hands on the towel tucked into his belt. "You'll get it next time. Alright, the boss man wants gun, spread left, 94," which was a four spread receiver formation with everyone running six-yard hitch routes.

Hondo threw a perfect hitch pass to Rayshawn Davis. However, Rayshawn took his eyes off the ball just before he caught the pass trying to see where his best run lane might be. The pass hit Rayshawn in the hands and shot up in the air. Safety Pete Logan intercepted the football and headed for the opposite goal line. Logan raced to the end zone for a clean Pick-Six interception.

"Not quite the execution we were looking for, huh, Sonny,?" asked Dempsey.

The scrimmage continued to go poorly for the offense. There seemed to be a major mistake on every series, especially on the offensive line, which ended up short fusing the offense's ability to gain any momentum. Hondo waited for a signal from the sideline for the next play but only saw Dempsey engrossed in conversation with Coach Walters. *Well, Coach D said to make a base call on my own if a call wasn't being signaled in on time.* "Let's try the lead option. Be ready for a quick pitch, Hug. Gun, slot left, lead option left on first sound," said the quarterback.

"Stay on my inside hip, Hug, if you get the ball pitched to you," said Ty. "Then, see if you can get your slow butt into the end zone."

"Got'cha, Ty," said Hug. "Hey, what'cha mean, slow butt?"

"Who called a play,?" asked the surprised head coach.

"Not me, Coach," said the new offensive line coach, Al Lopez. "I was talking to you."

"Set,!" yelled out Hondo as he took the shotgun snap and attacked the defensive end, Eduardo Ibanez. Eduardo rushed Hondo explosively in an effort to produce a tackle for a loss. At the very last second, Hondo pitched the football to Hug who was following Ty's arc block course.

Ty couldn't cut block as per Dempsey's scrimmage order. But he could drive his inside arm flipper up under the strong safety's pads. Ty's block was perfect as the strong safety went flat to his back with Ty falling on top of him.

"Great block,!" yelled out Coach Lopez.

"YES,!" yelled out Coach Dempsey as he pumped his right fist into the air. Hug sprinted to the end zone untouched, some 54-yards away.

"Now that's what we're looking for," said Dempsey. "Are you guys sure you didn't call that play?"

"I guess you better ask your quarterback who sent it in," replied Coach Lopez.

The offense sprinted to the end zone to jump on Hug and celebrate the touchdown. Hug looked around to find Ty. When he found him, Hug pointed at Ty and yelled "great block!"

Ty replied, "...now you owe me one."

"I don't know," said Hug. "You're a little slow to make a house call that long."

"Oh, so you two get all the glory," said the chagrinned Hondo. "What am I, garbage?"

Ty and Hug looked at the annoyed acting quarterback. They then looked at one another, smiled and said "yes" in unison.

Hondo jogged back to the sideline team area receiving pats on his back, fist bumps and words of praise. He then saw Dempsey smiling at him and waving for the quarterback to come over. "Hondo, who sent that play call in to you?"

"Well, no one did, Coach," answered Hondo. "You told me if there was ever a problem on the sideline getting a play in, I should make a basic play call of my own. You and Coach Walters were looking at each other on the sideline talk'n, so I called a lead option play. That's my favorite play! Did I do the wrong thing, Coach?"

"Uhhh, no. Not at all, Hondo. Good job, Kid."

"Ya know, Coach. I could call the plays all the time if you need some help," said Hondo with a big smile.

"No, that's O.K., Smart Ass," answered a smirking Dempsey.

CHAPTER 25

"Nice job by the defense," Dempsey said to Rod Franklin, the defensive coordinator as the scrimmage began to wind down. "You actually out-scored the offense two touchdowns to one."

"This is the last series of the scrimmage, Coaches," announced the head coach.

As Dempsey finished that statement, another scuffle, the third of the day, started. The Rough Riders' left defensive end, Eduardo Ibanez and the starting right offensive tackle, Eddie Holloway were locked on to one another, both throwing wild blows with their fists. The referees immediately blew their whistles and threw their red penalty flags.

"Knock that crap off,!" shouted Dempsey. "We can't have that kind of garbage going on if we want to win football games. What's wrong with you two?"

As the offensive and defensive players got to the line of scrimmage and started lining up for the final play of the scrimmage, Eduardo and Eddie suddenly started throwing knock out type punches at one another once again. Red flags immediately flew into the air and whistles quickly blown. Before the coaches could get back on the field to restore order, DeMarco Green, one of the defensive tackles, flew into the fisticuffs and slammed Ibanez to the ground with a vicious shoulder block. A sudden riot explosively broke out as the players on the sideline emptied out onto the field looking for targets to attack. There was so much sudden fighting that it was hard to figure out who was attacking who and why. Some players were striking their teammates with their fists, others with their helmets. Others delivered powerfully vicious kicks. Some players were doing their best in their efforts to break up the melee. Coaches pushed and pulled players away from one fight to only have to turn their attention to another. Players were blasting away with their fists at one another while others were wrestling on the ground trying to get the upper hand in an effort to pound the person beneath them. Some players were kicking their teammates as they lay on the ground. Some players, like Dino DeTaglia, Ty Douglas and Big Julie Goodman, tried to break up some of the battles only to get punched, or kicked, themselves.

Amidst all the hollering, kicking and punching, the sound of a loud 'HOOONNNKKKK!' from an air horn brought every player, and coach, to a standstill. They all stood motionless, looking at the enraged man who held the air horn, Coach Sean Dempsey.

"I want everybody to take a knee exactly where they're standing," said Dempsey with a low, but extremely firm, voice. "I said take a knee and do it right now," growled the head coach as some of the players stood around in fog-like trances.

"I might be wrong," said Dempsey as he now had the full attention of the players, "but I thought everyone on this team told me they wanted to be winners. How they wanted to play on a team that won rather than a loser like the old Roosevelt. And, you know what? I believed you. Like a dummy, I really did!" The players now had a tough time looking at their leader. Looks of shame and embarrassment were clearly seen on their faces.

"For the past few weeks you have worked hard, very hard. I've been very proud of you both as people and football players. And then you do this? In front of your families? In front of the young children here to see you play?"

"Tomorrow's an in-service training day for the teachers so there won't be any practice. That's probably a good thing because as your head coach, I'm obviously not doing a very good job right now. I need some time to think about all of this. I'm not very proud of what I've been able to do so far. That was certainly made obvious today by this fiasco."

"We'll meet in the team room at nine a.m., Saturday morning," continued Dempsey. "But, I think you guys need to do some thinking. Can you commit to what we're now trying to do here at Roosevelt? If not, maybe you should move on and do something else with your life. Today, we didn't do things the right way at the end," said Dempsey as he stormed away from the solemn group of players.

"Hey Coach," said Hondo, "...aren't you gon'na give us a Rider's break,?" with a questioning look on his face.

"No, Hondo. Team breaks are for unity. It seems very obvious that we're not very unified right now."

CHAPTER 26

Dempsey sat in front of his locker staring at the floor. The small coaches' locker room was cramped with the members of his staff. The look on the head coach's face showed anger and disgust. None of the assistant coaches dared try talking to him. Actually, they were doing everything they could to shower, dress rapidly and leave the grim room as soon as they could.

Dempsey sat on the bench in front of his coaching locker with his elbows on his knees and his head cradled in his hands. He had seen a lot in his days of football, but nothing like what he saw today. *That was an out-and-out rumble. You couldn't even classify it as a fight. And, to see such viciousness! Stomping their own teammates who are lying on the ground. I'm trying to get them to do things right on the football field and they can't even do things right as people.*

After the assistant coaches left, Dempsey stood up to a sudden rush to his head bringing on a strong sense of dizziness. Shaking his head in an effort to clear his mind, he gazed at his face as it reflected in the mirror of his locker. It was then that Dempsey saw Bo Harris in the mirror standing directly behind him.

Stop feeling sorry for yourself, Sergeant Dempsey, said Bo as he leaned back on the lockers behind him. *You're not getting soft on me, are you Sean? Hell, this was just a practice drill, Sarge,* as he struck a match to light up a cigarette, *You've been in situations like this a ton of times. Hell, Sean, they failed a drill that they needed to execute correctly. That's all. It's gon'na leave you with a great learning experience for those lads. It's now time for you to regroup and move on so you can ultimately complete your mission successfully. End of story, Sean. End of story!*

"Got'cha, Bo," replied Dempsey. When he turned from the mirror to see Bo, ...Bo was gone.

The team straggled off the practice field dragging their shoulder pads and holding the facemasks of their helmets. The players did not slow down to say hello to friends or family. They took a direct line to the locker room, deflated by the brawl. Once inside, the silence continued other than the tearing off of athletic tape or the slapping, banging sound of shoulder pads and helmets as they pounced on the tile floor.

The biggest surprise among the players was the feeling of having let down their head coach. In the short period of time that the players had been around him, the Rough Riders had come to like and respect the man who seemed to show a sincere concern for them. Many of them hadn't experienced such a sentiment very often in their lives. More often than not, they felt that they lived in a world where no one cared what they did or how they did it, ...as if they didn't matter.

"That wasn't good," said Ty as he broke the verbal silence. *Man, what the hell's wrong with these guys.* Ty was shocked by the team scuffle. He had never seen anything like it since he first started playing the game as a six-year-old, Pop Warner player. For an instant, he thought he was having a bad dream, actually a nightmare. Once again, he started to question his being a member of the Roosevelt football program. Since his early playing days, he had always been a part of disciplined, well-structured football programs. What he seemed to be experiencing now was unequivocal street, ghetto war. *Actually that wasn't even football at all. It was a rumble, ...a gang fight.* "You can't win games if you're fighting yourself. A full team riot? That's unbelievable!"

"It's been a normal event here at Roosevelt practices for a long time," answered Hug. "It's like how you proved yourself as a tough guy."

"Actually, that fight was nothing compared to some of the scraps we had last year," said Pete Logan. "And last year, they were almost every day! But, the funny thing is, this one didn't feel right at all. It was kind of like when you get in a fight with a member of your family and you end up hurting someone you really care about."

"We need to do something about this," said Big Julie. "This team's different from last year's where it seemed like we were fighting all the time, and not just with our fists."

"That stuff all shocked me," said Ty. "I've been around football fights but never a full team fight. It was like people wanting to hurt one another just to be nasty."

After a short, thoughtful delay, Ty spoke up again. "We need to have a meeting, a player's meeting. We need to get some things straightened out. If we can get some of this stuff taken care of, we might be able to be pretty damned good. Maybe even win some games."

"I don't know about a full team meet'n," said Big Julie. "I've been around some of those and all that ever seemed to happen was a lot of complaining and whining. There's too many selfish people on our team right now. I think we should just get together the guys who understand what it takes to win, the dudes who are willing to work hard and do what's right."

"I agree with that," said Pete Logan. "We need to find a group of people who can help lead this team to be winners."

"Dino's one of those people, I'll tell you that," said Ty. "All you have to do is watch the guy practice for a minute. He definitely gets after it! He'll like what we're saying."

"I know Leotis would be a good one to have with us," said Hug. "And so would Jarvis. Both of those guys give a damn."

"I know that Eduardo's fight with Eddie is what started this mess," said Hondo. "But, football and the team are very important to Eduardo. He's struggling in school but he's a great dude and works hard at everything he does."

"I also think Bernardo would be a good person to have," said Big Julie suggesting Bernardo Diaz, the team's center. "He hates losing and always gives you all he's got."

"This is good stuff, Guys," said Hug. "But when can we do this?"

"We're off school tomorrow," said Big Julie. "How about in the afternoon, right after lunch?"

"Of course it would have to be after lunch for you, Julie," said Hondo. "That would make it your fourth meal of the day by then."

"You know, I didn't think of it that way," said Big Julie. "Thanks for reminding me, Hondo."

"That sounds good," said Ty as he put a quick smile on his face. "But, where can we meet?"

"We can use my family's restaurant, ...The Burrito House. We have an extra dining room towards the back of the restaurant that we could use. I'm sure my folks would be glad to make us some tacos and burritos and not charge us."

"Those folks make some fine Mexican food," said Big Julie.

"But you'll have had your fourth meal of the day already, Julie, so you won't have to worry about eating when you get there."

"Yeah, right," said the big man.

"This all sounds good to me," said Ty along with a chorus of positive votes from the rest of the players.

"And, don't eat lunch, Guys," added Hondo. "Like Julie said, my folks will cook up some great Mexican food, and I'm not kidding. And, there will be plenty of it."

"I'm sure your family will take great care of us," stated Hug. "But, are they sure they'll understand that the Human Garbage Can will be with us?"

"And, just who might be this Human Garbage Can,?" asked Big Julie.

"Come on, Julie, ...who else can eat 31 Big Burgers at one sitting?"

"Like I've said before," stated Big Julie, "...eating's my hobby! What can I tell you?"

CHAPTER 27

"Tough day, huh Dempsey?" Mary Elizabeth had been so happy to see her man smiling again, flying around with fire in his eyes and displaying the old Sean Dempsey energy. However, she also observed how anxious and upset he could be worrying about the team and the players as he was tonight. The scrimmage ending brawl had created a definite challenge for the new head coach.

"Actually, calling it a tough day would be putting it quite mildly," answered Dempsey as he searched through the kitchen cabinet where the family medicines and vitamins were kept. "I don't think I'll need my pills today, Mary. But, I think I'll take them with me just in case. Bo helped me out on this one, Honey."

A dumbfounded Mary Elizabeth kept guardedly quiet about her husband's statement concerning his deceased Army buddy, Bo Harris. She took in a slow, deep breath and exhaled slowly. *At least he's being positive and not asking for more pills. And, thank God his hand's not shaking.*

"Mom, it was unbelievable," stated Ty. "It wasn't a fight. It was a rumble. There were guys really trying to hurt people. Wild, craziness broke loose. Right in front of me, one dude's pounding one of his own teammates with his helmet. Another guy is stomping a player on the ground. It was outrageous, ... absolutely hateful."

Addison Douglas listened with a sinking feeling in her stomach. She became sick the moment she found out her son would have to go to Roosevelt High School. Still, she never thought she would hear such words from her son. The mother knew Ty was a tough person and rarely complained about anything. "Just hang in there Ty. This is something your coach is going to have to handle. You said that you have a good feeling about Coach Dempsey. I'll bet he comes up with a way to fix this." *I sure hope he does. I can't believe I screwed up like this having to put my kid in that dump.*

"Coach Dempsey, ...this is Addison Douglas calling, Tyler Douglas's mother. Coach, I don't know what to do anymore," said the sobbing woman. I lost my husband two years ago in a car wreck and now all I have is Tyler. Coach, I grew up living in one foster home after another. I was rescued by the wonderful man and now he's gone. I just can't lose Tyler, Coach. I just can't."

"Are you still there, Coach," asked Ty's mother.

Dempsey took a deep sigh. "Yes, I am, Mrs. Douglas. Yes I am."

CHAPTER 28

"Rough afternoon yesterday," said the principal, Daryl Hoskins, knowing that it was only a matter of time before such a large-scale fight would break out. "You O.K. Sean? You look a little rough around the edges."

"A bad Thursday evening, Daryl. I didn't get much sleep. I'm sorry about that ridiculousness," said Dempsey as the two, old friends walked into the school auditorium for the school district's in-service training presentation. Dempsey was supporting a strong headache from the fighting episode. "Daryl, I'm starting to feel like it's caving in on me."

"Don't be sorry, Sean. Unfortunately, the Roosevelt football brawls have almost become a Rough Rider tradition. What you have to understand is that a day doesn't go by when I don't have to deal with some form of fighting. What's really scary is when the gangs get after one another. Then, there's guns and knives to contend with."

"Roosevelt is one tough place isn't it, Daryl."

"Unfortunately, it really is, Sean. But, I want you to know that I now realize that I'm the one who should say he's sorry, old friend. By not telling you about our academic problems and our constant fights on the field, I set you up. I was afraid to tell you about the situations, fearing you might not take the job. So, on that count, I'm guilty and I sincerely apologize. But, I'm also guilty about doing everything I could to get you here and I'm tremendously glad I did. Deep down, my gut told me that you could make a difference at Roosevelt and, so far, you most certainly have."

"What a change, Daryl. A month ago I was still knocking nails into two-by-fours. Now I'm trying to corral a group of diverse, inner-city kids to try to put together a football team that might not even be able to work together."

"Sean, it's not caving in on you. You had a set-back. But, you have to focus on all of the positives that you're making happen. Progress doesn't happen overnight as much as we might like it to."

"The one thing I promise you, Daryl, is that this fighting garbage is over. We might not win a damn game this year but that silliness is coming to a stop."

"Just stay with it. Hang in there, Sean. You're doing things the right way. Discipline is not a common word in these kids' vocabularies. The players are learning to respect and listen to you. You're making more progress in a short time than I ever imagined."

Dempsey let go a big sigh. He had become so happy to be the Roosevelt Rough Riders' Head Football Coach. Now he had some serious doubts. "I appreciate you saying that, Daryl. I really do. The thing is, I'm really starting to enjoy working with these kids which makes this incident all the more disappointing."

"That's because you're getting hooked onto this coaching stuff again," said Hoskins with a chuckle. "And you're finding out that we have a lot of great kids here despite what the outside world thinks. Are you going to have a tough practice tomorrow?"

"No I'm not, Daryl. I have something a little different in mind," answered the head coach as he shook his head quickly again in his effort to help get his headache to fade away.

CHAPTER 29

"How come you didn't go to St. John's or St. Mary's once you found out you were in the Roosevelt school boundaries and not the hotsy-totsy Eisenhower boundaries,?" asked Hug. Hug, Ty, Dino and Rayshawn Davis had all squeezed into Big Julie's car on their way to The Burrito House.

"Both schools said I was too late," answered Ty. "It seems like a lot of parents want to do everything they can to keep their kids from going to Roosevelt."

"Do you blame them,?" asked Big Julie. "Roosevelt's a dump and everyone knows it. My mom's a teacher and she wanted no part of me going to Roosevelt. Unfortunately, she just couldn't afford me going to either St. Mary's or St. John's."

"I didn't know your mother was a teacher," said Ty.

"Dawg, there's a lot of things you don't know about," replied Dino with a chuckle. "After all, you've been here with us for all of a month."

"And, how come you always wear that old New York Mets baseball cap all the time,?" asked Hug.

"This was one of my Dad's old ball caps," answered Ty. "He played at USC and was drafted in the 4th round by the Mets. He bounced around in the minors for six years before he realized he wasn't going to make it in the bigs. Unfortunately, he was killed in a car crash two years ago," said the teen dolefully. "Man, ...I sure miss him."

Ty was enthusiastically welcomed by his new, football playing friends. In the opposite vein, Ty felt a strange sensation that he needed to help protect them. He was able to quickly establish a strong sense of bonding with people he hardly knew. Ty had come to understand, in the vagabond existence of his mom and dad's constant job moves, that he never had the time to wait for friendships to develop. If he did, they probably would be short lived for another, quick, Douglas family move might be right around the corner. No, if he wanted to have friends, he had to be the one who stuck out his hand first. He had to trust his instincts and make friendships happen. Fortunately, for Ty, he had great impulses when it came to people.

As they were warned, Hondo's family gleefully opened their doors for a Mexican food fest at The Burrito House. The self-imposed leadership council for the Roosevelt Rough Riders ate until they nearly burst.

"So what are we going to do about this unity problem,?" asked Ty as the food stuffed player leaders wound down their eating. "We're not going to win against many teams on our schedule if we continue beating ourselves up." *Actually, we might not beat a soul if we don't get this stuff straightened out real quick.*

"Football teams at Roosevelt have always had lots of fights and brawls on the practice field," said Jarvis. "It's a Rough Rider tradition. Maybe we shouldn't make such a big deal about it and just focus on playing."

"No way,!" said Hondo. "We're awful! We lose! Our tradition sucks! People always say how Roosevelt has plenty of talent but we can't get our act together because we spend so much time fighting ourselves."

"And, when you add in our academic problems, we have nothing left by the time we get to the middle of the season," added Hug.

"I haven't been here very long," said Ty, "but it seems like we're one of those family comedies on T.V. that everyone laughs at because everyone is so screwed up. Those shows are funny because they show how stupid it is to be uncaring and selfish."

"But the funny thing is, I believe that most of the guys on our team really like each other," said Bernardo Diaz. "It's almost like the reason they fight so much is to prove how tough they are."

"I think all of you guys are pretty cool," said Big Julie in between bites of his latest helping of burritos. "We all just got'ta understand that we're a family and that a family can be made up of different types of people. But when things are tough, that's when the family has to be at its strongest, not at its weakest. We got'ta be just like those marines and soldiers that Coach D talks about, taking care of each other and covering each other's backs."

"Hey, who's the philosophical dude now,?" asked Hondo.

"That's some good thinking, Big Man," said Rayshawn Davis.

"That's because I have a full stomach," said Big Julie as he finished another plate of burritos. "I always think better on a full stomach."

"Then why don't we have separate talks with our own peeps," said Hondo. "Me, Eduardo, Ricardo and Bernardo can talk to the Hispanic kids."

"Me, Pete and Ty can talk to the white kids," said Dino.

"And Leotis, Jarvis, Big Julie, Rayshawn and me can talk to the Afro-American kids," said Hug.

"That's a start, Guys," said Ty. "We've got to be sure that everyone feels included. Kind of like those Three Musketeer movies where they say 'all for one and one for all.'"

"I love Three Musketeers," said Big Julie. "That's one of my favorite candy bars."

"I think Ty means a different type of Three Musketeers, Julie," said Hondo. "Why don't we tell everybody they have to take a pledge or they can't be on the team?"

"Man, that's pretty heavy," said Hug.

"Can we do that,?" asked Big Julie.

"Legally, probably not," answered Ty. "But, what the hell! We've got to do something and do it fast if we really want to have a chance to be any good."

"Maybe this group could chip in and buy one of those white signing balls and everyone who wants to be in has to prick their finger with a pin and put a blood print on it," said Hondo.

"Kind of like taking one of those blood oaths," said Bernardo.

"I don't know about no blood print," said Big Julie. "Someone might get the herp or something real nasty."

"Man, you're just afraid your fat ass will pass out when you see your own blood," said Hondo. "That's what happens when a person's soft like you."

"Hey, Little Man," said Big Julie. "I just might stick a whole box of pins right up your..."

"O.K.! O.K.!," said Ty. "I think we all get the point. And, I don't mean that figuratively."

"What's this figuratively word mean,?" asked Eduardo Ibanez.

"Guys,! Guys! Let's get back on track," interjected Ty. "And, I'll tell you what figuratively means later, Eduardo," worried that he had embarrassed his proud Mexican friend. "So we all sign the ball together."

"Hey, we could have a motto," said Hug. "Together!"

"That's rad, Guys," said Ty. "We could tack 'together' onto 'Riders' whenever we have team huddle-ups for breaks. From now on it will be 'Riders together!' What do you think, Guys?"

"I really think we got something," said Dino. "We better do something drastic or it's just gon'na mean another rotten season. I don't know about you guys but I'm sick of people calling me a freak'n loser. I'm not a loser."

"And, we can't overlook our academic problems," said Ty. "We can't afford losing two or three good players to academics no less half a team."

"You geniuses have to take care of that," said Jarvis.

"Yeah, but we all have to help make sure that all of the guys who need tutoring show up and get his work done," said Ty.

"On it,!" said Hug. "Does anyone else have something to say?"

Big Julie raised his hand a bit sheepishly. "Uhhh, I was wondering if anyone wanted that last burrito?"

"Ty, ...why don't you walk out with me for a moment,?" requested Big Julie as the leadership meeting came to an end. "That was great stuff today, Ty," said Big Julie. Ty noticed that Big Julie's speech didn't display his normal street jargon. "We really needed for someone to step up and lead to help get this team together. You did a great job of doing that today. You actually got everyone to agree to work together as a group of people, as a team, ...a real team. And, a white guy, no less," chuckled the big man. "And, of all places, at Roosevelt High School."

I know you're fighting taking on the leadership role, Ty, but the truth is, you're the only one who has the ability to do the job for us. You exhibited that today in the way you got everyone to jump up on the bandwagon and the sooner you realize that, the sooner we'll have a chance of winning, Like it or not, ...you're the man!"

"I was really surprised by the way the guys spoke up in the meeting," said Ty over the cell phone to Kayleigh. "I was starting to think our team was a bunch of losers, ...a bunch of jerks. The guys that showed up were all caring dudes. They want to win but it seems like there's so much negative history that the team simply can't break through it. It was, like, a lot of the guys were looking forward to such a fight to be able to show how tough they are, ...like they were trying to earn a bad guy badge or something."

"I think you're right on top of it, Ty," stated Kayleigh. "My brother Pete says no one's ever bothered to try to unite everyone on the team. Instead, it was always blacks, whites and browns trying to get the upper hand with macho, tough guy attitudes."

"If we're going to worry about separate people rather than the team, we'll never win," stated Ty.

"Maybe you better start thinking about becoming that leader if winning is as important to you as you say it is," said Kayleigh.

"That's what Big Julie says."

"I know," said Kayleigh sheepishly.

CHAPTER 30

Dempsey turned off the video projector. The wide receiver coach, Donny Walters, popped up to turn on the lights as the other coaches struggled to adjust their eyes. Dempsey was hoping he wouldn't see what he thought he had observed during the scrimmage. Unfortunately, he had witnessed the brawl all too clearly. Now it was time to get the problem fixed.

"So what did you see,?" asked a knowing Sean Dempsey of his staff.

"From a positive standpoint, I saw some of the kids trying to break the fight up," said Coach Williams.

"I saw that too," said Dempsey. "Hug, Ty, Luis, Hondo, Big Julie, Dino, they were all trying to do the right thing."

"Leotis and Jarvis were also trying to help as well," said Coach Franklin.

"What else, coaches,?" asked Dempsey. "There's something I definitely noticed. Something I felt very disturbing."

"It wasn't an offensive-defensive fight," said Coach Lopez, the new offensive line coach. "It was whites versus blacks, blacks versus Hispanics and Hispanics versus whites. It was a race war, a small version of a race riot, and a violent one at that."

"That's exactly right, Al," said Dempsey. "A fight between two players from different racial and cultural backgrounds turned into a brawl between white, black and brown faces. It was no longer a fight between two players or the offense and the defense. It seems to me that the problems, right now, are racial."

"Sean, what makes you think this team is any different than any other Rough Rider team in the last ten or 20-years,?" asked Coach

Roy Jefferies, the linebacker coach. "Roosevelt High School is definitely not the cultural melting pot here as much as people try to sell it that way. If anything, we have cultural disunity."

"Coaches, if we're going to have a chance of becoming any good, we have to find a way to break down some barriers so we can help these kids win," said Dempsey. "We're going to need some team building. It's our job to help these kids understand the importance of living, learning and playing together on, and off, the field. We're either going to work together as a team in our efforts to be winners or let ourselves fall apart due to apathy and disunity."

"Good short practice this morning," said Dempsey. "You don't have to practice long if you practice hard. Quality is always far more important than quantity. Do it right...."

"...Or do it again," chimed in the players.

"Well at least you're listening to some things I'm saying," said Dempsey. "For the rest of our time this morning, I've got a team building exercise I want us to work on. I think you'll all enjoy it. But first, there's something I've got to get off my chest in regard to our fight or brawl or whatever you want to call it from our scrimmage the other day." The players suddenly became dead quiet. There were no jests or wise cracks being made.

"I've already told you that we would have few set rules. Do what's right. Simply put, don't do anything that hurts the well-being of the team. You've also been told that you have to attend school and go to your classes. This new rule comes from me and me only. There will be no further discussion or exceptions to it."

"I don't ever want to hear the words 'Nigger' or 'Spic' again in our locker room, meeting room, on a practice or game field. I also don't want to hear any other such racially derogatory words, names or terms that attack a person whether he is black, white, brown, yellow, green or purple. End of story!"

"A team that is strong is a group of people who band together as brothers to achieve something important. True teammates show respect, concern and care for one another no matter what the make-up of the team. From now on, I demand that you show respect to every person here who calls himself a Rough Rider. Do all of you understand where I'm coming from,?" asked the stern looking coach.

"Yes, Sir," answered the throng of players.

"Then let's get inside, shower up and hustle to the meeting room. Bring it up!"

"Riders on three. One, two, three..."

"Riders together,!" screamed the players just before they sprinted off the field.

"Riders together,?" said Dempsey. "Maybe someone has found some leadership around here."

"I kind of got some information secretly that some of the players are trying to take on the leadership role by the horns," said Coach Franklin.

"That's fine as long as it's the right players," replied Dempsey.

"Trust me, Sean. It's the right players."

CHAPTER 31

"The coaches have placed you in six circles of six players," said Dempsey as he started to lead the team building exercise. "The coaches will be a part of the team building exercise alongside you. As you can see, each circle represents the great diversity of the various types of people whose backgrounds make up this team."

Each person has an eight-by-eleven card with a large Rough Rider helmet logo printed on it. Your name is in large letters across the top. The cards are meant for you to keep as a reminder of this exercise. You also have six, one-inch stickers and a pen.

You will, initially, tell everyone your name and where you originally come from. Then you will tell us about one of the most influential experiences in your life. This can be from a positive or a negative standpoint. Once that person finishes, every other person in the circle will take a turn giving that individual a personal compliment and place a sticker on the helmet with one or two words that they feel best represents that compliment. The two people will then look each other in the eye and shake hands. The person receiving the compliment will then give a sincere thank you to the person doing the complimenting. The coaches will go first to help get the exercise started," said Dempsey.

"I'm Sean Dempsey. I was raised in the Chicago, Illinois area. The experience that had the greatest effect on my life was a negative one. As a young, second-year coach, I ripped into our star player who cursed me out in front of the team. Losing my temper, I grabbed him in a crossbody wrestling hold, lifted him into the air and drilled him to the ground. I separated his shoulder. I was immediately fired from my teaching and coaching positions. I then enlisted in the Army and served for four years. After that, I fed my family as a skilled laborer, mainly as a carpenter banging nails. My college buddy, Daryl Hoskins, your principal, gave me a second chance to teach and coach. I'm very fortunate to now be part of the Rough Rider family. I feel like I've been given a second chance to fulfill my dreams and destiny."

After a short period of reflection, Jarvis Means placed a sticker on Dempsey's card that said "cares." "I'm very impressed by how much you show you care for the people on this team," as he placed his sticker saying "cares."

"Thank you, Jarvis," said Dempsey as the two looked one another in the eye and shook hands.

"Coach D," started Bernardo Diaz. "I like the way...."

For the next hour and a half, the team members opened themselves to one another. Many of the players started out slowly and shyly. However, as the players began to feel comfortable with one another and with the letting go of their private feelings, the words started to spill out from the young men like water from a faucet.

"After school, I'm not exactly sure where I'm supposed to go," said Rayshawn Davis. "My momma has lots of problems. I'm lucky though. I can always go to my grandma's house or to my sister's apartment for dinner. I'll end up sleeping on the couch at their places a lot. But, I guess I'm lucky that way. I really have three places where I can call home."

"After school and practice, I cook dinner for my family," said Hug Wilson with a proud smile on his face. "My mother works two jobs. She doesn't get home from her second job until after seven thirty. I always feel proud that we have a family dinner together every night and that she doesn't have to worry about coming home and having to cook when she's so tired. No cell phones or T.V. are allowed.

It's family time only. It makes me feel real good to see my momma relax, smile and have dinner with her kids. And, I'm a pretty good cook, ...if I say so myself."

"The big thing for me was coming to the United States," said Eduardo Ibanez. "It was very hard for us to sneak over the border to get here. Things were not so good for my family in Mexico. Things are not so easy for us here but they are much better. I am very glad to be here en Los Estados Unidos."

"I'm just glad I didn't get cut," said Brock Jamal, the tiny cornerback. "Everybody says I'm too small to play and that I'll get hurt. My brother was just like me when he was a sophomore and now he's playing in The League for the Chiefs. All I needed was a chance and now I can show everybody what I got."

"The biggest negative in my life has also become one of the most positive parts of my life," said Ty. "Constantly moving around because of my fathers, now mother's, jobs has been hard, very hard. You feel strange and alone the day you walk through the doors of another new school. I'm just fortunate to be an athlete and to be able to play ball. There's always been a lot of great guys on every team to help me adjust to new surroundings. The hardest thing for me is to have to leave those good friends behind and having to start all over again in a new state or town."

"It's really hard not having a father," said Wooley Woolridge. "Actually, I do have a father but no one seems to know where he is. All I ever hear is how I'm the man of the house which is O.K., I guess. Sometimes I wish I could just be a kid and have a father around to play ball and do things with."

"The most important thing for me," said Hondo, "is my family and our family business. I've helped work hard since I was ten years old. But, I love working with my mother, my Poppy and my sisters in our restaurant, The Burrito House and on our Burrito Bus. It's nice knowing your family depends on you and needs you even though you are only a kid. It's funny how you can go home after work feeling so tired. But then, you feel great knowing you helped the people you love."

"Most people would think that I would say eating is the biggest thing in the world to me," said Big Julie to the smiles and laughs of the players. "But it's not. It's my mother and you guys. Right now, that's all I really have that's important to me in this world."

"When I was younger, I had to share a bed with my older brother who was as big as me," stated Bernardo Diaz, "and the bed wasn't that big. I couldn't wait until he graduated and went into the Army so I could have the bed to myself. Then, one day, some soldiers came by the house and said my brother was killed in action. Now, a day doesn't go by when I wake up that I don't check to see if my brother's lying next to me. I'd give anything for that to happen."

The players and coaches walked out of Dempsey's class room with only a bit of whispering here and there. "That was really some heavy stuff," said Hug. "I always seem to think I'm the only one who has problems. When you hear what other people have to go through, it makes you realize that you might not have it that bad after all."

"I'm sure you all got something out of that team building exercise," said Dempsey. "I know I did. I want to end this session today by saying I really liked the words you used when you broke the team huddle this morning, 'Riders together!' Your challenge now is to see if those words are just that, words only, without true meaning. Or, are you really going to come together and do what you're capable of doing?"

"I was really surprised to hear Coach Dempsey spilling out his feelings to us like he did," said Jarvis Means.

"I think he showed us that he has a lot inside him to deal with, just like us," stated Bernardo Diaz.

I guess we won't know how good a coach he is for a while since he hasn't been here very long," said Big Julie. "But my gut feeling is that he's a fine man who cares a lot about us as people."

"That team building stuff makes for some heavy thinking," stated Ty as he and Kayleigh got into another serious conversation. "Kind of makes me feel like I've been a real, spoiled jerk. I complain a lot about all my moving and being so unsettled as a family. But, I have the most wonderful mother you could ever ask for. And, now I have this pretty, smiley girlfriend who's kind of crazy but is really a wonderful person to be with."

For one of the first times in her life, Kayleigh Logan couldn't think of a thing to say. After a few seconds, she simply leaned over and kissed Ty on his cheek.

CHAPTER 32

"Ow,!" yelled Hondo as his head collided with the metal frame of the window of Roosevelt High's football locker room.

"Shhhh!," said the players, all in fear that they could be caught breaking and entering into the school.

"You have to be quiet, Hondo," whispered Ty. "The security guard could hear you."

"Man, that hurt,!" replied Hondo. "I'm gon'na get a lump on my head!"

"Your head's already lumpy," said Big Julie as Hondo stood on his shoulders to use the giant tackle as a ladder. "One more won't make a difference."

"Why do you guys hate me so much,?" asked Hondo.

"Hondo, just shut up, climb in the window and open up the door," ordered Big Julie.

"Whoaaaa, C-R-A-S-H!," was heard by all as Hondo squeezed through the small window and fell on top of a stack of metal chairs.

"Get inside quick,!" ordered Ty as the team hustled to get through the opened locker room door.

"Dang-it, Guys," said Hondo as he rubbed the back of his head. "I feel like I just got run over by ten linebackers."

"Yeah, and your head dented ten chairs," added Big Julie.

"Man, this is like one of those spooky scenes you see in a horror movie," said Big Julie quietly as the last of the players made their way into to the Rough Riders' locker room.

"Those candles, ...the darkness and all the moving shadows on the walls give me the creeps," said Leotis Brown.

"What gives me the creeps is my father finding I sneaked out of the house in the middle of the night to be here," stated Jarvis. "Now that would truly be really creepy for me!"

"O.K., Guys," said Ty. "Is everyone here?"

"I got a text from Rayshawn," said Leotis. "All it said was 'sorry,' I fell back asleep."

"I got a text from Billy Pierce," said Seamus Collins. "His mother caught him. Billy didn't see their dog lying on the floor and stepped on him. The dog started howling and tried to bite him."

"Well, those guys can get this done tomorrow," said Ty. "Tonight, we're all here to make a pledge, to take an oath, together."

"What's the oath gon'na say,?" asked Leotis.

"What's the oath gon'na mean,?" asked Seamus.

"We're gon'na have a simple, two-word pledge, 'Riders together,' just as we have already started to use as our team motto," said Ty. "This pledge is to state that we're gon'na come together as a team, one group of teammates locking arms, side-by-side, covering each other's backs. That we're gon'na be a team that fights together, not one another."

"I'll sign that pledge," said Big Julie.

"So will I," said Leotis.

"So will I," said...

"Does anyone else have something to say,?" asked Ty.

"Yeah, let's get our butts the hell out of here before our parents find out we're not in our beds,!" said Jarvis.

“It was really spooky, Kayleigh,” stated Ty as the two Roosevelt students ate lunch together in the cafeteria once again. “It was jet black dark. Everybody’s waiting for Hondo to climb in the window to open the door. The next thing we know, a loud crashing sound scares the bejesus out of the team when Hondo falls on a stack of folding metal chairs. We thought we were going to be dead meat, for sure.”

“I wish you guys would have listened to Hondo and pricked your fingers with a pin and swore real blood oaths. That would really have been cool!”

“Girl, ...you’re brother sure tells you a lot, doesn’t he?”

CHAPTER 33

The preseason practices were over. It was "...game week, baby...," declared Big Julie. "Time to get it on!" Everyone felt the excitement of the start of the actual game season. You could even feel it in the air as the heat of the summer had just about faded and fall coolness had begun to take over. Even the fact that the Rough Riders opened-up the season with the perennial powerhouse of the Greater City Conference, the Eisenhower Generals, didn't tarnish the enthusiasm. After all, at this point in the season, every team in the conference was undefeated.

"That was a good preseason camp," stated Dempsey at the opening Saturday meeting of the first game week. Dempsey was correct. It had been a good pre-season camp for Roosevelt. The Rough Rider players had made great strides "We got an awful lot done and grew by leaps and bounds. But, we still have a long way to go. And, we have to keep making strides at coming together as a team. We need to make significant jumps this week in everything we do."

"Our offense is getting closer," continued Dempsey as the excitement in his voice was definitely noticeable. "We might have to rely on our defense for a while until the offense can carry more of the load. Getting in high gear is what we have to make happen in practice this week! Special teams are going to have to be a big factor if we're going to have a chance to win on Friday."

Coach Franklin flinched when he heard Dempsey's words. It wasn't that Franklin wasn't a positive person or coach. Realistic would be closer to the truth. In the last five meetings of Eisenhower and Roosevelt, Eisenhower had crushed Roosevelt by an average of 42 points. Actually, Roosevelt had only scored in two of those games, a touchdown in one and two in another.

"Practice hard this week,!" demanded Dempsey with a strong measure of intensity. Get yourself ready to fly around the field and get after these suckers! We've got to get in their faces from the get-go and not let them breathe for four quarters."

"Yes, Sir," chanted the players.

"When you practice, execute each repetition perfectly. How good can you be? How precise can you be? Remember, do it right..."

"Or do it again,!" chanted the team.

"Anybody got any questions,?" asked Dempsey as he displayed a definite anxiousness to get out to the practice field. "Anyone have anything to add?"

"Uhhh, I got one Coach," said Big Julie, a bit awkwardly. "Coach, did you drink a lot of coffee this morning or someth'n,?" to the laughter of the team.

"Naahh. I'm just a little fired up, Big Julie. Just like you said, it's time to get it on! Wait till Friday. Then you'll really see me get fired up."

"Oh Lordy. I can't wait to see that,!" said Big Julie seriously.

CHAPTER 34

"Hello, Dr. Hoskins," said Ty. "Coach Dempsey just went down to the equipment room to get a cup of Old Irv's coffee. He'll be right back."

"Not that he needs another cup," said Big Julie as he ate another greasy donut. "He drinks much more of that stuff and he's gon'na explode into orbit!"

Hoskins laughed. "So what's going on here? Is this an early, pre-practice meeting or something?"

"This is morning tutoring for our teammates who need help," answered Ty. "It's our goal to not lose any players at the mid-semester grade check like Roosevelt has done so often in the past. This is all a part of our goal to have a successful season."

"Let me get this straight," said the surprised Hoskins. "You guys have been having team tutoring sessions in the morning for players who need help,?" asked the astonished principal.

"Yes, Sir. Five days a week. Everyone in here is either a student tutor or a player getting tutored."

"Everyone in here except Big Julie," added Hug. "He just eats all the leftover donuts when we have some." A loud "buuurrrppp" was heard in the background to help support the statement.

CHAPTER 35

"Well, you lost that bet, Coach," said Chris Schermer, the Eisenhower defensive coordinator for Head Coach Don Watson as they both sat in the physical education office drinking coffee. Watson was the longtime head coach of the Eisenhower Generals football team. "Roosevelt's actually going to field a team. That'll be twenty bucks," as the assistant coach held out his hand for payment. *Who's kidding who,?"* thought Schermer with a smirk. *This guy wouldn't pay up a 25-cent bet if his life depended on it. He's the cheapest son-of-a-bitch I've ever known.*

"Not so fast, Schermer. It's still only Monday. They could fall apart in a matter of seconds. I heard they had one of their famous riots last Thursday. Now that they know they have to open up with us, they'll probably start shitting their pants like they always do. Just remember who we're playing, the absolute slop of the conference."

"Yeah, but supposedly, that was the only fight they had during all of their preseason practices. They used to have one of their famous brawls every day or every other day. It looks like Dempsey has a decent handle on those kids now."

"Yeah, right. They'll wear his butt out after the first couple of losses, just wait and see," said Watson vehemently. "Character is not something that's part of the Rough Rider vocabulary. Keep that in mind. We'll be playing a bunch of garbage! You hear me! Nothing but garbage!"

"Any special way you want to go after these guys," said the defensive coordinator. He hated it when Watson would fly-off-the-handle as he just did. Actually, he wished he could find another coaching job. He was flat-out sick of Watson and his antics.

"I heard this new, hotshot coach is trying to run a spread offense," said Watson with a chuckle. "What an idiot. Can you imagine trying to teach those kids a spread offense? I want you to blitz their balls off, Coach. I want a pressure on every play and use a different one every time. Can you imagine those idiots trying to block a blitzing defense? I want you to blitz them off the field. Do you understand?! Off the damn field!"

"I got it, Don," said the now nervous assistant. "I'll make sure they get far more than they can handle! Don't worry. I'll get you what you want."

"And that mini slot back, Rodriguez, is their quarterback,?" asked Watson with a knowing smirk. "They got'ta be kidding! How is he going to see what's going on when he gets under the center? All he'll be able to see is the center's ass. He's an absolute runt," as he and his assistant had a good laugh together.

"Guys, we're going to start off by playing the best football program in the conference," said Dempsey as his excited players sat in the team meeting room prior to Saturday's practice. "Eisenhower has been the conference champions for seven years in a row. As many of you already know, going over there to play is going to be a different experience. The Eisenhower program is the one school in our conference that doesn't have any money problems."

"What'cha expect,?" blurted out Hondo. "Eisenhower is where all the rich nerds live."

"You mean they don't have a Latimore Heights section at Eisenhower,?" asked Big Julie.

"Watch it, Dudes," said Ty. "I live in Latimore Heights."

"You need to stop telling people that," said Dino DeTaglia. "We're trying to cover up that fact for you, Dude! A Latimore Heights guy playing for Roosevelt? Get real, Man."

"How about you guys letting me speak,?" asked Dempsey.

"Unless one of you would like to come up here and run the meeting."

"Oh no, Coach, that's all right," said Hondo. "You do a great job. I wouldn't even think of try'n to talk for you."

"Why not,?" said Big Julie. "You try to talk for everyone else," as the players laughed aloud.

"AS I was trying to say," said Dempsey, "you're going to see the very best facilities that you would ever see in a high school. Their game field has a brand-new artificial turf. And, the stadium will be jam packed with well over fifteen thousand fans all wearing that putrid dark green. They have over a 200-piece marching band that performs across the country. They were in the Macy's Thanksgiving Day parade last year in New York City. Their cheerleaders have won a number of National Championships."

"I must say, they got some fine look'n hotties for cheerleaders,!" stated Hondo. "They..."

"Hondo,!" said Dempsey.

"Sorry, Coach," said the quarterback.

"Gentlemen, Eisenhower's good and they know it. They fully expect to win! What they don't know is that the Roosevelt Rough Riders have a new attitude, ...a new way of doing things. I'm actually glad we're starting out with Eisenhower,!" said Dempsey to a grimace on Coach Franklin's face. "It's now the 'Roosevelt Rough Riders' turn to make a statement!"

Slow down, Sean, thought Franklin. *This game can cave in on us in a manner of seconds if we're not careful.*

"Bring it up," ordered Dempsey. "Riders on three. One, two, three...."

"Riders together!"

"Did you really mean it when you said you were glad that we're starting out with Eisenhower," asked Franklin when back in the coaches' locker room. *Man, ...Sean has no idea what we're in for*!

"Hell no,!" said Dempsey. "Eisenhower is just what we didn't need! We needed a patsy to run over and gain some momentum."

"Then what you told them was a lot of garbage,?" asked Franklin.

"Naahh, ...more like one of those little white lies. Got'ta do what you got'ta do to get the boys ready, Rod. We need to get these kids ready to make it a fight, ...a four-quarter war!"

"Pete said these guys are really good," said Ty to Kayleigh as the two were working in a study group for a science assignment. The funny thing was that Ty and Kayleigh were the only students in the group. Both were excellent students and really didn't need any extra study help nor did they want any. However, they both felt it was the best way to attack their science work albeit more of a chance to be together.

"Eisenhower has been the definite bomb of the conference for as many years as I can remember," replied Kayleigh. "I can't even think back to when they last lost a game."

"Everyone thinks they're the next best thing to the Patriots or the Broncos," said Ty. "We're going to have our hands full, that's for sure."

"Think we have a chance?"

"Anybody you talk to will tell you we don't have a snowball's chance in hell and I'm not so sure they aren't correct,?" answered Ty. "But, on any given day, almost anyone can pull out a miracle win with some luck and good breaks. The problem is that everyone is saying that this might be the best Eisenhower team ever. And, unfortunately, we're predicted to be dead last in the conference with our biggest challenge being whether or not we can win a single game. I'll tell you one thing, Coach D sure believes we can beat them and that's what I'm going along with until someone proves him wrong."

"Good attitude, Douglas," said Kayleigh with an enthusiastic smile. "You're just going to have to use some of your magic dust."

"Magic dust? I didn't know I had some of that."

"Wait and see," replied Kayleigh seriously. "It won't be long before you realize that you do. And when you do, this conference is going to have to watch out."

CHAPTER 36

"A penny for your thoughts," said Mary Elizabeth as Dempsey walked through their home's back yard sliding door carrying a load of firewood into the family room. Dempsey loved making a fire in their large, family room hearth. The dancing flames were always mesmerizing for the head coach. They helped him to relax and think.

"Oh, I'm just reflecting about how far these players have come these past four weeks despite some set-backs," said Dempsey. "They're really a great group. I have a lot of screwballs and some hard liners. But, for the most part, they're great kids and a lot of fun to be with."

"They've changed you a lot, Sean."

"What makes you say that, Mary?"

"Well, for starters, you fly out the door most every morning with an excited look on your face. You're as happy as I've ever seen you in a long time. You have that old Sean Dempsey juice again, that's for sure. Nervous about tomorrow?"

"No doubt, Mary. I'm worried for these kids. I don't know how they're going to react when the bullets start flying. Their mind-set is so brittle. Win or lose, I want the kids to play hard and play well so we can have something to build on for the rest of the season. I don't want them to get pounded and see them lose confidence. When your claim to fame is a losing streak of 43 straight games, I'm afraid your psyche can be quite fragile. Actually, I just hope we don't get clobbered. I'm afraid they have too much fire power for us at this point."

"You've really gotten back into this coaching stuff, Sean. I'm very happy about that." *And, your headaches have lessened and so has your shaking hand. Thank you, God.*

"I just hope you can say that after tomorrow's game, Girl. What I'm afraid of is that the game might be the Roosevelt Rough Rider pint-sized team versus the monstrous Eisenhower Generals perennial state champions. Unfortunately, that matchup doesn't bode well for the little guys, and we're the little guys."

CHAPTER 37

The Rough Riders' school bus slowed down to stop at the walkway to Eisenhower's visitors' locker room. The players quickly noticed approximately three thousand students and fans milling around a platform. On the stage, the Generals' cheerleaders and pep band were stoking up the crowd. The horde was dressed up in wild and outlandish green and white outfits and costumes.

"Damn, it looks like Raider fans are here with the exception of green and white instead of black and silver," said Ty.

"I don't know, Man. It's a little bit early for Halloween, isn't it,?" asked Hondo."Hey, this is what these idiots do for pre-game," said Big Julie. "They even give a prize to whoever looks like the biggest idiot. Actually, we're lucky. They used to storm the bus and rock it back and forth as soon as the bus came to a stop. At least that was finally outlawed by the conference. Now we just have to go through their Death March."

"Death March,?" stated Hug with a question.

"Yeah, that's what they call it. You'll see," said Big Julie as the mass of people all started to run towards the walkway to the visitors' locker room. Within a matter of seconds, both sides of the walkway were packed three and four deep with outlandishly dressed Generals fans to taunt and razz the game's visiting team. Today, that visiting team was the Roosevelt Rough Riders.

Dempsey was as perplexed as Ty, Hug and Hondo and all other first time visiting Rough Rider players. Coach Franklin quickly saw that Dempsey was unprepared for the event. "I'll get this for you, Coach," said Franklin. "I want everyone to put on their helmets, right now! And, keep them on till you get into the locker room. Once you get off the bus, act like these morons aren't even there. Just keep your head and eyes down. Don't look at any of them. Don't say a word. They're going to try to intimidate you. Just answer them back by looking mean!"

"Hey Hondo, did they really have to special order a Pee Wee uniform for you,?" yelled a fan with green horns sticking out of his head. "You won't last a quarter, I promise you that!"

"It's a good thing you're fast, Hondo,!" said another. "That way you can run off the field before you get killed! The sideline is your best bet, you runt!"

"Raw meat, Hondo,!" growled another. "You're raw meat today! The Generals are going to grind you into oblivion."

"How'd you get so popular, Hondo,?" asked Ty with a smirk on his face.

"This ain't good, Guys," answered the alarmed quarterback. "This definitely ain't good!" The Rough Rider players rapidly picked up their pace. The Roosevelt team got to into the locker room as quickly as they could.

The Riders walked out to see the impressive Generals Stadium they had heard so much about. Stadium was the correct word to use. Eisenhower's seating complex was not a collection of aluminum stands. It was a steel and concrete structure whose seating stretched up over forty rows on each side of the field. And those seats were filled up each, and every, Friday night that Eisenhower had a home game.

"And this place is going to be all filled up,?" asked Hug.

"Jam packed," answered Pete Logan. "Fifteen thousand crazy fans, at least."

"I'm sure it's gon'na be a lot of fun," stated Big Julie facetiously.

Most coaches traditionally take a pre-game walk out to the game field where they will say hello and chat with the opposing coaches. It's also a pre-game ritual for the head coaches to stroll out onto the field to visit with one another. Dempsey waited for over fifteen minutes for Don Watson, the Eisenhower Generals' coach, to show up. He shrugged and walked back to the locker room once he determined he was officially being snubbed. *Well, I can't say I wasn't warned. Everybody says the guy's an ass anyway. I guess that's all true.*

Once the players were back inside, the Rough Riders' locker room was fairly quiet as most locker rooms are prior to a game. There were sharp sounds, shoulder pads crashing to the floor or a locker door slamming shut. Most of the noises, however, were the muffled hearings of one player quietly talking to another or the tearing noise of a roll of athletic tape as an ankle was being supported. There was also Hip-Hop, Rap and Country music being played. However, it was only heard through the muffled sounds of ear buds of other players. The players were allowed to listen to music as long as it didn't disturb others. They took full cups of water or a power, Gatorade-type drink, had a small sip or two and, then, nervously threw the remnants into nearby trash cans.

Dempsey's outward demeanor was focused and serious. On the inside, he was wound tight. Actually, his manner was no different than when he played the game back in his high school and college days. *We've got to hold onto the ball. We can't turn it over. We have to stay in this game as long as we possibly can so we can give ourselves a chance to win it late. We have to play hard and limit our mistakes. We...."*

"Captains please," stated the official.

"Our captains today are, for the offense, Hondo Rodriguez," said Dempsey to a quick, enthusiastic applause of the players. "For the defense, Dino DeTaglia. And, for special teams, Rayshawn Davis. If we win the coin toss, we'll defer to the second half."

"Show time, Hondo. Turn on the jets right away," said Ty.

"Take it to them, Dino," yelled another player. "Knock the snot out of them."

"House call, Rayshawn," said another. "Take it all the way!"

"OK, Riders, let's bring it up," said Dempsey. "First of all, I want everyone to take a knee and reflect or pray in his own way." After the short, personal period, Dempsey said his final pre-game words.

"Time to rock and roll, Riders! You've worked long and hard these past four weeks getting yourselves ready for this moment. Play hard, play fast and play smart! No dumb penalties! If someone cheap shots you, stay cool. Take his number and when you get a chance to get a clean block or tackle on him, do it forcefully, but do it the right way. The one thing I do want from you is to be sure that we walk off the field proud to be Roosevelt Rough Riders."

"Bring it up," ordered Dempsey once again. "One, two, three…."

"Riders together!"

CHAPTER 38

GAME 1:
EISENHOWER GENERALS

"Nice drive, Guys. Nice drive," said the Generals' head coach, Don Watson. "A five-play drive and seven-points. That's the way to get after these assholes. Way to pound the ball and stick it up their butts. Now, let's shut this crap down right now and show this Dempsey buffoon how champions play." The rowdy, normally crazed, Eisenhower crowd settled into their seats to fulfill their expectations of a crushing win over the horrific Rough Riders of Roosevelt High School.

The scoreboard immediately showed a 7 – 0 tally in favor of the Generals as a result of an easy, 71-yard drive as the air in the Rough Riders' footballs quickly seemed to be rapidly deflating. The here-we-go-again reality of defeatism suddenly seemed to rear its ugly head again inside the minds of the Roosevelt players.

"Let's go and get those points back, Riders," ordered Dempsey. "Just keep cool and execute like you're supposed to. This game has plenty of minutes left in it."

Rayshawn Davis, the speedy Rough Rider kick-off returner, took the high, floating football at his own seven-yard line. He immediately burst up field to get up into the pocket of the middle trap, kick-off, blocking design. Two of the Generals kick-off coverage players broke down directly in front of Rayshawn in an effort to tackle the fleet-footed, kick-off returner. As they did, they were suddenly blasted across the run path of Davis with explosive trap blocks by

Hug Wilson and Eduardo Ibanez.

"He's out,!" yelled Dempsey as he tried to start running up the sideline stride for stride with his kick-off returner. It was a feat impossible for the head coach to accomplish, but he tried anyway. "Go, Rayshawn! Go!, Go!, Go!" The returner burst through wall of tacklers and blockers into open green grass. He had a clear path to the end zone to help tie the game at 7-7.

"Atta boy, Rayshawn,!" yelled Dino as the kick-off returner jogged back to the sideline team area. "That was big time!"

"You the man, Rayshawn,!" shouted Leotis Brown. "You left those dudes in the dust."

"Great job, return team,!" said Dempsey. "Great block, Eduardo! Atta boy, Hug!"

"What the hell was that,?" shouted Coach Watson to his Special Teams' Coach. "We actually let those degenerates score! What's wrong with you idiots? This is Roosevelt we're playing, you morons! Roosevelt!"

On the next series of offensive plays for the Generals, the Eisenhower offense was stymied by an energetic effort of the Rough Riders defense. The Generals had to punt the football producing a three and out situation.

"Three and out? Are you kidding me,?" shouted out Watson. "Punt the ball to these fools,?" asked Watson. "We don't punt the ball to Roosevelt! Get this crap straightened out, Coaches, if you want to keep your damn jobs!"

On the next line-of-scrimmage play by the Rough Riders, a blitzing inside linebacker raced through the line unblocked to blast through Hondo and Ty's hand-off mesh point. "Fumble," shouted Dempsey as he suddenly felt as if he had acid poured into his stomach. "Whose got it, Donny? Whose got it?"

"They got it, Sean," said Coach Walters despondently. "They're on the 32 going in."

The Rough Riders' defense held up well on the first two downs of the new series. On a third and seven situation, the Generals' quarterback sucked up the middle linebacker, Dino DeTaglia, with a play action run fake. "Oh no," whispered Dempsey as the quarterback threw a high, soft, floating pass to their wide-open tight end for a 29-yard touchdown.

"Now that's more like it," growled the Generals' head coach. "Just make sure we keep the pedal to the metal and crush these turds."

On the next series, Eisenhower continued their heavy use of the blitz. On a third and eight situation for Roosevelt, Dempsey had a hunch that the Generals' defense was going to blitz the short side, boundary cornerback.

"Gun, slot left, lead option right," ordered Dempsey. The head coach was right. The Generals did blitz their short side corner. Hondo attacked the defensive end and executed a perfect pitch to Ty. Hug blasted the crashing cornerback opening up a big run lane. Ty then broke off of wide receiver Rayshawn Davis's block on the safety. The well blocked play produced clear sailing to the end zone for Ty to tie the game at 14-14. The small, but wild, Roosevelt fan contingent did their best to cheer for their vastly underdog team.

Ty and Hug sprinted at one another at top speed to jump in the air and hip bump one another. They were both so excited that their in-the-air collision antics knocked each other to the ground. The two buddies both got up laughing and then gave one another bear hugs.

"That was a great block," yelled Ty.

"Awesome block, Hug,!" said Dempsey as he also gave his big running back an energetic hug. "That was a great job, a great job. Way to put it in the zone, Ty."

"I swear, I'm going to fire all of you dumb asses," ranted Watson. His embarrassing game time antics were consistently scoffed at by opposing coaches as well as his own. Watson's behavior towards the Rough Riders, however, was always especially crude. What Dempsey didn't know was that Don Watson had a strong hatred for Roosevelt High School. To say the least, he had a strong dislike for all inner-city, minority people unless some of those minority people happened to be his own players.

The first half ended just after the Generals cashed in on another Rough Rider miscue versus one of Eisenhower's effective blitzes. On a quick pass play, a Generals' linebacker blitzed through the line of scrimmage untouched to bat the football into the air as Hondo released his pass. The floating football fell into the hands of the backside defensive end who raced 40-yards to the end zone for a Pick-Six touchdown. The score was now 21-14 at the half in favor of Eisenhower, much to the chagrin of the Eisenhower crowd.

The Rough Riders made their way across the field at halftime. As the visitors, the Roosevelt team was supposed to have the right of way to be able to cross the field first toward the visitor's locker room. At about the 35-yard line, the irate Generals' head coach rudely led his players on a cut-off course in front of the Roosevelt team. Dempsey immediately knew what was going on. He began to snicker as he, his coaches and one of the referees held the Rough Rider players back to avoid a confrontation.

"I thought the visitors were supposed to have the right of way to go first," said a smirking Dempsey to the referee.

"Coach, what can I tell you,?" replied the referee. "Watson is, shall we say, a bit different."

"Nice job, Guys,!" stated the Rough Riders Head Coach with grit and determination in his voice as the players huddled up in the locker room for the second half. "We're in a fight, Boys, ...a heavy-weight championship fight. We're only seven points behind. And, you're in the ring with the number one team in the conference, ... maybe the state."

"I first asked you before the start of the game to play hard, play fast and play smart. For the most part, you've done that while having to learn a new offense, a new defense and new special teams within a matter of weeks. We've made some mistakes. There's no doubt about that. But, you're doing a great job of hanging on to one another as a team, making this a true fight, slugging it out play-by-play on every down."

"Riders, let's snatch this game away from the Generals and show the entire conference, ...the entire state, what we're truly made of," stated Dempsey. "Out-execute, ...out-hit the Generals player in front of you. Kick some ass, Riders! Kick some ass!"

"Break'em down, Big Julie," ordered Dempsey.

The game continued to be hard fought in the second half. On the opening drive of the second half, Ty broke loose and got into a groove in his new role as a running back. Right off the bat, the transferred quarterback took an initial hand-off from Hondo on an inside zone run play and cut-back as he saw a large gap in the General's backside. Ty raced upfield for a 21-yard gain. On the next play, Ty took a pitch from Hondo and raced up the far sideline for 57-yards and a game tying touchdown to bring the score to 21 to 21.

"Great job, Ty," said Dempsey. "That's the way to get after their butts, Guys. Great job on the pitch, Hondo. Way to go, Riders! Great job up front."

"I can't believe this,!" yelled out Watson. "We're playing like dog shit! What in hell's going on? We're tied with Roosevelt?!"

On the next drive, the Generals scored again upping the score to 28-21. "That's better," growled Watson. "Now crank up that defense, Schermer, and shut this crap down. And, don't screw this up if you want to stay employed."

From the press box above, Chris Schermer shook his head from side-to-side. *What an idiot,"* thought the Defensive Coordinator. The Generals' did, however, shut down the Rough Riders allowing the Generals' to score again upping the score to 35-21 as the Generals' quarterback, J.J. Wickham, threw a perfect streak route pass to wide receiver Joe Tierney.

The Rough Riders came back for one last score when Ty threw

a halfback option pass to Wooley Woolridge to up the score to 35-28 as the Riders seemed to refuse to go away. From that point, however, the Rough Riders seemed to run out of gas. The Generals pounded away at the Rough Riders grinding out and chewing up yardage with the run game as the game clock kept ticking down unmercifully.

The Rough Riders played with great intensity and poise even though their inexperience definitely started to show. Watson's blitz plan worked effectively. It was the ultimate reason the Generals were able to wear down the Rough Riders. As the game wound down, Roosevelt got put into situations where they had to stretch themselves. It was far more than the Rough Riders could handle versus Eisenhower, their championship caliber opponent.

Rather than take a knee to end the game against the Rough Riders, Watson called for a time out. The football was three yards from the goal line with only three seconds left on the clock.

"This guy's really something, isn't he,?" said Dempsey referring to Don Watson's blatant show of poor sportsmanship. "Why does he hate us so much, Sonny?"

"It's hard to believe a coach would take it out on kids this way, no matter who the team was. No one will ever accuse Watson of having any class, that's for sure," replied Coach Walters.

On the last play, the Generals ran a sweep against the now exhausted Rough Rider defenders. The tailback ran into the end zone untouched to make the final score 49-28.

A perturbed Dempsey huddled up his team on the sideline before they went across the field to shake hands with their opponent. The Rough Rider players were easily able to pick up on their head coach's peeved demeanor. "I want nothing but class from all of you even if we feel we got disrespected at the end of the game. Shake hands and congratulate them. They won fair and square. They were the better team today. You played with toughness and class for forty-eight minutes. No matter what, I'm very proud of you."

Dempsey ran across the field to shake hands with the Eisenhower head coach. "Good game, Coach Watson," said Dempsey with an extended hand to be shaken.

"Who you kid'n,?" growled Watson, "We stunk up the field. I can't believe we let your trash score," said Watson as he turned his back on Dempsey, refusing to shake hands.

"Hey, Watson," said Dempsey. "I really thought your calling a time out with three seconds left in the game was a class act."

"Coach, if it was up to me, they'd bulldoze Roosevelt and Latimore Heights with everything and everyone there in it. You don't have 18-foot high cyclone fences around the school for nothing. It's to keep the animals in the zoo."

Sean Dempsey immediately felt the same violent rage that ran through his body when he was cursed out by Juron Potts eight years ago. He started to sprint towards Watson with his fists clenched tightly and with blood seemingly draining from his face.

"Bam,!" came the sound of a two person collision as Coach Franklin and Dempsey rammed into one another. "Oh, I'm so sorry, Coach,!" yelled out Rod Franklin. "I didn't see you," lied Dempsey's top assistant coach. "Get up slowly, Sean," ordered Rod at a low voice level. "Let it go. Don't blow it again. He's not worth it." Dempsey got up slowly, heeding Franklin's words. He took a deep breath as he realized what he almost did. *What the hell's wrong with me? I can't screw this up again. I can't!*

Dempsey walked off the field and towards the team bus totally spent, both physically and mentally. Mixed into those feelings was anger from his confrontation with Watson. He had his head down experiencing the first-time anguish of a defeated head coach. He took a split second to lift his head up to take a deep breathe. Behind the short fencing that surrounded the field was Mary Elizabeth and his three children. Suddenly, the four person Dempsey Cheering Squad let loose a round of cheers. A big smile came to his face as he jogged over to his family for a round of hugs.

As Ty walked off the field frustrated, he suddenly felt a soft arm slide under his own arm. He didn't have to turn to see who it was. "No magic today, Girl."

"I don't know about that. But, I certainly saw signs of it coming, Ty Douglas. You got better and better as the game went along and made some hellacious plays, especially in the second half."

"Thanks, Rod," stated Dempsey in regard to Franklin's intervention between he and Coach Watson as the two coaches walked back towards the school bus.

"Coach, I'm afraid you're a train wreck waiting to happen. You know I can't always be around for you like this. And, by the way, you're welcome, Sean," answered the Defensive Coordinator.

"I know that, Rod," said Dempsey with a long sigh. "And, that was quite a shot you gave me," said Dempsey with a humble smile.

"You're a load, Man," retorted Franklin with a small smile. "I had to use a cut block to take you off your feet, Sean. I figured that was the only way my skinny butt could stop you the way you were going after Watson."

"You did a good job of achieving that," said Dempsey with a smile of his own. "I already feel a sore bruise on my thigh. Actually, you should have let me go, Rod. I was all set to blast Watson. You could have become the new Roosevelt Rough Rider Head Football Coach."

"Naahh,!" replied Franklin. "You were the only one crazy enough to take this job."

"I owe you a cold one, Rod."

"No, as I see it, you owe three."

"THREE! How's that," replied Dempsey.

"Two for the two times I've had to step in for you to prevent you from doing something dumb with Ontario and Watson and one for the sore shoulder you just gave me. Make it an even six pack and I'll buy the pizza."

"You got it, Rod. And Rod, ...thanks!"

"Seriously, Sean. You need to listen to yourself."

"What do you mean, Rod?"

"You know, ...when you tell the players not to do anything that hurts the well-being of the team."

CHAPTER 39

"What are you thinking, Ty," asked Big Julie as the two sat in the same bus seat together on the way back to Roosevelt.

"You know, I was thinking how we played our asses off, Julie. They outmanned us by about 3 to 1. And yet, we gave them all they could handle. Two things ultimately beat us, ...they blitzed our ass off, which hurt us, and we got exhausted by the start of the 4th quarter. Otherwise we might have been in that game to the very end."

"What do you think, Julie?"

"I think you're a hell of a player and that with me blocking and you running, we're going to have a real good offense."

After the short twenty-minute drive, the Rough Rider bus pulled up to the players' locker room door. Sean Dempsey was the first person to get off the bus. He wanted to put himself in front of the bus's door so he could shake hands with each player as they came down the bus's steps to congratulate them on their efforts. Dempsey felt drained, ...absolutely exhausted. Standing next to the head coach was his principal, Daryl Hoskins, who shook hands and congratulated the players as well.

Once all the players departed, Hoskins turned to congratulate his head coach. "That was a heck of a job, Sean. I was very proud of how your team played. They played with intensity, toughness and class. It's been a long time since someone would say that about a Rough Rider football team."

Exasperated and disappointed, Dempsey replied, "at least we didn't embarrass ourselves."

"Embarrass yourselves? You've got to be kidding, my friend. You just scored more points in your first game than last year's team did in its entire season. And you scored 28 points against Eisenhower. Sean, they beat every team they played against last year by an average of 25 points."

"I know, Daryl. The funny thing is if we could have picked up the blitz even a little, we might have made a real run at them."

"I think they ran every blitz known to man, and maybe even some new ones," chuckled Hoskins. "But, Sean, your biggest accomplishment is the way you've gotten those kids to play hard and with discipline. Now, just rally the troops and go beat Adams. I've got a strong hunch that this is going to be a fun season for us."

Hoskins shook hands with his head coach again and started walking towards his car. "Oh, and there's one more thing. Seven A.M. tutoring sessions?! And, with your better students doing the tutoring! Sean, that's unbelievable. The best last year's coach could do was get kids out of the city's juvenile detention center so he wouldn't have to wake me up in the middle of the night."

"They kicked our butts, Mom," said Ty. "We hung in there in the first half. We were 14-14 in the second quarter and only down 21-14 at half. We even tied them up at 21. You saw it, 49-28. They just had too much fire power for us."

"Your team played hard," stated Addison Douglas. "And, you did a great job yourself. You definitely made some big plays and helped lead your teammates."

"We just weren't ready to take on such a good team, Mom.

They were too much for us to handle on offense and on defense."

"Hey, Son, that's why they've been conference champs for seven straight years. What you guys have to do now is focus on your next game and go get a win."

CHAPTER 40

The atmosphere in the team meeting room the next day after the Eisenhower game was definitely not as chipper as it had been for the buildup of the opening game. There was no joking or bantering among the players, no smiles, no tomfoolery. *Good, not winning, at least, seems to mean something to these kids,* thought the head coach. *Why the hell did we have to get Eisenhower out of the gates. We certainly didn't need that. Oh, well. Next!*

"I want to be sure to spend a lot of time on this video," said Dempsey. "That game was a lot closer than you think, Gentlemen. I know we had a lot of problems with the blitz. I put a lot of the fault for that on myself. I've got to get us ready for any situation that might occur in a game. If an opponent can blitz you, it's going to be a long evening. Unfortunately for us, it was."

"You're going to see that we made a ton of small, easy-to-fix mistakes that had a big effect on how we competed. But easy to fix or not, we have to put all of our focus on getting those problems corrected immediately. You played hard and you played fast, just as I asked you to. Now, eliminate a lot of those errors and we'll make a big jump in our improvement going into the Adams game."

After about fifteen minutes of video watching, Ty leaned over and whispered to Hondo, Hug and Big Julie. "Coach is definitely right. We made a lot of mistakes that are not hard to fix. The key now is to fix them."

"I hate Eisenhower," said Hondo. "They're a bunch of dicks."

"I'd love to play those guys again," said Hug.

"We will," said Ty as a surprised Hondo, Hug and Big Julie turned their heads to look at one another with questioning frowns pasted across their foreheads.

CHAPTER 41

On the following Monday morning, Sean Dempsey felt the need to get away for a few minutes during his prep period. He was ahead of himself in relation to his classroom teacher preparation and having filled out his football practice plan the night before. For some strange reason, he felt like visiting Old Irv. He had come to like the old timer and felt comfortable visiting him down in the ancient, basement equipment room and getting a cup of Old Irv's coffee.

"We sure got our butts kicked, Irv," state Dempsey. "That was an old fashion whupping."

"Yes, Coach Dempsey. Yes it was," replied Old Irv. "Them Eisenhower boys have themselves a fine team. They do a great job of recruiting. But, you know what, Coach. I have a strong feeling that we're going to have a fine team before this season is over. We have some dang good players on the team this year and they're only going to get better and better. You wait and see, Coach Dempsey. We're gon'na have a fine team, a mighty fine team."

"Thanks for saying that, Irv. That means a lot to me because you've been around here for a long, long time and you know what you're talking about. And, you're right, Irv. You do cook up a great pot of coffee."

"Like I said, Coach, you're welcomed anytime. Anytime at all," said the elderly equipment man with a soft chuckle. But, you know what, Coach? Our boys played their hearts out against one of the best teams in the state. They never quit, even when they were exhausted at the end of the game. And, they played with great pride and discipline. That hasn't been seen by a Roosevelt team in a long,

long time. You've made a great impact on this team, Coach D, and I know you're going to help these boys succeed."

"That was nice of you to say that, Irv. I greatly appreciate it. And, I certainly have come to appreciate your friendship in the short time I've come to know you."

"You're welcome, Coach Dempsey. But you remember what I've told you. We're gon'na be a fine team this year, a mighty fine team."

Dempsey finished up his cup of coffee, smiled and headed for the equipment room door. As he reached for the doorknob, he paused, "Irv, what did you mean when you said, they do a great job of recruiting?"

CHAPTER 42

"What do you mean, Eisenhower recruits," shouted Dempsey. "What the hell are you talking about, Rod. Public schools can't recruit players from other schools and other school districts. That's totally illegal in this state!"

"You're absolutely right, Sean," replied Franklin. "Recruiting is absolutely illegal for public schools and, actually, private and parochial schools by state mandate. But the Generals know how to do it and they do it well. They have been for a long, long time. Do you really think Watson would be as good a coach as he supposedly is without all the Afro-American kids he has on his team."

"How do they get away with it, Rod? Why don't teams in the league turn him in. This is a load of crap. Eisenhower has the largest student population in the school district and, for that matter, the state. On top of that, it's a super wealthy community. They have some of the best facilities in the state and now you tell me they cheat their asses off and illegally recruit."

"Sean, Watson and his staff don't actually do the recruiting. It's their booster club that does."

"And Watson, I'm sure, is the person who helps rule the roost," replied The Rough Riders' coach.

"You got that right, Coach. He has plenty of rich donors who easily take care of whatever Watson needs, ...a job for the mother or father, a cheaply priced apartment within the district boundaries, a handshake with five one hundred dollars being passed over from one hand to another. One way or the other, good football playing students from all over the state are suddenly enrolled at Eisenhower the first day of school."

What does the conference commissioner have to say about all of this,?" asked Dempsey.

"One of our past head coaches once asked the commissioner what he was going to do about the illegal recruiting at Eisenhower," replied Franklin.

"What did he say,?" asked Dempsey.

"He told the coach that he would be better off not bringing up such nonsense. After all, Eisenhower was the only high school in the state that was consistently on the USA Top 25 National Ranking List."

CHAPTER 43

GAME 2:
ADAMS PATRIOTS

Our scouting report says that Adams doesn't have a very strong team this year," said Coach Dempsey. His staff listened attentively as they chomped on pizza at their Sunday evening game plan session. "They don't seem to have a lot of talent." *I sure hope I'm right when I say that. There's no way we can take anyone lightly. Not when the program has lost 44 in a row.*

"They never do," said Coach Franklin. "And yet, they've always found a way to beat us. They're well coached and play smart. They don't make a lot of mistakes and always seem to hang around to win games late."

"That's what I see on the video," retorted Dempsey. "If we keep it simple and pound them, I think they'll have a tough time handling us. I also think they'll have a lot of problems handling our defense, Rod."

"I think you're right, Sean," answered the defensive coordinator. "We need to put the wood to these guys from the get-go and not give them a chance to breathe."

The home opener for Roosevelt was on an overcast day. The Rough Rider coaching staff was grateful that it wasn't raining. A dry field was a great advantage for the Riders' speed versus Adams. "Fast thoroughbreds don't do as well on muddy tracks," said Sonny Walters, Roosevelt's Wide Receiver Coach. "It looks like they're telling their defensive ends to sit and stay wide to take away the pitch option phase. I guess they're going to let us run inside with our zone runs."

"I think you're right, Sonny," replied Dempsey. "They don't want to let our speed get to the outside."

"I see it that way too," said Coach Walters. "But don't forget the zone bubble. They can't load up inside and take away the quick screens outside at the same time."

"Let's see if they can hold up with us pounding the ball inside at them," said Dempsey. "I don't think they can stop Ty and Hug for four quarters." *Pound them for four quarters with our horses and mix in Hondo's option threats. I really think that's the best way to go. Or, I hope it is.*

"I agree, Sean," said Walters. "Just pound them."

"That's the first time I've ever heard of a wide receiver coach anxious to run the ball, Sonny," said Dempsey.

"Coach, I just want to win a game and go home happy for once," replied Walters.

"O.K. Here we go. Hondo, I want gun, slot right, 3 zone."

"No triple, Coach,?" asked the quarterback, referring to the dive, pitch-option play.

"Not yet, Hondo. Let's get our feet wet with our base stuff and go right at them. I'll mix in the zone bubble so you can have some fun."

Hondo started to run out to the huddle, stopped and turned to address his head coach again. "Coach, what do you mean 'get your feet wet?'"

"Just get out there and run the play, Son. I'll tell you after the game."

"Got'cha, Coach," said the tightly wound offensive leader as he ran out to the huddle.

"The boss wants to pound these guys to loosen them up. Gun, slot right 3 zone. Ready...."

"Break,!" yelled the offense.

Ty was glad to be back on the field again after the tough loss to Eisenhower. Losing was definitely not a part of Tyler Douglas's make up. He was still a bit miffed about not playing quarterback. However, running with the football was, he found, a lot of fun. He knew he played hard against Eisenhower and that his team did as well. The converted running back knew he could live with that, for now. *This defense sure doesn't look like Eisenhower's. We just need to go after these guys right off the bat.*

Hondo handed the football off to Ty on a predetermined zone give. Ty found a crease inside of Big Julie's block and busted up inside for a solid six-yard gain.

"Nice job, Julie,!" stated Ty. "Good hole, Guys. Keep it up! Keep it up!" *Big Julie looks like a man among boys. I hope Coach Dempsey sees what I'm seeing.*

"3 zone," ordered Hondo as Dempsey wanted to continue attacking Adams on the ground with Roosevelt's inside runs. Hondo handed the football off to Hug who had to lower his pads to blast out some short yardage due to a missed block by the left guard.

"Third and one, Sean," reported Coach Walters.

"Gun slot right 2 zone lead," said Dempsey as Walters signaled the play in to Hondo. The zone lead was a double team, isolation block play. Hug isolation blocked the play side linebacker to lead Ty up into the hole.

"Good job," yelled Dempsey as the chain crew moved the chains for the converted first down. Hug had buckled the linebacker on his lead block giving Ty a hole to burst through for a five-yard gain.

The Rough Rider offense continued grinding up the Adams defense. On a first and goal from the four-yard line, the snap from Bernardo Diaz was short, unable to hit Hondo's hands. The result was a center-quarterback exchange fumble.

"The ball's out,!" shouted Coach Franklin. "They got it, Sean."

"Damn,!" screamed Dempsey. "We pound them for more than 60-yards and then cough up the ball! That's why we work on ball security drills, Gentlemen. The center and the quarterback must be able to exchange the football. That's bad football!"

Adams was able to pound out a first down on three consecutive run plays from their own three-yard line. On the next play, however, the Patriots ran a lead option to the field. Eduardo Ibanez, the big defensive end, froze in his position. He forced the quarterback to pitch the football. As the ball was being pitched, Eduardo exploded up field to swat the football down to the ground. The football bounced wildly into the Adams' backfield. Eduardo beat everybody to the football, scooped up the ball and raced into the end zone to put Roosevelt up 7-0.

"Great job, Eduardo," yelled Coach Franklin. "Big time, Son! Big time!" *Wow! That was a great play. Eduardo may not know exactly was he's supposed to do but he sure does make things happen.*

An intense Eduardo Ibanez walked to the water jugs as he was pounded on the back and high fived by the Roosevelt sideline. Eduardo then heard the voice of his head coach calling out to him.

"Hey, you're not going to leave me hanging, are you, Eduardo,?" said Dempsey as he held out his fist for Eduardo to bump with his own. The head coach had come to develop a strong like for the big, soft spoken, defensive end. "Way to go, Kid. That's the big time play I'm always talking about! You're getting good at this game, aren't you?"

"Si, Gracias, Coach," said Eduardo as he butted his own fist with Dempsey's putting a giant smile across his face. "I love to play American football especially when I can play at the defensive end. I like it out there."

"You keep playing like that and you can play out there all you want."

Dempsey kept grinding away on the Adams defense with the run game. The Rough Rider offense moved the ball consistently but kept stalling in the red zone. On a 3rd and nine situation for Adams, the Roosevelt defense struck again. Executing a four-streak vertical pass pattern, the Adams' quarterback threw a flat line pass to a seemingly wide open slot back. The free safety, Pete Logan, read the quarterback's eyes and broke on the pass before it was thrown. He intercepted the football just before it was about to fall into the hands of the offensive receiver.

Logan broke straight up field with the football securely tucked under his right arm. He ran through a poor tackling attempt by one of the offensive linemen and then broke to the outside sharply across the face of a wide receiver to an open run lane to the end zone. The defense had scored the second touchdown of the game to put the Riders ahead 14-0. Kayleigh Logan beamed with pride firmly announcing, "...that's my brother!"

Dempsey didn't like the fact that his offense kept stalling when it got close to the end zone. However, he felt great about the defense pitching a shutout through three quarters and scoring two defensive touchdowns.

In the fourth quarter, the Roosevelt offense kept churning up yardage against the Patriots. On another zone bubble play, Hondo read the stacked-in alignment of the outside linebacker in the Patriots effort to shut down the inside run game. Hondo caught the shotgun snap and threw a perfect bubble screen swing pass to Rayshawn Davis, the slot back. Davis then burst up the sideline. Just when it looked like he was going to be driven out of bounds, Rayshawn radically cut back to the inside to race untouched for the score.

The victory was a very conservative win for Roosevelt. Pounding the run game on offense and a stingy, opportunistic defense was just what the Rough Riders needed to secure a very important, and decisive, win, 21–0.

The Riders hooted and hollered as the referee held the ball up to signal the end of the game. Roosevelt's 44-game losing streak had finally come to an end! The Rough Riders may have beaten a weaker team convincingly for the win. However, the victory had a championship feel to it as the players and coaches rushed to the center of the field to congratulate one another.

"Great job, defense," yelled out Ty. "Two defensive touchdowns. That's big time!"

"Got a one game win streak going," shouted Big Julie.

"Get'n ready to make it two," said Bernardo as the team filed into their locker room with shouts of joy.

"Nice job, Ty. Nice job, Hug," said Hondo. "You two pounded those suckers. A hundred yards rushing a piece! That's some good stuff, Man."

"Big Julie and the boys got after them," stated Hug.

"I know you wished coach would have run some more of the option stuff, Hondo," said Ty. "I think Coach was just being careful that Adams was going to blitz the heck out of us like Eisenhower did."

"Naahh," said Hondo. "I was just happy we won. But I was a bit disappointed that he didn't turn this cannon loose on those guys," as he smiled and flexed his skinny, right throwing arm bicep. "Can you imagine what it's going to be like when Coach unleashes this weapon?"

"You mean those fifteen yard bombs you throw when Coach calls for deep passes,?" asked a smiling Big Julie.

"Are you talking about those monster throws you let loose that the wide receivers have to slow down to catch,?" added Ty, with a quick laugh.

"You dudes are brutal," stated a mockingly despondent Hondo Rodriguez.

The players all started chanting "...game ball, game ball, game ball!," as Dempsey walked to the middle of the locker room with two football held up high in his hand. "First of all, let's take a knee for a moment of silence," said Dempsey. After the brief moment for reflection and prayer, Dempsey stated, "that was a great win, Gentlemen. All wins are great ones as you will learn. But this one was definitely special. O.K., Men, who gets the game ball? Or should it be game balls?"

"Eduardo, Eduardo, Eduardo,!" yelled half of the team. "Pete, Pete, Pete,!" yelled the other half. "I guess that's why I brought two footballs," said Dempsey as he held both up in the air.

"Great job, you two," said Dempsey. "There's nothing better than a shutout and defensive scores as well. Big Julie's right, we now have a one game winning streak with eight to go."

"But Coach, we just play seven more games," said Dino DeTaglia.

"He means with a championship game, Dino," said Ty.

"Oh yeah," said the middle linebacker, embarrassed for not having thought about the championship game. After all, championship games were something you never thought about at Roosevelt for many a year.

"Coach, you keep giving out game balls like that and we're gon'na be out of footballs real quick," stated Old Irv with a big, happy smile spread across his face. "I'm only kidding you, Coach," said the equipment man just above a whisper. "You just keep winning and I'll get you all the game balls you need."

Dino had a bar-b-q victory celebration at his home. It was nothing fancy. Everyone brought some hot dogs or hamburgers to be grilled on Dino's backyard grill. Ty arrived with Hug and Big Julie, two players he had quickly become close friends with. Once at the party, his eyes searched the party for someone without success.

"Looking for someone,?" said a familiar voice from behind him. Ty turned around to see Kayleigh.

"No, not really. Just looking to see who's here. I did hear that there was this small, pretty looking blond-haired girl with long pig-tails cruising the party."

"You were looking for me and you know it," stated Kayleigh.

Ty just smiled.

CHAPTER 44

Marge Strausser briskly walked into Sean Dempsey's room just before the homeroom bell. "Congratulations, Sean," said the head coach's teaching buddy holding up a plate of homemade apple strudel. "My husband informed me that you ended a long Roosevelt losing streak. Now you know I'm not much of a football fan. But I, at least, wanted to tell you I'm happy for you. You sure have the school buzzing, Coach."

As the players walked into their locker room for Monday's practice, they noticed a concrete cinder block on the floor up against the wall. The sides were black, the face gold, the two colors of the Roosevelt Rough Riders. Black lettering on the gold face said ADAMS 21-0 with a big, painted, # 1. A vertical stack of the numbered spaces with 2, at the bottom, and 9 at the top were painted on the wall. Each space was just big enough to fit another Victory cement block as they were stacked on top of one another. The numbers were meant to signify another Rough Rider victory. On top of the numbers was the question "HOW MANY CAN WE GET?"

"The concrete block is meant to represent hard work, grit and toughness," said Dempsey to his huddled-up team in the locker room. "That's exactly what you just displayed to get your hard-earned win over Adams. I want you all to know that I was very proud of how hard you played and how you played with toughness and discipline."

"One block is not, however, a stack. To do that, we have to get another Victory Block placed on the top of the Adams' block. There has certainly been enough losing here at Roosevelt, especially over the past few years. Let's go and get another win this week so we can see the stack actually grow. By the end of the season, let's see how high we can get that victory pile."

"Break us, Pete," ordered Dempsey.

"Riders on three. Riders on three. One, two, three..."

"Riders together!"

CHAPTER 45

Dempsey blew his whistle to signal the end of the Monday practice. "Good job, Guys. But, unfortunately, we have some extra running to take care of," said Dempsey to moans and groans of the team. "As you know, if a player cuts class or school, he has to pay a penalty to stay on the team. Jaylon Shields decided to cut his third class this month. It seems that Jaylon doesn't like to go to Mr. Grainger's Intermediate Algebra class."

"That's not too smart, Jaylon," chimed in Big Julie.

"Nice job, Jaylon," said Wooley Woolridge from the back of the kneeling pile of players.

"The first time, you run ten Gassers by yourself. The second time you run with the players at your position. The third time you run with the offense or defense depending on what side of the ball you're on. And, understand this, Gentlemen, the fourth time is with the entire team if I allow it to get that far. Do you understand all this, Jaylon?"

The indignant young player didn't respond.

"Jaylon, I asked you a question."

"Yeah, I got it," grumbled the offended player.

"Coach, why do we do it this way,?" asked Dino.

"Because we're a team, just like those soldiers and marines in the Middle East. What you all have to understand is that a team is, often, only as strong as its weakest link. If one person is a slacker, it can mean devastation for the entire group. Those troops wouldn't want someone covering their backs who cheat the members of their squad as well as themselves. Instead, ...the group, ...the squad, ...the team takes care of the situation quickly and efficiently with peer pressure."

"I still don't think it's right to have to run for someone else who's screwing up when I'm following all the rules," stated Wooley Woolridge.

"Go ask a soldier if it's right for a squad to allow a slacker to shirk his responsibilities, Wooley, when such action could result in the lives of his buddies."

"Offense, on the line,!" yelled Dempsey.

"What's up, Chief,?" asked Dempsey as he entered the principal's office.

"Sit down, Sean. You need some coffee?"

"No thanks, Daryl. But I have to say, I don't like the look on your face, Boss. Did one of my boys get in trouble?"

"No Sean, not exactly. I just wanted you to know that the juvenile court has released Ontario Mosely and all of his buddies from the city's Juvenile Detention Center. They will all be reinstated to school tomorrow morning. The good thing was the restriction that they can't participate in any after school activities including sports. It's basically a house arrest having to attend school. So, hopefully, you shouldn't have to deal with him or his gang members."

"You know, Daryl, I felt bad when he was arrested. Now I'm disturbed that he's been released. He's a troubled kid who knows how to screw up." *I'm now going to have to discretely tell some of the boys to stick tightly to Ty. We certainly don't need any more problems between Ty and Ontario.*

CHAPTER 46

The third game of the season was against the Garfield Grey Hawks. The scouting report on Garfield was that they were significantly better than Adams. They had a greater amount of speed and a lot more athletes.

"These guys aren't bad," stated Ty as the offense watched video of Garfield's game efforts from the day before. "I don't think Coach is going to try to win this one with just defense. These guys know how to score. Our offense is going to have to put up some points."

"Here comes the option," stated Hug.

"It's about time that stuff starts earning its keep," said Hondo. "Hondo fakes to Ty and breaks up the alley. He slips the linebacker. He fakes out the safety but the safety gets a hand on Hondo's ankle. Hondo falls but executes an unbelievable pitch to Wilson a split second before his knee hits the ground. Hug is in the open, all by himself. Oh no, Wilson trips and falls flat on his face in front of 26 thousand screaming fans and his girlfriend."

"Very funny, you little runt," said Hug. "And I don't have a girlfriend."

"Of course not," replied Hondo. "With a face like yours, what girl would want to be your girlfriend. You're just plain ugly."

"You're getting real close to being blasted," said Hug as he held up a clenched fist.

"Problem is, you'd have to catch me first and we all know you're too slow to do that," continued Hondo.

Hug was just about to make a verbal counter when Ty jumped in. "I got an idea," not taking his eyes off the video monitor.

"You have more ideas than anyone I know," said Hondo.

"Just listen, will you,?" said Ty "We all know we're close on the option stuff. This video shows we're definitely going to need the option on Friday. So, why don't we get a football and go over and over the steps and the ball meshes at lunchtime for the rest of this week just like we did back in the preseason. I'm sure we can get some of the guys to give us the reads. The better we look in practice, the more Coach D will call the options. I'm sure of that."

"That sounds good to me. But, when are we gon'na get a chance to eat,?" asked Hug.

"Sounds like something Big Julie would say," answered Hondo. "If you'd skip a lunch or two, maybe you wouldn't be so slow."

"You're getting close, Man," said Hug. "Pretty soon your mouth is gon'na be the size of my fist!"

"So what do you Guys think,?" asked Ty.

"I'm in," answered Hondo.

"Me too, if I can figure out how I'm gon'na eat my lunch," said Hug.

On midday of Monday, Dempsey sat in the faculty dining room eating his lunch, watching some Garfield game video on his iPad. Ty's video analysis of Garfield was right on in regard to Dempsey's game plan. Dempsey saw the Rough Riders were going to have to score points if they were going to have a chance to win. That meant the Rough Riders were either going to have to rely on their passing game or their spread, run option thinking. Since the commitment to the option game had already been decided with the positional moves of Ty, Hug and Hondo, Dempsey felt the offense was much closer to executing the option run plays. *Time to get that sucker in gear. I can see we're going to need it if we intend to win this one.*

Dempsey looked out the window where he was able to see five of his key players on the practice field executing a full option drill. Hondo, Ty and Hug practiced their option execution actions over and over versus the defensive reactions of Jarvis Means and Eduardo Ibanez. *Well, at least we're on the same page in regard to getting the option game ready.*

As the team boarded the bus to Garfield, each player noticed a blank, black and gold cement block sitting on the dashboard. One of the first players to board the bus, the small, backup cornerback, Brock Jamal, patted the block to start a new Roosevelt Rough Rider tradition. Whether on the bus for an away game or on a table inside the team's locker room door for a home game, everyone now patted the blank Victory Block for good luck.

CHAPTER 47

GAME 3:
GARFIELD GREY HAWKS

On the first series of the game, Garfield took the football and ran directly at the Rough Rider defense. After seven straight runs, the Garfield Grey Hawks had the football first and goal on the three-yard line. "Strong left, strong left," yelled the middle linebacker, Dino DeTaglia. "Watch the flat route, Leotis. Be ready to switch, Jarvis."

"Set, ready, go,!" barked the Garfield quarterback. He handed off to his tailback on an off-tackle, kick-out play. The ball carrier broke into a large hole. It started to look like a big run for the Grey Hawks. Suddenly, Dino raced into the opening, lowered his shoulder and ripped his tackle through the inside thigh of the ball carrier's left leg for a two-yard loss.

"Nice job, Dino," yelled defensive coordinator Rod Franklin. "Do it again, defense. Do it again!"

On the next play, Garfield tried a toss sweep play into the boundary. Eduardo Ibanez, the big, powerful, defensive end stuffed the block of the tight end, shed him to the inside and tackled the sweeping tailback for a three-yard loss. On third down, Jarvis Means knocked down an attempted pass to the tight end. The Garfield head coach decided to kick a field goal that was good for an early 3-0 lead.

"O.K.," said Hondo. "Let's get this show rolling! Gun, left twins, 3 triple," read Hondo off his wristband. Hondo read the defensive end, pulled the football and attacked the alley defender. When the alley defender closed in on Hondo, he pitched the football to Ty. Ty burst through a gaping hole for a huge, 27-yard gain.

"What do you think about a deep throw, Sonny,?" asked Dempsey.

"No guts, no glory, Sean. Go for it."

"OK, Coach. I got'cha," said Hondo. "A little play action pass will do just fine. Gun, slot left, fake 2 triple pass," ordered the quarterback as he read his wristband. Hondo faked a zone run play. He then set up for the play action pass. Hondo saw that Rayshawn Davis was wide open down the middle of the field. He underthrew the pass. However, the athletic Davis was able to slow down to make the catch. The fleet slot back then burned up the remaining yards needed to get into the end zone to score.

On the next offensive series, Dempsey called for a naked bootleg pass. He had Hondo fake a zone run play to his left and bootleg back to his right on a 3rd-and-two situation. The coach had a hunch that the weak side wingback, Ty Douglas, would be wide open on his flat route.

Hondo took a quick read up field to check on the streak route of Wooley Woolridge. Wooley was wide open. On 3rd-and-short, Hondo had been taught to throw to the flrat route for a sure completion and a first down if open. Hondo decided to go for it all. He threw a perfect pass to Wooley for an easy six points.

"Good read and nice decision, Hondo," said Dempsey. "Great players do that type of stuff!" *The kid does have some balls, that's for sure.*

Hondo beamed with pride and, surprisingly, was speechless as the players on the sideline pounded on his back.

Garfield never took the lead again. The option plays came alive for the Rough Riders to help produce a 31-17 win for Roosevelt. For the first time in a long period of years, the opposing crowd left a Roosevelt game early with their team well behind on the scoreboard.

“Nice job today, Gentlemen,” said Dempsey after the return bus trip back to the high school. “That’s two great wins in a row! I want to be sure to give out a game ball after each winning game to the game’s player of the week. However, from now on, the winner of the game ball will now have a new, added job. He puts the Victory Block on top of the stack. By Monday, Irv will get it all painted up with win number two.”

“Let’s bring it up, Riders,” said Dempsey. “One, ...”

“Whoa, whoa, whoa,” chanted the team.

“Coach, you forgot to name the player of the game so he can put the Victory Block on the pile,” said Jarvis.

“Oh, Man. I’m sorry, Guys. I screwed up,” said Dempsey deceptively. “I guess this guy’s so miniscule, I almost forgot him. Big Julie, you might have to help him lift up the block to put it on the stack. Get up here, Hondo!”

A smiling Hondo Rodriguez walked up to Dempsey as the team applauded their quirky quarterback. “Coach, I can’t believe that even you’re on my case.” He then flexed the bicep of his right arm. “It’s this cannon that did it. Did you guys see the tightness of those spirals? Hey, what are you two jokers do’n,?” asked an annoyed Hondo as Big Julie and Ty were carrying the Victory Block to the stack.

“We’re helping you stack the block,” answered Big Julie. “It’s kind of heavy for a runt like you!”

“It’s obvious you’re going to need some help,” added Ty.

“Give me that thing,” demanded Hondo as he ripped the block away from his two friendly nemeses. He then placed the new Garfield Victory Block on top of the Adams Victory Block to the cheers of the team.

Two in a row, thought Dempsey as he flipped the game ball to his quarterback and said, “give them a break, Hondo.”

“One, two, three....”

“Riders together!”

"Big win, Son," said an excited Addison Douglas. "It looks like you're really getting that offense in gear."

"It really seems like it, Mom. The option stuff is starting to click."

"How are you doing not playing at quarterback, Ty?"

"I'm still disappointed. But, it's going better than I thought. Being a running back in this offense is fun. Coach finds ways to get us out on the green grass with the ball, that's for sure."

"Just keep grinding, Ty. Keep doing what you can to help your team win. Winning helps cure a lot of ills."

CHAPTER 48

"Every player but one has met the midterm requirements to be able to continue playing,?" Marge Straussser both stated and questioned. "That's unbelievable, Sean! How did you pull that off? There wasn't any hanky-panky was there, Sean,?" asked Dempsey's teaching buddy with her voice just above a whisper. A serious look suddenly became fixed on her face.

"No, Marge," laughed Dempsey. "It's been that good luck apple strudel you've been bringing in after our victories.

"I want everyone to take a knee for a moment," said Dempsey at the end of the Tuesday practice. "I have a special guest with us today who is a tremendous supporter of our program. He's here to say a few words to you. Let's give a warm Rough Rider welcome to a person you all know well, your principal, Dr. Daryl Hoskins."

"Thank you, Coach Dempsey," said Hoskins to a polite applause of the players. "I promise I won't take very long. First of all, I want to congratulate you all on two great wins in a row. It's been a long time since Roosevelt has achieved such a feat. Actually, it's been a long, long time since Roosevelt has won a game, no less two."

"What I'm especially proud of is that the football team, minus only one player, has achieved the necessary mid-term grades needed to continue playing for the remainder of the season. I can't tell you how happy I am to see those results. Congratulations on your hard work and your efforts as students and as student tutors. I'm very proud of what you have accomplished. My only disappointment has been to hear that your early morning, breakfast bag delivery man has not, ...EVEN ONCE, dropped off a glazed donut to go along with my morning cup of coffee.

"BOOO!!!," chimed in the players as Big Julie plastered what seemed to be an ear-to-ear smile across his face.

Ty was driving Kayleigh home from another study group session using his mother's car. This time, the study group was actually made up of five other students besides Ty and Kayleigh.

"Can you believe they let Ontario and his thugs back in school,?" asked Kayleigh disgustedly. "We go to school to try to learn something and the courts worry more about taking care of the dirt bags. Ty, I really worry about you and that Ontario creep. My brother told me he's vowed to get you. Supposedly, gangsters are big on making good on their threats."

Ty pursed his lips tightly. *Unfortunately, I think she's right. I have a strong feeling this is all going to lead to no good. No good at all.*

CHAPTER 49

GAME 4:
GRANT PRESIDENTS

On the offense's opening play of the game versus Grant, Dempsey reached into his playbook and called for a slot reverse off the fake of an option play. Hondo faked the zone run to Hug. He then attacked outside with Ty as the pitch back. The pitch, however, was not to Ty. It was to the speedy slot back Rayshawn Davis on a reverse. The opposing defense had bitten on the option fake. Rayshawn torched the field with his great speed for a 68-yard touchdown.

"Great job, Rayshawn," said Hug as he jumped on top of the touchdown scoring slot back. "You smoked them big time."

"Thanks, Man. Thanks, Man," said the speedy slot back. "That was almost too easy."

"That's all right, Rayshawn," said Big Julie. 'We'll take all the easy one's we can get!"

Dempsey didn't call for any of the halfback passes he had planned to use. He was hoping to more fully create balance for his offense by using the passing abilities of Ty and Hug. He didn't have to. He just kept calling the option and the lead option and a few zone bubble screens. Grant acted like they had never studied the exchanged game video. From the way they tried to defense the Rough Riders' offense, they probably hadn't. The Rough Rider offense exploded and looked unstoppable. Roosevelt's bench was cleared early in a 42-7 drubbing of Grant.

"Thanks for keeping the score down, Sean," said the Grant head coach as the two coaches shook hands at midfield. You could have scored a hundred if you wanted to. You're doing a heck of a job with those kids, Sean. It's really nice to see Roosevelt football have some success."

"Thank you, Coach," said Dempsey humbly. "I really appreciate your saying that."

Dempsey turned and started walking off the field when he heard the voice of the Grant coach once again. "And Sean, when you get to the championship game, do all the coaches in the conference a favor and kick Eisenhower's ass for us, will you? That jerk of a coach needs to be put in his place!"

Sean Dempsey was speechless. Deep down, he had hoped to shape up the Roosevelt football program and, perhaps, actually win a few games. Now a rival coach was telling him he was on track to go to the championship game.

"Coach, we got a long way to go to get to the championship game," said Dempsey with an appreciative smile on his face.

"You'll get there, Sean. You wait and see! You'll get there."

Rayshawn Davis, the winner of the game ball, hoisted the third consecutive Victory Block to what had now become the team's concrete Victory Shrine.

"Number three,! Number three,! Number three,!" chanted the team.

"Hey, Hug," shouted Big Julie. "How come you're not helping Rayshawn with the Victory Block like you had to do for Hondo last week," as the big tackle held up the huge sub sandwich he stashed in his backpack for his post-game snack.

"Ya know," said Hug. "Rayshawn actually has some meat on his bones. I'm not worried about him dropping the Victory Block on his foot like I was last week with Hondo."

"I'm gon'na show you guys how to run over a safety one of these days," said Hondo.

"Oh, please. Don't try to do that," said Big Julie. "We can't let you get hurt. You're much too valuable handing or pitching the ball off to Hug and Ty."

"Really,?" asked the quarterback as the rest of the team snickered.

"Hey, what'cha doing here,?" asked a smiling Ty as he left the players' locker room and saw Kayleigh standing off by herself.

"I'm waiting for you to take me to the Malt Shop to buy me a shake. That was a big win. We need to celebrate!"

"Oh, no," whined Ty after reaching to his satchel bag only to find no wallet. "I didn't bring any money with me this morning."

"That figures," replied the vivacious girl. "Don't worry. The treat's on me today. That way you'll owe me for a next time." As they walked away, Kayleigh reached to hold Ty's hand. The affection was much to the halfback's surprise but not to his displeasure. "I told you that you knew what you wanted to do."

"You certainly did, didn't you,?" answered Ty. "And, I'm glad I decided to not be selfish and go along with Coach D's idea. Winning is so fun. I've always known that. But it's so different for these guys. They win three games and you think we're going to the Super Bowl."

"Success is something so little of them have experienced," stated Kayleigh. "They finally have a leader to get them to understand what it takes to win."

"You're right. Coach D has done a great job getting this program turned around. The players really like him even though he can be so tough. They know he really cares about them."

"Actually, I was talking about another good leader," added Kayleigh. "He's one of the players. He wears number eight."

"Me,?" answered Ty.

"Yeah, you, Ty Douglas," answered Kayleigh as Ty pulled her in tight for a hug. "You might not think you're a good leader. But, you are. And, you're the best kind of leader. You lead by example, not with your mouth. That's why the players like you so much."

CHAPTER 50

Ty, Eduardo, Jarvis and Dino where talking about their upcoming game Friday against Kennedy as they walked down a corridor together to get to their next class. Ty noticed Dino smiling and nodding to Kimmie Colston, the pretty, blond haired cheerleader who sat next to Dino in their history class.

"Keep your mind focused," said Ty with a smirk on his face. "We have a big game this week. We don't need no love-struck middle linebacker for this one."

"I'm not love-struck," said Dino. "And, by the way, you have no room to talk, Romeo."

"She is a cutie," said Jarvis. "I will say that."

"I think she is very good looking," said Eduardo.

"Good observation, Eduardo," said Jarvis with a smile.

"What is this 'observation' word mean?"

Ty suddenly heard a familiar voice cry out. "No! Don't do this! Stop it! You're hurt'n me!" Ty fought his way through the crowd that had gathered around the disturbance. When he broke through, Ty saw Ontario Mosely and members of his gang trying to forcefully stuff Hondo into one of the school's hall lockers. Hondo's face was covered with blood as he fought to free himself. One of Mosely's accomplices was pinning down Hondo's arms as Mosely pounded his face with a barrage of punches.

Mosely suddenly felt the air going out of his lungs. After

charging the gang leader, Ty delivered a blocking flipper with his right forearm to Mosely's rib cage driving the gang leader upward and forward, smashing his face into the hallway lockers. Ontario's head and rib area exploded in pain. Ty then grabbed the back of Moseley's head by his hair and viciously slammed Ontario's face into the metal locker. "How's that, you scumbag,!" yelled out the enraged teen. "You don't have the balls to pick on someone of your own size, do you asshole. Well, I'm someone your damned size," spit out Ty as he continued the barrage of face slams into the locker. "And if you want more of this, just keep this crap up, Mosely."

Ty then realized he was being grabbed from behind by one of Moseley's buddies. He slammed his head backwards into the nose of the of gang member. Ty broke the gangster's nose as blood gushed rapidly from the thug's nostrils. With his arms released, Ty whipped up his left elbow to deliver a powerful blow up under the jaw of another of the gang members. He then whipped around in the opposite direction to deliver a blast with the back of his right fist to the temple of another.

Just as Ty was about to spin around to take on another of Mosely's thugs, the gangster took a powerful fist to the side of his face from Hug Wilson. Behind Hug was Eduardo Ibanez, punching another of the gangsters who, at this point had given up swinging his fists. Instead, he was covering up his head with both of his hands for protection. Jarvis was holding another of the gangsters by the front of his shirt with one hand and was punching him with the fist of his other. Dino dropped one of the other gangsters with a blast to the stomach. Big Julie, appearing from the throng of watching students, stood to the side of the melee holding up two of the gangsters in the air with powerful headlocks that had both screaming.

"That's enough! That's enough,!" yelled Dr. Hoskins as he, his assistant principal, Coach Walters and two other teachers arrived at the scene. "Put those two down, Julius!" Big Julie loosened his grip on the two thugs letting them both crash to the ground. "What is going on here? Coach Walters, get your boys down to my office right now. Mrs. Thompson, go get the school nurse please. Mr.

Ashley, Mr. Williams, get Mosely's people down to the vice-principal's office and stay with them until I get there."

Moments later, Dempsey entered Dr. Hoskins' office. Initially, he looked at his six football players without saying a word.

"All of the fighting was my fault, Coach D," said Ty. "All of the others were just trying to help me out."

"I heard about what went on," said Dempsey.

"How's Hondo,?" asked Hug.

"He'll be fine. He has a cut over his eye and a bloody lip but didn't need any stitches. His back is all scraped up. It's pretty ugly looking. But, he'll survive."

"Is he going to be able to play on Friday,?" asked Big Julie.

"Knowing Hondo, we'll never be able to keep him off the field," answered Dempsey. "Actually, I'm a lot more worried about what's going to be done about you guys. I've gotten a pretty good idea about the school district's No Tolerance Rule for fighting." *This is going to be dicey. It could mean a lot of trouble for us,* thought the head coach. *We were just getting on a roll and this crap has to happen.*

"But, we had to help Hondo," said Hug. "They were seriously hurting our buddy. That's not right, Coach!"

"I realize that, Hug. But, now I have to figure out how to take care of you guys. This could be a lot bigger problem than you think."

"That punk Ontario got what he deserved," said Ty. "I just wish his buddies weren't there to hold me back. That gutless asshole needed to be straightened out and get his ass kicked. Next time I'm gon'na..."

"Ease up, Ty,!" burst out Dempsey, almost to a shout. "You're the guy I have to worry about the most. Don't make this situation any more difficult for me than it is."

Ty continued to simmer as he stared at the ground.

"I kicked that creep's ass, Mom," stated an infuriated Tyler Douglas. "I wish those gangster buddies of his didn't grab me and hold me back."

"Well, Son, it sounds like you took care of those guys too," replied Addison Douglas. "Tyler! You have to calm down. I was told how you stopped the thugs from hurting your friend any more than this Ontario and his gangsters did. That was the right thing to do no matter what anyone says. I have your back, that I can promise. But, you have to ease up now, Ty, so I can work this all out. I'll see the principal myself. But, you have to calm down now."

This shit's really killing me, thought Ty's mother. *How can the courts let such garbage attack such a nice kid like Hondo? And, such a small, defenseless person at that. Now I have to worry like hell about my own boy all the more. They need to lock that bastard Ontario up for good!*

CHAPTER 51

All six of the Rough Rider players were immediately suspended. None of the students could be reinstated until a parent attended a conference concerning the fighting incident as per district rules. The next morning, principal Daryl Hoskins walked into the school's main office a few minutes before the starting bell. He was glancing at the sports section of the local newspaper when his administrative assistant got his attention.

"Ah-hum," said Hoskins' administrative assistant as she sat at her desk. She nodded towards the waiting area. Hoskins looked up to see nine adults waiting to speak to him.

Oh no. This is not going to be a good day.

"Why don't we all go to the conference room next door," said the smiling principal. "We'll all be a lot more comfortable there. Would anyone like some coffee,?" asked Hoskins as he took the seat at the head of the conference room table. No one took the offer. It was obvious that the parents were ready for a fight of their own.

"Dr. Hoskins, my father's English is not very good," said Maria Rodriguez, one of Hondo's sisters. "When he gets excited, it is very hard to understand him so if it is all right with you, I will interpret his Spanish."

"That will be fine, Maria. Thank you."

"My father says that it is wrong that the boys should be

suspended," said Maria. "He says that the boys who helped Hernando when he was being beaten up by those hoodlums should be given medals. Ontario and his gang are bad people and should all be put in jail. We need to get them out of our community."

"Mr. Rodriguez, I fully understand your concern and I am glad that your boy's friends helped to stop your son from being hurt any more than he was," said Hoskins. "Ontario Mosely and his followers are presently at the juvenile detention center since they violated the probations they already had with their actions yesterday. They will be going before a judge tomorrow. I'm very hopeful that the situation will be handled appropriately."

"But why are these good boys being punished,?" interpreted Maria.

"That's exactly what I want to know," said Addison Douglas, Ty's mother.

"I wish I had had friends like that when I was a kid," said Jarvis Means' father. "If our kids didn't come to the rescue, there's no telling how badly Hondo might have been beaten. A bunch of punks against one, small, sixteen-year-old kid isn't fair odds by any stretch of the imagination."

"Mi niño, Eduardo, he no go to jail, is he,?" asked the crying mother of Eduardo Ibanez.

"There better not be anything bad put on my boy's record or I'm gon'na sue this school district for a lot of money. And I mean a lot of money,!" stated Big Julie's mother, Geraldine Goodman. "I'm not gon'na let anybody stop my boy from getting a football scholarship. Maybe I should be calling my cousin at the NAACP. I know I can get some help straightening this mess out with them!"

The bewildered principal couldn't seem to get a word in amidst the verbal barrage of the parents. "Please, please, let's slow down here a bit," said Dr. Hoskins. "First of all, Eduardo is not going to go to jail Mrs. Ibanez. Secondly, what you have to understand is the problem I am facing. Our school district has a No Tolerance Rule for fighting and bullying. The thought is, why didn't any of Hernando's friends go to get help from a teacher or administrator?"

"Dr. Hoskins, Julius and Jarvis did initially look for a teacher or an administrator and none could be found," replied Mrs. Douglas. "My question to you is why wasn't there proper supervision in, what I have come to understand, is the most congested area of the entire school?"

"Mrs. Douglas, we did have a teacher on duty at that time," answered Dr. Hoskins. "The problem was that in a non-related incident, a male student turned the hallway corner quickly and slammed into a female student. The teacher had to help the young lady to the nurse's office as he attended to her bloody nose."

"One way or the other, it seems it took a long time for a teacher or administrator to come to the attention of Hernando's being assaulted," said Ty's mother. "If Hondo's friends didn't come to his defense, he could have been much more seriously injured. I don't want my son to be involved in such fights if he can avoid them. However, I also must say that I am quite proud to hear that my son, Tyler, was the first person to help protect his friend from being hurt any more than he was."

"Mrs. Douglas, I am quite aware of the actions of your son," stated Dr. Hoskins having clearly heard the word "assaulted" used by the intelligently spoken woman. "But, he also broke one student's nose and separated the ribs of another. That student also had to get six stitches above an eyebrow. Two others have concussions."

"And, that's because my Tyler came to the aid of a 150-pound adolescent who was being beaten up by an entire gang and I'm damn proud he did."

"Woo-weee!," declared Mr. Means. "I wouldn't want to mess with that boy. He's a fight'n machine,!" stated the father with an astonished look on his face.

"Mr. Means, please,!" said Dr. Hoskins. "No matter how much it may seem that Mosely and his people were in the wrong, I still am going to have to deal with the parents of those students."

"Maybe their parents should go to jail with them," growled Tony DeTaglia, Dino's father. "All of this would never have happened if there was some decent parenting."

"Let's keep this discussion in line with what we can do to help all of these students as best we can," replied Hoskins.

"Are you suggesting that we should get an attorney to represent us,?" asked Hug's mother.

"Or, at least, have this all brought up at the next school board meeting," added Mr. Means. "There's a lot of people on that board that would like to have that gang all thrown out of school for good."

I'm getting attacked from all angles. I knew I shouldn't have had all of these people in here together. That was definitely a bad idea. "Now, now, people," said Dr. Hoskins. "Let's not get ahead of ourselves. I don't think lawyers and school board meetings and the NAACP are what we need right now. By being here, your children are no longer on suspension. Of course, Hernando was the person who was attacked so he was never in any type of suspension situation."

"That's fine for now, Dr. Hoskins," said Mrs. Douglas. "But in all fairness, if this situation does end up putting a blemish on any of these boys' school records, we have decided, as a group, to seek legal representation," said Ty's mother firmly.

"Personally, I think it was about time that some kids stood up to Mosely and his delinquent friends and put them in their place," said Big Julie's mother. "It sure doesn't look like your teachers are doing that."

"Mrs. Goodman, I feel that we have made great strides at Roosevelt since I have been here," said Hoskins. "Our crime, drugs, fighting and bullying rates are way down. I'm sorry to see this situation develop. When it comes to your sons, we are talking about some of the finest young people that we now have here at Roosevelt."

"Let me work on this for a bit," continued the principal. "I need some time to get everything straightened out so I can come up with an amicable decision." *Would someone please get me some aspirins.*

When Ty left the principal's office with his mother, the first person he saw was Kayleigh. "Mom, this is Kayleigh," was about all Ty could get out of his mouth as his eyes looked down to the floor. Ty was peeved that he had had his arms held back when he felt he could have finished off Ontario Mosely for good. And yet, he knew this quandary was a long way from being over. He certainly wasn't concerned about fist fights. There, he could hold his own against most anyone his age. It was the knives and, possibly, guns that Ontario Mosely and his gang could bring to the table that troubled him greatly. He didn't want to see his friends or himself get seriously hurt.

Knowing her son as she did, Addison Douglas realized that it was time to give her son some space. "I have another appointment," lied Mrs. Douglas. "It was nice to meet you, Kayleigh. The next time we have a barbeque at the house, Ty will have to invite you."

"Thank you, Mrs. Douglas. That would be very nice."

"We'll talk more about this tonight, Ty," said his mother as she attempted a comforting smile. Addison Douglas then fumed once she turned away from Ty and Kayleigh. *One thing's for sure, ...I won't back-off this situation.*

"I screwed up again, Kayleigh," Ty finally was able to utter. "No matter where I go, I mess up. I always lose my cool and end up fighting."

"But you jumped in to help your friend, Ty, when those gangsters were beating the hell out of him. I know you're not supposed to fight in school. But, you did the right thing, Ty Douglas. You'd do the same thing again if it happened tomorrow and you know it. No matter what anyone says about your fighting, your sticking up for and your helping your friend is a part of you that makes you so special. That's one of the reasons I like you so much."

CHAPTER 52

"Wow!," said Marge Strausser as she, again, raced into Dempsey's classroom with her patented, fast-paced entry. "You're not looking too good, Coach. Too many adult beverages last night?"

"No, it wasn't that," answered the head coach.

"Sean, you've been taking your meds, haven't you?"

"I think I got this all worked out, Sean," said Hoskins. "Your kids will get the chance to play this week if they decide to accept some form of penalty. I'll leave that for you to take care of. But, it must be something realistic. It can't be frivolous. And, they must do some form of community service work. Maybe they can do a sweep of the trash around the fencing perimeter of the school. The problem is, I've got to cover my tracks about the boys fighting."

"There's one more thing I want you to do for me, Sean." continued Hoskins. "Your new player, Tyler Douglas. He seems to be a heck of a kid. He's a real good student too. I worry that he knows how to fight so well. And, he seems to have a short fuse. That can be a dangerous combination at a school like Roosevelt, Sean. We might not be able to help him the next time."

"I understand, Daryl. He is a good kid, ...a real good kid. But, there seems to be a lot going on in that head of his. He can flip a switch from a pleasant, mild-mannered individual to a street fighter in a heartbeat. And, as you have already said, Daryl, he damn well knows how to fight."

"Guys, here's where we're at," stated Dr. Hoskins as he looked at the worried football players involved in the brawl sitting in front of him. Dempsey sat behind his players. "The school district says I have to follow through on some form of disciplinary action whenever there is a fight. However, I have the leeway to lessen the severity of the consequences for first time fighting violations. With one small exception, you've all shown excellent behavior since you've been here at Roosevelt, which I am very glad to see."

"This has been a very difficult situation to deal with because you all came to the rescue of a fellow student, teammate and friend who was being injured. You will be given an option. You can accept a one game suspension from the team. Or, I can turn this disciplinary action over to Coach Dempsey. I told Coach it would have to be a meaningful enough punishment to make you think twice about such actions in the future. In addition, you will be required to do some form of community service work hours."

"I'll be sure to stay on top of all this, Dr. Hoskins," said Dempsey.

"If you don't have any other disciplinary problems for the remainder of the school year, as I fully expect you won't, this incident will be fully erased from your school records," said Hoskins. "Any questions?"

None of the players said a word.

As the players began to leave the office, the principal stated, "Tyler, I need to chat with you a little longer."

"May I stay, Dr. Hoskins,?" asked Dempsey.

"Please do, Coach."

"No more, Tyler," said the principal. "You're the one with the small exception I was talking about. You've only been here at Roosevelt for an extremely short time. I stood up for you because a number of people have gone out of their way to support you in the short time you've been here at Roosevelt. You're a smart kid and an excellent student. A broken nose, separated ribs, two concussions, stitches, it's time for you to start thinking before you act. You're not a little kid anymore, Ty. If you were an adult, which the state will declare you are shortly, you could have been charged with a felony since you have a black belt in karate. Do you understand what I'm saying, Tyler?"

"I understand," stated Tyler Douglas as he glared into the eyes of the principal. "But, I also believe that if someone attacks you, then you have the right to defend yourself. That's where I feel our administration is flat out wrong."

At the end of Tuesday's practice, Dempsey called up the team. Personally, he felt the disciplinary action was bogus. In actuality, he was proud of the fact that six of his players had come to Hondo's rescue. Deep down, he was glad Ty had pummeled Ontario Mosely. As a teacher and coach, however, he had to be careful. He knew his actions would be carefully scrutinized. "I know you all have heard about the decision for Eduardo, Hug, Ty, Big Julie, Dino and Jarvis to run at the end of the next three practices."

"I don't think that's right, Coach D," said Leotis. "Those punks beat the hell out of Hondo. And, if Ty and the other guys didn't get there in time, Hondo could have really been all busted up."

"Guys, ...I feel like I'm backed up into a corner," said Dempsey. "I understand that fighting has been a big problem at Roosevelt for a long time and our school district has been working hard to clamp down on it. At least our guys can earn the right to play this Friday by running and doing some community service hours. So, let's just support each other and get this over with."

"Big Julie, Dino, Jarvis, Ty, Eduardo, Hug, on the line." Dempsey suddenly noticed that seven players were on the line rather than six. "No, Hondo, you don't have to run. Hell, Son, you're the guy who was assaulted and beaten."

"These are my homies, Coach," said Hondo. "They had my back. Now, I got theirs. Riders together!"

Dempsey was at a total loss for words. He, simply, did not know what to say.

"Riders together," said the big defensive tackle, Ricardo Pena, as he walked to the line.

"Riders together," said Rayshawn Davis as he joined the group.

"Riders together," said Leotis Brown, Brock Jamal, Seamus Collins and Bernardo Diaz. For three consecutive practices, the entire football team ran ten Gassers with their punished teammates.

As Ty walked out of the players' locker room door, he found Hondo standing in front of him. Hondo stuck out his hand. "Gracias, Amigo! I had the right guy covering my back." Hondo then reached out to give his new friend a sincere hug. The emotionally silent Ty Douglas hugged back.

Defying his probation orders, Ontario Mosely left his dilapidated apartment building counting the money he had made on the streets that day dealing crack. Halfway down the block he heard a familiar, deep voice from the darkened alley he was passing.

"What's shake'n, Ontario,?" said Big Julie as he took a step forward so that the light would shine on his face.

"Uh, noth'n's up, Big Julie," answered Ontario nervously. "Noth'n at all, Bro." Big Julie was the one person in Latimore Heights that

Ontario Mosely was terrified of, especially when he was alone with Julius Goodman as he was now. As big as he was, Big Julie always seemed to have the ability to appear out of nowhere.

"Here's the deal, Ontario," said Big Julie quietly and slowly. "If you, or any of your gang buddies, mess around with any of my football homies again, I'm gon'na come looking for you. And, I promise I'll find you and I'll make sure it's when we're all by ourselves, just like now. Understand, Bro?!"

"Yeah, I got'cha, Man," replied the terrified gang leader.

Big Julie slipped back into the shadows with quiet and stealth.

"Mom, it was unbelievable," said Ty." The six of us who fought got on the line to do our penalty running and the next thing you know, everybody on the team says 'Riders together' and run with us."

"Well, as hard as this may be to say, Son, maybe that fight is exactly what was needed to help get the team to truly come close together."

CHAPTER 53

Football teams thrive on routine. They enjoy knowing what kind of practice they will have on a Monday and what they will be doing on other practice days. They like to know that Mondays and Tuesdays before Friday night games are usually long, physical, fully padded practices. They like knowing, and enjoying, the lighter practice day workouts of Wednesdays and Thursdays. Such a tapered schedule allows a team to focus on fine tuning and a freshening up of minds and bodies as a game's kick-off time gets closer and closer.

What often does not work well for a team is a break from such a routine, especially when that disruption is mental more than physical. Problems often crop up that make a team worry about what just happened or what the ramifications will be. Going into the big, upcoming game with the rival Kennedy Cougars proved to be a tough task for the Rough Riders.

"The offense seems a little off, doesn't it, Sean,?" asked Sonny Walters, the wide receiver coach. "They seem tight."

"Unfortunately, you're right on both counts," said Dempsey. He had barely slept the night before worrying about the focus and morale of his players. The players were dragging and it was definitely showing. *This could really be a tough one for us. We certainly don't need tired legs or tired players.*

"Good hard work, Guys," stated Coach Dempsey, after the entire team had, again, fulfilled the Gassers' punishment running drill. "You're doing a great job of pushing through our difficult situation. I'm very proud of how you've worked through this as a team." The head coach, himself, seemed to be exhausted. The P.T.S.D. syndromes seemed to be rearing up as a result of Hondo's assault. A hand was suddenly raised by one of the kneeling players.

"Yes, Ty," acknowledged Dempsey.

"Coach, we were kind of thinking that a fun-type competition drill might help perk everyone up a bit. It's a drill that pits the offensive guys and the defensive dudes, as the players giggled and smirked with the knowledge of what was coming. The losers do 10 push-ups. Each participant gets a shot at catching a deep punt from the Jugs machine."

"You put Ty up to this, didn't you, Sean,?" asked Coach Franklin, with a large smile plastered on his face.

"The hell I did," answered Dempsey. "I didn't have a thing to do with this, Rod."

"All right! Let's go defense! Offense, offense, offense,!" were some of the cheers that erupted from the players.

"May I take over the drill, Coach,?" asked the nervy running back.

"Go right ahead, Mr. Douglas. "It's your show now."

The ballsy running back waded through the pack of players amidst continued smiles and snickers. "O.K., Guys. We're going to call up six of the absolutely best athletes on the field, three from the offense and three from the defense, to attempt catching simulated punts from the Jugs machine.

"First up for the defense, ...Coach Carlton Williams," announced Ty to the coaching staff's bewilderment.

"You mean the coaches are the punt catchers,?" asked the frowning, but smiling, head coach.

"You got that right," yelled out Big Julie as all the coaches shook their heads from side-to-side whispering "...oh, no..." to themselves.

"Hey, we wanted to see how the best do it," stated Hondo.

"Let's go, Coach Williams. We don't have all day,!" stated Ty as the players and coaches laughed and smiled.

Coach Williams, the Defensive Line Coach, got wide-eyed as the Jugs delivery of football exploded into the air and fell down on top of him at what seemed to be warp-speed. He misjudged the course of the football as he desperately lunged forward for the football at the last, split second unsuccessfully. Coach Lopez, the new Offensive Line Coach was equally non-effective as the football hit the ground some ten feet away from him. Despite the ineffectiveness of the two line coaches, the players, on both sides, still cheered for their fumbling efforts.

Coach Franklin, the Secondary Coach and Defensive Coordinator, actually looked like an athlete as the ex-NFL safety smoothly made his punt catch. The same was true for Coach Walters who was an ex-college punt and kick-off returner. With the score tied two to two, the competition was down to Coach Jefferies, the linebacker coach and Head Coach Sean Dempsey.

Coach Jefferies had put on a few pounds since his playing days and was not quite the athlete he once was. He did a great job of positioning himself underneath the football as it dropped out of the sky. Unfortunately, he misjudged the tremendous speed of the football as it dropped on top of him. He reached up to catch the football at the last second. He was a bit too late as the football smashed into his head and bounced away to his side producing a comical scene for all who watched. The impact of the fast dropping punt on his head dazed the linebacker coach who collapsed to the ground and had a tough time getting up. Dino and Eduardo quickly ran over to help lift-up the sluggish and dizzy coach.

The contest was now in the hands of Coach Dempsey. Though not like Coach Jefferies, Coach Dempsey had also put on significant pounds since his playing days. Dempsey told himself to keep his eyes on the ball and stay slightly deeper than its descent, as was punt reception protocol. As hard as he tried to accomplish this feat, the ball did not hang high in the air as it did for the other coaches. Instead, it took off on a low, flat trajectory. This forced Dempsey to turn and sprint in an unlikely chance to intersect the flight of the football before it hit the ground. At the last possible second, Dempsey reached out as far as he could with his right hand as his fingertips closed around the fat of the football. He, impressively, pulled the football into his body as he crashed his opposite, left shoulder into the ground and then executed a forward roll.

The offensive players screamed and hollered as they sprinted to their spectacular catching head coach. Dempsey lied on the ground and held the football up with his right arm and hand. Dempsey got up slowly with the help of Hug, Big Julie and Ty as the players jumped and pounded on him in celebration.

With a painful grunt, Dempsey stated, "...you better break the team, Rod."

"Did you hurt yourself, Sean?"

"I think I separated my shoulder," uttered the suffering head coach. Dempsey was correct. He had separated his shoulder.

As Dempsey was dressing gingerly after his shoulder injury and post-practice shower, he noticed Coach Jefferies and Coach Lopez scurrying around the locker room, hustling out the door. As Dempsey walked towards his jeep, he now saw the same assistants carrying fan rakes and boxes of lawn trash bags out towards the school fencing that surrounded the athletic fields. As Dempsey curiously started to follow his assistants, he saw his entire team and coaching staff working to clean up the mountains of trash spewed over the grounds of the perimeter of Roosevelt High's school property.

"Need a trash bag, Coach,?" said Big Julie. "With that shoulder, I think that's all you can handle."

Dempsey looked around at his 33 football players and five

assistant coaches and said, "yes, I certainly do, Big Man. And, you're right. Holding a bag is about all I can do right now."

Standing at his office window, Roosevelt High School's principal, Daryl Hoskins, peered out to see the entire football team and coaching staff working together to fulfill the community service hours required of the six players involved in the fighting altercation. He had a small, sad smile across his face. Much as his head football coach, Hoskins didn't believe in the penalties dished-out for the six Rough Rider players. *The superintendent hung me out to dry on this one and I'll be sure to remember that.*

"Can we beat these guys,?" asked Kayleigh on their, now, nightly phone call.

"We can," answered Ty. "But, it's going to be tough. Kennedy is definitely one of the best teams in the conference. We seem to have lost a bit of our mojo since the fight to help Hondo. Right now, it looks like we're a tired football team. Our speed isn't quite there and we need our speed if we expect to win." *That fight stuff helping out Hondo might end up kicking our ass,* thought Ty. *The video shows that this opponent is too good to be fooling around with.*

"But, we must win,!" said a frustrated Kayleigh. "We finally have a team that's not a joke anymore. We've got to win this game!"

"Then we're going have to reach down deep to make it happen."

"And, you got'ta stop fooling around and start using that magic dust I'm always talking about!"

Well, I'm still not sure about this magic dust stuff, thought Ty. *But maybe Kayleigh's right. Something special has got to happen for us if we truly think we can win this game.*

CHAPTER 54

"Excuse my obstinance, Dr. Hoskins," said the menacing Addison Douglas as the mentally battered principal squirmed in his desk chair, "but I'd like to know what the hell's going on. My son, and five other football players, come to the aid of a 150-pound boy who's being beaten brutally and is being physically stuffed into a small locker by twelve, despicable gang members and he, and his friends, are being punished?! That's a crock of shit and you damn well know it!"

"I don't want to take a lot of your time, Dr. Hoskins. I'm sure you have a tremendous amount to take care being that Roosevelt is such a large school. I'm here to inform you that the parents of the six football players who are being punished, which includes myself, are looking into legal action concerning this matter. The last time I checked, people have the right to protect themselves when being brutally attacked."

On the Friday before the Kennedy game, Coach Dempsey took Ty Douglas out for lunch. "Want me to drive, Coach? It looks like you're struggling with your shoulder in that sling. I heard shoulder injuries hurt like hell."

"Naahh, I can handle this," said the chuckling head coach trying to feign that his separated shoulder was not bothering him that much. In reality, it was killing him since he didn't want to take any pain killers so close to game time. He wanted to be sure to be razor sharp and the pain from his shoulder was definitely helping him stay on high alert. Dempsey ordered two cheeseburgers and some of The Malt Shop's famous extra crispy, double fried French fries. When the head coach asked Ty if he would like a Coke, the running back politely requested the Malt Shop specialty, a chocolate malt.

"Got'ta go with the house special, Coach," said a smiling Ty Douglas. "Can't beat the chocolate malts here." Once again, Ty knew something was curiously up. You didn't get invited to lunch by the head coach for nothing. And, yet, Ty knew exactly what the lunch was all about. Anger management was the new term he had been hearing. It seemed that with every move there was a new name or term for what really was nothing but the simple word, ...fighting.

"So how's everything going for you, Ty? Getting treated O.K.?"

"Pretty well, Coach," said the apprehensive, junior running back, "other than my relationship with that gangster Ontario Mosely. Can I help you cut up that burger for you? It looks like you're struggling a bit."

"As much as I hate to admit it, I am struggling, Ty." *Who's kidding who ? This hurts so much that I'm ready to throw-up.* "Maybe you can cut that up into quarters for me. That might give me a chance to hold it so I don't get the ketchup all over me. As it is, my wife accuses me of being a sloppy eater no less not being able to move my arm very well."

"Anyhow, I'm really doing well in school. I got all A's in my classes so far. I'm having a lot of fun with the team. I really like the guys. They're quite a group, that's for sure. Some are definite characters, but really good people."

"Hondo, Hug and Big Julie alone would make a great T.V. sitcom, that's for sure," said Dempsey. "I'd probably have to throw you in for good measure just to provide some sanity."

"I don't know about the sanity, Coach. It seems like I've given you a few grey hairs already and I've only been here for a short time."

"You're right, Ty. You have given me a few, new grey hairs," declared the head coach with a soft laugh. Dempsey had come to like Ty Douglas tremendously in the short period of time that he had come to know him. He liked Ty's respectfulness for the teachers, coaches and his fellow players as well as his grit, toughness and determination. It was Ty's aggressive, fighting nature that had made Dempsey worry.

"You're a good person and a damn good player, Ty. I'm glad you're with us."

Ty took the words in as a sincere compliment. As most everyone else on the team, Ty felt his head coach was extremely sincere and honest, almost to a fault. He could be one, tough coach when he wanted, or needed, to be. However, working hard in a focused fashion and having fun doing it seemed to be the way the head coach was described by his players. A sudden, broad, Sean Dempsey smile normally brought a similar smile from the player, or players, involved.

"Thanks for saying that, Coach. I really am sorry about this situation concerning Hondo. I can only imagine how much of a problem it has been for you. And, I'm sure that's why we're having this lunch here together, isn't it Coach,?" as Ty then took a large swig of his chocolate malt. *Why the hell did I have to run into a turd like Ontario Mosely. And on the first day of school, no less.*

"Yes it is, Ty," said Dempsey as a strange, pensive look appeared across his own face. *What the hell am I doing,?* thought the head coach. *What right do I have to be here counseling such a sharp, dynamic kid as Tyler Douglas. Anger, a short fuse, trying to solve problems with his fists. Hell, that was my M.O. when I was Ty's age! How about right now? Well, I've always believed in fate and here I am being challenged to try to help a good kid succeed. But really, who am I to tell a Ty Douglas what to do. And yet, who better to understand his problems and difficulties. I might not be the person he needs. But, I can sure try to help. Half the battle is having someone in your corner who really cares for you. It might even help me to get some things in my own life straightened out.*

"Ty, I screwed up once, big time," said the head coach. "I lost it!

The linebacker I was coaching was a real talent. He was also a complete ass. A punk might be the best way to describe him. He cursed me out in front of the team and I lost it!"

"Did you punch him, Coach?"

"No, it was a body slam. I picked him up in a cross-body, wrestling cradle and slammed him to the ground. I broke his shoulder, much like I did my own the other day and my teaching and coaching career went out the window. Or, at least, it certainly seemed that it did."

"That must really have been a bummer. Were you married then?"

"Just got married that summer," replied Dempsey. "And, we found out that my wife was pregnant with our first child a few days before it had happened. As tough as things were, though, my wife stuck right by my side. She was, and is, a rock. That's the only way I can put it. I'm one lucky dumb ass to have her." *Am I ever,* thought Dempsey.

"So you enlisted in the Army?"

"Yes I did. I still had to let go some steam. The next thing I know I was an Army Ranger in and out of combat in the mountains of Afghanistan. You knew you were doing your job helping Americans and America. But, what a hell hole!"

"I'll bet that had a big influence on your life, Coach."

"That's putting it mildly, Ty. All of a sudden, I was a sergeant responsible for a squad of rangers now depending on me. There was no room for being a hot head anymore. And, I quickly learned that the tougher the situation, the cooler your head had to be. I couldn't go out and lose it anymore. I was too busy taking care of, and worrying about, my squad."

Ty stared at his head coach intently. It was obvious by the way his coach spoke that there was no pretention in his words. Coach Dempsey was a man who spoke from his heart whether you liked what he said or not. "And yet, Coach, my helping Hondo was my effort to help take care of my team, ...my family. I know I haven't been here long. But, one way or the other, I was brought up to know the difference between right and wrong and I feel what I did for Hondo was definitely right."

Dempsey felt befuddled. Here he was, trying to help a fine, young man with a definite problem. And yet, Dempsey felt glad that Ty did everything he did to help Hondo. After a few, pensive seconds, the head coach switched the course of the discussion. "Ty, what's your goal when it comes to playing football here at Roosevelt?"

"I want to earn a college football scholarship and play major college football and get a degree. And, Coach, my dream is to still do it as a quarterback. That's what I do best. To be honest, Coach, that's where I feel I can best help the team the most." *I still can't believe coach has taken away my position for a player who has never taken a snap in his life. I just hope Hondo doesn't fall apart. Against Kennedy, he just might.*

"Ty, that's all still extremely possible. To be honest with you, I can hardly sleep at night over the proposed move of you, Hug and Hondo. But I know you have the ability, smarts and toughness to be an excellent Division I scholarship player whether at quarterback or at another offensive or defensive positions. When those college scouts start coming around, which they will, I promise I'll be the first to sing your praises."

"But, I also have to say this, Ty," continued the head coach. "The more the recruiters like you, the more you get scrutinized. The scouts will start asking about you as a person as much as a student and athlete. They'll ask me if you've had any problems in school or in the community. They'll ask about the negatives of your personality as much as the positives. Have you been in trouble? Do you have a tough time getting along with people. And, Ty, I have to answer those questions honestly. If I don't and lie, or try to cover things up and they find that out, then they won't believe me when I'm trying to sell the next top potential Rough Rider recruit I may have. That's something I will never do. Do you see where I'm coming from, Ty?"

"Yes, I do, Coach," said Ty, ...a bit sullenly. *But I'll still never back down from a piece of shit like Ontario Mosely. I don't care what the school's rules are. If I get attacked by one of these would-be gangsters again, he better be ready for the consequences. Someone has to stand-up to this asshole.*

"I understand everything you're saying Coach," replied Ty. "And, I appreciate greatly how you are trying to help me. But, what's also very important to me are the words that have been drilled into me by my father who is now not with us. Like I've already said, right is right and wrong is wrong. I believe strongly that what I did for Hondo was right and nothing in my heart will ever let me think otherwise."

"How'd that go,?" asked Big Julie.

"It went pretty well, Big Julie," said Ty. "I really felt good about our talk. I really have the feeling that Coach Dempsey is on our side. I just think the administration is tying him up. But, if push came to shove, I feel Coach would be there for us."

CHAPTER 55

GAME 5:
KENNEDY COUGARS

The Rough Riders filed into the visitor's locker room at Kennedy High School for half time. The players were quiet as they grabbed paper cups full of water or sports drinks and took seats on the locker room benches. The only sounds came from the voices of the coaches as they enthusiastically encouraged the Rough Riders to pick up their intensity and play like they were capable of playing.

"Got'ta roll, Riders," yelled Coach Franklin. "We can get these guys but we got'ta turn up the heat! Get physical with Kennedy! They're a finesse team. They don't like it when someone gets rough with them."

"Get in their faces and knock'em off the ball," exhorted Coach Lopez to his offensive linemen. "They're blitzing a lot just like Eisenhower did. That's why we're running the zone plays so much. The zones pick up all of that blitz stuff if you keep your eyes up. You're better than these guys, Riders. Now go out in the second half and show it!"

"You tackles are playing too high," said Coach Williams, the defensive line coach. "Pad control, Guys! Stay underneath their blocks. We need some big plays from you dudes. I want you to go out and lead the charge this half. You almost had two sacks, Eduardo, ... don't hesitate. Once you decide to go, turn on the jets and sack the quarterback's ass!"

"Need better blocking by you receivers," said the wide receiver coach, Sonny Walters. "We missed some key blocks on the safeties that could have been big plays. I'll tell Coach D to throw a few deep play action passes to get the safeties back. If they suck up on the fake, we're over-the-top with a big-time play action pass."

"Be ready to pitch the ball quickly, Hondo," said Dempsey with his left arm still in a sling. "You running backs got to be ready for a quick pitch. If we can control the blitz, we'll have all the success we need out there, Gentlemen!"

The corrections and encouragements went on for about ten minutes. The Rough Riders were down by 14 points, 21-7 at the half. To this point, they had played like they practiced all week, as if they were in a trance of some type. The Riders were not playing sharply. They looked slow, like they lacked energy. The Rough Riders needed a wake-up call and they needed it soon.

"HOOOONNNNKKKK,!" blasted the air horn held high in Coach Dempsey's right hand. It was the same sound the players had heard to put a stop to the massive brawl they had a month ago. This time, however, the sound seemed to be magnified ten times greater in the small space of Kennedy's fully tiled locker room. All heads shot up. There was no sleepy looks on their faces now.

"Is this team we're playing better than you,?" asked Dempsey in a peeved manner.

"No, Sir," answered the team.

"WHAT?!"

"NO, SIR!"

"I guess those defensive linemen and linebackers are so good that we can't pick them up when they blitz. There's an old football saying, Gentlemen. You live by the blitz or you die by the blitz. We need to make these suckers die by the blitz!"

"Stand up, Bernardo. Can we block those people?"

"Yes, Sir!"

"Stand up, Big Julie. Can we?"

"Yes, Sir!"

"Offensive line, stand up. Can we block these guys?"

"Yes, Sir!"

"Eduardo, DeMarco, Ricardo, ...can we get to that quarterback and sack his butt!"

"Yes, Sir,!" yelled the defensive linemen.

"How about a pick back there, linebackers, ...safeties, ... corners?"

"Yes, Sir!"

"Receivers, catch the damn ball! Too many drops!"

"Yes, Sir!"

"Hondo, TY, Hug. Let it rip! Get to the outside and go!"

"Yes, Sir!"

"The coaches can't do anything for you now, Riders," said Dempsey. "You're the ones who said you wanted to win games, to not be the joke of the conference anymore. No one's going to make it happen for you, Riders. You're going to have to go out there and take it from them in their own house. And understand this, Gentlemen. That will not be easy!"

Bring'em up, Dino," said the determined head coach.

"One, two, three...."

"Riders together!"

CHAPTER 56

Dempsey kept the football on the ground on the Riders' first play with a zone run behind Big Julie. The head coach immediately saw what Coach Walters was trying to tell him. The safeties were flying down hard to help stop the run option plays.

"Here we go, Boys," stated Hondo as he looked at his wrist band. "Zoom, gun slot right, fake 3 triple pass on two, on two. Ready...."

"Break!"

Hondo took the snap and faked the run to Hug. The safety jumped up on the short, inside hook-up route of Rayshawn Davis. This left Wooley Woolridge open on his over-the-top post route from his split out, wide receiver alignment. It was a big throw for Hondo but he released the ball quickly and was able to hit Wooley for a 29-yard gain.

"Nice throw, Hondo," said Ty. "Just what we needed. On the money, Buddy!"

"Doctor Dempsey's get'n a little crazy, Guys," said Hondo. "Here we go. Gun slot right, fake lead option right pass on one, on one." Hondo ran the lead option and pitched the football to Ty. Rayshawn Davis and Seamus Collins both faked stalk blocks and then took off on streak routes. Both were wide open. Ty took the easier throw outside to Seamus. Although the pass was perfect, Seamus didn't catch the football cleanly. He bobbled the ball three times before finally latching on to it. The big wide receiver then smoked untouched to the end zone to bring the score to 21-14.

"Now that's what I'm talk'n about," said Hondo as he sprinted to the end zone to celebrate with Seamus. Ty and the rest of the offense were quick to follow as the energized Rough Riders now sensed the start of a momentum roll.

Kennedy rapidly responded. Their quarterback had a big arm. On the fourth play of the series, he hit his flanker on a hitch and go route that fooled Leotis Brown. This pushed the score back to a 14-point lead for the Kennedy Cougars, 28-14.

"That's all right, Guys," said Hondo. "We're smok'n now. They can't stop us." The quarterback was right. On the next offensive play, he kept the football on an option play and raced 46 yards to the Cougar 31-yard line. On the next play, Hondo pitched the ball to Ty on another option play. Ty burst through an outside opening on the line of scrimmage, broke a tackle of one of the Kennedy safeties and raced for 31-yards to the end zone to bring the score to 28-21.

"We're rolling, Boys,!" said Ty. "We got them on the ropes. Keep pounding them! They'll crack,! I know it!"

The game see-sawed back and forth the entire second half. The Riders couldn't be stopped by the Kennedy defense. However, Kennedy's offense was also excelling. With Kennedy ahead 35-28 in the middle of the fourth quarter, the Kennedy quarterback forced a pass over the middle. Dino DeTaglia tipped the football into the air and into the outreached hands of Jarvis Means. Jarvis returned the football to the Kennedy fourteen-yard line. On the very next play, Hondo kept the football on another option play. The quarterback looked like a blur cutting upfield to the left, then to the right. Finally, he shot straight up the field as he ended up walking into the end zone for the all-important score. The game was now tied 35-35.

"Nice read, Hondo," said Hug.

"Oh, I don't know," said Ty overhearing Hug's comment. "I think Big Julie and his three hundred plus pounds could have gotten through that hole. It was that big!"

"Come on, Ty," said Hug. "At least he got over the goal line and didn't fall or noth'n. You got'ta give the guy some credit."

"Man, you nerds really are haters," stated Hondo.

Kennedy got nervous after their previous interception and conservatively ran the football. The Cougars pounded the ball and slowly ran the clock down as they moved closer to the Rough Riders' end zone.

"Come on, Dino," screamed Ty. "Tighten it up, Man!"

"Watch for the play action pass," yelled the defensive coordinator Rod Franklin. On a 3rd and 4 situation on the Rough Riders' 9-yard line, the Cougars smartly called for a sprint-out pass to the right. The quarterback took the snap and sprinted to the outside. His first read was the quick-out route of the slot back who was wide open. The quarterback didn't hesitate. He threw accurately to the slot back. A white jersey suddenly flashed in front of the receiver and batted the ball to the ground.

"Atta boy, Means,!" screamed Big Julie.

"Great job, Jarvis,!" yelled Dempsey.

The Cougars decided to attempt a field goal to take the lead. "Is this guy any good,?" Dempsey asked Coach Walters, the Wide Receiver and Special Teams Coordinator.

"Not really, Sean," answered Walters. "He was pretty awful in warm-ups."

"It'll be about a 23-yarder," said Dempsey. "We'll find out soon enough," as the holder checked with the place kicker to see if he was ready.

The kicker shanked the football. The kick was a low, line drive that hit the left upright about a yard above the crossbar. The ball angled downward toward the crossbar, struck it, bounced upward and rolled over the bar for a three-point field goal. Kennedy was now in the lead, 38 - 35.

"Damn,!" yelled Dempsey. *When the hell is the ball going to start bouncing our way*? The burning sensation in his stomach had reignited as he popped some ant-acid tablets into his mouth.

"O.K., Gentlemen," stated Dempsey. "We have one last shot. There's a minute, 36 seconds on the clock. We have two-time outs. A field goal ties it and a touchdown wins it. Let's get it done, Riders." *Plenty of time. But, now is when I wish I had Ty at quarterback. This is going to be tough with Hondo's throwing ability.*

A poor kick on the kick-off allowed Rayshawn Davis to return the ball to the Rough Riders' *46*-yard line. "Hondo, let's see if we can start out and get a big chunk," said Dempsey. "Doubles left, 3 Back. Don't be afraid to hand the ball off to Hug if the pass isn't there. He'll get some damage done." *Maybe I should have started out with a draw to Hug right off the bat. We don't need for Hondo to get picked. Kennedy will probably play Man Free coverage. Or, maybe they'll play Two-Deep, Man Under. Damn, I should have just called for a draw. But, we need...*

Dempsey was right. The Cougar defense did spread out to stop the pass game and they did use Man Free coverage. Hondo correctly handed off the football to Hug, the big running back. Hug turned into a freight train. The big back burst through a huge hole at the line of scrimmage. Hug wasn't touched until he had already gained ten yards. He then broke one tackle and then another. He was finally dragged down late by three Cougar defenders. The big back blasted through the Cougar defensive front for 26-yards.

With the football now on the Cougars' 28-yard line, the offense hurried to line up in their two-minute formation. Dempsey signaled in the same play call combination with a flip of the formation. This time the defense condensed itself to stop the run. Hondo set up and threw an outside screen pass to Seamus Collins. Seamus had to lunge forward in an effort to get a hand on the poorly thrown pass. The football flew up beyond Seamus' reach towards a pursuing Kennedy outside linebacker. The football went through the hands of the linebacker. The football hit the top of the defender's helmet and bounced up into the hands of Rayshawn Davis. The surprised Davis immediately exploded up field towards the goal line.

"First down," said the signaling referee as Rayshawn gained 11-yards on the wild play.

"Well, I guess the ball does bounce our way," said Dempsey. "Sometimes!"

With the ball now on the 17-yard line, Dempsey called for a draw play to Hug. The blocking scheme got jumbled and Hug had to lower his head and create his own hole for a short three-yard gain.

"Time out," yelled Dempsey to the referee with 48-seconds left on the clock. "Let's see what a spread set will give us," said Dempsey as he called for an all quick-out, three-step-drop pass play.

"Just look over each side and throw to whoever has the softest coverage, Hondo," instructed Dempsey. "I don't think you'll see them press us at this point. They've got to worry about your running ability. Got it?"

"Got'cha, Coach," said Hondo. Hondo looked over the defense carefully before he started the cadence. On the snap, he picked the right receiver to throw to. Unfortunately, Hondo threw another bad pass.

"41 seconds, Sean," said Coach Walters as the incompletion stopped the clock. "And, you have one time out left. How about a post-corner route, Coach?"

"Not Hondo's best throw," said Dempsey. "I got exactly what I want."

Hondo looked at his wrist band and smiled. "The man's going for it all right here, Guys. Let's have some fun."

From a pistol formation with two of the receivers and Ty bunch aligned to the field, Hondo took the snap and attacked downhill towards the bunched alignment. He was faking a lead option with Hug acting as the pitch back. Ty, the slot back in the Bunch, took a pitch from Hondo off of reverse run action. The three remaining receivers, one being the backside split end, all crisscrossed the field. Wooley Woolridge, the outside receiver of the bunched formation, was open on his crossing route. Ty laced a throw in between two defenders perfectly for the much-needed, go-ahead touchdown.

"Great job, Wooley,!" screamed Hug.

"Nice pass, Ty," yelled Hondo. "Now of course, if I had thrown the ball..."

"Shut up, Hondo, will ya,?" said Bernardo. "If you don't stop talk'n so much, I'm not gon'na snap the ball to you. I'm gon'na go on strike."

With 31-seconds left in the game, the Rough Riders shut down Kennedy's feeble Hail Mary attempt to score as Roosevelt racked up its fourth win in a row, 42-38.

The exuberant Rough Riders piled into the Roosevelt locker room for what had become known as the Victory Block Party. Jarvis Means, the player of the game, hoisted block number four to the top of the Victory Block stack.

"Hey, that stack is actually starting to look like something," said the Rough Riders' elated head coach. At halftime, Dempsey thought they were done like scorched steaks on a barbeque grill. *This is good stuff. Not only have they learned to win, now they know they can come back and do it.*

"Bring it up, Guys," yelled out Jarvis. "Riders on three. One, two, three...."

"Riders together!"

"Hey, I was hoping you'd be out here," said Ty.

"Well, I'm out here," said Kayleigh. "But who said I was out here waiting for you?"

"Sure you were," answered Ty. "You like me!"

"You're getting real cocky, aren't you Douglas,?" responded Kayleigh with a big smile on her face.

"Naahh, ...I'm just mess'n with my girl."

"That was one heck of a game," stated Kayleigh as she and Ty sat in a booth in the 1950's style Malt Shop. The Shop, as it had, long ago, come to be known, had become Ty and Kayleigh's spot.

"Kennedy was a real good team," responded Ty. "They were

tough. They really had some ballers. It's a good thing we don't have someone tough next week. We need a breather. Thank goodness Jackson stinks!"

"Like I said before, you're getting real cocky, aren't you, Douglas?"

"That two-minute drive was big, Son," said Ty's mother. "Your last-minute throw on that trick play was perfect. I'm so proud of you."

"We pulled that one out of our butts, Mom," said Ty. "I think our team was really tired from all of the stress of the fight and the punishment running. Coach Dempsey sure woke us up at half time, though. He certainly got our attention."

"Good coaches find good ways to get things done," said Addison Douglas. "I'm glad you're smiling again, Ty. I could see a lot of pressure being built up inside you. I'm still pissed about the entire mess. But, I promise you, Son, we'll get through all of this like we always have. I won't take crap from any one of those dumb asses."

"Ty got up, out of his chair to cross the path to his mother. He wrapped his hands around her and squeezed firmly. "You and me. Mom. We're tough to beat."

CHAPTER 57

"Close one, Coach Dempsey," said Mary Elizabeth as she brought the hot pizza boxes into the house. The head coach smiled as he watched his children attack their mother to get to the family's favorite culinary delight.

"Did you get some pepperoni, Mom,?" asked Ryan.

"Of course I did," said the mother." She had quickly learned about the joy of winning when you were married to a victorious football coach. Most often it meant relief, fulfillment, happiness and gratification, if only for a matter of hours, or even minutes. Unfortunately, the next pressure filled challenge of a new game week was already at hand.

"I knew it was going to be a tough one, one way or the other. But I never dreamt it was going to come down to a two-minute drive to win it. We aren't built to be a two- minute offense throwing team. Hondo's an option guy. Hug and Ty came up big!"

"Who's next, Sean?"

"Jackson."

"Any good?"

"Their record isn't very good. They're 2–3. But, they've played tough in every game so far. The three games they've lost were by a total of 14 points. Eisenhower had to score twice late to beat them. I'll have to be sure to get our kids heads screwed on straight for this one. I'm sure it's going to be another barnburner. Our boys are going to have to realize that from the get-go."

"So you're worried about this one too?"

"Mary, with this group I worry about everything, 24, seven,!" answered her husband. "When you're a head football coach you have to worry about how players play, their academics, their behavior. You even have to worry about your assistant coaches, the administration, the councilors. It never stops, Mary Elizabeth, never, ...especially when you're at a school like Roosevelt! Now, are you going to let me have a piece of that great smelling pizza from Francesco's or are you going to keep tormenting me?"

Monday was a fun day for Hondo, Hug and Big Julie. As soon as the second period ended, they all rushed to the school library. There, they immediately jumped onto a vacant computer to scan on-line to the local high school sports section. It was fun to see the previous Friday's game scores and the standings and listings of the next games for each of the teams of the Greater City Conference.

"We're tied for first place in the Eastern Division with JFK," said Hug.

"That was a great win for us Friday, Dudes," stated Big Julie.

"Man, you can say that again," said Hondo. "Our offense stuck it to those guys in the second half."

"And, our defense made some key plays when we needed them to," said Julie.

"I'm glad we finally have an easy game this week, said Hondo."

"Doesn't sound like they're very good, does it,?" said Hug.

"No it doesn't. Maybe we could get up big by halftime and let some of the back-ups get some playing time, said Hondo."

"That would be cool, Man. We could be like those NFL guys who come out of the game, take their helmets off and put a ball cap on their heads," said Hug.

"Then they laugh and fool around," said Hondo.

"It would be a lot of fun to play a game like that for once," said Hug.

"What's wrong, Julie,?" said Hondo. "I don't like that look on your face."

"To be honest with you, I'm worried that we might be overlooking this team." said the big man. "This team has lost 3 games by a total of 14 points, ...all against tough competition."

"Man, ...you worry about stuff too much," responded Hondo.

"I wouldn't bet on that," said Hug, now definitely serious. "When Big Julie worries about something, ...it's usually time to worry."

The Rough Riders were seemingly having a good, efficient, Tuesday practice. However, Dempsey kept sensing that something wasn't right. Unfortunately, he couldn't quite put his finger on what it was. The team was working its offense and defense against the scout squads in an efficient manner. The practicing was going decently. The attitude of the players was a little loose. However, the make-up of the team had been to work hard when asked to and, yet, to have fun practicing whenever possible.

Dempsey watched the offense. He, suddenly, saw Hug, whose substitute was taking a drill repetition for him, joyfully flipping and juggling two footballs in the air rather than paying attention to the execution of the drill. He then saw Hondo, who was also not in for the practice play repetition, fooling around with one of the offensive linemen. Dempsey looked over to the defensive players and saw that hardly a player was paying attention to Coach Franklin's instruction. He watched DeMarco Green and Ricardo Pena shadow boxing one another playfully.

Dempsey let go three, loud, tweets on his whistle and shouted, "...bring it up!" The players quickly sensed that something was wrong by the look on their head coach's face. "Feeling pretty good about yourselves, aren't you? Hey, you just won your fourth game in a row. Who the heck would ever think a Roosevelt team could win four games in a season no less four in a row? You had a great comeback win over your rival. You guys are smoking. Man, ... you're on a roll! You've earned the right to cut back on your effort and focus a bit, right? You're 4 and 1 with a shot at playing for the championship. Maybe we should just take off the rest of the week and not practice, ...get nice and rested up."

"Do you know what Eisenhower had to do to beat Jackson this past Friday,?" asked Dempsey as he stepped up the intensity and sound level of his voice. "They had to score twice in the last five minutes to pull out a win. And that's the team that beat us by three touchdowns and scored 49 points on us, kicking our ass."

"Do you know when a head coach worries the most during a season in regard to an opponent,?" continued Dempsey with another question.

"When you're playing against the best team in the conference,?" answered Hug with a question of his own.

"Naahh,!" answered Dempsey. "Getting your team prepared for the best teams is the easiest job. That's when your players and coaches are the most focused, the most concerned about getting ready to play hard and play well. It's when your team is playing someone who doesn't seem to be one of the better teams in the league that a head coach worries the most. It's when his players start acting like all they have to do is show up to get the win, especially when they're on a bit of a roll like you are now."

"Jackson is 2 and 3," stated Dempsey. "They've lost three games by a total of 14 points, three in one game, four in another to Kennedy and by seven to Eisenhower. But, that's O.K., Men. We're so good now that Jackson shouldn't even bother coming over here. They should just phone in the win to us and start getting ready for their next game. Someone give us a break with that 'together' stuff so we can go home early and watch some Netflix."

Dempsey started to walk away as the stunned players stood in their places trying to digest what they had just heard from their disturbed head coach. Finally, Ty popped up and yelled to the head coach. "Hey, Coach D. We're not finished practicing! Everybody up! Riders on three, One, two, three..."

"Riders together,!" chanted the players as they all automatically ran back to their previous practice spots with a greater, more intense, focus.

The week's practices went a lot better after the outburst by the Rough Riders' head coach. However, Dempsey was still worried. Having carefully watched the opponent video of Jackson, he knew that Roosevelt could be in for a very difficult battle. To the dismay of the players, the head coach picked up on his on-the-field coaching practice intensely. *If pushing their asses is what's needed to light a fire under their butts, then that's what they'll get,* thought the tough-minded head coach.

"Hey, what's up,?" asked Hondo as he walked past Jaylon Shields' locker. The players were starting to file into the players' locker room after the final bell of the school day.

"His locker has been emptied out," said Hug. "Do you think someone broke into it and stole his stuff?"

"No, that's not what happened," said Dempsey as he walked through the players' locker room. After a heavy sigh, he continued. "I'll tell all of you what's going on as soon as we all get out to practice."

"Gentlemen, Jaylon Shields is no longer a member of this team," announced Dempsey. "As some of you know, Jaylon was declared ineligible to play at the mid-semester grade check period. I decided to allow him to stay on the team as a scout squad player in hopes of helping him to get his school work straightened for next year. Unfortunately, that did not work out for Jaylon either. The bottom line is, it's hard to stay up with your books if you cut classes, ...if you ditch school. As you know, his own fellow teammates have had to do incentive runs with him in an effort to try to help him see the light with peer pressure. Sadly, that didn't work either."

"Since Jaylon's only a sophomore, maybe he can get himself straightened out so he can return to the team next year. I've offered to help him get back on the right track in regard to his schoolwork. However, he's the one that has to get the work done."

"Too bad," said Big Julie. "Jaylon has a lot of talent. Now he's wastng it."

"Today's 'Perfect Thursday,' Gentlemen!," said the head coach after a quick reflection on Big Julie's words. "Let's get ourselves ready to win this one. Break'em, Leotis."

"Riders on three! Riders on three! One, two, three..."

"Riders together!"

"You have that sad look on your face," said Mary Elizabeth.

"Oh, I just feel kind of lousy about Jaylon Shields," replied her husband. "I couldn't get him to go to class. I just wasn't able to reach the kid."

"It's like I've heard you say so many times before, the players are keeping a close eye on you. If you let Jaylon slide, then you would be telling all the others they could do the same. I keep hearing from the coaches' wives how you've been doing such a great job of reigning in on these kids, helping them to learn to become disciplined, to be doing things the right way both at school and on the field. What you're doing with Jaylon is hard for you. I can see that. All you can do is to do your best to help your players. But, if they don't want to do things the right way, you simply have to let them go. You have a saying on your meeting room wall, 'Nothing comes before the well-being of the team!'"

"Remember, Sean. You can't save everybody."

CHAPTER 58

GAME 6: JACKSON STALLIONS

With the score tied at 14-14 just before the half, the Jackson quarterback faked a dive handoff to the left and ran a naked bootleg action to the right. The split end, on a deep comeback and go route, suddenly found himself wide open. The Rough Riders' cornerback, Leotis Brown, had taken the bite on the comeback fake and let the wide receiver get past him. The Stallion's quarterback threw a perfect touchdown pass to the open receiver. The score quickly became 21-14 in the favor of Jackson.

In the third quarter, Dempsey called for a zone run, bubble pass combination that had become very successful for the Rough Riders' offense. Hondo made a terrible read and threw the ball to the slot back even though he was tightly covered. The covering strong safety stepped up and intercepted the football.

"Oh, no," said Hondo. The fleet quarterback ran as fast as he could to catch up to the safety. He came close. But, the Stallion safety crossed the goal line for a Pick-Six touchdown just beyond Hondo's reach.

In the fourth quarter, Hug ran an inside zone run for eleven yards from the Rough Riders' own ten-yard line. He ran over two potential tacklers in his effort to break loose. As he spun out of the second defender's tackle effort, a safety drove his helmet through the arm pit that Hug held the football. The football flew up into the air. Jackson recovered it. Three plays later the Stallions ran the football into the end zone for another touchdown. Jackson beat Roosevelt 35-21.

When the Rough Riders entered their locker room, there was no Victory Block Party.

The distinctive noise of the sporadic crashing of wooden bowling pins dominated the air. It was easy to see that Ty's mind was not into the bowling that was the focus of the double date of Ty, Kayleigh, Pete and Pete's girlfriend.

"You're up, Slugger," stated Kayleigh to her despondent boyfriend. Ty sat on the bench angrily staring at the floor. "Ty, it's your turn. We need a couple of strikes to catch up." Ty gloomily rushed into his delivery steps and rolled a ball that that hung on just long enough to knock off the last two pins on the left side of the lane.

"Nice job,!" said Pete. "You're really killing'em. The good news is I won't have to pay tonight."

"Got'ta let it go, Ty," said Kayleigh as he sat back down next to her.

"That was awful! We should never have lost that game. Jackson wasn't even as good as I thought they'd be and they still kicked our asses. We were on the road to play for the championship and we blow it."

"Hey, you're still in it! You just have to win out and you can do that. As hard as it is, you have to let this one go and make sure you beat Washington." Having grown up with three football playing brothers, Kayleigh knew how much defeat could disturb a player's mental psyche. However, she also saw that Ty took it far harder than any of her brothers did. Succeeding in football was far too important for Tyler Douglas.

CHAPTER 59

"I can't get over that game, Mary Elizabeth," said Dempsey as the breakfast food on his plate sat untouched. "We gave Jackson that game! I can't believe how badly the team played. We made so many stupid mistakes! It was all my fault. I knew the team wasn't ready. Our practices stunk all week. The kids were overconfident after four straight wins. Can you imagine a team from Roosevelt being overconfident? I told the kids all week that Jackson was a lot better than their record. We..."

"Sean! You need to practice what you preach. There's nothing you can do about that game anymore other than to learn from it. That game's over! We lost and it's over! Just worry about beating Washington now. You're always talking about the importance of playing one game at a time. You're four and two. If someone told you after your first practice that you would be four and two after six games, you would have told them they were crazy. What you have to focus on now is that five and two is a heck of a lot better than four and three. Stop the self-pity and go and get yourself ready to whip up on Washington." *He'll rally again,* thought the head coach's wife. *He always does.*

"Coach Dempsey was right, Mom," said Ty. "We thought we were hot stuff going into the Jackson game. He told us how Jackson might only be 2 and 3 but had lost the three games closely, all to good teams. We heard him but we didn't listen."

"Well, that means you and your team better listen all the more intently this week to get ready for Washington. Be the leader, Son. The Washington game will be big for your team if you want to remain in contention to play for the championship."

"You got that right, Mom. This is a must game for us."

"Then make sure you do your part in helping to get your team to realize that, Ty. Someone's got to take the bull by the horns and get your team ready to win again and that someone seems to be you."

Damn! Another shot of that "be the leader" stuff, thought Roosevelt's star player.

With the staff having finished off the Saturday morning review of the previous night's Jackson game video with the team, Dempsey was eager to start getting into the new plan for the upcoming Washington Wildcats. "My first and prime thought for Washington is that I want the focus to be on our fundamentals this week. This is the time of the season that many teams get sloppy executing basic blocking and tackling skills because there's so much attention on game plan scheming. A new run here, a new pass pattern there, an extra blitz and all of a sudden there's not enough emphasis on fundamentals. I definitely believe we can beat Washington if we're sound and basic."

Deep down, Dempsey had a bad feeling in his gut about the upcoming Washington game. It was the same bad feeling that he had for the Jackson game. *Winning is tough enough no less trying to prevent a two-game losing streak. Mary Elizabeth says I always worry too much. I hope she's right.*

It took the disappointed head coach two full days to rally from the defeat to Jackson. On Monday morning, he jumped out of bed, shaved and got dressed, wolfed down some breakfast and sped off to the high school. Dempsey was fired up and ready to go. All he could think of now was beating Washington.

* * *

"What's the bucket for, Coach,?" asked Hondo.

"Á little Wet Ball drill, Hondo," answered Dempsey. "It's supposed to rain all weekend. We have to be ready to snap, handoff, pitch and throw no matter how wet the ball might be. We must ensure our ball security if it rains."

"Geez, Coach. The ball's not going to be this wet, is it? This ball's got'ta weigh ten pounds."

"Just keep working with it, Hondo. You have to get used to it. We can't let wet footballs stop us. Be sure to dunk that football in the pail every repetition," Dempsey said to the student manager. Dempsey was extremely concerned about the fact that Hondo had extremely small hands which is not what you want your quarterback to have on a cold, rainy, wet field.

* * *

Tuesday night was the Head Football Coaches Meeting for the Greater City Conference. The gathering gave the commissioner a chance to tie together the loose ends of the season as it started to wind down. In addition, it allowed for the start of preparation for the upcoming Greater City Conference Championship Game. Sean Dempsey was a bit late and entered the conference room slightly after the meeting had started. There was only one seat left open at the meeting table. That empty chair was next to Don Watson, the coach of the Eisenhower Generals. Dempsey gave a smile and a wave to the coaches across from him. The Adams coach, sitting to Dempsey's right, stuck out his hand for a welcoming shake. When he turned to Watson, the Eisenhower head coach lifted his right hand to signify a stop action.

"Don't bother," said Watson.

When the meeting was over, the coaches got up to go to the hotel's bar to have a beer or two or three with one another and share in on the coaching camaraderie. Dempsey turned to Watson. "You're really a class act, aren't you Watson?"

"Hey, Dempsey," replied Watson, "just go back to 'The Hood' with your brother pals and play that rap-crap music while you practice."

"Another cup, Coach D,?" asked Old Irv.

"Please," answered the blood-shot eyed head coach. Dempsey had not had a decent night's sleep all week. "I hope we can get this one for these kids and get everything back on track again."

"You know, Coach. This team is definitely different," stated Old Irv. "I sense that they're not like the Roosevelt teams of the past ten to fifteen years or so who expected to lose. Losing really bothers these kids. Winning has become super important to them since they've had a taste of it. They believe that they can win now, Coach D, but I think they're nervous that the winning might be coming to an end. They don't want to be known as losers no more."

CHAPTER 60

GAME 7: WASHINGTON WILDCATS

Hondo barked out the cadence from a shotgun alignment. Bernardo Diaz snapped the football. The ball flew over the top of Hondo's head. Hondo raced back to fall on the football for a 13-yard loss. "Get the ball down, Bernardo," yelled Hondo to his center. "The damn thing was over my head again."

"What do you want me to do, Hondo,?" asked Bernardo. "The ball's soaking wet. I can hardly hold it."

A few plays later, Hondo threw a pass that slipped off his hand and fluttered into the air without direction. Luckily for Roosevelt, there was no Washington defender in the area to make the interception.

With the opening kickoff of the game, the skies let loose a light drizzle. By the middle of the first quarter, the light drizzle turned into a steady rain. By the middle of the second quarter, steady rain turned into a downpour. Since the entire middle area of Roosevelt's football field was grassless, the hard-packed dirt turned into a quagmire of soupy mud.

"Set-hut, black 36, black 36, hut-hut," barked Hondo. He received a slow, wobbly snap from Bernardo. He turned towards the sideline to set in motion a lead option play. The defensive end closed down hard in an effort to put pressure on Hondo. As Hondo stepped to pitch the football to Ty, he slipped on the mud. The pitch of the ball floundered loosely on the ground in the Rider's backfield.

A pursuing defensive tackle fell on the football for a Washington turnover.

The game went back and forth throughout the third quarter. With neither team getting in the range to put the ball in the end zone, the score was zero to zero as the third quarter came to an end. "We've got to get going," said Ty. "We've got to find a way to make something happen."

Actually, both teams seemed to be getting a bit listless as the game clock started to wind down. The pouring rain, an increasing wind and a fast decreasing temperature seemed to put both teams into a stupor. That was until an exchange of the football from Hondo to Hug slipped through Hug's hands and fell to the ground. Hondo tried to pounce on the loose football but that effort only magnified the problem as the football squirted out from under his body, propelling it towards the Rough Riders' own goal line. The football was scooped up by a muddy, dirty-white uniformed Washington defender who plodded to the end zone untouched.

The Rough Riders on the sideline watched the Washington defender cross the goal line for the go ahead score in dead silence. The Washington players screamed in joy for the sudden good fortune. The Rough Riders stared at the Washington celebration in the end zone in disbelief.

"Damn,!" yelled Ty as he watched the horde of Washington players hooting and hollering in the Rough Riders' end zone. A roughly executed extra point kick that barely made it over the crossbar made the score 7-0. "Damn, damn, damn," fumed the Roosevelt running back as he started jogging back to his sideline team area. *Someone's got to get us in gear. Someone's got to light a fire under our butts even if it is pouring down rain. Someone's got to...*

CHAPTER 61

"What the hell's going on,!" yelled Ty as just about the entire Roosevelt team, including some of the coaches, stared into empty space. "This sucks,!" he continued. "We get some rain and cold and we decide to fold our tent and go home? That's unacceptable! Offense, bring it up! When the offense started to mope over to Ty, the fiery, ex-quarterback exploded again. "I said bring it up and I mean bring it up right now! Move!"

When the offensive players finally picked up their speed to make their way to Ty, he blew up once again. "We talk all the time how we want to win. We talk about being tough guys, ...how this all means so much to us, ...about being together. Well now we got one more chance to pull this out. We've got to stop the complaining and get this damn thing turned around while we still have a chance. Like coach said, no one's going to give us anything. We've got to go out there and take it ourselves and that's got'ta happen right now!"

Ty then ran over to his head coach. "Coach D, if you want to win this game, give me the football!"

Dempsey delayed commenting for a few, brief seconds as he studied the face of his brazen running back. Normally, he would never have tolerated a player talking to him that way. At that moment, Dempsey surprisingly felt as if a 100-pound bar bell plate had been lifted off his chest. "You know, Ty," said Dempsey with a strange smile suddenly appearing on his face, "...that sounds like a pretty good idea. Go get'em, Kid!"

The Wildcats kicked off with the wind pushing Rayshawn Davis back towards the end zone. As a result, a decent return was only able to get the ball back to the 26-yard line.

Ty solidified his authority by ordering Hondo to take the snap from under center instead of in a shotgun set and for Bernardo to be sure to snap the football up into Hondo's hands. He also told Hondo to be sure to press the football on the ballcarrier's belly on every handoff. "Knock these guys off the line of scrimmage, linemen," ordered Ty. He then called the first play of the series. "Right, 3 zone lead, on two," as given to him by Coach Dempsey with Ty taking a set position behind the quarterback that would have him carrying the football and with Hug offset to be the lead blocker.

As the huddle broke, Big Julie leaned in towards Ty. "Just stay behind me and we'll get our butts in the zone," said the behemoth offensive tackle with a knowing smile on his face.

Ty stared back at Big Julie and nodded assuredly back to the big man. On the snap of the football, Ty took the exchange from Hondo and angled towards Big Julie's zone block action. Ty exploded upfield behind Hug, the lead blocker for the linebacker as Big Julie knocked the defensive tackle back for 6-yards for a clean 11-yard gain by Ty. Although the rest of the offensive line did not block the play very well, Ty ran back to the huddle yelling "...do that again, Guys. Do it again!" Once he got in the huddle, he looked at Big Julie and gave his left tackle a confident thumbs-up signal. The big man smiled back at him and winked.

"That a boy, Ty," whispered Ty's mom. "Keep going, Son."

"First down," announced the referee.

On the next series of downs, Ty ran three lead zone plays in a row for 4-, 3- and 5-yard gains to help the offense garner another 1st down. On all three plays, Big Julie and Hug lead the way. "Keep pounding them, Guys. They don't know what's hit'n them right now,!" stated Ty.

"What do you want now, Sean,?" said Coach Walters, the excited sideline play call signaler.

"Keep signaling the zone lead for Ty and Hug," said Dempsey calmly. "Just mix up the formations for window dressing. I'll call most of those runs to the left behind Big Julie. The big man's blowing people up!"

On the ensuing 1st down play, Ty ran behind his center and left guard. He was forced to bounce to the outside. Big Julie cut off the defensive end and then worked upfield to seal off the linebacker. Ty burst into the secondary for 15-yards before a Washington safety could wrap him up. Ty spun out of grasp of the safety and carried two more ensuing tacklers for an additional 12-yards. When the whistle was blown to end the play, three Washington defenders had stopped Ty but they still hadn't been able to tackle him to the ground.

"Keep going, Ty. You're rolling,!" screamed Kayleigh from her seat in the stands. "Keep it up Ty! Keep it up!"

On a zone lead run to the right, Ty was stopped cold at the line of scrimmage when the mud didn't allow for much traction for the offensive line. Ty kept churning his legs and slipped through the grasp of two would be Washington tacklers for a hard fought, five-yard gain. The next call had Ty running a zone lead play to the left, once again behind Big Julie and Hug. It looked like Ty was going to explode into the secondary for a big gain but was tripped up by a diving Washington linebacker pursuing from the backside. As Ty started falling, he put his free hand on the ground to help himself regain his balance. He bucked his head up to take on the two Washington safeties. Ty gained additional yardage as he powerfully churned his legs in a refusal to stop driving forward.

"Don't stop, Ty," yelled out his mother from under her soaking wet umbrella. "Don't stop, Son!"

"This isn't good, Guys," said the Washington head coach. "Someone's got to stop that kid!"

"Just keep going, Ty," said Mary Elizabeth. "Get it in the end zone. Just get it in the end zone!"

"They're getting tired,!" yelled Ty. "Pound them! Pound them till they quit!" From the ten-yard line, Ty ran another zone play. He was stopped for what looked like a two-yard gain. However, the pile of would be tacklers kept moving backwards for an additional three-yards to the five-yard line behind Big Julie's bulldozer blocking action.

"Get it in, Ty,!" shouted Dino DeTaglia. "Take it to'em, Buddy!"

Ty then plowed forward for three more yards to the two-yard line. The soft turf and a stacked-up defense prevented him from crossing the goal line.

"Come on, Ty," said Roosevelt's Principal, Daryl Hoskins, as he stood on the sideline. "Don't stop, Kid! Don't stop!"

"Just keep pushing," said Ty to the offensive line. On 3rd-and-goal from the two-yard line, Ty slammed into the line. He slowly inched forward with each step until his footing slipped from under him.

"Fourth and inches, Sean," stated Walters. "What do you think?" Walters then signaled in Dempsey's decision.

Smiling, Hug said, "just follow us, Ty. Me and Julie will clear it out for you."

"Come on, Ty," said Dempsey. *Just one more time, Buddy.*

The call was for another zone lead play to the left. The offense exploded off the ball but was quickly negated by the gap eight alignment of Washington. The Wildcat's excellent middle linebacker, Lou Toth, flew across the top of the offensive-defensive log jam. His body was parallel to the ground. Just when it looked like the linebacker would stuff Ty for no gain, Hug Wilson exploded through the hole himself. The "whack" sound from the ensuing collision could be heard throughout the stadium. Both players seemed to fly off in opposite directions as Ty's body suddenly appeared, propelling over the top of the players lying on the ground. He dove into the end zone for the ever-so-important touchdown.

The offensive players wildly jumped on Ty, screaming, yelling and pounding him on his back for his lead in the 74-yard touchdown drive. Ty was yelling something to his team mates but they couldn't hear what he was saying. Finally, the players did.

"Are we kicking it or going for two,?" yelled out Ty.

Down 7–6, Dempsey had a tough decision to make. Should he risk attempting to kick an extra point try in an effort to tie the game and go into overtime? Or, should he go for two-points and try to win it right now with only 32-seconds remaining on the clock? The entire area on the field where the hold for the extra point kick would be was in awful shape, all puddles and soft mud.

"Time-out," yelled the Rough Riders' head coach to the referee. "Let's think this through and see what we have."

"I don't like the area where we would kick from," said Coach Franklin. "Bad footing."

"I agree," stated the place kicker, Bodie Swenson. "I don't know if I could stand still in that pile of mud, no less kick a football."

"What do we have for a two-point play,?" asked the head coach.

"We have our flood pass," said Walters as the coaches and offensive players all huddled up.

"The football is awfully wet and soggy," said Hondo. "I can hardly hold on to it."

"How about our special Octopus play,?" suggested Ty. "There's decent turf down near the goal line towards the hash marks since both teams have hardly been down there."

"Good thought," said Dempsey. "Do you think you can get off a pitch if you need to, Hondo?"

"Yeah, I can do that," answered Hondo. At this point, Hondo wasn't really sure what he could do. He was that disconcerted.

"Octopus personnel,!" yelled Dempsey. "Octopus personnel!" The funky Octopus play call told everyone the player personnel that was needed as well as the two-point formation and play. Utilizing such a unique call helped every involved player to remember his specific role for the special, two-point play.

"Tell the referee you want the football to be placed left of center, Hondo," instructed Dempsey. "That will give us the best turf and enough room to execute the pitch if we need it."

Neither team now had any time-outs left. At this point, that was a big advantage for Roosevelt. Washington was now unable to utilize a time-out to adjust their defensive personnel to the special personnel plan and formation they were about to see.

Roosevelt lined up in a two tight end formation with a Power I set to the offense's right. What was special about the play was that the fullback, with Hondo under the center, was the big, 245-pound defensive end, Eduardo Ibanez. The Power I back, stacked behind the right tackle, was Hug Wilson. The special formation and personnel usage alerted the defense that something strange was going to happen to the offense's right. "Watch 45,!" yelled Washington's middle linebacker, aggressively pointing at Hug. "Watch 45! It's an Iso. The ball's going right here," as he continued to point at Hug!

On the snap of the football, Hondo, Eduardo and Ty opened up to their left. The action was opposite the Power I backfield set that was used to create a diversion away from the option action. Hondo rode the option dive play fake to Eduardo. The interior front defenders of Washington all collapsed to the inside to shut down Eduardo's dive threat. The football, however, was not in Eduardo's hands. It was still in Hondo's. Big Julie seal blocked the defensive end to the inside enabling Hondo to read the tight end's block on the outside linebacker. The backer worked to the outside in an effort to shut off an outside pitch run lane to Ty, the tailback. Hondo worked down the line of scrimmage seeing a slight hole between the guard and Big Julie at tackle. Hondo faked a pitch action to Ty and broke up to the inside. Washington's backside linebacker broke free of Roosevelt's efforts to seal block the backside of the defense. The linebacker had a clean shot to blow up Hondo behind the line of scrimmage. Hondo, however, was able to plant his outside foot solidly and broke back to the inside like a bolt of lightning underneath the linebacker's course. All the linebacker saw was a muddy blur. Hondo broke in front of the linebacker to streak, untouched, into the end zone for the go ahead two points and a subsequent, 8–7, Rough Rider victory.

Pandemonium broke out. The Roosevelt bench emptied out into the Washington end zone. It seemed like the entire team jumped on top of Ty and Hondo, slapping and pounding their backs. Ty then broke loose to find Big Julie and raced to him to deliver a squeezing hug. Then, everyone started to jump up and down in place chanting "Riders!, together! Riders!, together!, Riders!, ...

"You were killing those guys, Julie," said Ty as the two teammates continued their hugs.

"I told you to just stay behind my big butt,!" said Big Julie with a huge grin spread across his face.

"You certainly did and you certainly were right," stated the running back. "I can't wait to see that video!"

"I can't wait to see if my Momma kept my roast beef hoagie dry," said the mountainous, offensive tackle. "I hate soggy bread."

"That was some big time playing, Son. You carried the team on your back on that last drive. I'm very proud of you, Ty," said Addison Douglas. "I'm so happy, Honey," said the mother as she hugged her son. "You were super! Just super!"

"You were awesome, Dude," said Kayleigh. "They couldn't stop you," as she kissed Ty on the cheek. "You were unconscious!" Ty became suddenly quiet, looking down to the ground. He then lifted up his head slowly, looking up, pointing to the sky. Ty saw his father smiling. *Proud of you son,* whispered the father.

After the pleasantries with his family and Kayleigh, Ty started to hustle back to the locker room. As he made his way across the field, he realized that his feelings were somewhere between euphoric and uneasy. He was ecstatic about the team's almost miracle win and felt great about having been such a big part in the victory. On the other hand, he felt extremely uneasy about taking it upon himself to attack his fellow teammates in an effort to arouse them for one last charge. He knew he really had no right to do so. *But someone had to do it,* thought the mud-caked running back.

As Ty approached the locker room building, Coach Walters was standing in the doorway. "Hustle up, Ty. You're the last player in. What's wrong with you? You're usually first."

"Sorry, Coach," responded Ty as he entered the boisterous, triumphant locker room with his head held partially down.

Once the boisterous, jubilant players saw Ty enter the room, everyone got quiet. After a few seconds of silence, Big Julie started clapping his hands chanting "Ty, Ty," softly and slowly. Hug and Dino joined in and started chanting "Ty,! Ty,!" a little louder and with a little more vitality. Then, the chanting exploded as Pete Logan and Jarvis Means and Bernardo Diaz and Leotis Brown and every other Rough Rider teammate chanted Ty,! Ty,! Ty! as loud as they could.

Ty, encouraged by the cheers of his teammates, carried the Washington Victory Block to the stack of Victory Blocks already in place. Instead of carefully placing the block on the top of the pile, Ty lifted the Washington Victory Block into the air with his two hands and smashed it down atop the Kennedy block. The power of his explosive delivery shattered the Victory Block into four pieces to the uproar of the team.

Dempsey shook his head from side-to-side. *I knew I should have bought an extra block.*

"The Man,!" shouted out Coach Franklin as Dempsey walked into the coaches' locker room. "Great job, Coach! And, can you believe the nerve of Douglas. I've never seen a player act like that and then go out and deliver big time."

"Rod, the only thing I did right was to agree with Ty," replied the smiling head coach.

"You sure surprised me on that one," added Al Lopez. "I thought you might bench him right there."

"It's funny, Al," replied Dempsey. "When he said 'give me the football,' something clicked in my head telling me that giving the ball to Ty Douglas was just what we needed. The kid's special and he showed that today. He's one tough sucker!"

When the excitement of the coaches started to subside, the smiling head coach happened to glance towards the back of the locker room. He suddenly saw his buddy, Bo Harris, leaning against the back wall with his left foot crossed over his right. Bo's arms were across his chest with a lit cigarette held in his left hand. Bo untangled his arms to allow himself to raise his right arm and, with a smile, give his friend a thumbs up signal. The victorious coach answered his Corporal with a head nod and a smile of his own. Dempsey then turned to close his locker. When he turned back to talk to Bo, ...Bo was gone.

"Hey, Hero. I'm over here," yelled a smiling Kayleigh Logan.

"Don't say that,!" replied Ty with an embarrassed look on his face as his eyes roamed from side-to-side to see if anyone had heard her words.

"But, you were the hero. When everything looked like it was falling apart and the game was over, you took out your magic dust, stepped up big time and you took the game over. And, maybe you don't want me to yell out 'hero' in front of all these people. But, you certainly were my hero today, Tyler Douglas," as she planted a big kiss on the side of his face. "I told you you had some of that magic dust and now it's kicking into gear, full throttle."

As the head coach of the Roosevelt Rough Riders left the locker room, he saw an attractive, 45-year-old woman standing in his way. "Hi, Coach," said Ty's mother. "I'm Addison Douglas. I'm Ty's mother," as she stuck out her hand for a shake.

"Nice to meet you, Mrs. Douglas. I've been hearing a lot about you."

"Not all bad, I hope," said Ty's mother.

"No, not at all," Mrs. Douglas. "You've done a great job raising that boy of yours," said the head coach with a polite grin. "He can be a little obstinate at times but I'm tremendously glad he's with us. He's a fine young man and I certainly enjoy having him with us."

"His dad had a lot to do with that," said the mother with a sad smile. After a few seconds to recover her composure, she continued on. "I just wanted to thank you for your guiding and mentoring my son, Coach. You've helped fill a big void in my son's life. Thank you," said the mother once again with a warm smile and tears running down her face. She then turned abruptly to melt into the crowd of players, families and friends.

CHAPTER 62

"Can you believe the condition of that field,?" asked Dempsey as he added firewood to the waning blaze. "I don't know if we'll ever be able to get those uniforms clean."

"Maybe they'll put in an artificial turf field for you now after seeing how badly the field held up to a hard rain," said Mary Elizabeth. She was so proud of her husband's success and so happy to see his exuberance. Most importantly, she was so thankful to see his headaches and shaking right hand subsiding.

"Yeah, right. Mary, I can't even get them to buy me a new blocking sled. The one we have now should be placed in the Football Hall of Fame. The dang thing's an antique!"

"Did you ever think Ty could do what he did? He tore it up big time!," said Mary Elizabeth.

"I had a feeling that he could explode at any time. He really went off, didn't he? He certainly took on the team leadership role today. And, he did it when we so drastically needed someone to fire up the team. He's a fighter and today he fought the right way, ...like a true champion."

Losing is awful. It can be dreadful, gut retching, depressing and humbling. Winning, however, is normally, wonderfully ecstatic. It can also be tremendously relieving. Or, winning can be a combination of both. An ecstatic Sean Dempsey was definitely relieved to have had his Rough Rider players pull out the astonishing, last ditch effort win over Washington.

The atmosphere in the Saturday morning team meeting room was definitely upbeat. There were lots of smiles and jokes and jesting. One of the great joys of winning a game is to come from behind and pull out a close one in the last, few, vital seconds.

"The lesson to be learned is that you never give up,!" said Dempsey to his players. "You never quit! You hang in there and play hard every play, play after play after play. You never know when the execution of one, single, basic technique might make all the difference in the world in regard to grabbing victory from defeat."

"Let's get ready to beat Lincoln."

"Ty, you can't let your team slip again," said Addison Douglas.

"But, Mom. I'm just one player on the team. All I can do is my own job as best I can."

"You have to knock that stuff off, Tyler Douglas, or I'm going to hit you on the head with this rolling pin. Whether you want the role of leader or not, you have become that person for your team, ...for the Rough Riders, Tyler Douglas," said Ty's mother. "I was proudly outside the locker room when they chanted 'Ty,! Ty,! Ty!' That chant honored you and no one else for leading your team to an unbelievable comeback victory with you in the forefront. And, now, your teammates have given the leadership baton to you. Being a leader takes on tremendous responsibilities, Son. But, when a person's actions pull his teammates and friends along to victory, there is no greater personal accomplishment. Like it or not, Ty, you now have that leadership baton in your hand. You've come to be the Pied Piper of this team. And, I'll tell you what, it's going be fun to see how you lead this team down the stretch. You have to admit that stepping up to the forefront and leading your team to a miracle victory had to be an unbelievably wonderful feeling. And, I know your Dad is so happy," said the mother with tears welling up in her eyes.

Ty listened to his mother's words pensively as his eyes looked down at the ground. The frown lines across his forehead supported that. Ty finally looked up to his mother's face as his own face lit up with a large, vibrant smile. The mother and son then locked into a long embrace.

"Well, at least we have a new streak going," blared out Marge Strausser as she dashed into Coach Dempsey's room again just before the Monday morning home room warning bell sounded. Congrats on the win versus..."

"Washington, Marge. We came back to beat the Washington Wildcats."

"Hey, take it easy! You even have me checking my computer in the morning to see if you won," stated Marge. "That's pretty big stuff for an old social studies teacher like me who doesn't know if the ball's pumped or stuffed. Well, congratulations Sean and good luck this week against whoever you play," as she turned to leave the room.

"Marge, no good luck strudel?"

The social studies teacher turned back to the head football coach with a New York wise guy look plastered across her face. "I just wanted to see if you pay attention, Dempsey. I woke up late this morning so the home economics teacher is doing me a favor and baking a whole batch right now."

"A whole batch,?" asked Dempsey.

"Yeah. Until my husband told me yesterday, I didn't know that you have assistant coaches." Strausser got to the classroom's door frame, turned backed and asked Dempsey, "...the ball is pumped with air, isn't it?"

CHAPTER 63

GAME 8:
LINCOLN LIONS

Versus Lincoln, the Rough Riders played their most complete game of the season. The offense, defense and kicking game all preformed at their best. As a result, the Rough Riders crushed the Lincoln Lions, 45–14. When the bus pulled up to Roosevelt High School, the players noisily and happily piled into the locker room.

"That was an excellent performance, Gentlemen," stated Dempsey. "A great win. I'm very proud of how far you've come this season. This trip together has been unbelievable. I wouldn't trade it for anything in the world. But, if you want all the hard work, effort and sweat you've put into this season to really mean something, then you have one more big challenge to meet!"

"Coach, we have two more big challenges, don't we,?" cried out Hondo. "Van Buren and then the championship game."

Hondo fell straight into the trap that Dempsey had set. "I'm glad you brought that up, Hondo. You're right. If we beat Van Buren and if Eisenhower beats Kennedy, then we, and Kennedy, will be tied for first place. And, since we already beat Kennedy, we would win the tie breaker and play for the Greater City Championship against Eisenhower."

"But that's two big ifs, isn't it, Gentlemen? And right now, we only have the ability to take care of one of those ifs. If we don't, we have to settle for a 6 and 3 record and a second place finish. But, hey, who ever thought we could finish in second place and have a winning record? 6 and 3 would be something we could all be proud of, ...an excellent year for a program like Roosevelt. Something..."

"Wait a minute! Wait a minute,!" said Leotis Brown. "Coach, you're mess'n with our heads, aren't you,?" asked the cornerback with a stern look on his face. Actually, everyone in the room now had a stern look on their faces as a result of their head coach's surprisingly submissive speech. This wasn't how their head coach normally spoke to them. This was especially true with something as important as a chance to play in and win a championship.

"You're damn right I'm messing around with you," replied the now simmering head coach. "The reality is that the only thing we can control right now is how we play against Van Buren. And, Gentlemen, that's exactly what we're going to do. We're going to put one hundred percent focus into beating the Van Buren Vikings. Does everyone understand that?"

"Yes, Coach, chanted the room full of mesmerized players locked into every word coming out of their head coach's mouth.

"In that case, we still have a block party to attend to, don't we,?" said the head coach to an explosive roar of joy and excitement. *And, to think I now have to root for Eisenhower.*

CHAPTER 64

"Hey," said Hondo. "Eisenhower and Kennedy are going to be on T.V. this Thursday evening at 7:00 p.m. They're the 'Thursday Night High School Game of the Week' on Channel 11."

"No way,!" said Hug. "That means..."

"We'll know if we are going to be playing for the championship or not before we play our final game against Van Buren," finished Hondo.

"Who told you that,?" asked Ty suspiciously.

"I heard Dr. Hoskins' secretary talking on the phone when I was waiting to see my guidance councelor."

"That's some heavy stuff," said Hug.

"That's no lie," replied Ty. "Man, this playoff stuff is heating up, isn't it?"

"Irv, Coach Franklin said you wanted to see me," said a smiling Dempsey as he entered the equipment room. "Still got that coffee pot going?"

"Hey, Coach. Thanks for coming," replied Old Irv. "And, yes. I certainly do have my coffee pot go'n. Sure do, Coach Dempsey. Sure do."

"Thanks Irv," said the head coach as he sat down in one of the old, beat up, yet comfortable, armchairs that faced Old Irv's desk.

"You like sugar, don't you Coach,?" asked Old Irv as he handed two packets to the head coach. Dempsey sipped the coffee from the hot, steamy mug. "You're sure right, Irv. You certainly do brew a great cup of coffee. So what's up, Irv?"

"Well, Coach, sometimes things come across my desk every now and then that I think are important for the head coach to know about."

"Irv, I can use all the help I can get. So, if you have something I should know about, I'd appreciate your telling me."

"Well, Coach. The word on the street is that Ontario Mosely is planning to 'do in' Tyler Douglas and he plans to do it soon."

"Do in Ty Douglas,?" responded Dempsey. "Just what do you mean, Irv?"

"Do in, ...like in beat up, Coach. Like in Ontario and his buddies attacking Ty when he's off by himself somewhere without his football buddies being around to help him. I've been around this type of situation a lot, Coach. If I were you, I wouldn't take this lightly."

"There's no doubt about that, Irv. I've already had more experiences with Ontario Mosely then I could possibly want. But tell me, Irv. What would you do?"

"Well, first of all, you as the Head Coach can, really, only do so much. The same is true for your assistant coaches. Heck, Coach, you have a family to raise and kids to teach in your classes. I think the people you have to rely on are your players. This is the best group of kids we've had on the football team in a long, long time. I'd round up a few of your best kids like Dino and Hug and Hondo, ... Pete, Leotis and Jarvis. But the guy who'll best get this straightened out is this team's boss man..."

... Big Julie," finished the head coach.

"That's right, Coach Dempsey, ...Big Julie!"

"Daryl Hoskins," said the principal as he froze the television to take the phone call.

"Daryl, this is Sean."

Not good, thought the principal. Evening calls were almost never good for a school principal.

"What's up, Sean?"

"I got info from Old Irv that Mosely's plotting to attack Ty with his gang, Daryl. I just wanted to let you know this as soon as I found out."

"I'm glad you did, Sean. Do you have a plan at this point,?" asked the principal.

"Not a full plan but I feel I have the key guy to help straighten this out," stated Dempsey.

"Big Julie,?" said the principal.

"Big Julie," said the head coach.

"Do you understand where I coming from,?" asked the head coach.

"Coach," answered Big Julie. "I'll take care of this."

CHAPTER 65

The Rough Riders practices were a mixture of excitement and hopefulness all week long. Dempsey focused on timing, ball security drills and efforts to freshen up his team, especially the players' legs. He wanted to be sure that the speed advantage in Roosevelt's favor would be ready to rip against Van Buren.

"I want quality," said Dempsey just before the Monday afternoon practice. "I want to wear Van Buren out with our speed and conditioning. We're going to have short, concise practices this week so we're ready to explode. Get your engines ready to roar, Gentlemen! We'll be in full pads today, Monday only. Half pads, helmets and shoulders pads on Tuesday. No pads on Wednesday and Thursday, ...helmets only. We'll keep to that schedule as long as you guys continue flying around in practice and maintain a good focus."

"All right,!" yelled out the appreciative players. "Way to go. Coach!"

"This is good stuff," said a hyped-up Hondo. "Man, it's like the play-offs in the N.F.L., you know what I mean?"

"Yeah, but we need to have a team we hate help us," said Leotis.

Ty enjoyed food shopping with his mother. Yes, it did provide an opportunity for Ty to get his mom to buy his favorite foods. However, he also thoroughly enjoyed the shared shopping chore together. As their shopping spree was about to come to an end, Ty disappeared for a few minutes only to find a large bouquet of roses in Ty's hands as they approached the check-out counter.

"Oooohhhh," said Addison Douglas. "Some pretty roses for Kayleigh. Just put them on the conveyer belt, Ty."

"That's O.K., Mom. I'd rather pay for them myself."

"O.K., Ty," said the mother with a smile. "I understand, Son."

The next morning, a sleepy Addison Douglas made a cup of coffee for herself. She knew that Ty had already left for school for early morning tutoring. She turned the corner to sit in the dining room and to read the morning newspaper. When she did, she saw a beautiful bouquet of roses on the dining room table with an attached note. It read, "Love You, Mom."

The easy-to-cry mother, ...cried!

CHAPTER 66

Thursday, non-padded practice, was going well. The players were excited about playing the Van Buren game and practiced with great effort. "The boys look like their legs are freshening up," said Coach Franklin.

"I'm happy about that," said Dempsey. "Van Buren doesn't seem to have a lot of speed. We might be able to heat them up pretty well."

"Coach Dempsey," called out a voice from behind the two Rough Rider coaches. Both coaches turned to see a sharp looking, well-dressed, handsome Afro-American man of about the same age as Dempsey hustling up in an effort to overcome his tardiness. The tall, well-built man stuck out a giant claw of a hand for the head coach to shake with a warm, genuine smile on his face.

"Sorry I'm late, Coach," said Sydney Broadhurst, the assistant coach and state recruiter from A&M. "There was an accident coming in on the interstate and my car hardly moved for over an hour."

"No problem, Coach," stated Dempsey. "I'm just glad you called this morning to let me know you were coming. This will be special for the kids, I'm sure."

"I'm glad I was able to get here in time to get an eyeball on some of your kids," said Broadhurst. "A lot of people are talking up your junior class. Got some good ones, I understand."

"We've got some good ones, Coach, that's for sure," stated Dempsey.

"I'll bet that hulk over there is Julius Goodman," stated Broadhurst. "I saw some video on him last week. He sure has great feet for such a huge man. Coach, he crushes people and not just once in a while."

"He's really smart, too," added Dempsey. "And, quite the character to boot. He knows how to make people laugh. He's a great kid. His mother's a teacher at one of the elementary schools."

"I really like your middle linebacker Dino DeTaglia," said the A&M coach. "He has great explosion and he sure can hit. He's an excellent tackler. Your outside linebacker, Jarvis Means, is sure active. And, I like Leotis Brown. He has great speed and is extremely athletic."

"Keep an eye on our tailback, the Douglas kid," stated Dempsey. "Believe it or not, he's really a quarterback and a real good one. I moved him to halfback to get both him and our other quarterback, Hondo Rodriguez, on the field at the same time. Hondo is a tremendous talent on this level, Sydney. But like I said, keep an eye on Douglas. He's a sleeper right now."

"I'll do that," said Broadhurst, unconvincingly.

After about an hour more of practice to allow Broadhurst to scout the Rider's top players, Dempsey stated, "...let me call the kids up so I can introduce you, Sydney. I really appreciate your willingness to talk to the players."

"Coach, the pleasure is mine," stated a sincere Broadhurst. "You don't often get a chance to come back to your old high school and talk to the players."

"Gentlemen, we have a special guest here that I would like to introduce to you so why don't you all take a knee," said Dempsey. "As you've noticed, over the past few weeks we've started to have college scouts visit us to take a look at many of the talented players we now have on our squad. Today, we not only have a college scout. We have a college scout who was a two-time college All-American, a five-time Pro-Bowler and a Super Bowl MVP. And what's most special is that when he was in high school, he wore the black and gold uniform of a Roosevelt Rough Rider."

"Man, that's Sydney Broadhurst," blurted out Bernardo Diaz. "Now that dude could play!"

"And he's Jarvis's uncle," said Leotis Brown knowingly.

"Thanks for stealing my thunder, Guys," said Dempsey with a

chuckle. "But you guys are absolutely right. Riders, meet one of the most famous players to ever play at Roosevelt, Coach Sydney Broadhurst from A&M." A loud and enthusiastic applause lit up the group of young players.

"Thank you, Coach Dempsey. Thank you so much, Guys. It's truly great to be back here to be with the Riders. Coach Dempsey has asked me to say a few words and I must say, right off the bat, that it's so good to see football success here at Roosevelt once again. And, when people in the area and the state start asking what's going on at Roosevelt, I'll now be able to say discipline, toughness and hard work. It's easy to see how true all of that is watching you fly around the practice field. And, it's great to see how you guys are taking care of business in school so that you can be considered for an athletic..."

"Coach," said Franklin softly as he jabbed Dempsey's right arm with his elbow to get his attention. He then nodded with his head and eyes for Dempsey to look to his right. Dempsey turned his head to see one of the city's local policemen quickly walking his way. Unfortunately, he wasn't smiling. The mesmerized attention of the players quickly transferred from the talk by the honored alumnus to the threat of the man with the blue uniform. Even Broadhurst's speech came to a dimmed halt as he, also, saw the scowling policeman approach Coach Dempsey.

"Hi, Officer. What can I do for you,?" asked Dempsey with a forced smile on his face.

"Coach, I have some bad news for you," answered the officer. "I have a warrant for the arrest of one of your players, a DeMarco Green. I'm really sorry, but I'm going to have to cuff him and take him away. If you look around your fence line, I have four officers stationed around your practice field right now. Whenever he's had troubles before, he's tried to bolt. We can't afford to lose him this time."

"Can I ask what he's accused of doing,?" asked Dempsey.

"Coach, I really can't say much other than it deals with drug trafficking," replied the officer. "We'll..., Oh no! There he goes,!"

said the police officer as DeMarco took off on a sprint. DeMarco ran to and jumped up on the cyclone fencing that surrounded the field. However, the pudgy player quickly lost his grip and fell to the ground as he tried to scale it. Two of the police officers quickly pounced on him, wrapped his hands and arms behind his back and cuffed him.

The Rough Rider players and coaches watched the situation unfold in front of them in a trance. Even though this was not the first time something like this had happened at Roosevelt High School, it was still crushing for the players and coaches to watch.

"I'm sorry to see this happen, Coach," said Broadhurst with a sad smile on his face. "Some things never seem to change at Roosevelt, do they?"

"Sean, this is tough stuff for you. I know," said Coach Franklin as the two coaches sat together in the coaches' locker room once practice was over. Dempsey seemed to be in a sort of shock as he tried to sort out what he had just witnessed.

"As I've told you before, you can't get too down about situations like this," continued Franklin. "Unfortunately, situations like this pop up all the time. It's almost like you have to build in a personal, self-defense mechanism to deal with such problems because they're going to happen and, often, at the most inopportune times. If you can't do that, Sean, then you'll go crazy and never last long here."

"I can understand that, Rod," replied Dempsey. "But, that doesn't make me feel any better right now."

"No, it doesn't, Sean," stated Franklin. "In the short time you've been here you've been able to grow attached to these kids in a big way. Roosevelt desperately needed a head football coach like you. But, if you're going to last here, you're going to have to deal with such situations on an almost regular basis."

"I know that DeMarco is a bit of a goof but he seems like a pretty decent kid," said Dempsey. "Why would a young kid like that throw everything away? For drugs? For Money?"

"It could be for a lot of things, Sean. Money, drugs. It could be that an older brother is selling cocaine and is forcing the kid to do some running. It could be because money is needed to put food on the table. It could be gang pressure."

"Have you been around such an abysmal situation like this before, Rod?"

"In nine years, I've been to five funerals to bury some of my boys. That's the ultimate bummer, Sean."

CHAPTER 67

"This is really going to be interesting," said Dempsey. "If that jerk Watson and Eisenhower win, then we're playing to get into the championship game. If he and Eisenhower lose, we're out. Oh, well. Go Generals. Go Coach Watson."

The entire Rough Rider football team piled into Hondo's family restaurant to watch the Eisenhower-Kennedy game. The players were excited but nervous. The Roosevelt players were going to have to root for the hated Eisenhower Generals, a tough chore for them, no matter what the stakes.

"I can't believe this," said Hug. "What a bunch of rich-kid snobs. I hate those punks."

"Hey, easy," said Ty. "I thought I was going to Eisenhower until I found out I was in the Roosevelt school boundaries."

"Yeah. But, we were able to straighten you out in time to be somewhat of a decent dude," said Dino. "Otherwise, you would have been a dweeb now, ...just like them."

"Thanks. I guess," responded a befuddled Tyler Douglas.

In a hard fought, see-saw battle, Eisenhower defeated Kennedy, 27-24 in overtime. In the first overtime period, Kennedy initially took the lead with a field goal. On Eisenhower's very first overtime offensive play, a tipped ball by a Kennedy linebacker ricocheted into the hands of a slanting Eisenhower slot back who was able to scamper into the end zone untouched for the Generals' victory.

The Rough Riders let go a roar of elation when they watched the Generals' slot back score. After a minute or so of celebration, Ty quieted everyone down. "Tomorrow evening, we're playing for the Eastern Division Championship berth of the Greater City Conference Championship Game! Win and we get to play against our friends, the Eisenhower Generals!" The room went wild!

CHAPTER 68

Another new Rough Rider tradition had been started early in the season before the Adams' game. Hug, Ty, Big Julie, Dino and Hondo all met to have an early, light, pre-game dinner together back at Hondo's family restaurant again, the Burrito House. After the Adams victory, the next week's pre-game Burrito House dinner swelled to nine players. By the Van Buren game, it had become a full team gathering. The players had gone so far as to invite the cheerleaders, the managers, the trainers and the coaches. Even Old Irv was invited and quickly became a popular, weekly, pre-game fixture.

"Has anyone heard anything about DeMarco,?" asked Jarvis.

"All I know is that he's at the Juvenile Detention Center," said Big Julie. "That's what his little brother told me."

"I told him to stop hang'n around Mosely," said Leotis. "Hang around with that turd long enough and you're gon'na get burned. The guy's poison."

"DeMarco's a good dude," stated Hug. "Why did he get involved with that stuff?"

"Money," said Big Julie. "His family desperately needed money."

Dempsey was conspicuously missing from the pregame dinner. He had not missed one of the dinners since the coaches had been invited by the players. When some of the players asked Coach Franklin where Dempsey was, the Defensive Coordinator responded with the comment "...he had some important business he had to take care of."

Halfway through the meal, Dempsey walked through the back door of the restaurant. With him was DeMarco Green. The room went dead quiet as all eyes moved towards the Head Coach and DeMarco. After a short, uncomfortable, period of silence, Big Julie stood up and said, "there's an empty seat over here, DeMarco. You're welcome to join us."

CHAPTER 69

"Even though they lost to Jackson, Roosevelt sure has come a long way since we beat them," said Don Watson's top assistant coach and Offensive Coordinator, Roger Zinski. He was sipping a can of soda in the coaches' office with Watson after Eisenhower had nipped Kennedy in the overtime nail biter the night before.

"Yeah, yeah," said Watson as he waved his hand at the assistant coach disparagingly. "After a million years, they win a few games on a soft schedule and everyone makes a big deal about them. If we play them again, I'll blitz every play and stuff that spread offense crap right up their ass. I want you to score your butts off. Don't even think about punting. I want this to be the worst beating in the history of Eisenhower and Roosevelt football. They're trash, every one of them! Trash!"

Zinski, used to Watson's tirades, said nothing in response. He knew better to question his head coach when in such a mood. *The problem is, he's like this most of the time,* thought Zinski, as he turned his head away from Watson to hide a knowing grin. *What a dumb ass I was to bring up Roosevelt. And, what an idiot I was to ever take this job.*

As the Generals' coaches were packing up to go home, Watson nodded for Zinski to come over to his locker. "If we play Roosevelt in the championship, I want to bury them, totally bury their asses! Just to see if they're doing anything new or different, I want you to send that new kid and have him watch Roosevelt tomorrow night."

"You mean scout them,?" asked the surprised coach.

"Yeah, you got any problem with that, Zinski? I'll have no problem firing your ass too."

"No, Don. Not at all," answered the intimidated assistant coach clearly knowing Watson was asking him to purposely break conference rules. Game scouting was not allowed by the Greater City Conference.

"Just tell him to wear a ball cap and a hoodie like those lowlifes do. And, tell the idiot not to put on any clothes that has our logo or name on it. You can you handle that, Zinski, can't you?"

CHAPTER 70

GAME 9:
VAN BUREN VIKINGS

The Rough Riders went through their pre-game stretch for Van Buren under the lights in front of over fifteen hundred family members, friends and students at Roosevelt's small, home game stadium. The number may not have seemed like a great amount for a high school game. However, it was an enormous amount for a Rough Rider home game.

"What do you think, Rod," asked Dempsey.

"The kids seem a bit anxious but I think they're ready to go."

"I do too. If we just play decently and don't make a lot of mistakes, I think we'll be fine."

"Well, we'll find out soon enough, Sean. Just score some points, will ya,?" in their, now, ritual, pre-game jest.

"You just hold them to under ten points and we'll do great," answered Dempsey in his best wisecracking voice. Dempsey turned around to face the stadium, the lights and the crowd. He suddenly felt a jolt of both pride and excitement. *What a ride,* thought the head coach. *I never came close to imagining such an outcome. I'm so happy for these kids. I'm so happy for Mary Elizabeth. Enough of this,* thought the melancholy head coach as he shook his head and took in a deep breathe. *Time to go to work.*

As Dempsey studied his play call sheet for the ninth time, a befuddled Rod Franklin sprinted up to the Head Coach. "Sean, Carlo Martelli is on the sideline talking to our kids."

"What,?" asked the Head Coach. "What the hell is going on, Rod?"

"Just what I said, Coach, ... Martelli's on our sideline talking to some of our players."

"Where the hell is he," asked the irate head coach as he tried to locate the fired, former offensive line coach.

"Wait, Sean, ...wait, wait, wait,!" said Coach Franklin as he held up his hands and tried his best to block the Head Coach from getting entangled with Martelli. "Sean, I have Dr. Hoskins coming up right now. Let him handle this. You concentrate on the game! You hear me, Sean? Concentrate on the game!"

"I got this, Sean. You just coach," said the principal as he arrived at the scene with two security guards in tow. Dempsey watched closely as the former Roosevelt Offensive Line Coach was being ushered off the field. For a brief, few seconds, Dempsey and Martelli locked their eyes on one another. Martelli gave Dempsey the middle finger. Dempsey smiled and winked at Martelli.

Wooley Woolridge opened the game by catching a short kickoff outside of the left hash mark. He immediately broke towards the middle of the field. Rayshawn Davis broke hard to the left to take a reverse hand-off from Wooley. The front line of blockers worked towards the middle of the field and then circled back to their left to set up a blocking wall. Untouched, the fleet slot back raced up the sideline 62-yards for his second kick-off return touchdown run of the season.

"Yeah, Rayshawn," yelled Hug as he was the first to reach the touchdown scoring player. He jumped on top of Rayshawn to start the pile of special teams' players.

"I'll take that start," stated Dempsey as he did a poor job of trying to disguise a smile. "Great, job," added Dempsey to his special teams' coordinator, Donny Walters. Walters pointed at Dempsey and nodded appreciatively.

The Van Buren Barons returned the kick-off to their own 44-yard line. On the first play of the series, Coach Franklin called for a blitz stunt by his two inside linebackers. The Van Buren offensive line picked up the first linebacker. Dino DeTaglia, looping around the first linebacker's charge, was left unblocked. The physical linebacker blasted the Barons' running back.

"Ball, Ball, Ball," screamed a number of the Rough Rider defenders. After a turbulent scuffle on the ground, the referee signaled for a Rough Rider possession.

"Hell of a job, Dino,!" shouted out Pete Logan. "You knocked the hell out of that guy!"

"You hit him good,!" said Eduardo Ibanez.

"Big turnover,!" yelled Coach Franklin. "Great job, defense!"

"O.K., Riders," said Hondo. "Let's put the screws to these guys real quick," as the quarterback went on to call for a triple option play sent in by Dempsey. Hondo gave the ball to Ty once he read the action of the defensive end. Initially, Ty cut back against the grain. He blasted through a pursuing backside linebacker and then straightened up his course as he bolted for the goal line. 38-yards later, the Rough Riders were quickly up by two touchdowns.

On the next offensive series for the Rough Riders, Roosevelt ran another triple option play. This time, Hondo kept the football, faked a pitch to Hug and broke up towards the goal line. The speedster put on a show making cuts that had defenders tackling air all the way to the goal line to up the score to 21-0.

On the following defensive series, linebacker Jarvis Means picked a pass meant for a Van Buren running back's flat route and returned it 26-yards for a pick-six Roosevelt touchdown.

When the Rough Rider offense got the football back," Dempsey called for another option play. This time, Hondo was forced to pitch to Ty who circled the defense, broke up the sideline and scorched the field for 56-yards and another Rough Rider touchdown. Later in the game, Hondo threw a play action touchdown pass to a deep cross route by Wooley Woolridge just before Hondo was taken to the ground by Van Buren's left defensive end.

Hondo limped off the field on a smarting right foot, ceding the rest of the quarterback playing time to sophomore back-up quarterback Billy Pierce. Pierce scored late in the game on a 15-yard option keep run. Even the diminutive cornerback, Brock Jamal, got into the scoring action with a pick-six interception while playing on some late, mop-up-duty. In a game of total domination, the Rough Riders won 56-7.

CHAPTER 71

As the Riders exuberantly left the field, the Roosevelt principal, Daryl Hoskins, stood by the entry way of the stands. He had noticed a man taking notes during the course of the game. The person hadn't realized that Hoskins had been eyeing him. When the individual made his way down the steps of the stands as the game ended, Dr. Hoskins addressed the suspicious looking person. "Hello there, Sir. I'm Daryl Hoskins, the principal here at Roosevelt. Could I talk to you for a moment?"

The young, Eisenhower coach froze when he heard those words. "You seem to look very familiar to me," said the principal. "Wait a minute. You're one of Coach Watson's assistants, aren't you!?"

"You O.K., Hondo,?" asked Dempsey. The hobbling player brought up the rear of the team as they boarded the bus to get back to Roosevelt.

"Oh, I'm fine," answered Hondo. "I just got stepped on during that last play and it hurts like hell. It's just a little tender now."

"Make sure you check with the trainer when we get back to school."

"Got'cha, Coach," replied Roosevelt's quarterback, matter-of-factly.

"And Hondo, ...awesome job today, Son," said Dempsey. "You did a great job keeping those two knuckleheads, Ty and Hug, straight out there."

"Thanks, Coach D," said Hondo with a grimace of pain running across his face. *And all this time, I thought I was the knucklehead.*

"I said you could still go to the championship game if you won out," stated Kayleigh after Ty came out of the locker room.

"How come you're so smart about football?"

"It's easy when you have three, older, football playing brothers. They never let me play with dolls. They'd rip them out of my hands and give me a football. You've never seen me throw the ball around but I'm actually pretty good till I have to throw deep."

"And, that's probably why you're so ornery," replied Ty with a chuckle.

"You'd be ornery too if you had brothers fifty pounds heavier than you using you for a tackling dummy. That's why you'd never see me wearing prissy looking dresses. They wouldn't let me."

"Well, you don't have to wear prissy looking dresses for me. I always think you look pretty, no matter what you're wearing."

For the first time in their relationship, it was Kayleigh who had nothing to say. She got up on her toes and kissed her boyfriend.

CHAPTER 72

"What do you mean, he caught you,?" screamed Coach Watson. "How the hell did he catch you, you idiot?! Did you wear a ball cap and a hoodie like I told you to?"

"Yes, Coach," answered Watson's young assistant. "I did, but he saw me taking notes. I never thought that might tip it off."

"You took notes? Are you kidding me? You're a complete moron. You know that? Now I have to go and explain this to that jerk principal of mine. Now, I have to stand up at the head coaches' meeting and confess this to those dummies and apologize! You're an idiot! A real idiot! Get the hell out of my sight. And, while I think of it, you're fired. I don't ever want to see your ass around here again. Got that, you stupid ass?"

When Dempsey's cell phone rang, both Sean and Mary Elizabeth broke from their focus of watching the sports segment of their favorite, local, nighttime T.V. news show. A definite look of concern was suddenly plastered across both of their faces. A late night call for a head football coach, like a principal, was never a welcomed event. Too often it meant nothing but trouble.

"Hello," answered Mary Elizabeth since the cell phone was sitting next to her on the family room couch. "Who's speaking please? Yes, just a minute, Juanita. It's Juanita Hernandez asking for you. She seems to be quite upset."

"Hello, said a now worried Dempsey. "Yes, Juanita." After a silent few minutes, a suddenly deflated Dempsey finally spoke up again. "Oh no! I'm so sorry to hear that. Well, when he wakes up, tell him how sorry I am. If it's O.K., I'd like to stop by to see him tomorrow. If there's any way I, or my wife, can be of help, please don't hesitate to contact either of us. Thanks for calling, Juanita. I'm sure that Hondo will be fine."

"Hondo broke his foot," announced Dempsey to his wife. "He had to have two surgical pins put in." *And, we got so far.*

CHAPTER 73

Big Julie had a strange, slightly sour feeling in his gut in the aftermath of the season ending victory over Van Buren as the Rough Riders team partied at The Malt Shop. He seemed to be only mildly interested in The Malt Shop's monster Kitchen Sink ice cream hodge-podge that sat in front of him. Such a lack of desire for food, especially an ice cream dessert, was a definite rarity for Big Julie Goodman. Actually, he well knew that his longtime buddy, Hondo Rodriguez, still being at the hospital, was a part of his sadness. *Something's up,* thought the giant offensive tackle. *X-rays usually don't take that long.* Still, there was something else that he felt was bothering him. He just couldn't put his finger on it.

The Rough Riders were at "The Shop," celebrating their in-season ending victory over Van Buren that had put them in the Greater City Championship Football Game. The mood in the ice cream eatery was one of joy and jubilation. The players danced in the isles with the cheerleaders to the 50's style jukebox music.

"Man, you got so much chocolate syrup on that thing that you can't even see where the ice cream is," said Hug as he sat down at the same table as Big Julie.

Such a statement from Hug would normally bring a quick, humorous, defensive retort from Big Julie. Instead, Hug got an innocuous "Uh-huh" in return. Big Julie lifted up his head to scan the party scene in front of him. His eyes locked onto Ty and Kayleigh who had just left his table and were waving goodbyes as they went through "The Shops" front door. The two hustled to enable Ty, using his mother's car, to drive Kayleigh home in time to meet her strict, 12 o'clock curfew issued by her parents. Big Julie kept an eye on his two, close friends. For some reason, things didn't feel quite right.

Ty and Kayleigh stepped up their pace to a quick jog to get to "The Shops" small parking lot. The parking lot was positioned across the street and slightly askew of the ice cream parlor. Big Julie suddenly observed two, darkly dressed figures in a crouch behind the car parked adjacent to Ty's. It was hard for him to see into the parking lot as he realized that the lights of the parking lot were, strangely, all out. Big Julie then saw another darkly dressed figure sneaking up to the first two stalkers. A flash of light from a car pulling away from the curb in front of "The Malt Shop" enabled Big Julie to recognize the group as some of Ontario Mosely's gangster buddies.

"PETE, CALL 911! JARVIS, HUG, DINO, EDUARDO, WITH ME,!" yelled Big Julie as the huge man flew out of his seat at lightning speed. The five Rough Riders raced out of "The Shop" with the rest of the team following once they realized that there was a problem.

As the Rough Riders raced through "The Shop's" front door and began crossing the street, they heard a loud scream from Kayleigh. As Big Julie and his teammates entered the darkened parking lot, they saw a large number of Moseley's gangsters holding down and pummeling, stomping and kicking a frantically struggling Ty Douglas. "Let me go you assholes," shouted out the distraught teen as his face was covered with blood. With one, last, powerful thrust, Ty was able to free his right arm to deliver a powerful punch up into one of the gangster's nose as the gangster screamed out in pain. Two of the thugs jumped on Ty's freed arm to thoroughly hold him down. Suddenly, a powerful shoulder block blow was explosively executed by the hard charging, massive Big Julie Goodman. The blow sent the hoodlums flying through the air, smashing them into adjacent parked cars.

"YOU GUYS HAVE THEM,!" yelled out Big Julie to his teammates. "Hold them for the cops. Watch out for knives!"

Big Julie dashed through the parking lot trying to find Kayleigh. He abruptly heard her screams from behind a shielding truck. When he turned the corner of the parked vehicle, he saw Kayleigh backed up against a brick wall with her blouse half ripped off her body. She was gouging the face of Ontario Mosely with her fingernails with all her might.

"You're filth, ...nothing but filth," screamed out Kayleigh as she clawed at Ontario's face and eyes, drawing gushing blood.

"You bitch," said Mosely as he let go a vicious swing of his right fist to her cheek bone. Kayleigh collapsed, slamming the back of her head on a car's back bumper. Blood quickly poured out of a gash on the back of her head as Mosely flicked open the switch blade knife held in his left hand. Mosely then raised the knife in an effort to slash across the front of Kayleigh's body. As Mosely began to drive the knife downward, Big Julie suddenly appeared to explosively deliver a punch to the side of Mosely's jaw. The punch threw Mosely's knife slashing efforts askew but he was still able to deliver a deep cut across Kayleigh's left arm. The gangster's body was forcefully grabbed and viciously spun 360-degrees into the air by Julius Goodman smashing Mosely into the brick wall behind Kayleigh.

As a groggy Ontario Moseley struggled to get up from the ground, Big Julie reached for a garbage can full of trash sitting off to his side. He picked up the trash can, raised it up in the air and smashed it down on Ontario's head, garbage and all. The giant Rough Rider player then picked up the glassy-eyed Mosely, lifted him up over his head and threw the gangster into an open garbage dumpster. Big Julie then forcefully slammed the dumpster's lid closed and spun around quickly in an attempt to assist Kayleigh. When he saw that Ty, Jarvis and Pete had arrived and were already attending to Kayleigh, he turned back to the dumpster, climbed up atop it and sat down on the dumpster's lid.

"WHERE'S ONTARIO,?" yelled out Ty. "I want his ass right now, Big Julie," said Ty. "And don't mess with me, Julie. Not now!"

"I'm not gon'na mess with you," said the monstrous man as he started unwrapping the emergency Snickers bar that he had stashed in his pocket in case he got hungry. "He's right here in this dumpster," answered Big Julie as Ontario's muffled voice and pounding on the inside of the dumpster could now be heard.

"Let his ass out, Julie! I'm going to finish this shit once and for all!"

"No, it's not gon'na happen today, my good friend," said Big Julie as he carefully unwrapped the bottom half of the Snicker's bar, with a knowing grin. "He's right here waiting for the police and you don't need to get in any trouble over this. You have a championship game to play next Friday and you owe all of your friends a chance to win the title. We don't need for you to get arrested. Go over and help Kayleigh, Ty. I got this covered. And, get that mess of a face you have fixed up, will'ya?"

Ty melted down when he heard Big Julie's words. With his eyes spinning, Ty hustled over to stay at Kayleigh's side. Kayleigh Logan was unconscious.

CHAPTER 74

The paramedics from the Latimore Heights Fire Department lifted the stretcher to lift Kayleigh into the ambulance. "She's gon'na be alright, isn't she," cried out Ty. "She's got'ta be alright! She's got'ta,!" as he grabbed ahold of the nearest paramedic. "I can go with her, can't I?"

"Are you a blood relative,?" asked the paramedic.

"No, I'm not," answered Ty. "But, I'm her boyfriend and she's in this situation because of me."

"Sorry, Buddie. Only relatives."

"I'm her brother," blurted out Pete Logan as he climbed into the back of the ambulance. "I'll let you know what's happening, Ty," said the shaken-up brother. "Say a prayer for her, Ty."

Ty looked up into the sky and took a deep breathe. "I'll need some help on this one, Dad," declared the scared teen to his deceased father. "I need for you to put one out of the park right now."

"Well, well, well, Mr. Mosely," said Sergeant Ed Lesley of the Latimore Heights Police Department as Ontario was cuffed and being escorted to a patrol car. Ontario stopped and turned towards the voice of the police sergeant with loathing and disgust spread across his face.

"I'd like to personally wish you a happy birthday," continued the smiling police sergeant as he checked Ontario's driver's license. Lesley was well aware of the troublesome presence of Ontario

Mosely in Latimore Heights over the past six years. "It was just yesterday, wasn't it? This means you're an all grown up, now, Ontario. An 18-year old adult says your driver's license. I'm sure you know that means you're a big boy now. You won't have to mess around with that little kid, juvenile court stuff anymore. Now, you'll have three, free hots a day and a rent-free, cozy cell to roam around in. Congratulations, Ontario."

"Kiss my ass, Lesley," said Mosely, well aware of the police sergeant's name. "Screw you and that prissy bitch!"

Lesley laughed. "Oh, ...and I'll be sure to bring you a birthday cupcake with a candle on it, Ontario," as he winked and turned his back on the gangster. "One more thing, Ontario. If I were you, I would change my cologne. Although, that Eue de Garbage aftershave seems to fit you quite nicely."

Big Julie walked back into "The Shop" and sat back down at the table he had been occupying before the fracas. He picked up his large, soup spoon to dive back into his Kitchen Sink ice cream delight. He looked down at the extravaganza, dropped his hand down with the spoon still in it and mumbled "Oh no." His Kitchen Sink dessert had turned into a cold bowl of soup.

"Yes, Jaunita," said Dempsey as he quickly answered the ringing cell phone.

"No, Sean. This is Sergeant Lesley."

"Sorry about that, Ed. I just got off the phone with my quarterback's sister and thought that was her again."

"Nothing serious, I hope,?" answered Lesley.

"Unfortunately for us, it is, Ed. My quarterback, Hondo Rodriguez, broke some bones in his foot in the game tonight against Van Buren. He'll be out for the championship game next week versus Eisenhower."

"Sorry to hear that, Coach. I know he's been a good player for you all season. Anyhow, Sean, I have some bad news and some good news for you. Tyler Douglas and a Kayleigh Logan were jumped and assaulted in the parking lot across the street from The Malt Shop by Ontario Mosely and his gang. Tyler is battered and bruised, but nothing serious. His girlfriend, Kayleigh, is unconscious and has a large laceration on the back of her head along with a deep knife cut on her left arm. I think she might have some cracked ribs as well. At this point, the Logan girl is listed in serious condition. The doctors think they'll know more in the next 24 hours."

Dempsey's demeaner seemed to melt as he heard the police sergeant's words. "I can't believe this crap, Ed. What the hell is going on?!"

"Well, on a good note, it seems that your big lineman, Julius Goodman was the hero of the day. He had a call placed to 911 immediately and then had the team surround Ontario's gang until we arrived. It also seems that he stopped Mosely's aggravated assault on the Logan girl. The report is that Goodman slammed Moseley into a brick wall, picked him up and threw him into a garbage dumpster. When we got to him, Goodman was sitting on top of the dumpster's lid eating a candy bar with Mosely holed up inside."

"So none of my boys are in trouble?," asked Dempsey as he shook his head from side-to-side and rubbed the ache forming in his head...

"Quite the contrary," answered Lesley. "Your team did a great job of stopping the assaults and holding the gang until we arrived. All of this was witnessed by three adults, verifying all of what I have just said. The best part of it all is that Moseley just turned 18 yesterday and will no longer be handled by the juvenile courts. Sean, we're not going to be seeing him for a while, thank goodness. Of course, sooner or later, some other clown will pop up to fill the crime leadership void."

"Thanks, Ed," said Dempsey. "I really appreciate your help."

"Good luck next Friday, Coach," replied Lesley. "I hope you beat the hell out of Eisenhower. They're pretty damn good as I'm sure you know. And, as you probably well know by now, that Watson's a total asshole."

Dempsey raced over to the hospital to see how Ty and Kayleigh and the rest of the team members were doing. As he entered the emergency room door, he ran in to an avalanche of his players who were being ushered out the door by the charge nurse.

"All of you will have to wait outside," said the nurse. "We don't have enough room for all of you and you don't belong here in the first place."

"Let's get outside, Guys," said Dempsey. "I'll go inside and try to find out what's up. It really might be best if you just headed home for the night. I'm sure we'll know more in the morning." None of the solemn players moved or replied.

Dempsey first bumped into Ty and his mother in the emergency room. Ty was a mess with cuts, scrapes and bruises protruding from any part of his body that wasn't covered by clothing. He held an ice bag over his left eye. His right eye was already swollen shut and deeply black and blue.

"Hello, Coach," said Ty. Ty's mother, with her arms folded across her chest, said nothing and just stared at her son.

"Hi, Ty. How you feeling, Bud,?" asked the chagrinned head coach.

"Kind of feel like I got hit by a truck," answered the rough looking player. "A big truck!"

"I'm very sorry about this Mrs. Douglas."

"It's not your fault, Coach. I'm just pissed, ...really pissed!" *I just wish I could go into a little room with one of your old baseball bats, John, and take a few swings at that son-of-a-bitch,* as she looked up towards the heavens.

CHAPTER 75

"You've certainly been quiet this morning," said Mary Elizabeth as she walked towards her husband as he sat at his desk in the family room. She well knew her husband was stressed, ...perhaps overly stressed. He had lost his starting quarterback due to an injured foot and now had to deal with the physical condition of Kayleigh Logan, Ty's girlfriend. Dempsey tried to make it up to Kayleigh's room at the hospital early in the morning but was also told "family only."

"You didn't say a word at breakfast," as she placed a fresh cup of coffee on the desktop. Once again, she wondered if he had taken his medicines. However, this was another time that she didn't feel it wasn't correct to ask if he had.

"To be honest, Mary Elizabeth, I'm just sick about the Logan girl. She's such a smart, vibrant, pretty, nice young lady. And, losing Hondo is a major blow to our offense along with the loss of DeMarco Green on defense."

"So what are you going to do at quarterback,?" asked Dempsey's wife.

"That's easy, Mary. "Ty goes into our quarterback spot."

"Do you think Ty's going to be able to play after the beating he took,?" asked Mary Elizabeth.

"Knowing the kid as I think I do, I doubt we'll be able to hold him back," stated Dempsey. "He'll play his ass off and do a great job with the leadership role as well. He's been released from the hospital. He's going to have to be checked out and released by his own doctor. But, I doubt that will be a problem."

"And, at the defensive tackle spot,?" asked the head coach's wife.

"Big Julie has to step in there and play both ways for as long as he can."

"Wow,!" said the head coach's wife. "Those are some drastic changes."

"Honey, ...that's the best I can come up with! We've just run out of quality players."

The next morning, Ty, Hug and Big Julie went to the hospital to visit Hondo. "We came to see you even though you're a big pain in the ass get'n hurt," said Big Julie facetiously as the threesome walked into Hondo's hospital room.

"You're soft, Man," stated Hug. "I can't believe you're out because someone stepped on your foot." Ty smiled slightly but was not in the mood to verbally wrestle with anyone, even in jest. He was too worried about Kayleigh.

"Come on, Dudes," replied Hondo. "Didn't you see the size of that gorilla? He was twice the size of Big Julie."

"First of all, no one's twice the size of Big Julie," said Hug. "The truth is you're just too scared to play Eisenhower a second time. And, what you were really afraid of is having to go on that Death March again. You know, all that tough guy Raider stuff is nothing but plastic toy hats and black eye shadow make-up, don't you?"

"Man, you dudes come to see me and all you are is haters,!" stated Hondo as Hug, Big Julie and Ty smiled at their buddy. "And by the way, what the hell happened to your face," as Hondo stared at Ty. "You look like you ran into a giant juice blender."

"Let's just say we had a scrimmage in 'The Shops' parking lot with Ontario and his boys," said Big Julie as he dominated the conversation. Ty acted despondently.

"What's the matter, Ty," said Hondo as the injured quarterback recognized Ty's glum disposition.

"Kayleigh got hurt badly when Ontario and his buddies jumped the two of us," answered Ty. "She's in this hospital right now and is unconscious. She has a couple of broken ribs and a slashed, cut arm. Unfortunately, she looks far worse than me. I can only be thankful for Big Julie taking over the situation. If he wasn't there, I don't know what would have happened."

"I'm sorry to hear that," stated a shocked Hondo Rodriguez. "Who won the scrimmage,?" asked the now serious Hondo.

"Big Julie saw what was happening from 'The Malt Shop' and led the charge," stated Ty.

"So you guys won the battle, right,?" asked Hondo.

"That's the one thing we did do," said a sullen Tyler Douglas.

CHAPTER 76

Dempsey's wife knew not to disturb her husband when he was in the family room planning. It wasn't that he would get mad, or annoyed, with his wife or children. It was that he felt most productive when it was quiet and there were no distractions. And, of course, he now had the extra mental burden of worrying about Tyler Douglas and Kayleigh Logan.

"Here's your lunch, Sean."

"Uh-huh," was all she could get out of him. She noticed that the floor was covered with what looked like a load of wadded-up paper. She knew they were the offensive ideas that didn't make the cut. Actually, she wasn't worried about the large number of discarded thoughts and ideas now sitting on the floor as she observed her re-ignited husband scribbling thoughts rapidly. That was a good sign. Her biggest concern was that there weren't any thoughts or ideas in her husband's "Keep" box.

"Got'ta get to school, Mary Elizabeth," said Dempsey as the staff would soon convene in his classroom for the start of a new week of game planning.

"Here's dinner for everyone, Sean. I even had time to make a batch of brownies," she said with a bit of a forced smile. The four married coaches' wives took turns making a dinner for each Sunday evening's meeting so the coaches could avoid being slowed down in regard to their game planning efforts. Sunday evenings ran long enough for the coaches without taking extended dinner breaks.

CHAPTER 77

"So we're all in agreement,?" asked Dempsey at the coaches' staff meeting knowing his plan was the only reasonably workable possibility to replace Hondo.

"I don't see what else we can do," answered Rod Franklin. "At least we're going to get the ball in the hands of our best players. I just hope Ty is able to handle it right now mentally and physically after that gang attack."

"What other choice do we have,?" asked Coach Walters. "Billy Pierce is not experienced enough to run the offense yet. He's a great kid. But, he's not ready in any way."

"Well, it will be interesting to see how Ty and Hug react to all of this," said Dempsey. "I think Hug will be excited about carrying the football more and I'll bet anything that Ty's raring to get this opportunity to get back to the quarterback position." *Don't worry about Ty,* thought a wry, smirking Dempsey. *Our boy will be ready to go*!

Dempsey flew into the meeting room, three minutes late. "Sorry guys, but I got great news from Dr. Hoskins that I was sure you would want to know. Pete's sister Kayleigh is now conscious and alert. It looks that she's going to be fine physically. The mental aspect, after that beating, could take a while for her to heal."

"Don't worry about that girl, Coach," said Dino DeTaglia. "She's tougher than most of the people in this room."

Ty pursed his lips tightly, starring at the ground.

"Ty, that's great,!" said Kayleigh as Ty, the new quarterback visited her at the hospital. Her injuries, cuts and bruises were all showing her discomfort. "I'm so happy for you. You wanted to be the quarterback from the start. And now, when the team needs you the most, you're going to get your shot!"

Ty looked at Kayleigh with an unexpected look on his face. "Ty, you're not worried about taking over the quarterback spot, are you?"

"No, it's not that, Kayleigh. I just feel so bad about our getting jumped by Ontario and his thugs and you being hurt so badly because of me."

"This wasn't your fault, Ty. And, it could have been a lot worse," replied Kayleigh. "But my brother, Big Julie and the team had our backs. Besides, the doctor said other than some sore ribs, I'll be back in great shape in no time. The best thing about all of this is that bastard Ontario is being charged as an adult since he just turned 18 the other day."

"The important thing is for you to get better, Kayleigh. And then, make sure that your magic dust stuff is working for us again come game time," said Ty with a warm smile spread across his face. "I have a feeling you might need to sprinkle out all that's left!"

CHAPTER 78

"Let's break down all the video we have on these guys versus offenses whose styles are similar to ours. Then we'll study every single blitz Eisenhower has used," said Dempsey to his staff in the team meeting room. "I want a spread sheet study of how and why they blitz. There has to be a pattern somewhere. No one can be totally random no matter how much they may try. Remember, Coaches, they're going to blitz us on every down and I expect us to find a way to shut that blitz garbage down."

"We're going to blitz the shit out of them on every damn down,!" shouted out Don Watson, the General's head coach. "The only reason they scored at all in that first game is because we didn't blitz enough. And, that's because you wouldn't listen to me, Schermer, you dumb ass. Don't even worry about watching any of their game film. They couldn't handle us when we pressured them in the first game. They're certainly not going to be able to handle us now when we turn up the heat. Run these guys into the ground! Remember, they're garbage. Nothing but garbage. Grind up that garbage!"

"I was ready to punch you in the face when I didn't get exactly what I wanted in that first game, Schermer," said Watson as he glared at his defensive coordinator. "And, you know exactly what I'm talking about," as Watson poked him in the chest with his index finger. I told you then I wanted you to blitz on every down. It's your damn fault they scored at all!"

Watson's defensive coordinator fumed. *When this game's over, I'm going to tell this fool exactly what he can do with this job. If it wasn't for the kids, I'd walk out the door right now. How can some-one dealing with kids be such an ass?*

"Don't you dare give me a look like that, Coach," continued Watson. "You think I need you, don't you? I got more knowledge about defensive coaching in my pinkie than you'll ever have in your entire life! I don't need you and I never will."

"That's fine, Don," said an enraged Chris Schermer. "So good luck versus Roosevelt. I hope they stick it up your ass because that's exactly what you deserve. I quit,!" said the fed up assistant as he angrily turned to leave the room.

"Hey,!" screamed Watson. "Don't you dare turn your back on me. No one quits on me. You're fired, Buddy, and you'll never get another coaching job. I can promise you that!"

Schermer turned around slowly with a large, calculated grin on his face. "Do you know how many coaches would love to have me on their staff just for me to tell all the stories about what type of a farce you really are?"

CHAPTER 79

Since it was Monday, Dempsey's busiest class schedule day, he found it impossible to find time to talk to Ty about changing back to being a quarterback. When he walked onto the practice field, he saw Ty already wearing a quarterback's red practice jersey warming up his right throwing arm. *What's that saying,* thought Dempsey. *Great minds think alike.*

Whatever we do, thought the head coach, *we better find out a way to slow down the blitz or we'll get flat out overrun again.*

"Ok, Riders, it's time to get ourselves ready to roll versus our friends at Eisenhower." It was the opening team meeting of the championship game week. "You all know we'll have our work cut out for us getting ready for the Generals, especially without Hondo."

"How's he do'n, Coach D,?" asked Leotis.

"Eventually, he'll be fine. Having to put in pins will slow down his recovery. But once it's healed, he'll be as good as new."

"I'll bet Eisenhower will be fired up about him being injured," said Hug.

"I wouldn't doubt that," said Dempsey. "We just have to be thankful for Hondo that the injury isn't more serious."

"As you probably have already seen, stated the head coach, we're going to have to make some personnel and formation set adjustments. First of all, we're moving Ty to quarterback." The team gave out a chorus of "ooooooo's."

"Did you check that out with Kayleigh, Coach,?" asked Dino. "She's his agent now, ya know!"

"Thanks, Dino. I really appreciate that comment," said Ty with a wry smile appearing across his face."

"And, Hug will be our new tailback," continued Dempsey with a smile of his own on his face as a result of Dino and Ty's verbal discourse.

"Booo! No way! You got'ta be kid'n," chorused the team good naturedly throwing wadded up paper at the big running back.

"One other change is that Big Julie is going to take some reps at defensive tackle so we don't get caught short without enough defensive linemen," added Dempsey.

Another chorus of "ooooooo's" filled the room.

"That's right. That's right," said the huge offensive lineman as he stood up and urged the team on with his hands. "Get ready to see some real defensive line play this Friday!"

"O.K.," yelled Dempsey. "Let's calm down. If I didn't know better, I'd swear that you guys were the one's maxed out on coffee."

"Coach, we're just fired up to go win us a championship," shot back Jarvis Means.

"Yeah, we don't need no coffee to get ready for these creeps," added Dino.

"Quicker, Ty," shouted Dempsey as he stood beside a practice passing target net, not giving the new quarterback a drop of mercy. Eight footballs were strewn around Dempsey's feet so he could quickly snatch them up and toss simulated, rapid-fire shotgun snaps to Ty. It was Ty's job to throw short, accurate, hot type passes to the target simulating quick, anti-blitz throws. "Catch the snap, draw it up behind your ear and let it go! Fast! No hesitation! Release that ball so quickly that they don't have a chance to get to you even if we do turn a defender loose."

Dempsey relentlessly stayed on Ty, the new quarterback, to produce fast, accurate, anti-blitz throws. "You have to be on your game, Ty. You'll have pressure coming at you from all directions. You're going to get hit. You're going get knocked down. Expect that. Just be sure you get up and get back in the fight."

"I'm get'n worn out," Ty said to back-up quarterback, Billy Pierce. "I just hope Coach D doesn't kill me before I actually get to the game. He's wearing me out, Man. And, that's no joke."

"The man is a little tight," replied Billy.

"Ya think,?" asked Ty. "I don't think you could pound a pin up his ass with a sledge hammer."

"Get your head around faster," yelled Dempsey to his slot back, Rayshawn Davis. "Fire the ball at lightning speed and be tight with the throw, Ty. That will get Rayshawn to look for the ball quicker. You've got to do it right, Rayshawn! We're depending on you!"

"No, Bernardo,!" exploded Dempsey. "You've got to secure that front side gap before you turn backside. See what the front side nose guard and the front side linebacker are doing! Remember, you're first job is insuring the front side gap."

"We better get to Friday as fast as we can," stated Big Julie to Ty. "At this rate, that poor man's gon'na have a heart attack!"

CHAPTER 80

The stage had been set. The players had all been given passes to the locker room to, supposedly, have their pictures taken for the upcoming championship game. Once they were there, it seemed to take an awfully long time to get set. Finally, Dempsey told the players they all needed to go with him to the gym. When they went through the gym doors, the astonished football team saw that the Roosevelt's student body had already filled the bleacher seats. The band blasted out the Rough Rider fight song. The cheerleaders all chanted and flipped across the gym floor. The Rough Rider mascot threw bit-sized pieces of candy into the crowd. The pep rally was in full tilt, ready to rip.

"So this is what winning is all about," said Hug. "Hey, there's Jenny Clauson who Dino's in love with, I got'ta say, ...she is a hottie. Maybe I'll ask her out one of these days."

"Yeah, right," said Dino.

"I kind'a like the girl at the end," said Big Julie.

"The cheerleader at the end,?" asked Hug.

"Nah! The one in the band who's play'n the tuba."

"You really surprised me when you said you wanted to have a pep rally, Daryl," said Dempsey. "I never pictured you as a pep rally type of guy."

"That's because you've never been a principal. When you're a principal and something good happens, you do everything you can to get positive publicity. When you're at a Roosevelt, you work it doubly hard. And, by the way, how's Kayleigh doing."

"She's still hurting, that's for sure," answered Dempsey. "The doctors are most worried about her head aches. She does have a slight concussion. It's a good thing she's a tough kid."

The light, no pad Thursday practice finally came to an end and, for the players and assistant coaches, not a moment too soon. Dempsey had been a wild man all week. It seemed like he saw every small mistake made in practice, offensively, defensively and on special teams. As soon as a mistake was made, he was all over it.

"You Guys have worked your tails off all week. There's no doubt about that" stated Dempsey.

"More like he tried to kill us," mumbled Hug. "My entire body aches."

"I've got a surprise for you," continued Dempsey.

"Oh no," moaned Big Julie. "Now he's gon'na make us run on a Thursday."

"That, or he's gon'na make us watch that Eisenhower blitz video again for the two thousandth time," stated Ty.

"Hey! Do you three numbskulls want to do a little extra running for the team since you're so interested in having a separate discussion?"

"Oh, sorry, Coach. We were just trying to be sure everyone was quiet so they could hear what you had to say," said Big Julie.

"Big Julie, you're so full of it," said Dempsey as the entire team laughed. "At this rate, you're going to drive ME crazy!"

We're going to drive HIM crazy,? thought Ty. *Coach has everyone walking around right now with a twitch. Another week of this and the whole team would need to see the school psychologist*!

"Anyhow, the surprise is that some of the parents have been nice enough to sponsor a special dinner for us after practice. Hondo's parents are bringing their Burrito Bus which I know you'll all enjoy."

"All right! Big Time,!" came some of the excited calls from the team.

"Oh, man,!" complained Big Julie. "There goes my stomach."

"What'cha mean,?" asked Hug. "You got a cast iron stomach."

"Ya' know," replied Big Julie, "I actually have a delicate stomach and sometimes Mexican food can give me a little gas."

"First of all," said Hondo as he hobbled around using his new crutches, "...the word 'delicate' has nothing to do with your stomach and when you pass gas it ain't a little. It clears out the entire locker room. You flat out stink, Man!"

The dinner was excellent and thoroughly enjoyed by the players and coaches. "Man, I love these tamales," said Hug. "I could eat a dozen all by myself."

"You're starting to sound like Big Julie," said Ty. "By the way, where is the big man?"

"When I last saw him, he was sitting on a box on the other side of my family's Burrito Bus," said Hug. "He had a large bowl sitting between his legs and was shoveling some beans into his mouth with a large serving spoon."

"We got'ta check this out," said Hondo. Dino, Ty, and Hondo, assisted by Hug, all hustled to get around the Burrito Bus to see what Big Julie was up to.

"Dang," yelled out the big tackle as he used a dishtowel to try to wipe off the large, brown stain from the beans he had slobbered onto his white shirt. As the four friends worked their way up to the immense man, they saw Big Julie toss the towel to the ground in annoyance and then continue to shovel the beans into his mouth.

"Julie, you're not eat'n that giant bowl of frijoles all by yourself, are you,?" said Hondo. "You eat too much of that and you'll explode!"

Big Julie smiled at his buddies. He then leaned over to one side and let go a gargantuan, smelly, fart. “RRRRUUUUPPPPP!” This quickly scattered his four friends in all directions noisily leaving Big Julie alone to laugh and continue eating his bean feast.

CHAPTER 81

Sean Dempsey wore a dress shirt and tie for the first time since the first day of school. Actually, he had a sports coat draped over his left arm as well as he banged around the kitchen trying to find his car keys. He had been wide awake since 4:30 a.m. He was awoken by another of his P.T.S.D. dreams. However, this particular dream was not the normal, horrific, dreadful type of dream that he had been painfully experiencing so often over the past, few years.

Dempsey dreamt that he was lying on the ground after the gate explosion at the Afghanistan compound. After shaking his head to clear the cobwebs from his mind, he felt his body to see if he was wounded. Strangely, he felt no pain as he abruptly sat up to assess the situation. He found himself alone, by himself, with the exception of Corporal Bo Harris, Sean's best buddy and brother-in-arms. Bo was squatted down, leaning back against the compound wall. He was smiling as he blew out smoke from the cigarette he was holding, "About time you woke up," said Bo. "I thought you were in for a long nap."

"Bo, we got to get out of here," stated Dempsey as he scrambled to get off the ground. "Where the hell are we?"

"We're just about finished with our mission, Sean. The new kid, Westy, just pulled one of our wounded guys back for some cover. He'll be back in a second to help you. By the way, the mission was a success."

"Let's get out of here, Bo," as Dempsey turned to draw back to the rest of the squad.

"You get along, Sean," as Dempsey looked back at his buddy.

"I'm gon'na kick it for a few more minutes till I finish my smoke. But, don't worry. I'll catch up with you down the road. I promise. Just remember, Sean. I'll always have your back, Buddy."

"Where you going,?" asked Mary Elizabeth as Dempsey tried to sneak out of the house without waking up his wife and children. "You're not going anywhere till I get to give you a good luck kiss. Want me to make you some breakfast? Pancakes? Sausage?"

"That sounds great, Hon," replied Dempsey, "...but I really feel I need to get to school early. I'll get some coffee and a bacon and egg sandwich at Doug's Deli. I have that pre-school interview with some of the T.V. stations and one of the radio stations. Getting in early will give me some time to watch some more video."

Mary Elizabeth smiled and laughed lightly at her husband. "Sean, you have every one of those videos memorized by now. But, I understand, Sweetheart. You get to school but give me a call later so I know how things are going. Now, get out of here before I decide to tie you down and keep you here longer," as she gave her man a peck on the cheek.

"Oh, and I had another one of my dreams," said Dempsey as he started to leave through the kitchen door. His wife cringed suddenly. "Don't worry, Honey. It wasn't a bad one. I just think Bo wanted to tell me something else."

CHAPTER 82

"You want the regular, Coach," said Dick Wylie, the owner of Dick's Deli.

"You got that right, Dick," answered Dempsey. "Can't change now."

"Yeah, I guess you can't, can you," replied Dick. "And, this is on me, Coach."

"You don't have to do that, Dick. But, thank you. That's real nice of you."

"Don't worry about it, Coach. As it is, I'm trying to soften you up to allow me to name the sausage, Swiss cheese and egg sandwich a Dempsey Delight for my Breakfast Board menu after you win the championship tonight.

"Coach, you've had an unbelievable season as a first-year head coach after being away from the sport for eight years," stated Lainey Boldin from KZAR-5 Television at the early morning, pre-game press conference in the Roosevelt High School cafeteria. "How have you been able to meet such success?"

"By having an excellent staff and a great group of kids who were able to put up with me," said Dempsey with a smile and a chuckle. "And, I know that wasn't easy to do at times. This has been a wonderful group to work with. This season has been a tremendous experience amidst many challenging highs and lows."

"Do you really think you have much of a chance to win tonight against a powerhouse championship program that crushed you the first game of the season by 21-points," said Ike Shackleford, sports-writer for the Chicago Tribune.

A slightly annoyed Sean Dempsey responded to the negative sounding question. "I think anyone who makes it to the Greater City Conference Championship Game has a legitimate chance to win," answered the Rough Riders head coach. "This is a great conference. There's tremendous balance. The excellent, overtime game between Eisenhower and JFK just proved that."

"So, you feel that way even though you've lost your starting quarterback, an explosive player who has been so productive all season,?" asked Shackleford as he continued to probe for pre-game information.

"Ike, we darn well know what we're going up against when we take the field versus Eisenhower. We're not kidding ourselves. We'll be fielding 27 players tonight versus a powerhouse football team that has a roster of 80. The amazing thing is that there's little fat on that 80-man roster. They're loaded with excellent players and have excellent depth."

"And, yes, we've lost our excellent starting quarterback for the game," continued Dempsey testily. "Win or lose, we'll come to play and I guarantee you we'll play hard, very hard. In the end, win or lose, that's all we can do. The most important thing for me is to be sure that we fire all of our bullets for 48-minutes so that when the smoke clears, we can be proud to be Rough Riders."

"So, it seems that you're going into this game with a dose of reality then. Would you say that's true Coach,?" continued the prying Schackleford.

"Ike, do you know who Shug Jordan was?"

"I think he was a great, old-time college basketball coach," answered the newspaper reporter.

"Well, he did coach basketball at Auburn and Georgia for fifteen years in the 30's and 40's. However, he's known for more of his football coaching career at Auburn during the 50's, 60's and 70's. Anyhow, one of my favorite quotes is from Shug. He said, 'Always remember that Goliath was a forty-point favorite over David.'"

CHAPTER 83

When the interviews were over, Dempsey quickly walked down the hall from the main office to get to his classroom in time for the home room attendance roll. He still held his sports coat as it draped over his left arm with his tie tucked away in his inside coat pocket. As he made the right hand turn to get to his classroom hallway, he suddenly heard yelling and screaming and saw an avalanche of frantic students running in his direction. He jumped to the side of the hallway and physically inched forward in an effort to get to his classroom. Once there, he quickly saw an empty room.

Marge!

Dempsey fought his way through the remainder of the students fleeing to get away from the confrontation he was about to see. As he entered Marge Strausser's classroom, he saw his teaching buddy make a slow, dizzy, unstable turn towards the classroom door. She held her right arm as her dress sleeve was drenched in blood. The head coach sprinted to the teacher, catching her as she started to fall to the classroom floor. Dempsey was immediately able to see blood pulsating and squirting through the long tear in her dress's right arm sleeve as he gently laid her down to the floor.

"SOMEONE CALL 911,!" yelled out Dempsey to no one specifically. The coach quickly tore off his white dress shirt and tie and used them to directly apply pressure to Strausser's arm wound. "911, call 911," repeated Dempsey.

"I didn't mean to do that,!" yelled out JaQuire Abraham. "She got in the way, Man! I didn't mean to hurt her,!" stated the student as he held his switchblade knife in a threatening fashion towards the face of Jesus Morales. Three other Hispanic students were bottled up behind Jesus. "I really didn't mean to hurt her! But, I'm still gon'na carve up this Spic's face."

"Put that knife down, Son," ordered Dempsey in a firm, but calming, voice.

"Whoa," said Coach Walters haltingly, now back in his normal school time role as a security officer as he entered the classroom. Behind him was a teacher, Marie Kelly and the principal, Daryl Hoskins.

"Let's everyone take it easy right now," ordered Dempsey as the nervous JaQuire continued to yield the threatening knife in front of Morales's face. Mrs. Kelly, please take over for me and keep applying pressure to Mrs. Strausser's arm. Coach Walters, please call for EMT assistance immediately. Dr. Hoskins, we might be needing more help."

"On it,!" said Hoskins. "JaQuire, you need to listen to Coach Dempsey. He's here to help you now, Son," as the principal stepped back outside to make cell calls in the hallway.

"Huh! No one's here to help me and you know it," replied JaQuire.

"JaQuire, I am here to help you," said Dempsey as he turned over the pressure being provided to Strausser's arm to Mrs. Kelly. "But, first of all, it would be best for everybody if you let the other three students go, JaQuire. It doesn't seem like you have any beef with them. We don't need any innocent people getting hurt."

After a short, pensive delay, JaQuire responded, still acting in a nervous, threatening fashion with the knife in his hand. "They can go. I have no problem with these Beaners."

Dempsey calmly signaled for the three students to circumvent the scrap. "Every one go slowly," said Dempsey as he put a forced smile on his face.

"Not you," countered JaQuire as Morales attempted to join the other three students. "We still have business to finish."

"JaQuire, do you really want to hurt somebody,?" asked Dempsey. "You already hurt your teacher by accident and I can tell you're feeling badly about that." As the coach made that point, the paramedics, housed across the street from the school, noisily entered the classroom. Seeing the knife altercation, they quickly quieted their efforts.

"They're just here to help Mrs. Strausser, JaQuire," stated Dempsey. "I know you want her to get some help."

"I really didn't want to hurt her. I really didn't," said the now teary-eyed student.

"Give me the knife, JaQuire," said Dempsey. "That way this situation won't get worse."

"Not till I carve up this Spic's face," stated JaQuire.

"No, JaQuire," said Dempsey evenly and calmly. "You really don't want to do that. You're a good person who just got caught up in a mess. Let me help you. Let me have the knife, Son."

The teen suddenly started to tremble. He then slowly lowered his hand as tears now started falling down his face. Dempsey slowly reached out and gently took the knife. JaQuire collapsed into one of the school desks and cried.

Hell of a job, said Bo Harris as the former sergeant, Sean Dempsey, looked up to see his corporal smashing out the remains of his lit cigarette on the bottom of his shoe in the corner of the class room. *You did good Sarge saving your teaching buddy and that troubled kid. I'm proud of you. You did good, Sarge, ...real good.*

Dempsey looked at Bo in amazement. He closed his eyes and shook his head briskly and focused back on Bo. But Bo was gone once again.

"Addie, please get Mary Dempsey on the phone for me," requested Daryl Hoskins of his administrative assistant. "And, get ahold of Coach Franklin as well. "Tell him I'd like to see him here as soon as possible."

"Mary Elizabeth, this is Daryl Hoskins calling. We had an incident here at Roosevelt and Sean helped us out tremendously. He's fine and he wanted me to let you know as soon as I could. He's with the police now helping with the report. Otherwise, he would have called himself."

"Did he get hurt, Daryl?"

"No, but he needs for you to bring down a complete set of clothing for him," replied the principal.

"Did he get dirty or something?"

"No, Mary Elizabeth. All of the clothing he has on him are stained with blood. Fortunately, it's not his."

"Rod, you're Sean's top assistant. I need for you to stick with Sean for the rest of the day," stated Hoskins. "Make sure we dot every I and cross every T until kickoff. I'm sure Sean is going to be distracted. He has a lot of confidence in you so I know you will be a big help. You know how I worry about him."

"I'll stay on top of everything, Daryl," stated Franklin. "I know why you're worried, boss. But, to be honest with you, I have a strong feeling that Sean will do the same great job tonight as he did today."

"This is Curtis Neally, from KJAZ-11 Television. What you're watching here on the screen behind me is a blood-soaked Sean Dempsey, the Head Football Coach at Roosevelt High School here in Latimore Heights. It was this morning that Coach Dempsey came to the aid of a fellow Roosevelt teacher, a Margaret Strausser, who was stabbed by an unnamed Roosevelt High student. It is reported that Coach Dempsey stopped excessive bleeding by Strausser. He then talked the alleged student, who was threatening another student with a knife, to surrender. It seems that black and Hispanic racial overtones were the cause of the conflict. This is the same Sean Dempsey who is the head coach at Roosevelt Rough Riders who play for The Greater City Championship tonight against the perennial champion Eisenhower Generals. Strausser is listed in stable condition at Queen of the Most Holy Rosary Hospital."

"Not a great way for a head coach to get ready for a championship game, Dan," continued Neally. "Back to you, Dan, in the studio."

Daryl Hoskins, the beleaguered looking principal, entered the coaches' locker room looking for his teacher and coach. The first thing he noticed was the pile of blood-stained clothing sitting on the tile floor as Dempsey stepped out of one of the shower stalls.

"Sean, ...Rod," said the principal. "How's it going, Guys,?" he asked somberly.

"We're hanging in there," answered Dempsey as he dried himself off. "How are you doing, Chief?"

"I'm really not sure," answered the frazzled looking principal.

"I feel I know where you're coming from, Daryl. That was a

flashback to my soldiering days. I'm just glad that it seems that Marge will be O.K."

"You did a great service for Marge and this school this morning, Sean. And, just like I told you on my first phone call, I needed a teacher and coach who could physically and mentally handle himself at a school like Roosevelt. You certainly did that today and I wanted to let you know how much I realize and appreciate that, Old Friend. Thank you."

Hoskins strongly urged calling in a substitute teacher for Dempsey for the rest of the school day. The head coach politely and calmly refused such assistance. He did miss teaching the first two of his five classes as he waited for his wife to arrive with clean clothing. Dempsey now calmly and quietly, sat at his desk waiting for his next class of students to arrive. He displayed no feelings of agitation or depression nor did he reach into his briefcase for his headache medications. If anything, the ex-Army sergeant felt steadily in control for the first time in a long time. He was back from his mission having helped save one of his own soldiers in the form of his buddy teacher, Margaret Strausser. He now felt confidently prepared to lead his football troops versus the Eisenhower Generals that evening with the championship at hand.

First a battered mugging and then a blood-stained assault all in the span of a week, thought Dempsey. *Daryl's right. Roosevelt High School is one tough place, to say the least. This is surreal.*

CHAPTER 84

Dempsey sat by himself behind the bus driver on each away game trip. For some reason, he liked being tucked away behind the bus driver in the seat closest to the window with the entire team behind him. Coach Franklin sat in a similar seat on the opposite side of the bus. But, first it was Franklin's job to stand outside the parked player bus to check off the team roster as the players boarded.

As the players climbed the bus's stairwell, they immediately made eye contact with their head football coach. All well knew about what had happened that morning. Each player softly uttered "Coach" or "Coach D" as almost all of the players nodded their heads towards him in acknowledgement of his feat. Some stuck out a hand to shake or bump fists. The head coach gave each player a quick nod in return with a slight smile and a first name recognition for each. The only person to say anything of substance was Ty Douglas.

"That was big time, Coach D," stated Ty. "Are you doing O.K.?"

"You know, I'm doing just fine, Ty. Thanks for asking."

"Your team has your back, Coach. Riders together."

"I know that Ty. Thank you. Riders together."

CHAPTER 85

The Rough Riders' bus pulled up on the south side of Eisenhower's open campus, the opposite side of the Greater City Conference Championship Game. The location was directly opposite the normal drop-off point of visiting teams when playing the Generals. The bus driver let the players and coaches off, waited five minutes as per Coach Dempsey's directions and then drove on.

The Rough Riders stole through the campus with its buildings shielding off the near five thousand, crazed, Generals fans waiting to harass the visitors on Eisenhower's infamous "Death March." The team entered the gymnasium, housing the visitors' locker room, through a back door opened by Old Irv, as planned. At the same time, an empty Roosevelt school bus pulled up to the normal, team debarkation spot at the curb leading to the walkway of the "Death March." The mass of the nasty, green and white clad Generals' fans stood dumbfounded when the empty school bus door was opened.

"Sean, I have an important quick call for you," stated Daryl Hoskins as he held up his cell phone for Dempsey to grab.

"It's not another news reporter, is it,?" asked Dempsey.

"Not quite," answered Hoskins with a huge smile spread across his face.

"Sean, this is Marge," said Dempsey's buddy teacher. Her voice was definitely not the strong, booming quality he was used to hearing from her. "Thank you, Sean. Thank you so much for helping me."

"I'm glad I was able to be of assistance, Marge," stated Dempsey. "It's great to hear your voice. I'm just glad that you're so tough, Girl."

"I don't feel so tough right now," said Marge meekly.

"You'll be fine, Marge. I know you will."

"It sounds like I owe you a new shirt."

"Naw! We'll let Dr. Hoskins take care of that."

"Good luck in the championship game, Sean."

"Thank you, Marge."

"And by the way. Who are you playing?"

CHAPTER 86

CHAMPIONSHIP GAME: EISENHOWER GENERALS

Dempsey had no thought about giving a long, pre-game, rah-rah, pep-talk as the players all took a knee in front of him. *"Well, at least Marge is O.K. Now it's time to take care of my boys. I have a feeling this one's going to be a tough one.* "I really don't have to say much to you for this game, do I?"

"No, Sir," answered the players.

"Here's what I want you to do," said the Rough Rider leader. "I want you all to close your eyes. I'm not kidding. Right now, close your eyes. I want you to visualize the pile of concrete blocks in our locker room. See the seven Victory Blocks on the pile right now, Adams, Garfield, Grant, Kennedy, Washington, Lincoln and Van Buren."

"Now, I want you to visualize what was painted on the wall at the top of that stack today. What does it say?"

"CHAMPIONS,!" shouted out the team.

"Play hard, play fast and play smart," said Dempsey. "Bring it up. Break'em, Ty."

"One, two, three..."

"RIDERS TOGETHER!"

"This is Ralph Phillips from KJAX-11 Television with color commentator Bill Travers. We're bringing you the Greater City Championship Game between the perennial champion Eisenhower Generals and this year's surprising Cinderella team, the Roosevelt Rough Riders."

"Surprising is definitely the word, Ralph," said Bill Travers. "Coach Sean Dempsey has done a marvelous job of reviving a football program that has not won a game in four years."

"What we have, Bill, is a team with a 26-game win streak and seven Greater City Conference Championships in a row, the Eisenhower Generals. On the other side, we have an upstart group with a 43-game losing streak going into their season opener, the Roosevelt Rough Riders," said Phillips.

"And, that opener for Roosevelt was against these same Generals, in a game that was won handily by Eisenhower in the season's opener," commented Travers. "And, just this morning, Ralph, KJAX-11 television learned that Roosevelt's fine option quarterback, Hernando Rodriguez, was hurt in last week's game versus Van Buren requiring surgery for a foot injury. Unfortunately, he will not be able to play today."

"That's a terrible break for Roosevelt," said Phillips. "Hondo, as he's called, has been the sparkplug of the spread offense of Coach Dempsey's Rough Riders all season long. They'll miss his tremendous speed and ball handling abilities with those two excellent running backs, Hug Wilson and Ty Douglas."

"That leaves the Rough Riders with young, sophomore Billy Pierce to carry the quarterback load for Roosevelt tonight," added Travers. "Billy has seen very little action for the Riders this season which does not bode well for Roosevelt."

"And, for those of you who haven't heard, Head Coach Sean Dempsey came to the aid of a fellow, female teacher who had been stabbed by a Roosevelt student just this morning," said Phillips.

"Dempsey applied initial emergency medical aid and then talked the student into surrendering the knife he used to stab the teacher," added Travers. "The female teacher is listed in serious condition. Such experiences help to better put our lives in perspective, Ralph. I've only met Sean Dempsey once. But he certainly seems to be a good man. Kudos to Coach Dempsey as he now takes on the challenge of the Eisenhower Generals in this Greater City Championship Game."

"There has also been some intrigue in the Eisenhower Generals' camp," stated Phillips.

"That's right, Ralph," added Travers. "And, a bit of a controversy at that. Chris Schermer, Eisenhower's fine defensive coordinator, has resigned this week. He stepped down, reportedly, over disputed game plan philosophies for the upcoming championship game against the Rough Riders with Coach Don Watson."

"Coach Watson says it was a firing, Bill, on an explosive interview with the KJAX-11's Evening Sports News Show last night."

"One way or another, that can't help the Generals even though Coach Watson, himself, has stated he's taking over the defensive play calling role for the championship game. We're going to take a short break here. This is Ralph Phillips and KJAX-11 Television with today's Greater City Conference Championship Game between the Eisenhower Generals and the Roosevelt Rough Riders. We'll be right back."

"This is going to be one crumby game, isn't it,?" asked Travers.

"I'm afraid so, Bill," answered Phillips. "Roosevelt has surprised some people but I don't think that's going to happen for them today. Not with a quarterback who hasn't played a lick this season."

CHAPTER 87

Dempsey looked out and scanned the game field, studying the freshly cleaned uniforms and the touched-up, painted helmets that shimmered under the stadium lights. He then glanced at the large crowd of fifteen thousand plus fans working their way into the stadium all wearing the dark green and white of Eisenhower or the black and gold garb of Roosevelt. *This sure beats pounding nails into two-by-fours,* thought the first-year head coach as a warm smile spread across his face.

Come game time, most head coaches like to lead their bunched-up teams onto their stadium sideline area. Such head coaches would, normally, give one last rousing word of encouragement and then lead, hopefully, his excited players onto the game field to the roar of their fans and, probably, the jeers of their opposition. Sean Dempsey felt more comfortable letting his captains excitably lead the charge onto the field as he followed his team from behind at a jog.

Since Roosevelt was the visitor, Dempsey was expecting an outpour of booing and chastisement from the dark green and white Eisenhower fanatical fan base. As the visiting Rough Riders entered the stadium, he quickly noticed an almost deadly silence from the crowd with the scant exception of the small group of rowdy Roosevelt rooters stuck in the far, back corner of the stadium. Initially, he thought it might be some form of an Eisenhower fan ploy such as the Death March used back in the first Roosevelt-Eisenhower meeting of the season in September. Suddenly, the home town crowd nearest Dempsey started politely applauding from their seats. Like a wave on both sides of the field, the

Eisenhower crowd first clapped and then stood and clapped. As Dempsey advanced towards his gathered team, he was approached by his top assistant coach.

"What the hell is this all about, Rod,?" asked Dempsey. "Is it some form of trick or something?"

"No. Not at all, Sean," answered Franklin as he smiled. "Sean, they're applauding your action from this morning. You came to the aid of a distressed teacher who had just been stabbed by a student and in your successfully disarming the student so others could be safe. And, I'm sure, there's probably a measure of them respecting your turning around the worst football program in the state in one season."

"So, what should I do now, Rod?"

"Just tip your hat casually to each side of the stadium."

"You're kidding, Rod. Aren't you?"

"No, Sean. I'm not. So just tip your hat quickly so we can get ready to win this thing."

Sean Dempsey tipped his cap quickly to each side of the field as the applause continued.

CHAPTER 88

"Remember, Billy. You're going to go with the first team during warm-ups," instructed Dempsey. "And all the reps will be with Hug and Ty in a split back, shotgun alignment. We're going to hide the Pistol action for as long as we can. No sense giving Eisenhower any extra time to make adjustments."

"Got'cha, Coach," said the nervous, young, backup quarterback.

On the opening kick-off, with a deafening roar of the crowd, Eisenhower received the football. Maurice Hightower, their speedy cornerback took the kick-off on the 15-yard line and headed up field.

"Hightower finds a crease," announced Phillips. "He's up to the thirty, the forty, the fifty."

"Oh no," mumbled Dempsey. "We can't start this way!" *Damn it! How did we let this happen!*

"He's in the open,!" shouted Phillips. "He's going all the way! T-o-u-c-h-o-w-n, Eisenhower! 85 untouched yards by the speedster, Maurice Hightower!"

"We sure didn't need that," stated a quickly deflated Dempsey. Getting off to a fast start was, the Rough Rider coaches believed, a major key to an upset victory. "O.K., Riders. Let's go and get those points back."

"That's the way to shove it up their butts, Generals," said Watson. "Keep it up! Keep putting pressure on them. They'll crack in no time. Lay the wood to them right off the bat! Don't let them breathe."

"O.K., O.K.,!" yelled Dempsey. "Let's go out there and execute. It's going to be a long game, Gentlemen. There's a lot more football left for us to knock these guys off."

On the ensuing kick-off, the Eisenhower kicker drilled the football all the way to the Rough Riders' goal line. Rayshawn Davis waited for the ball to drop down to him. He tried to look down to see where the best return lane was developing. This forced him to take his eyes off the football for a split second before he was about to make the catch.

"Davis bobbles the ball! It's loose on-the-ground,!" yelled Phillips. "There's a mad skirmish on about the one-yard line. Who has it, Bill?"

"The Rough Riders have it,!" stated Travers. "That would have meant total catastrophe for the Rough Riders."

"Whew! This is too much excitement for me. We haven't even played a full minute of this game, Bill."

"Well, you better calm down, partner. I have a feeling this is going to be one, wild game."

"Roosevelt's falling apart already," said Phillips once they were off the air. "Too bad the championship wasn't the Eisenhower, Kennedy game. That was a hell of a battle."

"Let's take a shot," said Dempsey. "I don't think they'll be anticipating a play action pass on the one-yard line. Maybe we can get out of the hole quickly. Ready to crank up that gun of yours, Ty?"

"Yeah, I'm ready," answered the confident, substitute quarterback. *I've been waiting for 10 games. I wasn't sure what to expect being a Rough Rider but it sure has been a trip. Now it's time to finish this story. Like Kayleigh says, it's time to use some of that magic dust stuff, that's for sure.*

"Roosevelt breaks their huddle. Wing to the left. Twins set to the right," announced Phillips.

"Hey, Ralph," said Travers. "That's not Billy Pierce at quarterback. That's Ty Douglas, the outstanding Roosevelt running back."

"And that's Hug Wilson behind Douglas, Ralph. Roosevelt's aligned in a Pistol set."

"Douglas takes the snap," announced Phillips. "He gives the ball to Wilson. No! It's a play action fake! Seamus Collins is wide open on a streak route from the slot position. Douglas launches a beauty! Collins has it! He's in the open! To the 50, the 40, the 30, the 20, the ten! T-o-u-c-h-d-o-w-n, Roosevelt! A spectacular 99-yard touchdown pass from Douglas to Collins!"

"That's a heck of a way to start your career at quarterback for Roosevelt," said Bill Travers. "That pass was perfect. He hit Collins right in stride allowing the speedy wide receiver to burn up the turf."

"It was just like you said, Bill. That wasn't any just a get-the-ball-to-him type throw," added Phillips. "That was one big-time pass! What a way to open up a game. We aren't into this game for a full minute and the score's 7-7. Hold on to your hats, Ladies and Gentlemen! This looks like we could be in for a barnburner."

"Atta boy, Ty!," yelled Dempsey. "Hell of a throw!"

"Great pass, Ty,!" yelled the still battered and bruised Kayleigh Logan from her seat in the stands sitting between Kayleigh's and Ty's mothers. "His first throw as a Roosevelt quarterback and he throws a truly great deep pass!"

"That's my boy," said Ty's choked-up mother. "Keep it up, Son."

"That's the way to shove it down their throats, Ty," growled Daryl Hoskins. "Let it rip, Kid!"

"That stinks to high heaven,!" screamed Watson. "I told you I wanted a shutout, Coaches! I guess firing the defensive coordinator wasn't enough. Get that garbage straightened out or I'll fire all of you idiots!"

"And people wonder why he leads the conference in the number of assistant coaches that go through his program," mumbled one of Watson's assistants.

"What's that, Coach,?" asked Watson as he heard the assistant coach grumbling.

"Just said we got to put the brakes on these guys," lied the assistant.

"Yeah, I'll bet that's what you said."

"Now cut the crap,!" screamed Coach Watson to the Generals' offensive players. "Let's pound this one directly at them and start shutting the door right now." Eisenhower did pound the football down the Rough Riders' throats, running the football directly at Roosevelt to up the score to a 14-7 lead halfway through first quarter.

"I told you these guys would fold their tent if you put some pressure on them," said Watson. "They got lucky on that pass play, that's all."

Actually, Roosevelt didn't fold their tent. Instead, Ty Douglas went to work slicing and dicing the General's defense. He may have played running back all fall but the experienced quarterback quickly, and efficiently, fell back in line with his old quarterbacking skills. "Douglas keeps the ball," said Phillips. "He bursts up field for a nine-yard gain."

"He's an explosive kid, Ralph. The Generals better make sure they don't give him too many good running lanes.

"Douglas gives the ball to Wilson," announced Phillips. "He's stopped for a four... No! Wilson spins out of the grasp of a General's defender and bulls his way forward for another eight yards and another Rough Rider first down."

"The Rough Riders sure look smooth for a group that just put in a new offense in one week," added Travers.

"Douglas gives. NO, he keeps the ball! He breaks back inside, cuts up field. He's in the open! 30, 20, ten, five. T-o-u-c-h-d-o-w-n, Roosevelt!"

"Douglas is a lot faster than I thought, Ralph."

"And how about his throwing, Bill? This kid looks like a big-time college prospect right now and he's only a junior. And, the score's 14-14 as we end the first quarter."

"Wow,!" said Ralph Phillips as he checked to make sure the microphone was turned off. "I don't know how long Roosevelt can keep this up but that was one hell of a first quarter for both teams.

"Surprised the heck out of me, I can tell you that," said Travers.

CHAPTER 89

At the start of the second quarter, with the Generals in the red zone driving for another touchdown, cornerback Leotis Brown studied the quarterback's eye movement as the passer set up to throw. Leotis cut to the ball's throw path as the quarterback released the football. The cornerback had a good interception angle to the flight of the ball but was just short of being able to make a clean pick. As a result, Leotis slapped the football into the air. Fortunately for Leotis, the slapped football popped up into the air giving him the ability to reach out and make a diving interception.

"Damn-it,!" barked Watson. "What the hell kind of a pass was that,?" yelled Watson at his quarterback as the player hustled off the field. "I'll tell you what kind of pass that was. It was a shitty pass, Wickham! A totally shitty pass! All-State my ass! You're playing like a jackass. Get the hell out of my sight. I'm sick of you!"

On the first play after the interception, Ty threw a post-corner route to Wooley Woolridge for a 28-yard gain. "Nice job, Wooley," shouted out Ty. "Great route! Keep it up, Wooley. Keep it up!"

On the next play, Ty kept the ball again on an option play for thirteen yards as Big Julie crushed the play side linebacker into the backside linebacker to block two defenders with one block. On the next play, Ty dumped a pass off to Hug on a swing route. Hug bowled over a cornerback for a 17-yard gain. "Great run, Hug." stated Ty as Hug jogged back to the huddle. "You crushed those dudes!"

Ty and Hug each ran the ball on the next two plays. Both gained three yards as the football was now well into Rough Rider scoring range. On a third-and-four situation, the Rough Rider right tackle,

Eddie Holloway, missed a block on the outside linebacker resulting in a sack on Ty and a five-yard loss. A field goal attempt by Bodie Swenson was wide right resulting in no points.

"That's all right, Bodie. We'll get those points back,!" said Ty as the place kicker hung his head at the failed attempt. *Damn! We can't blow such scoring opportunities against these guys. We need every point we can get just to stay in this thing.*

"A nice drive by Roosevelt goes all for naught as they come away empty handed," said Phillips.

"I still like what I'm seeing here from the Rough Riders, Ralph," said Travers. "And, Douglas has been a man among boys so far today. Eisenhower hasn't been able to stop him."

"Green, Texas, green, Texas," barked Eisenhower's quarterback. He took the snap, executed an effective run fake and dropped back to set up for a play action pass. The flanker ran a deep post route to hold the Rough Riders' cornerback and safety. This opened up a deep out and up route by the flexed tight end. A mix-up in coverage between Leotis Brown and Pete Logan allowed the post route to come wide open.

"Uh oh," said Coach Franklin. "The post is open!" The flanker never had to break stride for the perfectly thrown football. He scampered for 72 yards untouched for another Eisenhower touchdown. The Rough Riders were now down 21-14 in the middle of the second quarter.

"I want more of that," yelled Watson to his offensive coordinator. "They can't stop the run. They can't stop the pass. They stink! Bury this crud, Coach! Just keep scoring! Pound these animals into the ground!"

Down by seven, Ty went right back to work. "Douglas hands off to Wilson," announced Phillips. "No, it's a play action fake. Douglas throws a deep out to Woolridge, complete for a 17-yard gain."

"Douglas keeps on the option. He breaks to the outside. He's up the sideline for a pickup of 16-yards."

"Douglas is on a roll, Ralph," said Travers with a grin as he began to enjoy the quarterback's run and pass style.

"A give to Hug Wilson for six more, Bill. The big horse is bowling people over."

"What a great one, two punch for the Rough Riders," said Travers. "Got to hand it to Sean Dempsey, the Roosevelt Head Coach. So far, the drastic offensive adjustment is paying out in full dividends."

"The Rough Riders line up with a bunched formation to the right," stated Phillips. "Single split end left. Douglas, in the Pistol set, takes the snap and throws a bullet to Collins. The ball hits Collins in the chest! The ball pops up in the air! A white shirted General has it! It's Maurice Hightower! He's all by himself. T-o-u-c-h-d-o-w-n, Generals! Eisenhower now has a commanding two touchdown lead, 27-14."

"The P.A.T. is good making the score 28–14," added Travers. "This is not what the Rough Riders needed, Ralph. They needed to play an almost error free game to have a chance to win this one. This Pick-Six by Eisenhower certainly doesn't help."

CHAPTER 90

"Stay cool, Guys," said Ty as the second quarter was starting to run out of minutes. "We can do this! A touch or a field goal will put us right back in it going in at half. Be ready for a Clock play." Ty threw a quick pass to Woolridge on the first play of the series for an easy nine-yard gain. Hug then carried on an option run for four yards and a first down. Ty then threw another strike to Wooley on a wide receiver screen. Wooley burst up field for a quick eight-yard gain before he was blasted by the Generals' play side strong safety.

"Fumble,!" yelled Phillips. "The ball's scooped up by the Generals! It's Maurice Hightower, again! He's to the 30, the 20 and is knocked out of bounds by Douglas at the 14-yard line!"

"This is not good for Roosevelt," stated Travers.

"Not good at all, Ralph. The Rough Riders can ill afford going into the locker room at half time, down by three touchdowns. Not to a team as good as Eisenhower."

"Just keep pounding them," said Watson. "They're packing their bags right now. They want no part of a game like this! Bury this crud! No mercy, Generals! No mercy!"

The Generals threw another play action pass for a completion that put the football on the Rough Riders' three-yard line. "Put the nail in the coffin right now, Eisenhower," yelled out Watson! "Make them fold their tent. They're a bunch of losers! That's all they are,

Generals, a bunch of losers!"

We definitely need a stop here, thought Dempsey. The defensive players surrounded their head coach on the sideline after a called time out. *We can't go into the locker room down by three scores.* "Big challenge, Guys! We're now down by two touchdowns. Three would be awfully tough to overcome. Put a stop on them here and we'll win it in the second half. You can do it, Guys! I know you can." *I sure as hell hope they can! Or, deep down, do they just think I'm full of it?*

"Break'em, Dino," ordered Dempsey.

"Here's our chance to shine, defense,!" said the teams' stellar middle linebacker. "Lay it out on the line, Riders! One, two, three..."

"Riders together!"

The Rough Rider defense had not played well to this point in the game. The defense ran back out onto the field to huddle up. Once they got there, they all held hands. This was something they had never done before.

"Remember, Guys, together,!" said Dino intently as the defense broke to align to the Generals' goal line formation. "Power I left,!" yelled Dino to the left side of the formation. "Power I left, to the right side. Watch for the off-tackle kick-out!"

Dino's guess was correct. The Rough Riders left defensive tackle did a great job of blowing up the double team block that was the focus of the off-tackle play. The defensive tackle powerfully pushed the offensive guard and tackle's double team block back into the offensive backfield. This allowed Dino to fill the off-tackle gap and wrap up the tailback's legs for no gain.

"Atta boy, Dino,!" screamed out Ty. Actually, the entire Rough Rider sideline was screaming some type of encouragement amidst the desperate situation.

"Great job, Big Julie,!" shouted Dino to the transplanted,

makeshift defensive tackle. "I guess you are tough enough to play defense," said the middle linebacker.

"No problem," replied Big Julie. "These guys act like they're afraid."

"I might be afraid of you too if I saw your big rump lined up in front of me," said Dino.

"Nice job by Dino DeTaglia," stated Phillips.

"And, how about Big Julie Goodman filling in at the left defensive tackle spot for the suspended DeMarco Green to help provide some extra pop," added Travers. "That would be like having somebody placing a mountain in front of you and being told to knock it backwards."

"I guess that's what it means when you want a defensive lineman to eat up a double team block," said Phillips.

On second and goal, the Generals pounded an isolation blast play behind their right guard directly at Big Julie and Dino. Dino took on the isolation block of the fullback as per the offensive play's blocking design. Big Julie stymied the offensive blocking scheme once again as Dino exploded forward and bent his knees to lower his body. He ripped up under the fullback with a powerful, inside arm flipper blow, stopping him in his tracks. The surprised tailback hesitated. The delay allowed Dino to shed the fullback and wrap up the tailback forcefully for a one-yard loss.

"Dino,! Dino,!, Dino,!" chanted the Rough Riders standing on the sideline.

"Keep it up, Dino,!" yelled Dempsey. "Keep it up Big Julie!" *I need two more of those, Guys. We've got to have a stop right now*!

"What kind of a soft, mush-mouth block was that,?" yelled Watson. "Come off the damn ball! Cram-it! Cram-it down their throats! Run the same play! Pound that linebacker until he gives up! Get that damn ball in the end zone!"

On third down, Eisenhower substituted two extra offensive linemen to be the blocking backs to load up their power I run play formation. "Do you think they're bluffing, Rod,?" asked Dempsey. "Maybe bootleg the other way or, at least, run away from Big Julie?"

"Not this guy, Sean," answered the defensive coordinator. "He's too much of a thick head. He'll come at us again and probably right at the same spot."

Coach Franklin was 100 percent correct. The Generals ran a wedge play straight ahead, directly behind their right guard. The wedge blocking, with the extra, big linemen, was low to the ground, but still ineffective. The scheme was still unable to get a push on Big Julie Goodman. The tailback, however, saw that he could jump up and over the top of the pile of bodies lying on the ground. He exploded powerfully like a missile blasting off a launch pad. But, so did Dino DeTaglia. Dino and the tailback collided with a crashing sound that could be heard by everyone in the stadium. The hit was so forceful that the two players knocked each other sideways in opposite directions. The tailback ended up one-yard short of the goal line.

"Big hit, Dino,!" screamed Coach Franklin. "Great push, Julie!"

"Dino rocked him on that one," said Dempsey. "Dino and Big Julie are playing their tails off! What do you think, Rod? You think he'll kick it."

"Are you kid'n, Sean,?" answered Franklin. "Watson's not going to kick it, run it outside, throw it or anything else but run it directly at the same spot."

"Six-two, double Bonsai," signaled Franklin to Dino.

"Eight-man blitz. I like it, Rod," stated Dempsey.

"I hope you'll still like it in a few seconds."

True to form, Coach Watson called for another isolation blast play right at Dino, the blitzing linebacker. "Let's see if that kid has it in him four times in a row,?" said the Generals' head coach with a sneering confidence that Dino could not.

"One more time! One more time,!" came the encouragements from the Roosevelt sideline.

"Blow'em up, Generals,!" yelled Watson.

The result came fast. A resounding "whack" was heard by everyone in the stadium. Dino had blown through the center guard gap eluding the lead isolation blocker and knocked the tailback backwards for a three-yard loss. The referee quickly signaled first down going the other way. The Dino DeTaglia and Big Julie Goodman led defense had held up against the mighty Eisenhower Generals' offense.

Big Julie was the first Rough Rider to get to Dino to congratulate him. "Awesome, Dino! Awesome,!" yelled the new defensive tackle. Big Julie then realized something was wrong. "Dino's not move'n!"

CHAPTER 91

Dempsey and Franklin sprinted to the end zone. So did the trainers and doctors from both sidelines. Since there was four seconds left on the clock, both teams had to remain on the field for the last play of the half. The bewildered Rough Rider players stood around staring down at their defensive leader and friend, all in a state of shock.

"He ain't move'n, Man! He ain't move'n,!" said Jarvis.

"That was one heck of a hit," said Big Julie.

"He'll be O.K.," said Pete Logan. "I know he'll be O.K."

"What's going on,?" yelled Watson. "It's probably a ploy by these clowns to get some extra half-time rest!"

"Players, I want you all out of the End Zone and on the other side of the field," ordered the trainer. "I need the end zone clear for the ambulance."

The players all did exactly as they were told. The Roosevelt defensive players were all grouped together when Big Julie said, "... maybe we should all take a knee and say a prayer or someth'n."

All of the Roosevelt defenders on the field followed Big Juilie's suggestion. The rest of the Rough Rider players on the sideline then walked out on the field to be with their teammates. After a minute or so, the Rough Riders looked up to surprisingly see Eisenhower's offensive players walking amongst them. The Generals' players took knees and joined hands with the Roosevelt players. The Eisenhower players on the General's sideline then started walking toward the two-team huddle.

"What the hell do you think you're doing,?" questioned Watson.

"A player's hurt, Coach," said the Generals' defensive captain.

"We're going out there to give support."

"Get your butts back on the sideline," said Watson.

"I'm sorry, Coach Watson," said the captain stubbornly. "We decided we needed to do this and we're going to follow through on it." Watson froze in disbelief of his player's audacity.

Dino was carefully placed on a gurney. His right foot twitched back and forth from side-to-side as the medical assistants lifted and carefully placed him securely in the ambulance.

"Man, that doesn't look good," said Leotis as the Rough Rider players watched in a daze.

CHAPTER 92

The shell-shocked Rough Riders executed a quarterback sneak to eat up the final four seconds of the half. The Riders then made their way back to the visitor's locker room, not really knowing they were doing so. Once there, Dempsey immediately broke the team down to get with their assistant coaches and talk about needed scheme and technique adjustments. He wanted his team to focus on something other than Dino's injury. Dempsey called over Ty, Hug, Jarvis and Big Julie.

"Guys, we've got a big problem," said the worried and desperate head coach. "We don't have anyone who I could put in at linebacker right now who could hold up to Eisenhower's offensive line. You've both practiced as backup linebackers all season. I'm going to need both of you to help fill in at middle linebacker in the second half. I really don't have any other possibilities. I'll alternate you both on each series to try to help keep you fresh. And, Big Julie, I'm going to need you to take more of the reps at the left defensive tackle spot. What do you think, Guys?" *I hope I'm not being stupid risking the only person we can use to play quarterback right now. But, what the hell else can we do?*

"I'm in," said Hug. "I can't wait to put some hurts on those rich dudes. I'll crush that tailback."

"No problem, Coach," said a determined Tyler Douglas. "Running back, quarterback, middle linebacker. Coach, I'll run out from the sidelines with the water bottles if it can help beat these guys!"

"No worries, Coach," said Big Julie. "Actually, I kind of like messing around with these offensive line dudes. They're kind of soft, to tell you the truth."

"Guys, I'll just need for you to do your jobs," said Dempsey. "Play hard and smart! Hug, you take the first defensive series. Ty, the second. Alternate each series after that. Jarvis will help you with the calls. Big Julie, just let us know if you're getting tired by tapping your helmet if you need a break."

"That won't happen, Coach," said the huge lineman. "I'm ready to roll."

"Don't be afraid to ask," said Jarvis. "I'll get you straightened out on whatever you need. You dudes will do great."

"You'll meet the challenge. I know it," said the head coach. "Guys, you don't get many chances in life to have people call you champion. I need you all to bring home the trophy."

After a short period for the review and his talk with Ty, Hug, Big Julie and Jarvis, Dempsey called up the team for the ending half of the season. "Let's bring it up nice and tight so you all can hear me and so I can see all your eyes."

"Ty once asked which of all those sayings that I had hanging on the walls of our meeting room was my favorite. I answered, the one by Vince Lombardi. 'It's not whether you get knocked down; it's whether you get up,' meaning you have two things you can do when football, or life, knocks you down to the ground, flat to your back. You can lay there, quit and accept defeat. Or, you can get back up and get back into the fight. Getting back into the fight doesn't guarantee success. But, staying on the ground, lying on your back, certainly guarantees failure."

"Eisenhower just gave you everything they had in an effort to break you, to get you to give up, to get you to quit. But our defense bucked up and said no! Big Julie jumped in to help seal up the defensive line big time! Dino, who played so hard he knocked himself silly, led the charge with an awesome effort. You didn't break. You didn't quit. You didn't give up."

"Riders, now it's our turn," said Dempsey. "Play hard, play fast and play smart! Defense, play like you did on that goal line series, with toughness, aggression and determination. Hug and Ty are going to share the reps at the middle linebacker. Big Julie is going to stay in at the left defensive tackle spot for as long as he can. Offense, the Pistol stuff we put in is working. Just keep scoring! Special teams, be the difference-maker like we always talk about!"

"And lastly, when we win this game, I don't want you to go crazy like our win was a great upset," stated the Rough Rider head coach. "I want you to act like you expected to win," as the Rough Rider players' eyes flared open wide to intently focus in on their head coach. The one thing that the players had learned about their coach was that he was a genuinely honest person, not one to blow smoke up their butts. A strong, strange, concrete feeling of confidence suddenly filled their hearts and minds.

"I want you to act like it was no big deal, ...like you knew you were going to win all the time. Then, we'll go home and do our celebrating at our Block Party, back at Roosevelt, ...Roosevelt High School, ...home of the champion Roosevelt High School Rough Riders. Got that, Riders?"

"Got'cha, Coach,!" answered the aroused team.

"Bring'em up, Riders,!" said Dempsey. "Break them, Leotis."

"One, two, three..."

"Riders together!"

CHAPTER 93

Rayshawn Davis ran the kick-off back and returned the football to Eisenhower's 45-yard line. A desperate lunge and ankle tackle by one of the Generals' kick coverage defenders was all that stopped Rayshawn from going all the way. On the first play of the series, the Rough Riders showed an unbalanced spread set formation for the first time all season. Eisenhower's defense acted confused and didn't align properly, not having enough defenders to the strong side of the unbalanced formation.

"That's an unbalanced formation," whined Watson. "Who does this guy think he is? Unbalanced formation! This is a lot of garbage, Coaches! Your damn defense can't even get lined up right!"

"Set, hut, hut," barked Ty. The quarterback attacked the defensive end to the strong side of the formation with lead option action. The end tried to play cat and mouse with Ty. Ty faked the pitch and explosively broke up inside to daylight. The free safety cautiously came up to tackle Ty. Ty flipped the football out to Hug, his pitch option wing man, who trailed Ty perfectly on his pitch phase course. Hug caught the pitch, tucked the football away under his outside arm and sped towards the end zone for a 35-yard gain.

"Great job, Hug," said Ty. "That was big time!"

Ranting frantically, Watson ripped into his coaches. "How many big plays are we going to give up, Coaches?"

With the football on the 11-yard line, the Rough Riders used the unbalanced spread set formation once again. This time the Generals aligned to the overloaded alignment, the strong side, leaving an imbalance of defenders to the weak side.

"Set, red, 39, red, 39," barked out Ty to check the call made in the huddle back to the weak side. "Hut-hut," shouted-out Ty as he ran the weak side lead option. The defensive end was put in a bind with the quick, quarterback, lead option pressure. Ty pitched almost immediately. Hug caught the pitch and raced into the end zone to bring the score to 28 - 21.

"We're gon'na win this game, Ty," said Hug as the two friends hugged one another in the end zone.

"We will if we keep executing like that," answered the smiling quarterback.

Watson threw the water bottle he was holding back at the defensive bench hitting a defensive lineman in the face. "What's going on, defense,?!" screamed Watson. "Our defense is stinking up the field, Coaches! I can't believe we can't shut this crap down."

"Great job, offense," said Dempsey. "Keep it up, Guys. Just keep scoring and we'll win this thing. We got these guys reeling."

CHAPTER 94

"O.K. Let's get our tails back on track with a nice, long scoring drive," stated Watson. "The replacement for that Dino kid is supposedly a runt. Pound them right up the middle. It's time for us to grind these guys into oblivion."

On the first play of the Generals' new series, Eisenhower ran a straight ahead, blast, isolation play. A thunderous explosion was heard as part of the ferocious tackle of the Eisenhower tailback. "Who made that tackle,?" yelled out Watson. "That doesn't look like some runt to me!"

"That's number 45, the Wilson kid," said a Generals' assistant coach. "Hug Wilson. He's a load, Coach, ...a real good player."

"Just what we need now, an All-American at middle linebacker," said Watson. "This sucks, Coaches. It sucks big time."

On the next play, Hug displayed his excellent lateral speed as a linebacker and ran down the tailback on toss sweep action for a tackle and a three-yard loss. On third and long, Eduardo Ibanez sacked the Eisenhower quarterback as he tried to avoid Hug on a blitz stunt up the middle.

"Let's see if we can get this one," said Dempsey. "Double outside block," ordered Dempsey.

"The Generals are going to have to punt the ball away," announced Phillips. "There's pressure from the left side from Ibanez." The "thump-thump" sound reverberated throughout the stadium. "It's BLOCKED,!" yelled out Phillips. "And, the ball bounces up into the hands of Leotis Brown rushing from the opposite side! Brown's all by himself! The 20! The ten! T-o-u-c-h-d-o-w-n, Roosevelt!"

"Can you believe this, Ralph,?" said Bill Travers. "The little guys are going toe-to-toe with the big guys and the little guys simply won't give up!"

From the end zone, Leotis spun around and ran back directly to Eduardo Ibanez. "Great job, Eduardo," yelled Leotis to the hard-breathing, wide-eyed defensive end as the defensive players jumped on and pounded the likeable player. "You tied the game! What a great play! Way to go, Man. Way to go! That was big time!" The score now quickly became 28 – 28.

On the opposite side of the field, Coach Watson fervently punched out with both of his fists into the chest of his punter's personal protector. Actually, he double punched the personal protector a second and then a third time as he continued ranting and raving. The havoc finally came to an end when two of the General's assistant coaches jumped in to block off Watson's path to the player. As Watson finally pulled away from the scuffle, the head coach's bombastic mouth yelled out a series of shockingly profane words that many of the Eisenhower fans could clearly hear.

CHAPTER 95

"This is ridiculous," groaned Watson. "How can this happen? How can we stink so bad to a team like this? Enough is enough, Gentlemen. Time to turn this ridiculousness around."

On the next series, the Generals got back on track. Their excellent quarterback, J.J. Wickham, started clicking and hit three straight medium range passes. On the next play, the Generals popped a lead draw down to the 15-yard line of the Rough Riders. After two stellar tackles by Ty, now in at middle linebacker, the Generals found themselves third and seven on the 12-yard line. The Generals quarterback threw a perfect flag route pass to his tight end into the back corner of the end zone. A white shirted flash suddenly appeared. Jarvis Means undercut the route, leaped up into the air and slapped the football out of bounds.

"A great play by Jarvis Means keeps the Generals out of the end zone,!" said Phillips.

"What do you think Watson is going to do, Ralph,?" asked Travers. "Joel Hendricks has done a credible job of place kicking for the Generals this season. A field goal will put them up by three."

"Do you want us to kick it, Coach,?" asked the Generals' special teams' coach.

"I can't believe we've got to kick a field goal against these clowns," said Watson. "Kick the damn ball!"

Just as Dempsey was about to send out the field goal block team, Big Julie trotted up to the head coach. "Coach D, ...I can block this thing. The kicker kicks low and I can get through the center-guard gap. I know I can get it for you, if you want me to."

Dempsey was initially foggy from Big Julie's request, frowning heavily. The head coach hesitated since Big Julie was not on the field goal block team and had never practiced with that special team before. But, strangely, Dempsey had a real good feeling about the possibility of a block by the humongous man-child. "All right Kid. Let's give it a try," said the head coach somewhat hesitantly. Get in the left-center guard gap. Key the ball! Whatever you do, DON'T go off sides. A root beer float if you get it," added Dempsey with a quick smile.

"I'd rather have a chocolate malt, Coach," said the big offensive tackle seriously. Big Julie was one of the quickest and most athletic players on the field. He just rarely displayed it. He never wanted anyone to think he could run as fast as he could so he wouldn't have to put forth great running efforts during conditioning drills.

Big Julie lined up in the left-center, guard gap just as he was told, the side of the center's right snap hand. On the snap of the football, the Generals right guard tried to cut block Big Julie low. The big Rough Riders' tackle quickly jumped over the guard's attempted block and exploded into the face of the field goal kicker. Big Julie was right. The kicker did kick with a low trajectory. The football hit Big Julie directly in his raised hands.

"BLOCKED,!" yelled Ralph Phillips, "by big Julius Goodman!"

"And the football has bounced right back up into Goodman's stomach,!" said Bill Travers. The behemoth of a young man suddenly displayed the tremendous speed he had strategically disguised from the coaches all season long. It was almost funny to see such a large human being running so fast.

"Goodman's to the 40, the 50, the 40," said Phillips. Big Julie was in full throttle at the 30-yard line of the Generals when he started to run out of gas. However, his wide eyes and flushed face told he was giving it his all. At the 13-yard line, a Generals' player caught up with Big Julie, dove out and grabbed one of his extremely large ankles. Big Julie stumbled at the 7-yard line, dove out, stretched his massive frame parallel to the ground and reached the football out, just crossing the goal line.

"T-O-U-C-H-D-O-W-N, R-O-O-S-E-V-E-L-T! for a dramatic lead for the Rough Riders," stated Phillips. "Roosevelt now, unbelievably, leads in this Greater City Championship game 34-28," as the Rough Rider sideline erupted in euphoria.

Hug Wilson wrapped his arms around Coach Al Lopez and spun the offensive line coach around with him in a comical dance in which the coach was doing all he could to not fall to the turf. Ty Douglas grabbed and shook Hondo Rodriguez until he saw the horrified look on the injured quarterback's face as Hondo tried to stabilize himself on his crutches. "Oh, Hondo. Sorry, sorry! You O.K.,?" as the small, but thunderous group of Rough Rider fans roared as loudly as they could.

"Can you believe what we just saw,?!" screamed the play-by-play announcer. "Big Julie Goodman looked like the proverbial 'runaway freight train!'"

"Talk about special teams' play making a difference," stated Travers. "That play will be one of ESPN's Top Ten Plays of the Day, Ralph. I'll guarantee you that!"

Big Julie jogged back to the team area where the players and coaches hugged him, pounded on his back and gave him fist bumps. The big man huffed and puffed as he jogged up to Dempsey. "Ya know, Coach D, maybe that root beer float is a good idea, as long as they don't put any of that diet soda stuff in it."

Dempsey smiled and then laughed at his giant offensive tackle's words. "Great call on the blocked punt, Big Man. I think you're going to be a great coach someday."

"Nah," said Big Julie, You coaches have too much aggravation."

"Make that 35-28 as Bodie Swenson knocks the ball cleanly through the uprights for the extra point," reported Phillips.

Coach Watson ranted and raved on the opposite sideline. For whatever reason, it seemed as if no one on the Eisenhower sideline was listening to him.

CHAPTER 96

On the next series for the Generals' offense, Eisenhower stumbled once again. Hug made a tackle for a loss on an off-tackle power play on first down. On second down, Hug batted down a pass to a short square-in route by the tight end. On third down, Leotis Brown out-jumped a significantly taller Eisenhower wide receiver as he ran a streak route. Leotis knocked the football out from the grasp of the receiver for what seemed to be a sure first down catch. On fourth down, the Generals punted the ball away. A shanked kick led to only a 25-yard punt as Coach Watson continued to fume.

"25-yards,?" yelled out Watson as his punter jogged off the field. "Hell, I can kick a ball farther than that. You choked, you asshole, ...you know that don't you,?" shouted out the Generals' head coach. "You're nothing but a damn choker."

"Here we go, Guys," said Ty, having read the play call off of his wrist band. "Everybody does their job and it's a touchdown! Gun, doubles right, slot fly, double pass on one, on one. Ready, ..."

"Break!"

Ty handed the football off to the motioning slot back, Seamus Collins. Collins ran an across the formation to enact a fly sweep run play.

"Collins pulls up and throws back to Douglas," announced Phillips. "Douglas looks downfield. Rayshawn Davis is wide open! Douglas launches A BEAUTY! T-O-U-C-H-D-O-W-N ROOSEVELT!"

"YES,!" shouted out Ty. *We're roll'n, man,* thought the junior quarterback. *We just have to keep this up. We GOTTA keep this up. We can't forget who we're playing!*

"Wow! A big-time trick play to put the Rough Riders ahead 42 to 28 after another Bodie Swenson extra-point kick as we come to the end of the third quarter," said Travers. When off the air, Bill Travers continued. "What a game, Ralph! I still don't believe what I'm seeing, can you? The little guys are kicking the big guys' asses."

"We'll be back in a minute after a word from our sponsors," said Phillips. "Roosevelt might pull this off, Bill! They have Eisenhower totally out of whack right now."

"This could be a heck of a fourth quarter," stated Travers.

"What the hell's going on,?" blurted out Watson. "We're losing this game, Coaches. Can you believe that? We're losing this damned game and we're losing it to Roosevelt!"

"Great pass, Ty," said Rayshawn. "Right on the money."

"That was a great reverse throw, Seamus," said Ty as the Rough Riders were in control, ...for now.

"What do you think, Rod,?" asked Dempsey as he looked up at his enemy, the scoreboard.

"We got twelve more minutes to worry about," answered the defensive coordinator. "Our kids are playing on adrenalin right now. I don't know how much gas we have left in the tank, Sean. But, if I were you, I'd keep the pedal to the metal against these guys for as long as I could. We're still playing the champs and they know how to win."

"Unfortunately, I agree with all of that one hundred percent, Rod," said the head coach with a nervous smile. "I think we have to keep attacking but do everything we can to milk that clock.

Make sure our ball carriers work to stay inbounds to keep the clock running."

"I'm with you, Coach," reinforced Franklin. *We have to hold on a little longer, ...only a little longer."*

CHAPTER 97

The Eisenhower Generals weren't The Greater City Conference Football Champions for seven years in a row for nothing. They may have had a highly disliked, despotic tyrant for a head coach. However, the Generals had been in tough situations like this many times before. They confidently felt this was, simply, time to roll up their sleeves and get back to work. Even Coach Watson shed his crassness and rantings to lock into the all-important tasks at hand.

"We have plenty of time, Generals," stated Eisenhower's veteran head coach. "We have twelve minutes left to flip this thing around. The only thing we have to worry about now is to take the football, ram it down Roosevelt's throats and get seven points. Then, we'll only be a touchdown away from tying this thing up."

The Generals were all business on the ensuing offensive drive. None of their play calls were fancy. Watson was going to take the most direct route to the goal line by attacking straight ahead with his run game and play action passes. "A 7-yard pick-up by the General's fullback, Gerard Simons, on that trap play," stated Ralph Phillips.

"That was a big tackle by number 77 for the Riders," said Bill Travers. "That's, errr..."

"Bill, that's Big Julie Goodman playing defensive tackle again in place of DeMarco Green," interjected Phillips to assist his confused partner. "Coach Dempsey is pulling out all of the stops in his effort to slow down the Generals' offensive juggernaut."

"I think that's going to be Roosevelt's biggest problem as we go down this fourth quarter stretch," stated Travers. "Roosevelt only suited up 27 players for this game, Ralph. Eisenhower has three times that number. The Rough Riders have played their tails off to this point but they seem to be wearing down."

"That's what happens when you have to use your best players on both sides of the ball, Bill. A pick-up of 7-yards on that off-tackle play," announced Phillips matter-of-factly.

"A five-yard pick-up and another Generals' first down. The Generals are looking formidable at this point, Bill and the Rough Riders seemed to be getting more and more tired."

"A quick pass to the Generals' Joe Tierney off of an excellent fake to the tailback."

"The Generals are rolling, Ralph!"

"A give to Evan Waters, the Generals' fine tailback. He bursts through a big hole produced by the Eisenhower offensive line. He's to the 20, the ten! T-o-u-c-h-d-o-w-n, Generals! We now have a one score game, Bill," as Roosevelt now only has a one score, 42 to 35, lead. "You better keep us off the field for a while, Sean," stated Franklin. "Our defense looks exhausted! I don't know if we can hang on much longer."

"Got'cha, Rod," stated Dempsey as his eyes flashed up to the scoreboard to check the time left on the clock.

"O.K., let's go get those points back," ordered Ty after a kick-off return of only to the 22-yard line. Much like the KJAX color commentator, Bill Travers, Ty Douglas also started feeling that the powerful Generals were cranking up their fire power and the Cinderella Rough Riders were starting to show definite signs of wearing down. "Let's make sure we leave everything we've got out on the field, Guys," said Ty as he looked at his fatigued teammates. "Just hang in there a little longer and we go as home champs."

On the first play of the new series for the Riders, Ty handed off to Hug for an 11-yard pick-up on an option play.

"First down," shouted out the referee.

"That a boy, Hug," muttered Dempsey. "Just keep going, Guys."

"Great job, Ty," shouted out Addison Douglas even though she realized that her voice was probably being drowned out by the raucous crowd.

"Douglas gives to Hug Wilson versus the blitz," stated Phillips.

"No, it's a fake as Seamus Collins takes the quick hitting pass from Douglas. Collins is to the 40, the 50, the 40, the 30, the 20! He's finally brought down at the General's 18-yard line!"

"It looks like Douglas is willing Roosevelt to win, Ralph. The clock winds down to under six minutes in this unbelievable Greater City Championship Game."

"So far, Ty Douglas has been the difference all over this field, Ralph. Now the question is can he keep it up for another six minutes?"

"Keep going, Ty," yelled Coach Dempsey's wife, Mary Elizabeth. "Just keep going!"

On the next two plays, Hug Wilson pounded the football at the Eisenhower front for only two-yards. Eisenhower had quickly called for time-outs after both plays to stop the clock and conserve time.

"What do you think, Sean," asked Coach Walters. "Ty's asking for another slant."

"I don't know," responded Dempsey. "I'm afraid to go to that well too often. Eisenhower has to be looking for our slants. Let's go with a quick, double speed-out combination off of a quick play fake to the opposite side to hold the linebackers."

The quick, double speed-out pass pattern combination was a great idea. It did everything both Ty and Dempsey wanted to see as the play developed. Ty drilled a perfect bullet of a quick speed-out pass to the wide-open slot back, Wooley Woolridge. Wooley let the well thrown football slip through his hands. Directly behind Wooley was a Generals' cornerback.

"The ball's picked," yelled out Phillips. "Rashad Jennings, Eisenhower's all-conference cornerback, makes the interception and returns the ball to the Generals' 38-yard line. And with that, KJAX television says we're going to take a break in this tremendously exciting championship football game between the Roosevelt Rough Riders and the Eisenhower Generals as the two teams vie for the Greater City Championship."

"One way or the other, we're going to be sorry when this game is over," said an elated Bill Travers. "This is exactly what a championship game should look like. Two heavy weights going toe-to-toe for twelve rounds."

"This may be as good a high school championship game as I can ever remember announcing," stated Phillips. "But I don't know about the two heavy weights analogy, Bill. It's more like a powerful heavyweight in the form of the mighty Eisenhower Generals versus a gutsy, undermanned, lightweight in the form of the under-powered Roosevelt Rough Riders. The fun part, Bill, is that the little guy is hanging in there to the very end as the Rough Riders still lead."

"But don't forget, Ralph. We still have over four minutes left in this game and the Generals now have the ball."

From the 48-yard line, the Generals' quarterback, J.J. Wickham, cranked up a high, deep streak that dropped in perfectly into the hands of star receiver, Maurice Hightower. TOUCHDOWN GENERALS!," announced Philips. "And, once again, we're all tied up with the extra point kick being good as the scoreboard reads 42 – 42, with three minutes and 48 seconds remaining in this awesome championship game."

"This game's a barnburner, Ralph, ...a real barnburner," stated Travers.

Ty Douglas, with his hands on his hips and a glazed look in his eyes, slowly shook his head from side-to-side trying to contemplate what was now needed to be done to reignite a Rough Rider spark and get the Rough Rider offense back on track. *We can still do this,* thought the stubborn, determined quarterback.

A deep kick-off by the Generals into the end zone puts the ball on the Rough Riders 25-yard line. "Like I said, Bill, I still think the wear down factor is Roosevelt's biggest enemy at this point of the game."

"Douglas hands off to Wilson on an inside zone run play for the Riders," stated Phillips. "Wilson cuts to the inside. He sees some daylight for a solid four-yard gain. Coach Dempsey is trying hard to get this game into overtime to regroup and catch a breath for his team. The Generals quickly call a time-out."

"Good, tough run, Hug," said Ty, "Nice job, o-line."

"We're going to be just fine," said the Generals' head coach with a smirk spread across his face."

We've got to get out of this hole, thought Ty. *We need to get two first downs to use up the clock and get a chance to go into overtime.*

"O.K., Ty," said Dempsey. "Let's go with a 36-counter. If we can seal the line of scrimmage so we don't get penetration, we should be able to get a good chuck of yardage."

"I like that call, Coach," said Ty. The play call seemed to be a good one until the offensive line did give up some penetration. The 36-counter lost three yards. Once again, the Generals called out for their second time out. To this point, the Rough Riders had only been able to burn up seventeen seconds of the clock.

"Three minutes and seven seconds are on the clock, Sean," informed the defensive coordinator, Rod Franklin.

"And we're going to take another T.V. time out," stated Phillips. "Too bad, Bill. Roosevelt put up a heck of a fight," said the play-by-play announcer once the station was off the air for commercials.

"Ralph, this one isn't over yet. You seem to forget that Roosevelt and Eisenhower are still tied."

"Yeah, but not for long. The Generals are going to stuff Roosevelt on third down, force them to punt and then have enough time to run right over the top of them once they get the ball back. Roosevelt won't even know what hit them."

"I guess I wouldn't bet against that right now," replied Travers. "However, you yourself said it, ...'IF' the Generals get the ball back. Let's see if Ty Douglas has any more magic left up his sleeve. He's been the sparkplug for the Rough Riders all game long."

CHAPTER 98

"Tired,?" Dempsey asked of his huddled-up team during the time out. It was easy to see that they were.

"No, Coach,!" said the weary team in unison.

"Naahh, you guys are full of it," said Dempsey with a smile. "You're as tired as all get-out. You're tired and you have a right to be. You've played hard for over 40-minutes against a team that has a lot more player fire power than you do. And yet, you're still in the thick of the battle with a great chance to win!"

"I want you all to think back to our very first practice. It was steamy hot and we looked dreadful that day. If I had asked you then, how would you like to play Eisenhower for the championship in the championship game this year, you would all have been fired up, wouldn't you?"

"Yes, Sir," answered the team.

"Well, here you are, right smack dab, in the middle of that championship game all tied up with Eisenhower, 42 to 42 with three minutes and 26 seconds left in the game. Riders, for three minutes and 26 seconds, make this a fight you refuse to lose. Let's go out there and execute every single play with everything we have left in the tank to finish this thing up right here and right now. Anyone got anything to add?"

From the back of the huddle, Hondo said, "Riders together!"

"Riders together," said Ty and Eduardo and Big Julie and Hug and Leotis and..."

CHAPTER 99

"It's up to the offense now," stated Ty as he stepped into the huddle. "Whoever you line up against, out-fight him just a few more times. Refuse to lose, Guys. Refuse to lose!"

"Just let it rip, Ty," said Big Julie. "We got your back, Man."

"The Rough Riders break their huddle and line up on their own 26-yard line," announced Phillips. "This is an extremely important third and three situation. The flanker is into the boundary, slot alignment to the field. The Generals are hugged up to the line of scrimmage tightly."

"Ralph, Coach Watson wants to heat the Rough Riders up right off the bat. Here comes the blitz! Douglas takes the snap. He quickly launches a high, arcing fade pass to Wooley Woolridge on the sideline. Wooley DROPS the ball! The Rough Riders are going to be forced to punt."

"Too bad," said Travers. "That's two great passes that have gone down the drain as the Rough Riders are now forced to punt."

"Say what you want, Bill. At least the Rough Riders are still in this thing," said Phillips. "Who knows what can happen?"

"Well, I certainly wouldn't want to bet a lot of money on the Riders at this point," added Travers.

"Hug Wilson, Roosevelt's punter lets go a high, floating punt. "I don't think there will be much distance to this one, Bill. The Generals are going to take over on the 50-yard line in great field position once again."

Two plays later, the Generals changed the scope of the game.

"J. J. Wickham, the Generals' quarterback let's go a deep one. Joe Tierney's wide open on his post route. He's GOT IT as he lays out for a spectacular, dividing catch! The Generals now have the ball on the Riders' fourteen-yard line!"

Oh shit, thought Dempsey.

"Oh no," whispered Ty Douglas to no one but himself.

"This can't happen," uttered the extremely uncomfortable Kayleigh Logan. *You're going to have to use every bit of that magic dust that you still have left right now, Ty Douglas,"* thought Ty's precocious girlfriend.

And here I thought we had them when we were up by two scores, thought the flustered principal.

Eisenhower quickly ran two, inside zone runs in a row garnering a total gain of seven yards grinding up the game clock unmercifully for the Rough Riders. On third down, Hug Wilson wrapped up the ballcarrier's legs for a five-yard loss.

"That's horse shit blocking you know that," yelled out the crass Generals' head coach to his right guard. *At least this helps keep the clock running* thought Watson as he acted somewhat sanely for a few seconds. "Now just kick the damn ball so we can beat these degenerates and run around the field like a bunch of idiots because we supposedly accomplished something." Eisenhower kicked the field goal to up the score to 45 to 42 in favor of the Generals with 31 seconds left on the clock.

"O.K., Guys, we still have 31 seconds left," stated the head coach. "A touchdown wins it and a field goal ties the game up and puts us in overtime. We can do this, Riders. I know we can."

The Rough Rider players nodded affirmatively, ...but not assuredly.

"Hey, ...cut the shit right now," growled Roosevelt's quarterback leader. "You heard Coach Dempsey. We can still get this done. We've come too damn far to give up now. We got 31 more seconds. Play your ass off for 31 more seconds. We can do this Riders! We can definitely do this!"

The Generals' place kicker boomed his kick-off to the 5-yard line. A well-blocked return effort allowed Rayshawn Davis to return the ball to the Riders' 33-yard line. "Trey right flex, 50 scramble right," ordered the Rough Riders' head coach. The "Set-Hut" call put the designed scramble pass pattern play into motion. Ty dropped back three steps from the shotgun set purposely hesitating for a long second and then deep scramble-ran to the right as assigned. His first read was to check the three, fanned-out, deep streak receivers from the sideline to the middle of the field. When Ty saw that none of the three streak routes were open, he scanned back underneath to see a wide-open, deep-crossing Rayshawn Davis working hard to get to the sideline. Ty laced a tight throw to Rayshawn who made the catch with a foot in bounds at the Generals' 32-yard line.

"Great throw by Douglas," stated Phillips.

"And that allows Davis to get out-of-bounds with 16 seconds left on the clock," stated Travers.

"We still need a chunk, Coach," said Sonny Walters. 49-yards is just too much for Bodie," said the special teams' coordinator.

"Let's go with max protection and see if we can get a deep one-on-one comeback iso for Seamus on the sideline," said Dempsey. That would get us 15-yards quickly."

"Douglas fires a rocket to Collins for 16-yards and the big split end makes the catch and immediately goes out of bounds at the 34-yard line with 10 seconds left on the clock," stated Phillips.

"That was a big-time throw by Douglas," said Travers. "I just can't believe the effectiveness of Ty Douglas having to step in for Hondo Rodriguez and only getting in a week of practice."

"On-the-line, slot right, on-the-line, slot right" called out Douglas as the chain gang and referee moved the sticks. "261 Sailor, 261 Sailor," barked out Ty to each side of the formation calling for the slot square-out pattern that Dempsey had signaled in to the huddle.

Ty took the shotgun snap but immediately found himself under pressure from the field side. He darted quickly to the short side of the field only to find the Generals' defensive end in hot pursuit. Ty saw that Rayshawn Davis had broken free on his slot route as he felt a grasp of his left ankle forcing him to stumble towards the ground. Before he hit the turf, Ty flicked a sidearm throw that was low and outside of Rayshawn's reach. However, Rayshawn dove out parallel to the ground to reach out and make spectacular diving catch.

"TIME-OUT! TIME-OUT!," screamed Dempsey as did the rest of the coaching staff. The clock was stopped with 2-seconds left in the game.

"The Riders now have the ball on the Generals' 24-yard line with two seconds left to go in this fabulous Greater City Championship football game," exclaimed the excited Ralph Phillips.

"In goes Bodie Swenson for what will be a 41-yard field goal attempt and a tied up, overtime situation," stated Phillips.

"That seems to be a long way for Bodie Swenson," stated Bill Travers. "And that's a lot of pressure for the youngster with a championship still on the line."

"Come on, Bodie," ordered Daryl Hoskins, the principal.

"Oh, please make this, Bodie," prayed Addison Douglas.

"I hope you gave Bodie some of that magic dust, Ty," said Kayleigh.

"Billy Pierce handles the ball cleanly on the snap. Swenson's kick looks good, ...a straight shot towards the goalposts. It looks high enough! It looks long enough! IT'S, ...short."

Ty took about three seconds to let his head hang down. He then popped up to run out onto the field to grab Bode Swenson. "That was a hell of a try, Bodie. Almost, Buddy! Almost!"

Ty Douglas, Hug Wilson, Hondo Rodriguez, Leotis Brown and the rest of the Rough Rider players and coaches somberly watched the Generals wildly celebrate another Greater City Championship. The Generals jumped for joy, slapping each other on their backs, screaming and yelling and dumping jugs of water and Gator Aide on their assistant coaching staff since they would never think of dousing their head coach in any way. The cheerleaders chanted and flipped high into the air twisting and turning, hopefully into the hands of their male counterparts. The General's band blared their fight song and the fifteen thousand crazily dressed Generals' fans ranted and raved as exuberantly as they could.

"Almost," said Ty.

"Almost," responded Hondo.

"Next year," said Hug.

"Next year," declared Ty. "We'll definitely get them next year."

"Damn," said Dempsey.

Fifteen thousand screaming Generals' fans went crazy. The Rough Rider fans were completely numb. The Eisenhower Generals were the Greater City Football Champions again. The Roosevelt Rough Riders were the Greater City Football Championship Runner-Ups.

CHAPTER 100

The two teams lined up to shake hands. The Rough Rider players firmly shook hands with each of the Generals' player's and peered into each of the Eisenhower player's eyes as they had been taught by their head coach. The Generals' players returned the procedure with a great respect for the tremendously underdog group from Roosevelt High School. In addition, the Generals showed a sincere concern for the well-being of Roosevelt's standout middle linebacker Dino DeTaglia.

After the hand shake lines dissipated, Dempsey and his staff herded up the Rough Rider players to begrudgingly accept the runner up trophy for the Greater City Championship. As Coach Dempsey mentally struggled to raise the actual trophy, a small chant of "Roosevelt, Roosevelt" was heard. The chant quickly grew louder and louder as Coach Dempsey raised the runner up trophy into the air. Within seconds, the mass of Eisenhower fans joined the Roosevelt fans chanting "ROOSEVELT!, ROOSEVELT!, ROOSEVELT!"

"What the hell are they doing now, Rod," asked the morose head coach.

"They're honoring our team, Sean," said Coach Franklin.

"Maybe these people do have some class after all," stated Coach Walters.

"Let's not get too carried away," said Coach Franklin. "This is still Eisenhower we're talking about."

The deflated, but proud, head coach tipped his ball cap to both side of the stadium as the General's fans continued their honoring.

Even though his team had pulled out an amazing, come-from-behind victory, Coach Watson, again, made no attempt to shake hands with Coach Dempsey. He, simply, walked off the field stewing over what he felt was a lousy performance by his team and coaches. *How could we have played so badly? We stunk up the field against Roosevelt!, ...ROOSEVELT!*

CHAPTER 101

As Sean Dempsey walked towards the south end zone, he saw his lovely wife, Mary Elizabeth, in the stands hugging and shaking hands with the other coaches' wives, parents, friends and fans. A warm, comforting smile was spread across her pretty face. A small, sad smile was on Dempsey's. His wife looked up and saw the man she loved so much. The Head Coach gave her a firm thumbs up signal. She returned the signal with one of her own as tears filled her eyes.

"O.K., Guys, O.K. Let's get ready to wrap this up," said the disappointed head coach as his team huddled up and kneeled underneath the stadium's south goal posts. "First of all, I do have some great news from the hospital. It looks like Dino's going to be fine. He had no idea who we just played but wanted to know the score. Let's all take a moment and give thanks and focus our thoughts and prayers towards our friend and teammate as well as giving thanks for allowing us all to be an unbelievable part of the Rough Riders this season."

After a brief few seconds, Dempsey continued. "Wow!," said the head coach with a look of sincerity and a warm, but disappointed, smile spread across his face. "Close, close, close! But, let's get something straight. When you lose a tough, close one like we did tonight, every one share's in the loss. You can grade out at your position with an excellent ninety percent. However, that still means that you didn't get the job done ten percent of the time. A coach can call the best game of his life and yet make one or two bad calls in a game like this that could have made all of the difference in the world. One more successful play by you and you and you and me," as he pointed-out randomly, "could easily have made the difference in this loss," as he tried to ease the pain of the missed, last second field goal attempt by Bodie Swenson.

"I've got to say this, though. What you have accomplished this season is nothing short of a miracle," continued Dempsey. "I'm extremely proud of all of you and want to thank you for allowing me to join and be a part of the Rough Rider family this past season. You played with grit, determination and heart all season. And, now, I'd like to leave you with one of my favorite sayings. Getting back up after you've been knocked to the ground does not necessarily guarantee you success. But, if you do get up, you just might slay the dragon."

"So, if you will allow me, I'd like to lead us in one last Roosevelt Rough Rider cheer of the season. One, two three..."

"Rider's together!"

One player hung back in an effort to be the last one to depart from the stadium field. That was Ty Douglas. Ty stepped up, smiled with a warm grin and stuck out his hand to be shook by his head coach. "That was one hell of a season coach," stated Ty.

The head coach smiled back at Ty and reached out to grab his extended hand. "You got that right, Ty. That's for sure. And, you had a great season yourself."

"Thanks, Coach. I appreciate you saying that."

"So what's all this I'm hearing about you transferring to St. John's next year, Ty."

"Depends, ..."

"On, ..."

"Whether or not you're the head coach here at Roosevelt," said Ty. "Word on the street is that Coach Watson is going to retire and you're going to take his place at Eisenhower."

"Wow! That's one I haven't heard about," said a chuckling head coach, as he slowly shook his head from side-to-side. Neither individual said another word. Instead, they ended up with a quick, but sincere, hug.

CHAPTER 102

Ty steered Kayleigh's wheel chair toward the Logan family's SUV. Kayleigh was exhausted by half time. However, she hung in there to the very end. "Almost," said the pretty teen with a pretty smile on her battered looking face.

"Almost," responded Ty as he returned a smile of his own. "You'll just have to reload my stash of your magic dust for next year."

"Hey!," yelled out a huffing and puffing Big Julius Goodman from behind Ty and Kayleigh. "I was trying to find you guys but the crowd was all over the place. "Pete said you wanted to see me, Kayleigh."

"That's right, Julie" said the weary teen as she extended out her arms. "I need a hug, Big Man" After the warm hug, Kayleigh uttered, "thank you, Julie. Thank you."

"Ty!, Ty!," yelled out a 50ish year old man wearing a red jacketed sports coat. "Ty, I'm Coach Dale, Head Coach at the 'U' and it's nice to meet you and your mom."

"I know who you are, Sir and it's very nice to meet you," said Ty as Addison Douglas beamed. "I'm a big fan of the 'U'."

"Now that's what I like to hear, Ty."

"And, it's nice to meet you, Mrs. Douglas," stated the Head Coach. "I'm glad I was able to catch up you. And, this goliath must be Big Julie Goodman. What do you think, Ty? Can this guy block for you at the 'U.'"

"I don't think, Coach. Big Julie's the real deal," stated Ty. "He can block, ...that's for sure."

"I like meeting you too," said the excited Big Julie as his flushed face and big eyes made him look even bigger than he was. "So you're really the Head Coach at the 'U?'"

"I certainly am," said the 'U's head coach with a laugh as he reached out to shake hands with the massive tackle..

"Now I can't really talk to you yet since you're still only juniors by NCAA rules," said Dale. "But that was some show you two put on out on that field today and I just wanted to let you know how much the 'U' is going to be interested in recruiting you. You're going to look good in red and blue as will your lady friend there. And, tell Dino and Jarvis I said hello, Guys."

"So long, folks. Be seeing you soon," as the head coach smiled, waved and disappeared amidst the departing fans.

CHAPTER 103

"Derrick Whitman, Daily Examiner," said one of the local newspaper's sports columnists. "Coach, it looks like you now have a quarterback controversy going into next season between Hondo Rodriguez and Ty Douglas. Would you comment on that?"

Dempsey was totally taken back by the question and a bit frustrated with the sports columnist. "Derrick, we almost pulled out a miracle, championship season. Until you just mentioned us now having two excellent quarterbacks, the situation never even crossed my mind. Heck, we were just fortunate enough to have a talented athlete like Hondo Rodriguez lead us to The Greater City Conference Championship game and a versatile, explosive athlete like Ty to take over at quarterback to help give us a chance to win."

Once off the recorder, Dempsey bit back at Whitman. "I'm surprised by you, Derrick. Roosevelt, of all people, almost pulls out a miracle win and the only question you have for me is about a possible quarterback controversy for next season. You're better than that, Derrick," said the head coach as he stormed away from the newspaper columnist.

"This is Jack Lounsberry with KNIK-5 T.V.'s Daily Sports Report. I have with me Sean Dempsey, head coach of this year's Greater City Football Championship runner ups, the Roosevelt Rough Riders. Coach, you were loaded with juniors this season. With all those excellent players returning, what can you tell me about the rumor of you moving on from Roosevelt. There's even been a mentioning of you replacing Coach Watson at Eisenhower with the talk of a Watson retirement."

A discombobulated Dempsey stared at the television sports commentator with a blank look spread across his face. Six months ago, Sean Dempsey was working as a house framer shooting nails into two by fours. "You're kidding me, right,?" asked the head coach. "My kids played their butts off for 48 minutes and that's all you have to ask me. You're really something, Jack. I just don't know about you media people, that's for sure."

Bill Travers, the color commentator for KJAX-11 Television was right. Big Julie Goodman's field goal block and subsequent remarkable touchdown return run made it to ESPN's Top Ten Plays-of-the-Day. Actually, it was #1.

CHAPTER 104

Coach Sean Dempsey won the Greater City Conference's Coach of the Year Award by a landslide vote, eight to one. Guess who didn't vote for Coach Dempsey?

THE END

AUTHOR - STEVE AXMAN

Steve Axman started out as a high school assistant football coach at Freeport High School in Freeport, NY and Bethpage High School in Bethpage, NY. He then became the Head Football Coach at General Douglas MacArthur High School in Levittown, NY before moving on to coach on the college level. Later in his career, Steve coached as an assistant football coach (quarterbacks) at Perry High School in Gilbert, AZ.

Steve first started his college coaching career at East Stroudsburg State College and on to coach at Albany State University, The United States Military Academy at West Point, The University of Illinois, The University of Arizona, Stanford University, U.C.L.A., The University of Maryland, Northern Arizona University for eight years as Head Coach, The University of Minnesota, The University of Washington, The University of Montana, The University if Idaho, Simon Frazier University in Burnaby, B.C., Canada and Nichols State University as interim Head Coach.

Steve also coached on the professional level in the U.S.F.L. for the Denver Gold, The Indoor Football League for the Arizona Rattlers and The American Alliance of Football for the Arizona Hotshots.

In addition, Coach Axman has written and had published fifteen football coaching texts with a sixteenth, DESIGNING AND STRUCTURING A SUCCESSFUL PASS GAME to be out soon.

CPSIA information can be obtained
at www.ICGtesting.com
Printed in the USA
FSHW022014140421
80503FS